JUST UNTIL FOREVER

NOUHA JULLIENNE

JUST UNTIL FOREVER
BLUE COLLAR BILLIONAIRES: SEATTLE
NOUHA JULLIENNE

Editing by Jennifer Innamorati, Sleepy Night Owl Edits
Proofreading by Gill Travers, traversingfiction
Cover Design by Dream Echo Designs
Artwork by Vita

CONTENT WARNINGS

This story includes explicit sexual content (mild impact play, mild somnophilia). It also touches on divorce, custody conflict, child abandonment, and an emotionally manipulative ex-partner, alongside references to grief and loss, including the death of a parent.

For those who chose each other again and again. Because the family we build is often stronger than the one we're born into.

1

Worth

"Ah, fuck," I grunt.

The brunette on her knees in front of me moans in response, mouth full and hands already down the front of her panties.

I like when a woman knows what she wants.

I like giving orders even more.

"Lift your skirt. I want to see your ass." She doesn't hesitate to obey.

I'm in my corner office at the top of Miller Towers, getting my dick sucked by my receptionist—and I couldn't be more bored.

You'll rarely hear a man complain about getting head, but this is just maintenance. A stress-relief exercise. After thirteen hours—and still counting—at the office, my tension is through the roof, and she knew exactly what to suggest when she walked in, pretending to be remorseful for misscheduling a supplier call.

I'm not even convinced it was an accident.

Shaina is decent at this, I'll give her that. She's also the only one bold enough to offer, and I'm too busy to seek out anyone else. The convenience outweighs the effort. I don't have time for dates or emotional labor—I barely have time to sleep.

Still, I'm staring at the starless sky instead of her mouth. Thinking about the past instead of the present. Wondering how the hell my life became this tightrope of responsibilities and isolation.

I used to feel something once. Pleasure. Maybe even the illusion of intimacy.

The last time I let someone in, she tore my world apart on her way out. My ex-wife didn't just leave me—she gutted the part of me that still believed in love. Took it with her like one final, cruel souvenir.

So now I keep things simple.

Surface-level. Temporary. Unattached.

Another box to tick before moving on to the next task.

I sink my hand into Shaina's hair and tilt my hips forward, pushing deeper. She gags a little, tears streaming down her face, but she doesn't stop.

"Touch yourself until you come," I tell her, voice flat. She's close. I can feel it in the way her moans vibrate against my cock. I grit my teeth and chase the end. When I come, it's hard and fast, pouring down her throat like it means nothing.

Because it doesn't.

She wipes her mouth, smooths her skirt, and leaves without a word. That's part of the arrangement—no talk, no delusions.

I tuck myself back in, loosen my tie, and lean back in the chair.

I glance at the time. 8:57 p.m.

Shit.

I shove the résumés for the junior designer position I'd been reviewing into my briefcase and lock up, pausing as I pass by Shaina's desk. It's empty, but the scent of her strong, nauseating perfume still lingers. There's a lipstick-stained coffee mug sitting beside the keyboard and a sticky note on her monitor that says 'teach me a lesson tomorrow for messing up ;)' in bubbly cursive.

I stare at it, then rip the note off the screen, crumpling it in my fist. I toss it into the trash.

I should fire her for being so fucking bold and inappropriate. But I won't, because that would mean confronting the fact that I've let this go on far too long. That I've blurred the lines and pretended it was harmless. I shake my head and sigh. I'll deal with Shaina another day.

As I hit the elevator, my phone rings. I pick up without looking.

"Yes?"

"Hi, Dad."

My daughter's voice immediately cracks something open in me.

"Hey, sweetheart. I'm on my way. I'll be home soon to say goodnight."

Guilt tightens my chest. I missed dinner. Again.

"I'm thirteen, Dad. You don't need to tuck me in."

I chuckle. "God forbid anyone finds out I still kiss you goodnight."

The elevator doors open. I see Shaina heading toward me, and I jab the button to close the doors like my life depends on it.

Brianna giggles on the other end of the line. It's the sound I live for. The one thing that still feels like joy.

"Maggie made me call to check if you're still alive. She said, 'make sure your father hasn't worked himself into cardiac arrest.'"

I roll my eyes, though Bri's impression is spot-on. "Tell Maggie I'm taking my vitamins and drinking plenty."

"She says whiskey doesn't count as hydration and that you need rest. R-E-S-T."

I laugh, walking through the underground garage to my car. Brianna is barely a teenager and is already teaming up against me with our nanny.

When my marriage imploded, Maggie never tried to take anyone's place, but she filled in the cracks. Always steady and dependable. Now, she's become a second grandmother figure to Brianna.

"I'll be home soon," I promise again.

But *soon* won't matter forever. Brianna is getting older. There will come a time when I won't be able to fix things with a bedtime joke and a forehead kiss. When she won't need me at all.

And maybe I deserve that.

I think about what Maggie said the other night.

"Brianna needs stability, Worth. You either show up now or you lose her later."

But how do I show up for my daughter when I can barely keep my own head above water?

Maybe that's why Henson, my brother and the company's Chief Financial Officer, has been pushing me to restructure the business, hire a junior designer, and delegate more. So I can make room to actually be present. Both in my daughter's and in my own life.

I unlock my car, throw my jacket on the passenger seat, and slide behind the wheel. My head hits the seatback.

The blowjob didn't help. I'm still stiff.

I grip the steering wheel until my knuckles go white.

Thank God it's Friday.

A while later, I walk inside my house and hang my suit jacket on the hook by the door. The rest of my things drop to the floor by the wall. My bag slouches down, and my body wishes it could do the same, but I'm always tense, wound tighter than a suspension cable. Some say my personality is the same—they're not wrong.

I tried being the easy going guy once. That version of me got used, taken for granted, especially by my ex-wife. So now, I'm sharp edges and short tempers.

The grand staircase stretches ahead of me under the domed ceiling. I head towards it and call out, "Brianna? You up there?"

No answer.

I step further into the foyer.

The kitchen is spotless. Dishes put away. Counters wiped down. It looks like no one has been here in days, but I spoke to Bri less than an hour ago. Where the hell did they go?

I check everywhere. Kitchen. Dining room. Living room. Theater. Office. Bathrooms. Nothing.

My pulse spikes as worst-case scenarios flood my brain. What if someone broke in? What if they were taken? I start searching harder, my voice echoing through the too-big house. Who the hell needs this much square footage anyway?

I curse myself for buying this place. It's just Brianna and me now. I've got five too many rooms and not nearly enough peace.

I turn in circles calling their names, and I'm met with dead silence.

The basement is the only place left. My feet slam against the stairs as I head down. When I hit the bottom step and round the corner, two bodies tackle me, hard. I stumble, arms flying up to protect my face.

"What the fuck is going on?" I bark.

"Language, Worth!" Maggie scolds.

I lower my arms to find Bri and Maggie laughing hysterically, standing over me on the carpet. My vision clears, and I see their smug faces. They look at each other, then double over in another fit of giggles.

"I thought you were hurt!" I yell, breath still catching up to my brain.

"It worked!" Bri shrieks, throwing her arms around Maggie. "We got him!"

I stare, speechless, as they celebrate their little ambush.

"You're both dead," I mutter.

"You're so dramatic, Dad." Brianna tries to muffle her snort.

Maggie offers me a hand. I grab it and yank her down beside me.

"Ah-ha!" I grin as she hits the carpet with a shocked gasp.

Bri and I burst out laughing while Maggie glares at me, lips twitching.

"How does it feel now?" I ask, smug.

"Yeah, Mags," Bri chimes in. "How does *that* feel?"

I shoot my daughter a wicked look. "You're not off the hook yet, Piglet. You better run."

She squeals and bolts up the stairs. I give her a few seconds' head start before chasing her, pounding up behind her like the big bad wolf—a game we always used to play when she was younger. She darts through the first floor and zips up the back staircase, finally slamming her bedroom door shut in my face.

"Little pig, little pig," I say in a gravelly voice, "let me come in."

"No!" she shouts, giggling from the other side.

"Come on, little pig. I just want to *talk*."

The door doesn't lock—deliberate design choice, thank you very much—so I turn the knob and push against her weight.

"I'm not a pig, Dad!" Bri squeals.

I shove the door open and she leaps into bed, hiding under her blanket.

"Too slow."

I dive in and tickle her until she's snorting again.

"You sure sound like one," I tease.

Her laughter is contagious. Loud, free, and full of life.

My heart swells. This is the part of me that still works. Being her dad.

"Okay," I say, brushing hair from her face. "Time for bed, Piglet. Get ready while I check on Maggie."

She nods, cheeks flushed, and I step out.

No amount of money compares to spending time with my daughter. Not the empire I've built, not the penthouse views or tailored suits, or even the boardroom wins that keep piling up like trophies on a shelf I no longer admire.

I don't know who I'd be without Brianna.

Probably some lonely, bitter billionaire screwing his way through meaningless nights.

I find Maggie in the kitchen, rummaging through the pantry.

"What are you doing?"

"Feeding your ungrateful arse," she replies without looking up. "Even though you tackled an old woman."

"Oh, piss off," I grumble. "You're not *that* old."

She laughs and gives me a little shove on the shoulder. "I'll take that as a compliment."

After bedtime routines and dinner, Maggie leaves and I head to my office in the back of the house, pour myself a glass of whiskey and sit at the desk, staring down the mountain of résumés.

The junior designer interviews start in two days and I haven't even looked at any of the interviewees.

I down the drink, take a breath, and dive in.

It's almost midnight when I spot a name: Mya Dessen-Jones.

Barely any experience, but top of her class. 4.2 GPA. Excellent recommendations.

HR must've flagged her for her academics alone.

I linger on her file a little longer than I should, wondering if she might be the right person to finally fill the role. We need someone hungry who can execute.

Then I leave everything on the desk, check on Bri one more time, and head to bed.

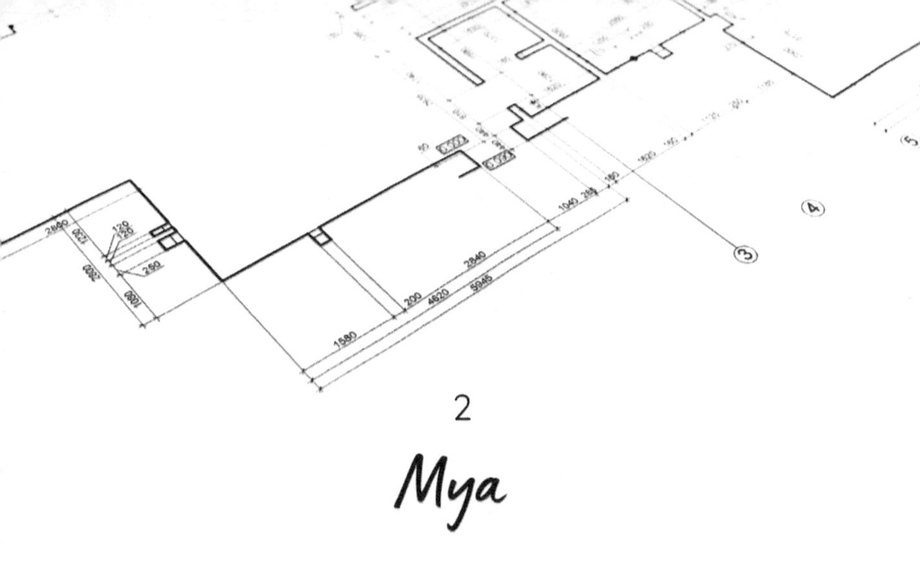

2

Mya

"MYA DESSEN-JONES!" A familiar voice shouts from my left.

My hand jerks and boiling hot coffee splashes from the reusable cup all over the expensive machine. I hiss in pain as it hits my skin, dropping the cup and scrambling for a rag.

"Shit," I mutter, patting the mess frantically.

I didn't even realize I was still holding the lever. I was in another dimension entirely until my best friend-slash-manager-slash-sister-from-another-mister snapped me out of my trance. Tiana stares at me, tilting her head to the side toward the client in line.

I glance up, flustered, only to meet the impatient silence of the man waiting for his double shot Americano mist. He doesn't say a word, just grunts and goes back to scrolling on his phone like I'm some glitch in the matrix he can't be bothered to acknowledge.

"Sorry about that."

Of course, he doesn't look up. *Prick.*

He's tall and broad-shouldered, in a tailored charcoal suit

that looks like it was stitched directly onto him by a very expensive Italian man, with a very precise measuring tape. His hand, still gripping the phone, has perfectly manicured nails. Not a hangnail in sight. *Who even has time for cuticle maintenance?* I bite back a scoff as I finish remaking his drink.

Then I catch a glimpse of his profile as he leans forward, enough for the overhead light to graze the sharp edge of his jaw and the striking contrast of his salt-and-pepper beard.

I don't even need to see his entire face to know that he's stupidly handsome. Like, *rude*-level handsome. His hair is just as perfect as the rest of him.

My brain short-circuits for a half-second as I slide the drink across the counter.

"There you go."

Nothing. Not even a twitch.

He takes the cup, gives the barest nod, and walks out without ever lifting his head.

"You're welcome!" I shout after him.

Asshole.

Classic corporate Seattle—rude, passive-aggressive, and severely caffeine-dependent.

There's still a line of groggy people waiting to get caffeinated, but I need a moment. Thankfully, Demi's on cash and Eric's covering baked goods. They'll survive without me for a few minutes.

I sigh, tug off my apron, and head to the back.

"I told you to stay home today. You were up 'til an ungodly hour working on that project," Tiana says, following me into the kitchen.

"TJ," I groan at my step sister.

My biological father, Marcus Dessen, was a design consultant. When I was eight, he died in a work accident after falling from a structure during an on-site visit.

I was still too young to understand the loss, but I've grown up carrying the echoes of it. My mom was the doctor on duty when they wheeled him into the emergency room. Her husband of ten years, broken and fading on a gurney in front of her. I can't even begin to imagine the kind of pain that must have ripped through her as she worked, torn between the roles of wife and physician.

Two years later, she met Devon Jones. They eventually got married and, just like that, I became Mya Dessen-Jones. Our parents blended our families when I was ten and Tiana was seven.

She and I hit it off immediately. We were practically twins in energy and chaos. A few years later, our little brother JJ was born. Jackson has my curls and brown eyes, and Tiana's nose and warm skin tone. We always joke that he looks like our love child.

"I told you I'd be fine. I just need a shot of espresso and some cold water. I'll be good."

"You've had four shots already and it's not even eight," Tiana snaps, arms crossed. "You need to go home. Don't make me put on my manager pants."

Gah. I hate when she does this.

Even though I'm twenty-four and three years older than Tiana, she acts like the older sister. Always has, but especially now that she's my boss at the café. She never misses a chance to remind me of it, wielding that manager title like a crown. And the worst part is that she knows how to keep me in line, even when I don't want to admit she's right.

"Tell you what. If I mess up one more time, I'll go home. Otherwise, I'm staying 'til the end of my shift."

Tiana exhales like she's debating body-slamming me. "Fine."

"Fine."

She spins and leaves, and I collapse onto the break room chair, kicking my legs up on another. I'm fried. TJ is right. I was up until four a.m. finalizing my capstone project. It counts for the bulk of my final grade, and I'm proud of it. But now, I'm running on fumes.

I've worked here at Willow's since second year in college, when Tiana offered me a part-time gig.

I love this place. The energy is comforting. Familiar. Even on a shitty day, the smell of fresh coffee and the sight of Demi's chaotic highlighter notes taped to the espresso machine help me reset. Unless a corporate jerk like that guy walks in.

Still, I should've stayed home today.

But I'm restless. The wait for final grades and the anxiety over job applications are gnawing at me.

I don't want an internship. I want real responsibility and experience. I want to be seen and respected. Not someone's coffee runner or personal assistant. I worked my ass off for this degree. I'm graduating top of my class. I followed in my father's footsteps for a reason: to make him proud.

Of all the firms I applied to, W.H.M. Construction is the dream. They are massive, with projects all over the world, endless resources, and a creative division that lets designers pitch and build their own concepts. If I land this job, it could change my entire career.

My heart pounds just thinking about it.

I wipe my forehead and shuffle away from the oven before I melt into the tile.

As if on cue, the timer blares and my phone vibrates at the same time.

I yelp, nearly launching out of my chair. I fumble for my phone and nearly drop it twice before I see the caller ID: W.H.M. Construction.

Oh my God.

"OH MY GOD!" I'm screaming, and not just in my head anymore.

Tiana rushes back in, fanning smoke. "What's going on? Did you burn the cookies?"

Shit. The cookies. I forgot them.

I try to answer the phone as I wave what I hope is an apologetic hand at her, but my fingers don't work. I'm panicking. Sweating. Possibly dying. Eventually, I press accept and croak out, "Hello?"

A woman starts speaking on the other end. "Is this Mya Dessen-Jones?"

"Yes, that's me."

She starts shooting information at me, but I have no pen or paper. TJ has her back to me, salvaging the baked goods. I flail my arms to get her attention. Nothing.

I whisper-shout her name. Still nothing.

So I do what any rational adult would do—I throw my shoe at her.

It hits her square on the butt. "Ow!"

No time for apologies. I wave her over.

She hurries to me, and I grab her phone, typing furiously into her Notes app.

"Okay. Thank you, Shaina. I'll be there. Goodbye."

I hang up, hands shaking. My heart is trying to claw its way out of my chest.

Tiana just stares at me. "Well?"

"I just got a call from W.H.M. I have an interview in two days. I can't breathe."

We scream. We jump. I cry.

My sister hugs me tight, and I feel relief and pride in my bones.

"I'm so proud of you, MJ. You're going to kill it."

I wipe my tears and nod, trying to savor the high before the nerves creep back in.

"Thanks, sis."

After another hug, TJ heads back out. As she reaches the kitchen door, she throws a grin over her shoulder.

"Oh, and MJ?"

"Yeah?"

"You messed up again. The cookies. You're out."

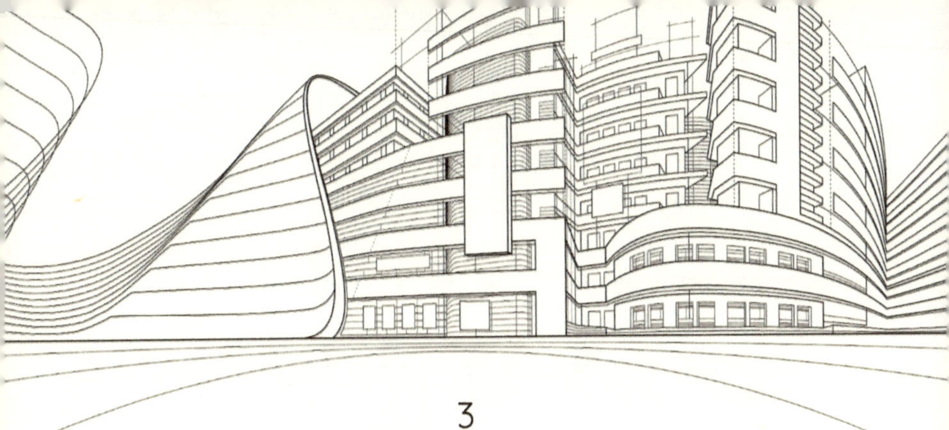

3

Worth

I step off the elevator and my phone vibrates in my hand.

A name flashes across the screen—one I recognize immediately and wish I didn't.

I close my eyes for a brief, long-suffering second.

I have a rule. A very clear one. No woman more than twice. This one clearly didn't get the message—or chose to ignore it.

I don't respond. Instead, I slide the phone into my pocket. I don't owe anyone an explanation, and I refuse to clean up confusion I never invited.

I barely have time to breathe before I'm immediately ambushed.

"Mr. Miller!"

Francine, one of our interns, comes jogging towards me with a stack of documents. I can already feel the migraine forming. Andrée—my assistant and the office manager—must be triaging fires again.

"Andrée said to give you these right away. It's the Lau Construction agreement," she blurts. "Apparently, it needed your signature yesterday."

"Everything needs my signature yesterday," I mutter with a sigh.

I grab the papers from her hands as I swipe my badge at my office door. "Next time, don't rush me before I've had coffee."

She stammers something apologetic, but I'm already inside, gesturing at her to follow me.

I sit at my desk, rub my temple, and scan the agreement.

"Legal's looked this over?" I ask without glancing up.

"Yes, sir," Francine says from the doorway.

"And the board?"

"Reviewed late last night."

I sign the pages and push them towards her. "Take them."

She grabs the documents and scurries off like her shoes are on fire.

I glance at the stack of interview folders in front of me. Meetings start in ten minutes, but I haven't bothered to check the order. Doesn't matter. I'll figure it out on the fly like I always do.

Seconds later, Andrée steps in with her clipboard in hand, and gives me her classic no-bullshit look, bringing me back to the present. "It's time, boss. The first candidate is waiting."

I follow Dre into the boardroom, head down, distracted by a message from Henson finally confirming we received the building permits we'd been waiting for. The other board members greet me but I barely acknowledge them as I sit at the head of the table.

Then I look up.

And everything fucking shifts.

Familiar, piercing brown eyes are watching me, posture perfect, nerves radiating from every angle.

It's the barista from Willow's. The one I didn't even thank for my drink. Here. Interviewing for a job at my company.

My lips quirk at the memory of her shouting at me only a few days ago.

I had stopped in for caffeine while waiting on an update from Henson about zoning permits for a project. The place was loud, cramped, and smelled like lavender.

I used to take Brianna to that cafe all the time when she was little on Saturday mornings. Hot chocolate with extra whipped cream for her, black coffee for me. She'd sit on my lap and sip her drink, leaving foam on her upper lip and giggling when I'd wipe it off with a napkin. Now, between school and my schedule, and Brianna becoming a teenager, those mornings are long gone.

Which explains why I'd never seen that barista before.

Now that I'm getting a real look at her, without the distractions, I realize why she stuck in my head in the first place. She's stunning. Striking, even. Beautiful curls, curves to die for, dark doe eyes.

"Mr. Miller?" someone says. "Sir?"

I feel a light kick under the table. "Worth," Dre hisses.

I snap out of it. "Yes. Sorry." I reach for my water bottle, twist the cap too hard, and take a giant gulp to hide my own reaction.

What the fuck is wrong with me?

Dre begins her intro, outlining the interview format, introducing everyone on the panel.

I can't hear a word.

All I can see is the woman sitting in front of me. Her lips. Her eyes. Her tight pencil skirt and the way she's biting her bottom lip like it's a nervous habit. I shouldn't be noticing that. I really, *really* shouldn't.

My gaze lingers too long on her mouth. Our eyes meet. Her pupils dilate and her chest rises like she's holding her breath.

I am too. This is bad.

"And this is Mr. Miller," Dre finishes. "He'll be leading the interview."

I clear my throat. "Right. Thank you, Andrée."

I lift the papers in front of me to break eye contact and buy myself a second to get it the fuck together.

"Name?"

"Mya," she replies, her voice a little shaky. "Mya Dessen-Jones."

The same name I saw on that résumé two nights ago.

"Mya," I repeat, letting it settle on my tongue. "Tell me about yourself."

Mya shifts in her seat. "Um, I'm a senior in the Graphic and Architectural Design program at U of W."

Young. *Too* young.

"I'm graduating with my master's with high honors in Sustainable Architecture," she continues, finding her footing. "I'm driven, detail-oriented, and passionate about design—"

"I read your file," I cut in. "You don't have field experience. This is a multi-billion dollar firm, Ms. Jones. We don't hire just anybody. So, what makes you special enough to be an exception?"

Mya goes still.

Then, slowly, she exhales. I can feel Andrée looking at me, probably scolding me telepathically for my tone.

"My father—" Mya starts. "He worked in construction. He'd come home with blueprints in his hands, and he'd light up when he talked about what he was designing. He loved his job.

He loved design. When I was little, he'd explain site plans to me like they were bedtime stories."

Her voice wavers, but she doesn't stop.

"He died in a fall on-site. I was just a kid. But I remember how proud he was of what he did. I fell in love with design, and I made a promise that I'd carry that pride forward. That I'd finish what he started. It's why I'm relentless about succeeding. If you put me on a project, I'll give it everything I have."

Something in my chest tightens at the obvious grief she's feeling, but my gaze keeps betraying me, sliding to the curve of her mouth, the shine of her brown eyes under the harsh fluorescence, the way her blouse stretches just enough when she breathes in.

It's ridiculous. I don't get flustered, but this woman's presence is like a live wire buzzing under my skin, and it's scrambling every logical thought I've got.

I grip my pen tighter, forcing my focus back to the page in front of me. Ask a question. *Any* question. But when I open my mouth, the words dry up, and all I can think about is how her voice tickles places in me that haven't woken in years.

If I don't dismiss her now, I'll say something I can't take back or worse, and everyone in this room will know exactly what I'm thinking.

I nod once. "Thank you, Ms. Jones. That'll be all."

She blinks. "I didn't show you my portfolio."

"You can leave it on the table. We'll review it."

She straightens. "With respect, the work reads better when I can walk you through the constraints, budgets, and sustainability targets I met—"

"And with respect," I interrupt, eyes still on the page, "out there, you won't have time to narrate competence. It should be obvious on the paper."

"It *is* obvious if you'll just look."

My eyes lift, meeting hers. A challenge. Heat climbs my collar.

Mya slides the folio closer. "If you're going to pass on me, pass on the *work,* not the assumption you made thirty seconds into meeting me."

The room thins to the two of us. I hold the silence until it bends.

"Noted," I say at last. "You're dismissed."

Mya sets her jaw. "Thank you for your time."

She adjusts her blouse, and walks out with her head high.

As soon as she steps out, I turn to Dre.

"We can't hire her."

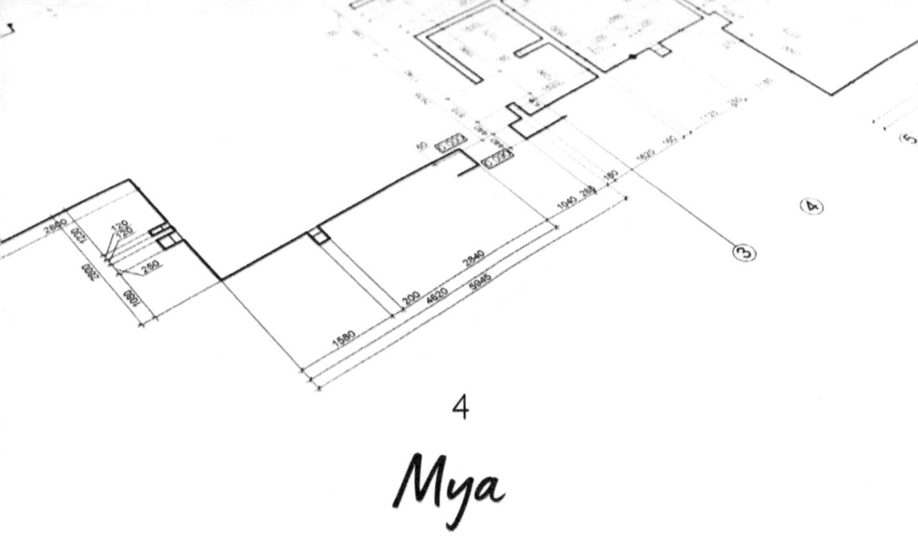

4

Mya

"*We can't hire her.*"

Mr. Miller's words echo into the corridor just as I step out of the boardroom.

My spine stiffens. *Asshole.*

"Worth, with all due respect, she has so much knowledge and skills she can bring to the table. And that project proposal of hers—" Andrée says.

"I don't care. We can't hire her."

I rush down the hallway before I can hear anything more and collide with a man carrying a tablet.

"Hey! Watch it!"

"I'm so sorry!" I say, stumbling backward, cheeks burning.

Way to go, MJ. Not only did you bomb the interview, you're now the girl who causes traffic jams in the hallway after arguing with the CEO in front of the *entire* board. Who does that? Of course that's what cost me the position.

I knew I shouldn't have come. What was I thinking, applying to the biggest construction firm in North America with no experience?

And worse than all that? I ogled Worth Miller like I was under some kind of horny spell.

What the hell is wrong with me?

There was something familiar about him that I couldn't place, until his gaze clipped mine and recognition sparked for both of us. Worth Miller was the rude prick from Willow's. Even with that same irritated set to his mouth of that day, I couldn't make myself look away.

Although, to be fair, *he* started it.

His stare wasn't neutral. His eyes raked over me like he didn't know whether to devour me or dissect me like I was some new species. I was caught in it.

Goosebumps shot across my skin the second his gaze landed on my lips, and when it dropped to my chest, I could barely speak.

Get it together, MJ.

There's no way the billionaire CEO of W.H.M. Construction was actually looking at me like *that*. He was probably sizing me up as a liability, which he made perfectly clear when he cut me off and dismissed me like I wasn't worth another minute of his time.

Besides, even if he *was* looking at me like that, it's probably just part of his routine to add another notch to his tailored, tabloid-famous belt. Seattle's very own blue collar playboy. I've read the gossip sites. I know his type. And I'm not auditioning to be his next meaningless distraction.

I spin in slow circles, scanning for a bathroom. My skin feels clammy, my cheeks are on fire, and I'm pretty sure I'm one second away from a full-blown panic attack.

I spot the sign for the women's restroom and practically sprint towards it.

Once inside—blessedly alone—I blot cold water on my cheeks, chest, and the back of my neck.

I will *not* cry.
I will not leave this building looking pathetic.
I pull out my phone and type with shaking hands.

> I fucked up.

TJ:

Nooooo! What happened?

> The CEO hated me.

TJ:

Impossible. No one hates you.

> Well, ask Worth Miller and he'll tell you he hates me.

Her reply doesn't come immediately.
My phone buzzes again a minute later.

TJ:

sends image

THIS is who interviewed you???

WTF, MJ? I'm drooling!!!

thought he'd be old! Since when are billionaires this hot???

A laugh bursts out of me.

> You're ridiculous 😆 I didn't know billionaires came with an age requirement.

TJ:

Shut up. You know what I mean. How did you even stay composed? I would've passed out.

> That's what I'm trying to tell you. It was a MESS.

TJ:

I'm sure you're overreacting. Have you seen yourself? You're young, hot, and brilliant. Who wouldn't want you?

Worth Miller. That's who.

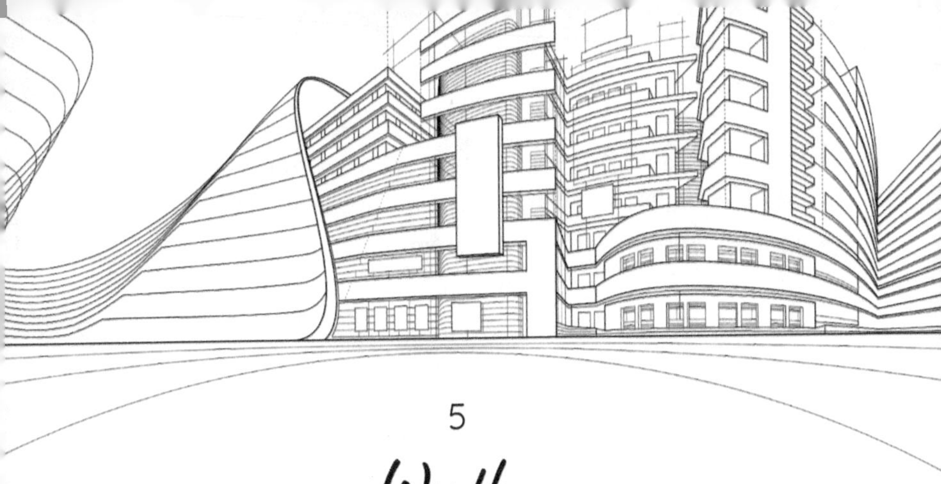

5

Worth

Standing in the kitchen, I scroll through my inbox with one hand, mug in the other. Henson has already sent over the agenda for this morning's meeting.

As I'm going over the information, a text comes in from my brother in the group chat I share with him and my best friend, Griffin, the company's chief of operations and lead architect.

HENSON:

Big day, boys. Meeting at 9. Bring your game faces.

GRIFFIN:

I always bring my game face.

HENSON:

Your "game face" looks like you're at a funeral.

Griff grew up with me and Henson in Mid-Island Nantucket. We built forts out of two-by-fours and shared every stupid childhood dream. We even worked the same crews after high school, doing grunt work and learning the trade with our hands in the dirt. When Henson and I decided to start W.H.M. Construction, Griffin was the first call we made. We didn't just want him on board—we needed him.

> It's too early for this shit.

HENSON:

> Awww, morning Sunshine. Did you sleep okay or did your pillow not fluff to your liking?

GRIFFIN:

> Don't poke the bear, Hen.

> You're both idiots.

HENSON:

> Love you too, big bro.

I scoff, toss the phone onto the counter and glance at the clock. Bri is usually halfway down the stairs by now, hair still wet from her shower, and muttering something about how I "micromanage breakfast."

Her sneakers are by the door, laces half-untied the way she always leaves them. Her backpack is missing from the hook. Normally, I'd hear the faint thud of music leaking through her earbuds, or the bathroom door slamming shut as she rushes to grab her things.

But the house is quiet.

"Brianna! Let's go, kiddo, we're gonna be late!"

I stand at the bottom of the stairs, phone in one hand, car keys in the other, waiting for the familiar thump of her footsteps coming down or for her to yell and complain about the little time I've given her. But not today.

I try again, louder this time. "Bri, come on!"

Still no answer.

Irritation sparks in my chest. She knows we have to be out the door in a few minutes. I set the keys on the hall table and head upstairs, my socked feet barely making a sound on the hardwood.

Halfway down the corridor, I notice the bathroom door is shut. I knock lightly. "You okay in there?"

There's a long pause and then, "I'm fine!"

I know my kid. She's not fine. That's her *leave me alone before I combust* tone.

"Bri..." My voice softens. "Can I come in?"

"No!" The answer comes fast, almost panicked.

I straighten, my hand still resting against the doorframe. "What's going on?"

"I—uh—" She stammers, stops, starts again. "Nothing."

It's the kind of nothing that screams something.

My mind stumbles for a second, flipping through every possibility until it lands on the one that makes the most sense. And then it hits me.

Oh.

She's thirteen, wants privacy, and her voice has that edge of discomfort I've only heard a few times before.

"Brianna, honey... Do you need me to call Maggie?"

There's a beat of silence. Then, quieter, "No. It's okay. I'm fine. We've... talked about this before."

I lean my forehead against the door, eyes shutting for a moment. Guilt presses in hard. In these moments, Bri shouldn't be on her own, having to be navigated by a dad awkwardly guessing through a closed bathroom door.

I do my best, and we have Maggie, thank God. But she can't be here all the time to fill in every blank space where her mother should be.

My shoulders tighten. It's hard not to picture my ex's face—hard not to imagine her justifying walking away, abandoning her daughter long before Bri would need her most. My chest heats with anger.

Not now.

I force the tension out of my voice. "All right. You sure you don't need anything? I can run to the store, grab whatever you—"

"I'm *fine*," Brianna says again.

I wait another moment before saying, "Okay. Just know I'm right here. Always."

The latch clicks, and the door opens an inch, then another. She steps out, face pink, eyes darting to the floor. My kid, who's usually all sass and chatter, suddenly looks uncomfortable, embarrassed.

I pull her in for a hug. She fits under my chin perfectly, still small enough that I can wrap her up, still young enough to let me. Her arms tighten around me for a second longer than usual.

I should drop her off at school and head straight to the office. I've got that meeting with the team for a big project, the kind of deal most companies dream of locking down. But the rest of the day can wait. My brother and best friend can handle it on their own.

My daughter needs me.

I lean back enough to see her face. "Hey, we've got some time before school. How about we swing by that coffee shop we used to go to, grab a snack?"

Her lips twitch in a smile. "I'd love that."

I'd cancel a dozen meetings just to see that smile.

"Grab your bag and meet me downstairs. We'll make it a slow morning."

Bri disappears down the hall, and I pull my phone from my pocket.

Won't make it to the meeting. You've got it.

Before Henson or Griffin can respond, I fire off another message to Dre to clear my morning.

By the time Bri comes down, backpack slung over her shoulder, I've got my keys in hand and the front door open.

I'm already picturing the warm smell of roasted beans and that corner booth Brianna used to like.

That place has been sitting in the back of my mind for days now, though I haven't bothered asking myself why.

It's not because I've been thinking about that barista since I walked in there last week.

Or because I'm curious about the same woman who interviewed at W.H.M. and stole my breath away.

And most definitely not because I've been thinking about her more than I should.

When Brianna and I walk into Willow's, I'm immediately hit with the heavy scent of coffee and fresh pastries.

"So what are you gonna have, Piglet?"

My eyes instinctively go to the bar, and I try to tell myself I'm *not* looking for Mya.

Memories of long, brown curls tumbling in every direction flash into my mind. Skin the warm shade of honey and bronze, like sun-kissed caramel. Mya looked... ethereal that morning.

And then, when she walked into W.H.M. for an interview a few days later...

The way I felt when I stepped into the boardroom was something I hadn't let myself feel in years. Desire curled in my gut, where I thought I'd buried it for good.

It was dangerous and unwelcome.

"Dad." Brianna's voice cuts through the noise of my thoughts. "Did you hear me?"

I shake my head, dragging myself back to the present. "Sorry, sweetheart. What did you say?"

"A hot chocolate with whipped cream, please." She repeats it slowly, like I'm hard of hearing. Then she smirks and nudges me in the side. "What's got you so distracted, huh?"

I laugh, the sound loosening the knot in my chest. The awkward tension from earlier at the house has melted away, and seeing her tease me like this feels like a gift. I'm just glad she's in better spirits.

"Got it, Piglet," I say, ruffling her hair. She pushes my hand away with a laugh. "Want to wait for me at a table?"

Brianna nods and heads for the booth by the window.

I turn back towards the counter, stepping closer. My gaze sweeps the line of baristas again, but Mya isn't there. Maybe she's not working today. *Pull yourself together, Miller.*

Then I catch movement below the bar. A cascade of familiar curls, disappearing out of sight.

My brow furrows.

Did she just... duck under the counter?

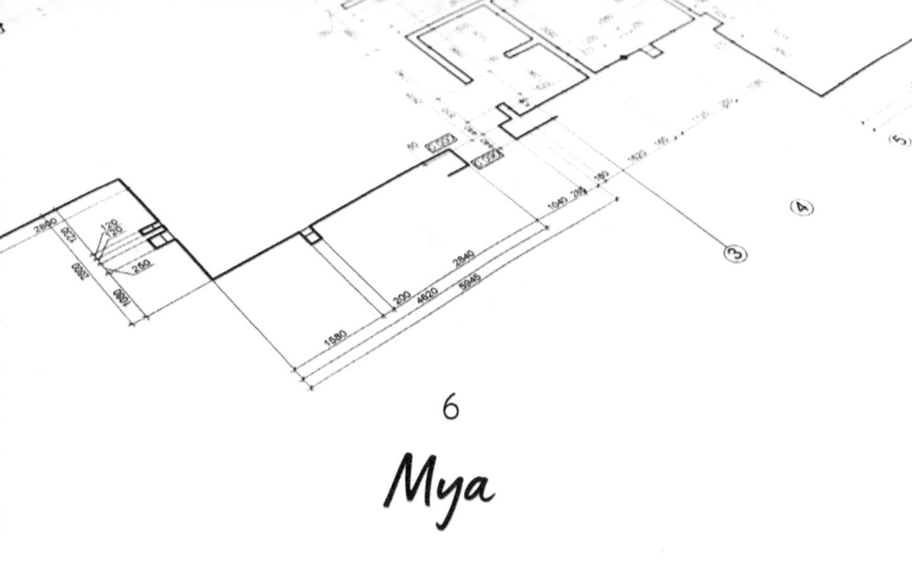

6

Mya

I t's a typical Tuesday morning at the café.

The sound of the espresso machine fills the quiet as I pull my hair into a messy low bun.

It's been a week since my interview at W.H.M. HR hasn't called, but I'm not holding my breath. They said we'd have answers by the end of this week—I already know mine. I'm still haunted by Mr. Miller's words like a verdict I can't appeal.

We can't hire her.

Part of me thinks he's right. I don't deserve the job.

I shake my head.

A few rebellious strands of hair fall around my face, but I don't bother fixing them.

Like an idiot, I even mentioned my dead father. Who does that? Who drags their grief into a work interview?

Apparently, me.

But my dad is the reason I even wanted this career in the first place.

However, what I really can't shake—what I *hate* that I can't shake—is the rush that went through me when Mr. Miller looked at me.

My stomach twists as I think about the interview again, about Worth Miller's penetrating eyes and the way his dismissal still rings in my head. He doesn't want me there. He made that perfectly clear.

Apron tied at my waist, I'm halfway to the cash register when the front door swings open.

One of my co-workers, Eric, shuffles in, hood up, sunglasses on, muttering something about how he should still be in bed.

"Morning to you too," I tease, stepping aside so he can pass.

"Ugh," he groans, dragging his feet towards the counter. "Never doing tequila shots on a Monday again. Who even thought that was a good idea?"

I chuckle and pat him on the back. "Sounds like you had fun, though."

"Fun, sure. Though my liver disagrees." He grins at me through his hangover. "You should come out with us next time. We're doing trivia night at O'Malley's this Thursday. Cheap drinks, good music, bad decisions. You in?"

My smile falters before I can catch it. "Maybe! We'll see," I hedge, turning my attention to the register.

I remember when I used to say yes to nights like that without a second thought. In my first year of college, I went out constantly—drinks with friends, late-night takeout, spontaneous weekend trips. I lived like I had an endless supply of cash, swiping my credit cards without blinking. Two cards, actually. Both maxed out before I'd even graduated.

Being twenty-four and thousands of dollars in debt isn't how I pictured starting my life. When I finally faced the reality of the hole I'd dug for myself, I slammed the brakes on all unnecessary spending. No more trips. No more random bar tabs. No more "fun" if it came with a price tag.

I push the thoughts away before they drag me under and start counting the till, sliding crisp bills into place.

The shop doesn't open for another thirty minutes, so Eric puts on a 2000s pop playlist, and we fall into our usual prep routine. He loads the baked goods display while I replenish the coffee cups, both of us singing badly and loudly to Britney Spears' *'Stronger.'*

Eight o'clock arrives faster than I expect. I flip the sign to *Open* and unlock the door for the first wave of customers.

As I hurry back behind the counter, the bell above the door jingles again. I glance up.

My body freezes, a jolt shooting straight down my spine. No. It can't be.

Worth Miller?

I don't even have to get a good look to know it's him. His presence has been lodged in my head for days.

What the hell is he doing here, anyway?

I scold myself. *He's here to get coffee like everyone else, duh.*

I keep my head down and hide behind one of the machines, like if I don't make eye contact, maybe he won't notice me.

Then I hear a softer, feminine voice answering his lower tone.

Before I can think better of it, my head snaps towards the sound, completely ignoring the fact that this means risking him seeing me. Not because I'm embarrassed about working here, but because after my dumpster fire of an interview, I'd rather not face him again.

It also doesn't help that the man is *gorgeous*. In a clean-cut, *should-be-illegal* kind of way. Meanwhile, I look like Ursula just crawled out of bed and decided to sling lattes for the day.

Dammit. I knew I should've washed my hair this morning.

When I finally focus on who he's talking to, my brow furrows. Standing beside him is a teenage girl—thirteen, maybe fourteen—tall, with sharp cheekbones and the same greyish eyes as his.

She's smiling at something he says, nudging him in the ribs.

He has a daughter?

The young girl heads straight to the booth in the far-left corner by the window, sliding in like it's her usual spot, even though I've never seen her here before.

Worth turns from her, scanning the café, and his eyes land on the bar.

I duck so fast behind the counter, my knees slam on the floor.

"Ow."

At the same time, Demi steps out of the kitchen and freezes when she sees me crouched like a fugitive. "Mya, what the hell—"

"Shhhhh!" I hiss, pressing my index finger to my lips.

Her mouth twists. "My bad." She tiptoes away, disappearing to the opposite side of the café like we're in the middle of a spy op.

If any customers notice my ridiculous behavior, they don't comment.

Thank God Tiana isn't here. She'd have a field day with this.

As if on cue, my phone buzzes in my apron pocket.

TJ:

> Why are you playing hide and seek at work, MJ? Are you drunk?

My gaze shoots up towards the security camera. How could I forget? My sister has remote access to the feed on her phone.

Tiana takes her job a little too seriously. But I get it. The owner, Mr. Patel, is a sweet older man who's been hinting for years that he's ready to retire and sell the place. TJ's a social media influencer—good at it, too—and even though she likes what she does, she's always had bigger plans. She was supposed to start a business degree before her brand blew up. And when the followers and sponsorships hit, Tiana pressed pause to ride the wave. It's worked for her, but she's not about to pass up a real foothold in the business world. Owning something of her own has always been her dream, and she loves Willow's so much she treats it like it's already hers.

I can respect that, but it doesn't change the fact that she's a total creep for watching me like some café security overlord.

I glare at the little black dome and flip it the finger.

Another vibration.

> TJ:
>
> You're fired.

> Buzz off. I'm kinda freaking out here.

> TJ:
>
> Why???

> Look at who's in line...

A three-dot bubble appears for a second, then her reply pops up.

> TJ:
>
> Gasp! It's the blue collar playboy in the flesh.

I slide to the floor and crawl towards the kitchen. Eric glances over mid-pastry prep, one brow raised, but he doesn't say a word.

Something hard taps the top of my head. I look down to see a cardboard cup rolling to a stop by my hand.

I turn towards him, narrowing my eyes and mouthing, *What the fuck?*

Eric smirks and mouths back, *You owe me*, before turning on the charm for the next customer like nothing happened.

Finally in the safety of the kitchen, I let out the breath I've been holding and fish my phone out again.

> Do you think he saw me?

My phone rings almost instantly.

"Why are you hiding from him?" Tiana demands the second I answer.

I pace in a small circle. "Well, we didn't exactly *get along* at the interview. Plus, if he sees me here again, he'll realize I left Willow's off my résumé, and that might tank my already nonexistent shot at the job."

There's a pause. Then she bursts out laughing.

"Mya, you're overreacting. He's not gonna care that you have a job. If anything, it shows you're responsible. You're a graduate with bills to pay. He's probably been there himself."

Maybe she's right. I've read a few articles about Worth since the interview.

Strictly research for the job, of course.

Most of the articles weren't about construction or business. They were about his *other* reputation—the man is always photographed with a different woman on his arm at every gala or charity event. Then there were paparazzi shots of him shirtless on a yacht in Saint-Tropez, swim shorts hanging low on his hips, sunglasses shielding his eyes while the sun lit up the salt-and-pepper scruff on his jaw. His body was chiseled, unfairly so, and the image burned into my brain before I could click away.

I shake my head hard, dragging myself back to reality. Nope. Absolutely not. I can't think about him like that. He's my potential boss, for God's sake.

"You should seize this opportunity and go back out there to talk to him! It'll show initiative, and you'll most likely leave a mark on him, if you haven't already," she says, her tone filled with mischief. "Show him that you're interested. I'm sure he won't bite... Actually, maybe you do want him to bite you, if you know what I mean."

I can practically hear the waggle of her brows.

Rolling my eyes, I mutter, "Focus, Tiana."

She's not wrong, though. This could be my last shot at showing Worth I'm serious about the job. I need this—not just for my career, but to keep up with my bills. Not that I'd ever admit that part to her.

"Okay, I'll do it. Let's just hope I don't embarrass myself again."

The memory of me talking about my deceased father, my voice wobbling, eyes stinging, flashes uninvited. Nearly crying in front of the entire hiring board... Perfect first impression, really. And then practically arguing with the CEO on top of that? I cringe.

"You'll be fine. Go get 'em, tiger!" Tiana roars into the phone, making me shake my head with laughter despite myself.

I hang up and draw in a deep breath, forcing my shoulders to relax and my pulse to slow.

The plan is simple: walk out there, greet him like he's any other customer, and when I *pretend* to finally see him, I'll stop by his table for a quick, casual chat. Easy.

Hopefully, he won't mind me crashing what's clearly a daddy–daughter outing.

Daddy.

The word sends a sudden rush of heat down my spine, and I immediately clamp down on it.

No, Mya. Get your mind out of the gutter.

I'm aiming to be his employee—his subordinate. Not

someone who daydreams about him in ways that would definitely violate a HR policy. And besides, I'm too young for him. *Way* too young.

Either way, this is a big gamble. He's already made it clear he didn't want to hire me.

But what do I have to lose?

I step back out, cheeks still warm, a timid smile tugging at my mouth. I can feel the embarrassment in my eyes as if I've been caught doing something I shouldn't have.

Worth is at the counter, and his gaze immediately lands on me. His brow furrows, like he's only just placing me.

"Good morning, Mr Miller."

"Mya, is it?"

"Uh, yeah. Hi. Nice to see you again." I extend my hand before I can overthink it.

He waits a beat too long. My smile falters and I start to pull back, mortified, when his fingers close around mine at the last second.

A spark shoots up my arm. My pulse spikes, and for half a second, the room narrows to just the two of us.

We both let go quickly, and I try to pretend nothing happened.

What was that?

"Likewise," he says flatly.

I yank my hand back and stuff it into my pocket like I can smother the zing still humming under my skin.

"I didn't realize you worked here."

Heat crawls up my neck. "I figured it wouldn't help my chances," I admit. "It's just temporary anyway." I shift my weight and tuck a loose curl behind my ear, wishing it would behave.

Eric slides Worth's order across the counter—two drinks

and a bag with muffins. Worth nods to him, then to me. "Thanks. Well, best of luck, Mya."

I paste on a polite smile in return.

As he turns away, I stand there with a thousand bad ideas crowding in.

Should I go over and explain that I wasn't trying to be insubordinate at the interview? That I panicked and my mouth outran my judgment? I should definitely apologize, at least.

I glance toward his table. He's already seated, jacket off, sleeves rolled, smiling at his daughter as she digs into one of the pastries.

You could walk over there, Mya. Own it.

Or you could leave with what little dignity you have left.

I wipe my palms on my apron. Then I square my shoulders and make myself move.

"Sorry to interrupt you, Mr. Miller. I was actually wondering if I could have a word?"

He glances up. "Sure," he says, leaning back in his seat.

I turn to the young girl across from him and soften. "Hi, I'm Mya."

She smiles politely. "I'm Brianna. Nice to meet you."

I draw a breath, fingers knotting together to stop them from shaking. "I just wanted to apologize if I came across unprofessional during the interview. Bringing up my father and speaking to you the way I did was inappropriate. I don't know what I was thinking; I promise that isn't how I normally conduct myself."

The word *father* scrapes my throat raw. My eyes gloss and I blink. He doesn't say anything, just stares.

"I'm probably just making this worse," I mutter, already stepping back.

"Apologies don't retroactively make an interview stronger,"

he finally responds before I can leave, his voice even. "Your portfolio will either hold up or it won't."

I swallow. "Understood." I should go now. Instead, I hear myself say, "For what it's worth, I wasn't trying to be dramatic. It was context." Worth nods, and I straighten. "But I'm aware of timing, Mr. Miller. I also thought owning a misstep mattered."

His mouth tips. "Owning it. Noted."

My cheeks flame again.

Worth exhales, looking at my fidgeting hands. "I don't know what it's like to lose a parent," he says, a little less clipped, "but I understand loss. When you lose someone or something you thought would always be there, it leaves a big hole. Sometimes it closes. Sometimes it doesn't. But either way, it changes you. That's all."

Then he adds, almost dismissively, "You're still young. You have time to find your footing again."

The way he says 'young' lands like an insult. As if grief has an expiration date. As if pain means less when it comes in a younger body.

I swallow the anger down.

Because from someone like Worth Miller, I believe it's the closest thing to comfort I'll ever get.

He clears his throat and checks his watch. "If you're asking for an answer, I don't have one for you. If you're selected, you'll hear from HR by week's end."

I nod, throat tight. "Thank you for your time."

He gives a single, dismissive dip of his chin and glances at Brianna. "I need to get my daughter to school."

"Of course." I force myself to turn away, feeling the sting of his cold professionalism like frigid air on an open wound and hating that a part of me still wants to look back.

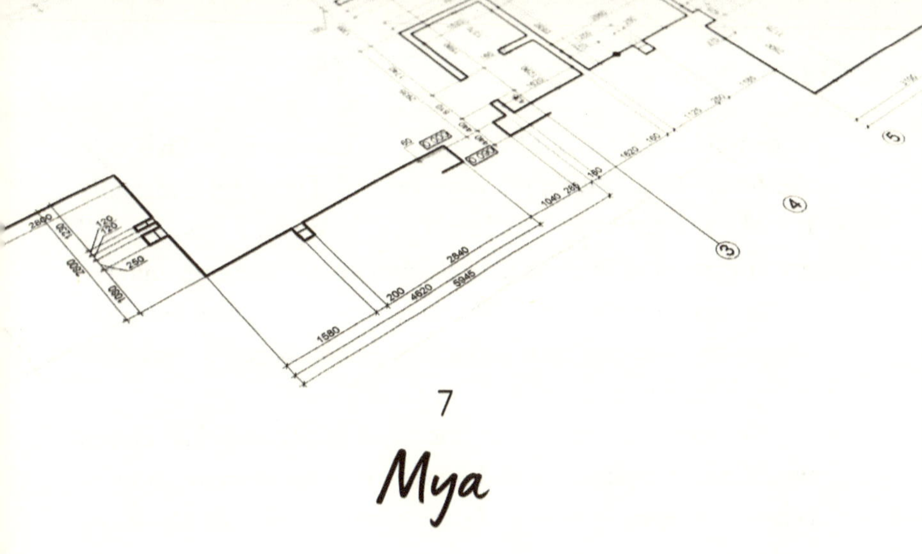

7

Mya

My stepdad walks into the kitchen just as I'm putting the final touches on my famous seven-layer dip that he begged me to make for game day. He's wearing a Philadelphia Eagles jersey, and I resist the urge to roll my eyes.

I'm a Cowboys fan, inherently because of my dad. But Devon is an Eagles fanatic, which makes us arch-nemeses.

We're a huge football family, so Sundays aren't just for dinners in the Dessen-Jones household.

"You ready to lose, loser?" When he doesn't respond, I look up; his expression is solemn, and I immediately go into worry mode.

"Are you okay?"

He heads to the fridge, grabs another beer.

"I'm just thinking..." he starts, his serious tone making my stomach flip, "about how sad you're going to be once my team kicks your ass!" He breaks into wicked laughter as he hunts for the bottle opener.

I swat the back of his head playfully. "Don't be an ass!"

My stepdad and I have always had a great relationship.

When he came into our lives, he brought sunshine with him in the form of his smiles, his warmth, and Tiana, who instantly felt like a sister to me. At first, I was hesitant. I was ten, still grieving my dad, and the idea of another man stepping into the picture felt like a betrayal. But even at that age, I could see how happy he made my mom. The house soon began to feel alive again; brighter days replaced the gloomy ones.

My mom sat me down once and explained that Devon would never replace my dad, never erase his memory. And he echoed the same promise. That's why we still talk about my dad openly, and why his pictures still hang proudly on our walls.

Devon pops the cap off his drink and takes a swig, smirking at me over the rim.

"You know, when the Cowboys choke this season—and they *will* choke—I'll be here with tissues and your seven-layer dip to comfort you."

I scoff, grabbing the tortilla chips. "Please. The Cowboys have more fight in them than your precious Eagles. I'd start stocking up on tissues for *yourself*, old man."

He lets out a dramatic gasp. "Old man? You wound me, MJ." He flexes his arms like he's in a commercial, which only makes me laugh harder. "Do I look old?"

"Like a fossil," I shoot back, grinning. "But a lovable one. Don't worry, Mom still thinks you're hot." I grimace and gag a little at the thought.

Devon chuckles, shaking his head. Then, his expression softens as he watches me fuss with the dip. "So, any word on that job interview yet?"

The question is like a punch to the gut and my hands freeze on the cheese. I force a smile that doesn't quite make it to my eyes. "Nope. Never got a call back." I try to keep my voice light, but the lump in my throat betrays me. "Guess I wasn't good enough for them."

Devon's brow furrows. He sets his beer down and steps closer, nudging my shoulder with his. "Hey. Don't do that. Even if they didn't pick you, that doesn't mean you're not good enough. It just means they weren't smart enough."

I huff out a shaky laugh, blinking quickly before my eyes can betray me. "Yeah, well, doesn't make it sting any less."

"Of course it stings. But you've got grit, Mya. And that's worth more than any one company's decision."

Just then, Mom walks in, wiping her hands on a dish towel. She takes one look at me and narrows her eyes. "What's wrong?"

"Mya's beating herself up about the job." My step dad gives her a look that says *help me out here*, and before I know it, they've flanked me, like some kind of motivational tag team.

Mom cups my cheek. "Oh, sweetheart. Listen to me. One job doesn't define you. You are brilliant and hardworking; anyone would be lucky to have you."

I glance between them, my chest tightening at the way they're both looking at me, like I'm capable of so much more than I ever give myself credit for.

"You two really need to take your act on the road," I murmur, trying to disguise just how much their words mean to me.

Mom laughs, pulling me into a hug. "We'll be your cheerleaders as long as you need us."

"Even if it means wearing Cowboys gear," Devon adds with a groan.

That gets a real laugh out of me, and the heaviness in my chest feels a little lighter.

Devon finally drifts out of the kitchen but Mom lingers,

leaning against the counter. Her eyes soften, and I already know what's coming.

"Hey. There'll be other jobs. Plenty of others. You'll find your place."

I swallow hard, trying to focus on smoothing out the dip. "I know... It's just hard not to feel like I'm disappointing Dad." The words slip out before I can stop them.

Mom pushes away from the counter and steps closer, taking my face in her hands again so I have no choice but to meet her gaze. "Sweetie, your father would never see you as a disappointment. He'd be so proud of the woman you've become."

Her reassurance should ease the guilt gnawing at me, but it only makes my throat tighten more. "I want to make him proud. And every time I fall short, it feels like I'm letting him down."

"You're not," she says firmly, her voice carrying that no-nonsense edge I've known my whole life. "The only person putting that pressure on you is *you*. Your dad would want you to be happy, Mya. That's all. And I know for a fact he'd tell you the same thing I'm telling you right now."

Her thumb brushes away the tear I didn't realize had escaped, and I lean into her hand.

"You carry him with you, Mya," she whispers. "Everywhere you go, in everything you do."

My chest aches with the truth of her words. Grief has a cruel way of twisting love into expectation, making me believe that if I stumble, it somehow erases him.

"I'll try to remember that."

Mom presses a kiss to my temple, her hand lingering at the back of my head the way she's done since I was a kid. "That's all you can do."

Before I can respond, Tiana struts into the kitchen, tossing her purse onto the counter. She takes one look at Mom holding me like I'm on the verge of collapse and quirks a brow.

"Yikes. Who died?"

I roll my eyes, wiping quickly at my face. "Really, TJ?"

Mom chuckles and gives my arm one last squeeze before stepping away. "I'll let you girls talk."

Tiana eyes me for a second, then she smirks. "I know what'll make you feel better."

I narrow my eyes. "What?"

She bumps my hip with hers and grabs another chip. "Let's go out tonight. Blow off some steam. A little dancing, a little drinking... there's nothing a few cocktails won't fix."

"You're ridiculous."

"Ridiculously *right*," she fires back, grinning. "C'mon, MJ. You need this. One night out won't kill you."

I sigh, already knowing where this is headed. "Tiana..."

She widens her eyes like I've just said no to free money. "Don't 'Tiana' me. You've been moping around for days waiting for that call. You need to stop sulking and live a little."

I cross my arms. "I'm not really in the mood."

"Exactly why you should come. You sit at home, you'll stew. You come out with me, you'll laugh, dance, maybe even flirt a little. Boom. Problem solved."

I give her a flat look. "You make it sound like some kind of miracle cure."

"It *is* a miracle cure." She loops her arm through mine dramatically. "Now say yes before I blackmail you on my socials."

Despite my resistance, a chuckle slips past my lips. My sister is impossible to argue with.

"Fine. One night. But you're buying the first round."

Her grin spreads wide. "That's my girl."

THE COWBOYS DO, IN FACT, LOSE, AND MY STEPDAD IS *insufferable.*

He struts around the living room like he personally led the charge, jersey stretched over his chest, a smug grin plastered on his face. I swear, if he says "told you so" one more time, I might retire from watching football altogether—and throw my dip at him.

Eventually, dinner is served, and the noise of victory chants is replaced by clattering silverware and laughter. My little brother finally bursts through the door, back from his friend's house, and the table feels whole again.

A while later, when the plates are cleared, Tiana grabs me by the arm and drags me upstairs to get ready for our night out. Instead of going home to change, I decide to borrow one of TJ's outfits.

We're halfway through hair and makeup when my phone buzzes on the nightstand.

An email notification.

From *Worth Miller.*

My heart lurches and my vision blurs for a second.

"Uh... why do you look like you just saw a ghost?" Tiana asks, eyeliner in hand.

"Worth Miller just emailed me. Why would he email me on a Sunday night at eight p.m.?"

Her eyes widen. "Oh my God. Open it!"

"I can't."

"Mya."

"No, I'm serious, Tiana. What if it's bad? What if he's telling me I didn't get the job? Or worse?"

"There's only one way to find out."

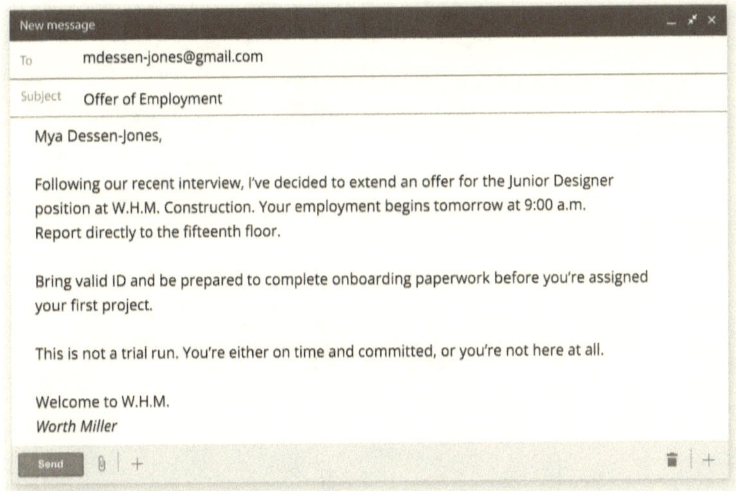

My heart slams against my ribcage, my eyes darting back and forth across each line.

"I—oh my God. Tiana." My voice cracks. "He hired me."

Tiana's jaw drops, her mascara brush freezing mid-air. "Wait—what?"

I thrust my phone towards her with shaky hands. She snatches it, scans the email, and then looks back at me like I just announced I won the lottery.

"You're starting *tomorrow?* At nine a.m.? Oh my God, Mya!"

I nod frantically, barely able to contain the giddy scream bubbling up in my throat. "I can't believe this. I was sure I didn't get it. And it's Sunday night! He sent it from his own personal email! Who even does this?"

"Worth-freaking-Miller does this," Tiana says, her grin splitting wide across her face. She sets my phone down and grabs my shoulders, shaking me.

"Girl, I guess we're celebrating tonight!"

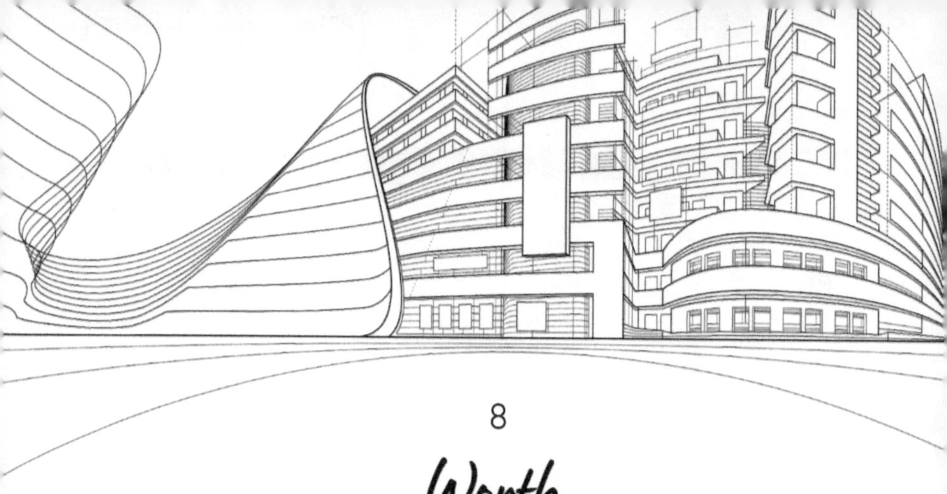

8

Worth

"What do you mean you offered her the job *last night*, Worth?"

Andrée's voice cuts like glass. She's the only person in this building—other than Henson and Griffin—who dares to call me by my first name, and when she does, it's never good news.

And she's right. I fucked up.

When I woke up this morning and realized what I'd done, I nearly launched my phone across the room.

I had been set on my decision. HR had already made the calls to the new hires, and Mya was not one of them. That should've been the end of it. But last night, after one too many glasses of Lagavulin, I pulled her résumé back out of my drawer.

The more I stared at it, the heavier that knot in my chest grew. Guilt. I don't know why. I don't know her. I don't owe her a damn thing. But the way she spoke about her father in that interview, and how raw and unpolished her grief was when I saw her again at Willow's—it stuck.

And the mouth on her. Most people fold when I cut them

off. But Mya didn't. She pushed back, and her sass landed low and immediate, right at my crotch. My control almost slipped. I had no business feeling that pull of arousal in the middle of a boardroom.

But underneath all that, Mya has grit that you can't teach and could be a great asset to the team.

It made me wonder if I had made a mistake.

And then, tipsy and restless, I opened my personal email and offered her the job. Starting today.

Andrée's eyes are practically shooting lasers at me now. "That was so reckless, Worth. You can't just email an applicant from your *personal* account, at eight o'clock on a Sunday night, telling her to report here the *next morning*. Do you realize how unprofessional that looks?"

I rub my temples, my skull throbbing in agreement. "She never even responded. So either she didn't see it, or she doesn't want the job. It's not a big deal, Dre."

Her brows shoot up. "Not a big deal?" She glances at her watch. "What if she shows up in twenty-five minutes?"

I lean back in my chair, letting out a humorless laugh. "Then we have HR draft her paperwork and find her a desk."

Andrée doesn't laugh. She just crosses her arms, eyes narrowed. "Is there something you want to tell me?"

It takes me a second, then I get what she's implying. I straighten in my chair. "No. There's nothing else to share."

Her expression doesn't soften. "It'll look bad on both of you if this is anything more than professional."

I inhale slowly. "I know." I swivel back to my computer, jaw tight. "I have work to do. Let me know if she shows."

Dre studies me for another beat, clearly unconvinced, then shakes her head and walks out of my office.

I stare at the blank email draft on my screen, but I can't focus. My fingers drum against the desk. The truth is, this already looks messy. And if Mya walks through those doors today...

I pull my phone out and scroll to my best friend's name. If anyone's going to give it to me straight, it's Griffin. He's the only one who knows when I'm bullshitting myself.

> Need you in my office. Now.

I hit send before I can second-guess it.

A beat later, the dots appear on my screen.

GRIFF:
> I'm busy.

> I might've done something really fucking stupid.

GRIFF:
> On my way.

I drop the phone on my desk and scrub a hand over my face. For the first time in a long time, I feel like I may have lost control of the narrative.

A few moments later, Griffin pushes my office door open and strides in, dropping into the chair across from my desk.

He waits, eyes narrowed. Griffin's patience has always been his most irritating weapon. I cave quicker than I'd like.

"I might've offered someone a job."

His brows shoot up. "Okay. And?"

"From my personal email. Last night." The words taste bitter coming out.

"Who the hell did you hire on a Sunday night?"

I hesitate. "Her name is Mya."

Griffin's eyes flash with recognition, and he lets out a low chuckle. "The one you told me about? The boardroom girl you couldn't stop staring at?" He leans forward, elbows on his knees. "The one you said *not* to hire?"

I shoot him a glare, but he doesn't flinch. "Yeah."

He shakes his head, a smile tugging at his mouth. "You're walking a fine line here, brother. Do you have *any* idea how bad this looks? Andrée will have your head."

The ache in my temple pounds harder now. "I know. I just —" My voice falters, and I hate myself for it. "She got under my skin. And I just felt like I made the wrong call. She's good."

"Under your skin, huh? That's not like you."

"No, it's not. And it won't happen again. She's an employee now. Nothing more."

He lets out a short laugh. "Just like that?"

"I don't have a choice."

"Maybe not, but you're already bending rules. That tells me something."

My jaw clenches. I hate that he's right, but I'm not about to hand him the satisfaction of hearing me admit it. "This is business. She's talented, and we need fresh blood. That's the end of it."

Griffin raises a brow. "Then what did you drag me in here for if you claim to know what you're doing?"

I exhale slowly, leaning back in my chair, eyes fixed on the skyline outside my window. "Because I needed someone to tell me I'm not losing my goddamn mind."

"You're not," Griffin says flatly. "You're just breaking your own rules. Which, for you, might be the same thing."

"She's an employee," I say again, more firmly this time. "Nothing more."

Griffin studies me for a second, then lets out a chuckle. "Jesus, Worth. You actually like her."

"No. I don't. I don't even know her."

The words feel hollow the second they leave my mouth.

Two brief interactions, and somehow she's lodged herself in my mind like a splinter I can't dig out. It's irrational. I don't do this. I don't *feel* this anymore.

And yet... There's something about her that lingers in my subconscious.

I shove the thought down. I've got no business mixing work with anything else, let alone this. I have rules for a reason. And beyond that, I'm raising Brianna. I'm not dragging women in and out of her life. I won't do that to her.

I clear my throat. "It's all good, Griffin. I've got it handled."

He gives me a long look, nodding once and stands. "Fine. Just remember what I said." Then he leaves, the office door clicking shut behind him.

The second he's gone, I reach for the phone on my desk, fingers tightening around the receiver before I can think better of it. I dial the one person who's *un*complicated. The one who never asks questions.

Shaina.

"Come to my office. Lock the door behind you."

I hang up before she can respond.

Maybe if I burn this out of my system, the way I always do with any type of feeling, I'll stop thinking about soft curves and wide brown eyes.

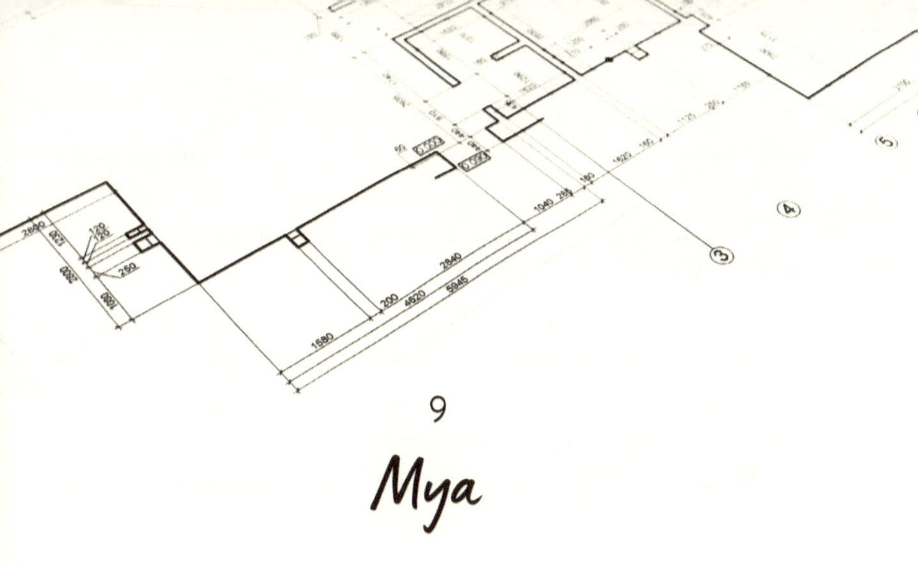

9

Mya

It's my first day at W.H.M. Construction, and I'm nervous as hell.

After receiving Worth's email, my excitement skyrocketed. I had something real to celebrate.

When Tiana and I went downstairs to share the news, my mom immediately wrapped me in a hug, while Devon clapped my shoulder with a grin. *"Congrats, kiddo. They finally came to their senses."*

They did question how I managed to get an offer so late on a Sunday, but I brushed it off. Beggars can't be choosers. A small part of me wondered if it was a scam—the email had come from a personal account, not the company's—but I refused to let paranoia ruin the moment.

Since I had to be up early the next morning, we kept our celebration lowkey. Tiana and I went to a lounge, shared an appetizer, and laughed until my cheeks hurt. I definitely didn't want to risk showing up hungover on my first day.

Now, standing in the lobby of Miller Towers, I'm instantly

taken aback. The building is stunning. My pulse jumps with awe. *Whoa.*

The designer of Miller Towers, Christopher Lowe, is a genius. We studied his work in my Architectural Theory and Design class, and his approach to clean lines, natural light, and sustainability has always been what I look up to most. The way he integrates modern function with eco-conscious choices makes every one of his projects feel alive.

To be here, in a place that carries his signature touch, is surreal.

A uniformed security guard greets me from behind the front desk, his expression professional but kind.

"Hi. It's my first day. My name is Mya Dessen-Jones."

The guard flips through a clipboard of papers, his brow furrowing. "Sorry, ma'am. Your name isn't on the list of new hires."

My stomach drops. *Shoot. Maybe Mr. Miller didn't have time to notify HR.*

Or worse... maybe this was all some bizarre hoax.

I force a smile that feels shaky. "Could you maybe call HR? Just to double-check?"

He nods once. "Give me a moment."

While he steps aside to make the call, I stand awkwardly in the middle of the lobby, clutching the strap of my bag. Nicely dressed employees stride past me, their shoes pattering against the marble floor. I hear another nervous voice at the second security station—a woman introducing herself as one of the new hires. She's greeted warmly, handed a badge, and directed towards the elevators.

Minutes crawl by before the guard returns. "Miss," he says carefully, "HR confirmed you weren't hired."

Heat floods my cheeks. *Well, this is awkward.*

"I have an email from Mr. Miller confirming my employment," I say, pulling out my phone and sliding it across the desk for him to see.

He leans closer, scanning the screen with a skeptical frown. "I'll call up to his office."

Again, I'm left standing there like some kind of lost puppy while polished employees stride past me without sparing me a glance. My palms are damp, nerves buzzing under my skin as the minutes tick by.

He returns, looking regretful. "I'm sorry, but I can't get through. Mr. Miller's receptionist isn't at her desk and his assistant is busy onboarding the new hires."

A groan builds in my throat, but I force it down, pasting on the most polite smile I can muster. "I understand that you're just doing your job..." I glance at his badge. "Constantine. But I really need to get inside. I don't want to be late on my first day. Now, please just let me up to the fifteenth floor. Escort me if you want, but I'm not missing this opportunity. And I'm sure you don't want to be the reason I get fired before I even start."

"I'm sorry, Miss—"

"Please, call me Mya."

"Mya," he corrects. "It's protocol. I'd be risking my job."

Before I can argue further, a tall, bulky man approaches from the elevators. Broad-shouldered, built like he belongs in a lumberjack calendar, with neck-length ginger hair and a neatly trimmed beard to match. He claps Constantine on the shoulder, briefly glancing my way "Hey, Stan. What's going on?"

Before Constantine can answer, I jump in. "Apparently, my name isn't on the new hires list, but I was offered a position here. I'm supposed to start today."

That gets his attention. His green eyes snap to mine. "You must be Mya."

Relief washes over me as he extends his hand. I study him quickly—ruggedly handsome, the kind of man who looks like he could chop wood with one arm and draft a skyscraper with the other. But the attraction dies as soon as our palms touch. Not my type.

"I'm Griffin," he says. "Worth mentioned he was expecting you this morning."

I let out a breath. "Great. So you'll be able to take me upstairs?"

He nods and murmurs a few words to Constantine, who finally waves me through the barrier.

The walk to the elevator is short and quiet. Once we're inside, I notice the faintest smirk tugging at Griffin's mouth.

"What is it?" I ask, my voice shaky despite my best effort to sound casual.

He shrugs me off with a chuckle. "Oh, nothing. Just thinking about how the boss messed up."

"I don't get it."

"You will soon enough." The elevator doors open on the fifteenth floor, and he steps out, leaving me no choice but to follow.

I'm hit with a cacophony of sound—phones ringing, conversations overlapping, the clack of keyboards filling the air. The space is buzzing with good energy, focus and chaos.

This is it. My new world. My new beginning.

Griffin gestures around as he guides me through the bustle. "W.H.M. spans several floors, but this is where the magic happens. Over there is the design team where you'll be stationed. On this side, spaces for our contractors. And at the far end—" He points towards a row of private glass-walled offices. "The executive wing. CEO, CFO, and mine."

"You're an executive?" I blurt, surprised.

He crosses his arms, cocking a brow. "Is that hard to believe?"

"No, sorry. I didn't mean anything by it. I just thought—"

"Relax, Mya. I'm just giving you a hard time. I know I don't exactly look the part." He gestures at his jeans and plain white tee, shrugging. "But I'm usually on-site more than in the office. Besides, Worth and Henson are like brothers to me. They can't say shit." He winks, then continues towards the corner offices.

Heat creeps up my neck. Griffin seems nice and easygoing. But as we get closer to those glass doors, my nerves kick back in with force, heart hammering. Am I about to face Worth again?

The thought rattles me. I keep seeing flashes of him—how hot and cold he was in the interview, his detached intensity in the café, and how soft he was with his daughter.

I need to snap out of it. He's my *boss*.

"Since your employment offer was... unconventional, I'll take you to Worth instead of his assistant, Andrée. She's handling the training, but he'll probably want to talk to you first."

I remember Andrée from the interview. She was professional, yet kind. I'd much prefer her over Worth right now.

When we round the corner, I notice the front desk is empty. Then, a door swings open. A woman slips out, smoothing her blouse and tugging at her skirt, like she's readjusting it. My eyes flick automatically to the gold plaque on the door. *Worth Miller.*

I roll my eyes.

Of course he's banging his receptionist. Why am I not surprised? The man's reputation precedes him. A forty-something billionaire playboy still living like a twenty-something frat star.

Any fantasy I had about him, any ridiculous thoughts I let myself entertain, melt away under the ice-cold bucket of reality.

But then, I remember the man at the café. The father with

his little girl. He looked... different. I guess that was just another mask.

Griffin clears his throat, jolting me back. "Mya?"

"Y-yes. Sorry."

"You were staring."

"What?"

"At Shaina. The receptionist."

I plaster on a smile, though I know it looks fake. "Just getting a glimpse of the kind of colleagues I'll be working with."

Griffin shakes his head, as if he can read every single thought in my head. "This is going to be interesting," he mutters under his breath.

Before I can press him on it, Shaina turns to him. "You can go in, Mr. Hayes."

Griffin thanks her, then gestures for me to follow.

He cracks the office door open and steps aside for me. "Worth. Your new protégé is here."

Worth glances up from his monitor. His eyes skim over me once—barely even a second—before returning to his screen.

"Take her to the boardroom," he says flatly. "Andrée just started the introductions."

Griffin narrows his eyes at him. "That's not in my job description. So how 'bout no? You do it."

Worth finally looks up at us again, his gaze lingering this time. "Fine. You can go, Griff."

Without hesitation, Griffin backs out, tossing me a quiet, "Good luck," before leaving me behind.

"Ms. Jones. Take a seat."

I glance at the chair, then back at him, every instinct in me screaming to bolt. But I want this job. I *earned* this job. And I will not cower in front of the big, bad CEO.

Either way, I'm not the one who emailed me on a Sunday night to offer me a job. Clearly he wants me here for a reason.

I sit, crossing my legs. My skirt shifts a little higher on my thigh, and I catch Worth's gaze lowering to the exposed skin. Heat creeps up my chest. I quickly tug it back into place, pretending I didn't notice.

"Thank you for coming in today. As you can imagine, the way I hired you goes against HR protocol. I would appreciate discretion on how you received the offer."

I force a polite smile, keeping my tone neutral. "Of course, Mr. Miller." Nothing more, nothing less. The last thing I need is anyone thinking I got here through favoritism.

One day, I'll ask him what made him change his mind after our interview, why his sudden offer came out of nowhere. Just not yet.

He nods once, satisfied. "Good. I'll have my receptionist take you to the training room." Then, without another glance, he turns his attention back to his monitor—a clear dismissal.

Without another word, I rise quietly and leave his office.

The image of the man I saw at the coffee shop—the one who smiled at his daughter like she was his whole world—fades like smoke. Maybe this is the real Worth Miller: cold and uninterested.

For my own sanity, I need to stay as far away from him as possible.

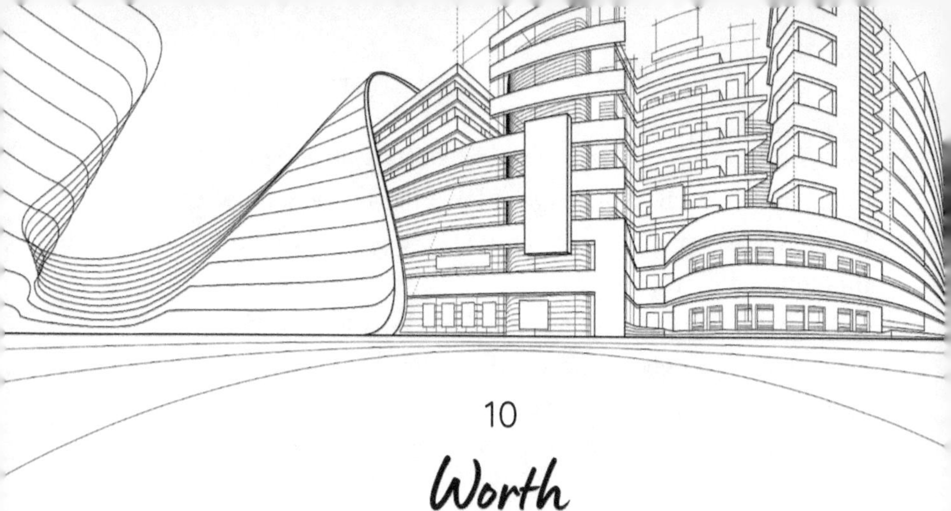

10

Worth

I'm so screwed.

Mya's scent still clings to my office, sweet and maddening, and I find myself inhaling the air like some pathetic hound searching for its master.

My cock twitches against my slacks, straining, and I glare down at the traitor.

Ridiculous. I should be satisfied. Hell, I just emptied myself into Shaina's overinflated mouth ten minutes ago. But that release did nothing to quiet the pull I feel towards my new employee.

For fuck's sake.

When she was right in front of me, I managed to mask the hitch in my breathing, the way my fingers dug into my mouse, hard enough to ache. Pretending not to notice the bare skin and curve of her legs when she crossed them. Pretending not to *want.*

Griffin is a dead man walking.

There was no reason for him to march her straight into my office. He could've taken her anywhere. Andrée, the boardroom

—the goddamn break room. No, he wanted me rattled and off-balance.

Well, congratulations, Hayes. It worked.

Scowling, I reach for my phone, thumb hovering over the screen.

> I ought to strangle you with my bare hands.

HENSON:

What? Why? What did I do?

> Not you, dumbass. But the fact that you immediately think you're the culprit is concerning.

HENSON:

I plead the fifth.

GRIFFIN:

It was a test.

> Test what exactly? How many lives you have? Because you're about to lose one.

HENSON:

Whoa. What did I miss, brethren?

> Griffin thought it was a good idea to parade one of the new hires in my office.

HENSON:

Why? Is she hot?

GRIFFIN:

Yes.

> Shut up, Griff.

HENSON:

Oh… sensitive…

> I better not hear from either of you for the rest of the day.

HENSON:

Griff, I'm calling you for the scoop.

GRIFFIN:

I'm ready.

Worth, it was a test to see how you'd react to her at the office. From what I saw, you passed, so why are you all pissy?

I don't want to be part of your stupid tests.

HENSON:

Who is this girl?

GRIFFIN:

Worth's next ex-wife.

HENSON:

Lol. I can already tell that you fucked up, Worth.

GRIFFIN:

If what you told me this morning is true, then you have nothing to worry about. Her presence shouldn't affect you, right?

Right.

I'm trying to convince myself as much as him.

And that's what I need to remember. If I let her get under my skin, Mya Dessen-Jones could dismantle every piece of the perfectly curated life I've built for myself.

It's after lunch, and I haven't caught another glimpse of Mya since she sat in my office this morning.

Griff ended up running his mouth to Henson about my so-called "dilemma" and, sure enough, my brother called me demanding why I hadn't told him about her earlier. I argued there was nothing to tell, I wasn't planning on hiring her. But in my almost-drunken lapse last night, I offered her the job anyway.

Henson let me off the hook faster than I expected, though not without giving me the same look Griffin had, also reminding me to "be careful."

I'm a grown man. I don't need anyone telling me how to conduct myself.

On my daily rounds through the office, I pass the glass-walled boardroom. The new hires have been corralled in there all morning, learning about W.H.M. Construction, the firm's structure, and the projects on deck. Soon they'll be split into teams and given their first assignments.

A sudden motion catches my eye. Curly brown hair, tilting towards the window.

Mya turns her head at the exact moment I pass, and for a split second our gazes collide. Hers darts away immediately, but mine lingers.

I shouldn't want to affect her. But hell if I'm not glad I do.

At least I'm not the only one who feels the pull.

I've had more women than I can count, but something about Mya... She's not like anyone I've entertained before. There's a grit beneath her nerves, something bright that makes her hard to ignore.

Not that it matters. Nothing can ever happen between us.

Even though my cock begs otherwise.

AT THREE O'CLOCK, MY PHONE VIBRATES IN MY POCKET. I fish it out, glance at the caller ID, and answer on the second ring.

"Hey, Piglet."

"Hi, Dad. I just got home."

"Great. Is Maggie on her way?" I lean back in my chair, tugging at the knot of my tie, loosening it just enough to breathe.

"Yup! She's bringing dinner from home this time."

"Alright. Don't forget to do your homework, Squirt."

Brianna stifles a laugh. "Why do you call me ridiculous names?"

"Because why not?"

I can practically hear her eyes roll through the phone, and it makes the corner of my mouth twitch despite the stress knotted between my shoulders. Still, a thought nags at me. The fear that the more my daughter grows, the more she'll slip away. Ever since she "became a woman" last week, I realized there are parts of her life I won't be able to reach. Parts I can't help with. That distance scares the hell out of me. Maggie does what she can—and I'm grateful—but it doesn't fill the hole her mother left behind.

My hand drags down my face, my jaw tightening.

"I'm almost fourteen, Dad. Nicknames are for kids," Brianna argues, exasperated.

"You *are* a kid, and you'll always be my little girl. You could be married with children and I'd still call you Piglet."

She groans, but I can hear the smile she's trying to hide. "I don't think my future husband would understand that."

The thought of Brianna with a husband—or worse, some hormonal boy sniffing around her—twists my gut. "Well, fuck him. Stay single forever and live with me."

Her loud laugh bursts through the speaker, and I swear it's the best sound in the world. "Dad! First of all, language. Second, that sounds crazy. What if *you* find someone?"

"I won't, kiddo. It's just you and me."

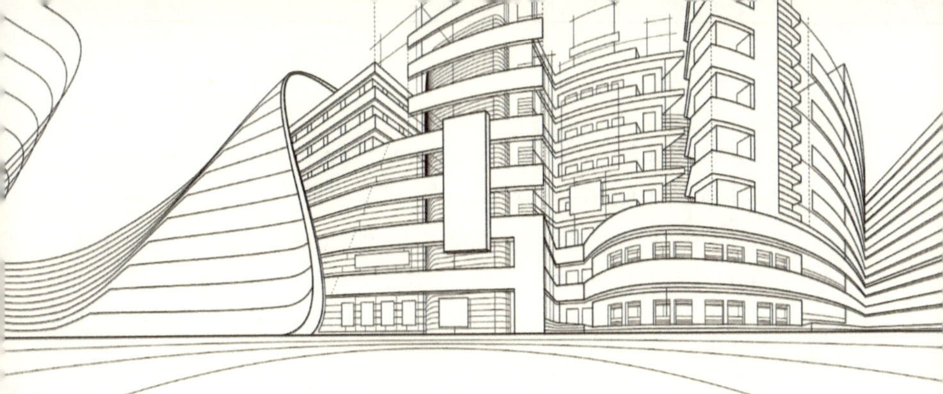

11

Worth

The floor is dead. It's past seven and everyone is gone.

A supplier changed delivery dates this afternoon and blew up the schedule, so I'm here fixing plans for a meeting at eight a.m tomorrow morning with our partners. If I don't clean this up tonight, we will lose weeks. I'm halfway through the terrace sheet when my phone lights up with an unknown number.

I answer. "Worth Miller."

A voice I haven't heard in months echoes through the phone. "Worth."

Cold slides under my skin. "Vanessa."

"I didn't expect you to pick up."

"Yet you still called."

Brianna's mother is still the rawest nerve in my life. The way she left us, like marriage and motherhood were disposable titles, still boils my blood. Last I heard, she was floating through Asia with some boy toy, not a care in the world.

I don't keep in contact. I just pay a PI to check in every now and then. Not because I give a damn, but in case Brianna ever asks, I'll have the answer ready.

She never does. Never even says her name. But I know Bri wonders. I know she misses her mom in ways she won't admit.

But I don't miss my ex-wife. I don't think about her unless I have to.

Vanessa laughs awkwardly. "Still working at the office late, I see?"

"Clearly."

"How's... how's work?"

"Same as always." I flip a page. "Say what you called to say."

A pause. "I saw a photo of Bri. The one Maggie posted of her science fair thing? She looked tall. Older."

"She is."

Another pause. "How is she?"

"Fine."

She exhales. "Does she sleep okay? Is she eating? Still drawing all the time?"

"She's fine, Vanessa. Cut the shit." I'm tired of the circling. "What do you want?"

"I want to see her."

"No."

"Right out the gate?" She clicks her tongue. "Still charming."

"You said that last time," I say, eyes on the darkening Seattle skyline. "And the time before that. You never show. I'm not doing this again, Vanessa. It always ends with my kid crying into her pillow."

"I had a job, Worth. I had things—"

"You always have things."

"You make me the villain every time I try," she snaps. "I want to be present. She's my daughter."

"She's *our* daughter," I correct. "And Brianna needs consistency more than your apologies."

"I can do next Sunday," Vanessa rushes out. "Two hours, public place. You can sit at the next table if that makes you feel more in control."

"What makes me feel in control is knowing my daughter won't spend time getting ready for someone who won't arrive."

"You think I don't feel sick about that? You think I don't—"

"I don't think about you," I cut in. "I think about *Brianna.*"

"God, you're impossible." A jagged breath. "Fine. Keep her from me. Keep playing the perfect dad—"

"I'm not perfect," I say. "But it's more than you'll ever be."

Another silence. When she speaks again, it's low. "If you don't let me see her, I'll call my lawyer."

"Then do it," I say, tired and done. "Your lawyer knows mine."

"Worth—"

"Good night, Vanessa." I end the call and set the phone face down, rubbing my temples to ease the eminent headache.

Then, I sense movement in the hallway.

I pivot.

Mya stands just outside the door, laptop hugged to her chest, guilt written across her face like she's been caught trespassing.

Of course she'd be here late. She has been every day of her first week here. She's the only other person who voluntarily lives in their work.

I press my thumb into the bridge of my nose, exhale once, and wave her in. "Come in, Ms Jones."

She steps in, careful, closing the door behind her. "I'm sorry. I was going to ask about the terrace detail, and then you were on the phone and I—"

"It's fine." It comes out sharper than I mean to. Her mouth presses into a thin line, but she nods.

"How can I help you?" I ask, gesturing to the desk.

Mya sits hesitantly, and sets her laptop down. "Are you okay?" Something that looks like concern flashes in her eyes.

"I'm working," I deflect, flipping a page I'm not even seeing. "What do you need for A9?"

She doesn't take the bait. "I know I'm a new employee and basically no one to you, Mr. Miller, but if you ever need to talk, I'm here."

I exhale through my nose, but the frustration from the call doesn't abate. "That's not in your job description."

"Neither is staying 'til seven, yet here I am."

I should send her back to her desk. Instead, words I haven't said out loud in a long time spill out.

"My ex called," I say, jaw tight.

Mya's expression softens. "That must be complicated."

"It's not," I bite off, heat burning under my skin. "She left us, and now she suddenly wants back in again." My fingers drum on the table. I drag a breath through my teeth.

"We were happily married for five years before Brianna was born. Then it just went downhill." My throat tightens as I speak. "She suffered from postpartum depression; we got her the help she needed. After that, she just seemed so disconnected. She began traveling all the time, leaving Bri with our nanny while I was at work, building the company."

My jaw locks, and I stare past Mya to the dark pane of glass. "We barely saw each other. I felt like it was my fault, like I wasn't there enough, and that's what made her seek happiness elsewhere. The more money I made, the less present Vanessa became."

I flatten my palm on the desk, steadying myself. "When I confronted her about what she was doing—who she was seeing, where all the money was going—she flipped, packed a bag, and walked. She didn't even say goodbye to Brianna." I swallow hard, the memory hitting like a body blow. "I had to explain her disappearance to a three-year-old."

I don't say that it gutted me, too.

How the house went too quiet at night, that I'd stand in the doorway of Bri's room, counting her breaths, because it was the only thing that was still steady. How I slept on the couch for months, because sleeping in our bed felt wrong.

I don't say that work wasn't just work after that—it became my escape. If I kept the numbers growing and the schedules tight, then at least something held. If I made the company impossible to shake, maybe *I'd* stop shaking. You learn to lock it down and make the face that tells everyone you're fine—until you almost believe it yourself.

I don't say I'm still angry at how much it hurt.

Brianna needed a spine, not a puddle. So I took the hit, packed it behind my ribs, and kept moving.

Mya's throat works. "I'm sorry."

"I'm not looking for sympathy."

"I didn't offer sympathy," she says gently.

I stare at the skyline beyond her shoulder. "She called tonight, saying she wants to make it right." I huff a laugh that isn't real. "You can't make right what you never stayed for."

Mya folds her hands, thinking. "Do you want Brianna to see her?"

"I want Bri to be okay." The answer is automatic. "Every time Vanessa promises and bails, I'm cleaning up the fallout. I'm not running that play again."

"Maybe if Vanessa really means it, she'll keep showing up. And if she doesn't, you protected your daughter from another hit."

I nod once. The muscle in my jaw finally loosens. "Yeah."

I don't know why I'm saying any of this to Mya. Maybe it's the hour. Maybe it's the way she listens, like she can quiet the static in my head just by standing there. This is dangerous. Lines blur fast when you let someone make the noise stop.

I pull the mask back on and file my vulnerability away, back in the drawer where I keep things that hurt.

"Now, how can I help you?"

"Oh, yeah. The terrace detail. Your note about drainage was right. I rerouted the scupper here." Mya turns the laptop, walks me through the change.

I look where she points. It's good. "Fine. Push it."

Mya nods and starts to stand, then glances at me. "I meant it, by the way. If you ever need to talk."

Something in my chest warms, but I shut it down.

"I'm good. This isn't a therapy office after all," I say, back to clipped. "If you're done, you can go home."

She nods, her lips pressing into a thin line. "Good night, Mr. Miller."

"Night, Ms. Jones."

THE NEXT MORNING, MYA AND I HIT THE REVOLVING doors of Miller Towers at the same time.

"Morning, Mr. Miller," she says, before giving security a nod. Constantine beams at her and she flashes those pearly whites back.

I'm irritated for no good reason. He's being friendly. But I'm not an idiot. I know what he's looking at. Anyone with eyes can see she's gorgeous. Most people would trip over themselves to get her attention.

I flash my badge; Mya does the same beside me. We move through together.

"Good morning," I finally respond.

It's not exactly awkward between us, but it's definitely tight around the edges.

I shouldn't have said that much last night. I went home, stared at a dark ceiling, and mentally tore into myself for handing over pieces I don't hand to anyone. It was too personal, but what's done is done.

We walk towards the elevators in silence, and step in together when the car dings open. Without looking, we both reach for the panel.

Our fingers touch.

A clean, electric brush of skin against skin. A spark snaps up my wrist. Mya freezes; so do I. Her breath hitches, audible in the small box, and her chest lifts once, like she's trying to force oxygen to her ribs.

My gaze flicks to her mouth, then away, but I don't move my hand.

She's the first to break, hand curling back to her side, knuckles whitening around her laptop sleeve.

I press fifteen, and the door slides shut.

The air hums as the floors tick up, one by one. Out of the corner of my eye, I see the pulse at her throat beat fast. Mine does the opposite.

Finally, the bell chimes and fifteen lights up.

The doors part, and I gesture for Mya to get out first. "After you, Ms. Jones."

"Thank you, Mr. Miller."

She steps past, poker face back on, and we peel off in opposite directions down the glass corridor, both pretending the static didn't follow us out. *Christ.* Whatever that was needs to be buried for the rest of the day.

I walk into my office, drop my brief on the credenza, and head to the conference room. It's already loud; two of our building partners, Lang and Pierce, are tag-teaming excuses when Griffin slips into the chair at my right, sleeves rolled up. He gives me a sideways nod.

The wall screen pings and Henson pops on from Vancouver, tie loosened, hotel art behind him.

"We can't absorb those penalties," Lang insists. "Your revisions pushed the timeline—"

"My revisions kept your tower from shearing in high wind," I say from the head chair. "You're welcome."

Pierce slides a folder across. "We'll need W.H.M. to participate in liquidated damages—"

Griffin taps the folder back with one knuckle. "You'll need to participate in reading. Section 12.2 excludes safety-driven changes."

On the screen, Henson lifts a brow. "And your procurement window closed before those revisions locked. You cheaped out on glazing, gentlemen. That's not market conditions. That's a gamble."

Pierce bristles. "We value-engineered per—"

"Correction," Griffin says, calmly. "You gambled and lost."

I look from one brother to the other. Before the skyscrapers, the suits, and the glass office with a view, I was hauling demo debris at dawn. None of us grew up rich, but we grew up solid. Our parents taught us to hustle and build from the ground up. W.H.M. wasn't born from a trust fund or a loan—it came from sweat equity, second jobs, and the kind of risk that keeps you up at night. We built this company brick by brick. So I don't take it lightly when people try to take me for a ride.

"You're asking the wrong house for charity," I finish. "Here's what you'll do: lock your steel order by noon, revert to the approved glazing spec, and stop pretending you can save a dime by spending a dollar."

Henson holds up a single page to his webcam. "Your homework. Send us a revised schedule by three p.m., weekends included. If you want W.H.M. to babysit, add a zero to the retainer. Otherwise, do your jobs."

Lang starts, "We—"

I lift a hand and tap the contract. "Meeting adjourned."

Chairs scrape, and they file out, chastened. Griffin leans back, mouth ticking. Onscreen, Henson watches them go.

"Should've brought cupcakes," he says dryly. "Everyone takes bad news better with frosting."

Griffin huffs a laugh. "Or bourbon."

Henson's gaze swings back to me. "So... How's it going with the new junior designer?"

Griffin muffles another laugh into a cough.

"Good," I snap. "Why?"

Griffin studies me like I offended him. "Only that you go taut like a tripline when she's around."

"I don't." It's the opposite. Somehow, I'm less taut with her in the room, as if the noise drops and my breathing evens out—even if my face refuses to admit it. I won't tell these idiots that.

"Sure," Henson says, voice dry. "And I don't eat carbs."

Griffin tips his head. "She's sharp and holds her ground. You like that."

"I like competence," I retort.

"Uh huh. *Competence.*" Henson mimes quotation marks.

I give my brother a deadly look through the screen.

He grins. "Relax. I'm kidding. But your *vibe* isn't chill—at all."

"It's purely professional."

It is, right? Not entirely. And last night, Mya listened like my words mattered, and that's a drug I don't intend to sample. Not again.

Henson leans closer to his webcam. "Listen, man. I know

why you keep steel walls up. But not everyone is a breach. Some just... stand with you."

I flick my eyes to him then Griffin. "Is this a feelings meeting now? Should I get a candle?"

Griffin lifts both hands in surrender.

I collect the folders off the table. "We done?"

Henson salutes the camera and Griffin pushes to his feet, still smirking. At the door, he pauses. "For what it's worth, she's good for the team. And you look... a little less miserable."

"Get out," I say, but there's no heat.

The door shuts behind him and the room goes quiet.

I stack the files, trying not to think back to touching Mya's skin in the elevator, and the way her voice threads through the static and turns it down.

Around noon, Mya steps into my doorway with a file.

"Do you have five minutes?"

I check my watch, even though I already know the answer. "Three."

She crosses to the table, close enough that her perfume slips into the space between us, and drops a folder onto it.

I plant a hand on the hard surface and keep my voice even. "Are those the preliminary drawings for the community housing project?"

Mya nods. "That's what I'm here to show you."

"You know you don't have to bring them to me, right? Griffin is your direct superior. He should approve your drawings."

"Oh. Yeah. You're right. I'm sorry." She clears her throat. "I shouldn't have bothered you. I just thought you'd want to see them since I came to you about this yesterday."

She's rambling, and it's cute as hell. I smother the smile trying to get out.

"Relax, Mya. I'll take a look." Her name slips out before I can catch it. Shit. I keep my face neutral. "I meant you don't need my sign-off. I trust your vision. If you need help, Griff is the guy."

Her gaze lifts to mine for a moment, and then she's laying the sheets out, talking me through the set. I try to focus on the drawings, not her mouth.

"These are strong," I say, flipping to the last page. "Good work."

A glint sparks in her eyes at the praise. "Thank you, sir."

I almost groan. Every time she calls me *Mr. Miller*, my cock tightens in my trousers. But *sir* is a straight shot to the blood pressure.

"Anything else, Ms. Jones?"

"No, Mr. Miller," Mya drawls, like she knows exactly what she's doing, gaze locked to mine.

"Good." I break first. "Close the door on your way out."

She does.

When the latch clicks, I drag a hand over my face, turning toward the glass.

Fuck me.

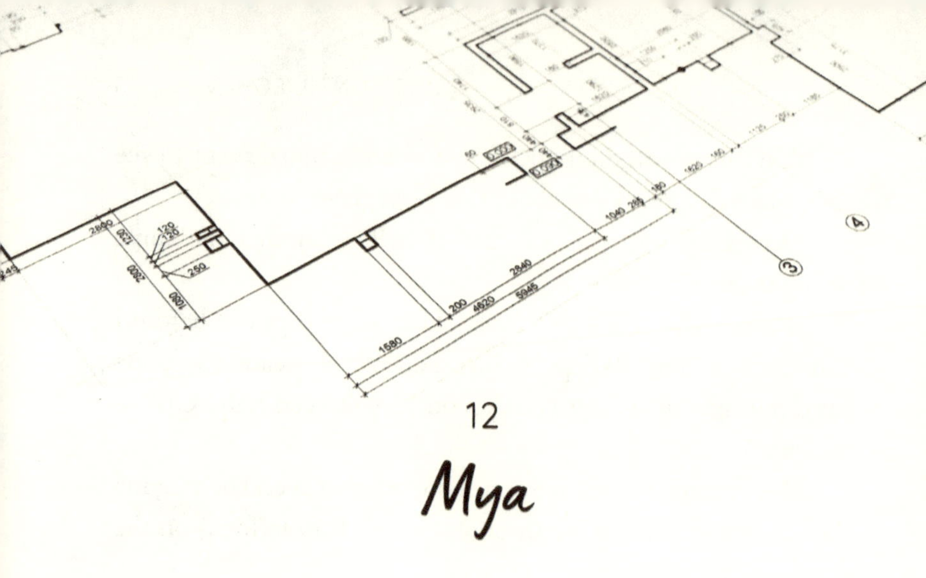

12

Mya

I've been working at W.H.M for a couple months now, and I'm finally finding my groove.

The nerves that ate me alive on day one have mostly disappeared. My team welcomed me faster than I expected, and I've developed an easy bond with them. We joke, brainstorm, and argue like we've known each other forever. They've taught me things I didn't learn in school, and they actually value my input.

Griffin has been a big part of that, given that he oversees the entire design team. He checks in often, and somewhere along the way, our conversations turned from strictly professional to friendly. He's approachable, quick with sarcastic comments, and doesn't hold back if an idea needs reworking. He pushes me, and I like that.

Somewhere in those conversations, I also learned he's a single dad to a little boy. Widowed, though he didn't offer details. His face turned grim when he mentioned it, so I didn't press.

I've been placed on an international project with Lau

Construction in Singapore, a partnership that carries a lot of weight around here. Being trusted with that responsibility makes me want to pinch myself. I thought I'd start at the bottom, grinding on scrap assignments while everyone else worked on the "real" projects. But here, it's different. At W.H.M, they treat every employee like they matter.

Well, everyone except Worth Miller.

Before I even make it to my desk, I do what I probably shouldn't and scroll through my phone while walking off the elevator.

A headline screams at me as soon as I open Instagram.

WORTH MILLER SPOTTED WITH TECH HEIRESS ALEXANDRA VALE — CEO'S NEW BAE?

The smile I didn't realize I was wearing fades.

There's a photo beneath the headline of Worth in a tailored coat, walking beside a gorgeous woman I've seen featured in other gossip articles. Alexandra Vale is polished, wealthy in her own right, and the kind of woman magazines love to call *powerfully enigmatic*. They're not touching, but the implication is loud enough.

My stomach twists in a way I don't appreciate.

I lock my phone and shove it into my bag, annoyed with myself for caring at all. It's none of my business. Worth Miller's personal life isn't exactly a guarded secret, and I'm not naïve enough to think men like him stay single out of sentiment.

Still.

The man is so hot and cold, and has perfected the art of grunting in place of actual words. If I pass him in the hall and say hello, he barely looks at me. And when I try to ask him questions, he doesn't even bother to be civil. *"Go talk to your superior, not me."*

I reminded him once that he is, in fact, a superior. His response was to threaten to fire me for having a "smart mouth."

The only reason I'm still here is because Andrée—a literal angel of patience—stepped in before the man could self-combust.

I honestly don't know how she does it. Dre is sweet, thoughtful, and level-headed, the exact opposite of the fire-breathing dragon she works for. If it takes a village to raise a child, then it must take a saint to handle a CEO like Worth.

The worst part is that I wish I didn't notice him at all. But ignoring Worth Miller is like trying to ignore a thunderstorm rolling in—loud, oppressive, and impossible to miss.

Speaking of the devil, it's Monday morning, seven a.m., and he's already here.

I sigh. So much for having the office to myself for at least an hour of peace and quiet. I wanted to get the final touches done on the draft drawings for the Infinity Towers in Singapore, but of course, Worth Miller had to ruin my plans.

At first, he doesn't notice me, which I silently thank the heavens for. But as he passes by the area where my desk is, he freezes. He doesn't turn, doesn't speak, just stands there, staring at me for what feels like an eternity. I don't look at him.

What the hell is he doing?

Then, just as suddenly, he continues to his office like nothing happened.

Deciding to be the bigger person, I gather my courage and head to his door a few minutes later. Whatever this tension between us is, it needs to stop. I've done nothing to deserve his cold shoulder, especially when he's the one who wanted me here.

It's as if that night he opened up about his ex-wife never happened, like he shoved every vulnerable word back into a vault and snapped it shut.

I knock softly.

"Come in," he calls, already sounding annoyed.

I push the door open a crack.

"I told you not to interrupt me before eight, Shaina. What do you need?"

When he finally looks up and realizes I'm not Shaina, his eyes widen before he slips back behind his mask of indifference. But I catch it.

"Can I help you, Ms. Jones?" he asks, all clipped and professional.

I cross my arms over my chest.

"Good morning to you, too, Mr. Miller. I just wanted to greet you like a normal human being, but apparently, decency isn't in your vocabulary." My voice comes out sharp. "Mind telling me what I've done to offend you, sir? Last time I checked, you're the one who *hired* me, though I'm guessing someone twisted your arm, because it feels like I'm being punished for it now."

Something shifts in Worth's expression, too quick to pin down. Instead of snapping back, though, his mouth twitches as if fighting a smile.

He rises from his chair slowly and comes around the desk, leaning back against it and folding his arms to mimic me, as if daring me to keep pushing.

He's in a charcoal three-piece suit today, and damn it all, he looks devastating. The vest pulls across his broad shoulders, the crisp white shirt is impossibly smooth, and the knot of his tie is perfect.

He shouldn't look that good this early in the morning.

My stomach flips, my pulse betraying me, and annoyance burns hot in my chest. Because I notice everything about him. And I'm almost certain he knows it.

Worth smirks, and I want nothing more than to wipe it off his stupidly perfect face.

"I'm glad that I'm amusing you, Mr. Miller," I spit, heat rising in my cheeks.

He doesn't say a word and just keeps watching me. His silence unnerves me, gnawing at my composure until I shift on my feet.

"You're not being punished for anything. I hired you because I knew you'd have potential," he finally says, his tone maddeningly casual, as if that's all there is to it.

I scoff. "So why did you say *'we can't hire her'* right after my interview?" The words tumble out before I can stop them. I slap a hand over my mouth. Shit. I didn't want him to know I overheard.

Worth straightens, his hard gaze locking with mine. "It was a mistake."

Confusion snakes through me. "Hiring me?"

"No. Saying that after the interview. I initially didn't think you'd be a good fit."

My brows knit. "So what changed your mind?"

He shrugs. "My gut."

A sarcastic laugh slips past my lips. "Well, tell your gut I say 'thanks.' That still doesn't explain why you've been an asshole to me these past few weeks."

In a flash, Worth moves closer, invading my space until there's less than a foot between us. He lowers his head just enough for his breath to ghost over my skin.

"Watch it, Ms. Jones," he growls out. "You're walking a thin line talking to your superior like this."

His voice hits me like a live wire. Goosebumps erupt all over my skin, even though my brain screams that this is wrong. His tone sounds angry, yet there's something else buried in it. *Arousal?*

"Punish me then, Mr. Miller." My words come out breathier than intended. "Fire me."

His gaze drops to the bow of my blouse, right where it ties at my chest. Slowly, he reaches out and tugs on the ribbon, just enough to feel the fabric give beneath his fingers. My pulse skyrockets.

What are we doing? He's my boss. I'm his employee. I should not be provoking him like this.

Reality slams into me and I stumble back. But Worth closes the distance again, as if retreat isn't an option.

"I'd suggest you watch the way you talk to me, Ms. Jones. I'm a very decent man, but I don't take kindly to people pushing my buttons." His gaze sweeps over me, dismissive in a way that makes my spine stiffen. "Especially someone as young as you. You'd do well to remember that, when walking into the lion's den."

I narrow my eyes, refusing to shrink. "My age seems to unsettle you more than my qualifications ever could, Mr. Miller. I didn't put it on my résumé, so tell me... Why are you so fixated on my 'youth'?"

His jaw flexes.

"You don't scare me, Mr. Miller. You hired me because I'm good at what I do. Because I bring value. Not because I'm young, or naïve, or easy to intimidate. I know my worth and so do you. Respect works both ways."

A dark chuckle rumbles from his chest, and he finally backs off. He returns to his desk, the distance between us suddenly cavernous, but there's a spark of something in his eyes now, almost like admiration.

"Have those draft designs on my desk in an hour, Mya." His tone is final, as he sinks back into his chair. I ignore the tingle at hearing him call me by my first name again.

"Fine."

"Fine," he echoes.

I spin on my heel and storm out, but by the time I reach my desk, my heart is still pounding against my ribs.

What the hell was that?

By the time I've put the finishing touches on the draft drawings, the office is buzzing with life. It's past eight now, and the illusion of privacy from earlier is gone.

The last thing I want is to step into Worth's office again, so instead of handing him the designs myself, I slide them onto Dre's desk.

She smiles warmly, always the calm in the storm. "Got these ready already? You're quick."

"Trying to stay on top of things." I force out a smile.

Her eyes narrow as she looks me over. "You okay? You look a little... flustered."

I let out a small laugh. "Just stressed about the project. That's all." A lie. The real reason still lingers on my skin like static, every nerve reminding me of Worth's low voice, his proximity, the tug on the bow of my blouse.

Dre seems to accept my answer, though her brows are still furrowed. "Don't let him get under your skin. He's... a lot. But he's fair."

I nod quickly, not trusting myself to answer, and rush off before she can ask more.

In my haste, I nearly collide head-on with a tall figure rounding the corner. My chest bumps into solid muscle, and I let out a startled gasp as strong hands grip my arms, steadying me.

"Whoa there," Griffin says, his mouth curving into a half-smile.

"Sorry," I mumble, heat flooding my cheeks.

"Running somewhere important?"

"Just back to my desk," I answer lamely.

He studies me for a moment, then tilts his head. "You okay?"

"I'm fine." Too quick. I scramble for a subject change. "I dropped the draft designs off. Worth asked for them this morning."

"Huh. Usually, I go through everything first before he gives the final approval. He must be in a hurry." Griffin shrugs it off, his hand lingering on the small of my back as he guides me towards my desk.

"I actually wanted to circle back to the community housing project," he says. "We've been refining the design to better integrate green space. It's something I'd love to get your perspective on. Fresh eyes and all that."

I nod, though my brain is only half registering his words. His presence is comfortable, friendly, the kind of energy that makes me feel appreciated. But as we stop at my desk, a shift in the air prickles my skin.

My gaze drifts unintentionally towards Worth's office.

And there he is, leaning against his door, eyes locked on me like I've committed a crime. His stare is scorching, and I can practically feel the intensity from across the room.

What the hell did I do this time?

I swallow hard and try to keep my attention on Griffin, who's still talking about the project, but then I notice Worth's gaze land squarely on Griffin's hand still resting lightly on my back.

His fingertips curl into small, white-knuckled claws against his leg.

Heat curls low in my stomach. I hold his gaze. Before I have a chance to wonder what his reaction means, he retreats back to his office without another glance.

13

Worth

Griffin's hand is still on her.

It's nothing, really. It was barely resting on her back as he walked her to her desk. But to me, it feels like a fucking violation.

Heat scorches through my chest, and I have to curl my hands into fists just to keep from putting them through the glass wall of my office.

What the hell is this? *Jealousy?*

It can't be.

I don't get jealous. I don't care who Mya talks to or who puts their hands on her. She's an *employee*. One of a hundred. Replaceable. That's what I should be telling myself—but all I can think about is ripping Griffin's hand off her and reminding him exactly who the hell is in charge here.

Jesus Christ.

Yes, I find Mya attractive. And I'd love to bury myself so deep inside her that she forgets her own name. Especially after this morning, when she dared to storm into my office and call me an asshole.

I should've fired her on the spot or, at the very least, repri-manded her for her insubordination. But instead, all I could think about was how badly I wanted her to keep running that smart mouth while I pulled her hair back and fucked her into my desk.

When Mya looked me dead in the eye and told me to punish her, I almost lost it right then.

I'm shocked she didn't notice the way my trousers strained, how close I was to coming apart at nothing more than her defi-ance. That clever tongue, those fiery eyes.

She's dangerous.

And that's exactly why I've been keeping my distance since she started.

Not because she's incompetent—she's already proven herself on the Lau project with the Singapore drafts. If anything, Mya's sharper than half the people here.

I just don't trust myself around her.

And now, watching Griffin stand too close, watching her smile back at him, I know I was right to keep her at arm's length.

What's wrong with me?

She's young. Off-limits.

And yet... All I want is to tear her away from everyone else, lock her in my office, and find out just how many names she'd call me while bent over my desk.

Fuck.

This is bad.

Griffin leans down, pointing something out on Mya's laptop, and her nose scrunches in that way I shouldn't notice but always do.

My blood boils.

I don't even look away when she catches me staring. Her

gaze darts up from Griffin to me, but I hold it. I don't waver. If anything, I double down, daring her to look away first.

A couple of minutes feel like two hours before I've had enough.

I shove off my door and storm back into my office, ignoring Dre calling my name from her desk.

I grab my phone and then turn right back around.

"Dre. Give me the new employee files."

She blinks, confused. "Whose?"

"All of them."

"Why?"

"Just give them to me."

The edge in my voice makes her swallow her questions. She hands them over reluctantly, her brows furrowed like she knows I'm up to no good. I snatch the folder and disappear back into my office, shutting the door behind me.

Flipping through the papers, I eventually find what I'm looking for: Mya's personal number.

Worth, you're acting fucking crazy.

But I'm way past giving a shit now.

I punch her digits into my phone, save them, and type out a short message. Then I lift my head and watch through the glass.

Seconds later, Mya glances down at her device, discreetly sliding it towards her. Her nose scrunches again. She taps the screen and reads the message.

> Stop flirting with your superiors, Ms. Jones.

Slowly, her eyes lift towards my office.

Straight to me.

MYA:

> How'd you get my number?

And I'm not flirting.

Then explain Griffin's hands all over you.

She furrows her brows, before a small smirk spreads over her lips.

MYA:

Breathe, Mr. Miller. Jealousy doesn't look good on you.

I'm not jealous. You're simply being unprofessional on company grounds.

MYA:

Well… from here, it looks like green is your favorite color.

As if to drive the knife deeper, she puts her phone down and leans in closer to Griffin, laughing at something he shows her. Then she rests her hand on his arm like it's nothing.

He doesn't shrug it off.

Once again, Griff's a dead man standing.

I push back from my desk and stride out into the bullpen. My voice cuts through the noise like a blade.

"Ms. Jones. My office. *Now*."

The room falls silent. Dre's face drains of color, like she's already drafting the HR email in her head. Griffin smirks like a bastard, practically vibrating with 'I told you so'.

Mya's eyes go wide, but she doesn't argue. She hurries after me, heels clicking fast against the floor.

Inside, I slam the door and yank the blinds shut. The space is instantly smaller, hotter. She stands stiffly, looking nervous, all of the earlier bravado gone. Good. She should be.

"Mr. Miller, I'm sorry if I—"

I don't let her finish. My arms cage her against the wall. Her breath catches, eyes wide.

"Worth. What the hell are you doing?" she rasps.

"Oh. We're on a first-name basis now?" I mutter.

She rolls her eyes. Goddamn brat.

"I'm only going to say this once more, Mya. Do. Not. Flirt. With. My. Employees."

Her teeth grind, and she points her finger at my chest. "You. Do. Not. Own. Me."

She's right. I don't. And it's unfortunate.

"I might not control you outside of these walls, Mya. But in here? I can damn well dictate what you do. No fraternizing." My pulse is pounding, and from her rapid breathing, I think hers is too.

She glares at me like she wants to burn me alive. "You are insane, Mr. Miller."

"You have no idea."

I have truly lost it.

Mya ducks under my arms and straightens her blouse, chin tilted high. "For the record, I wasn't flirting with Griffin. He's my boss, just like you. I'm not interested in fraternizing with *anyone* here."

She turns to go, hand on the knob. Then pauses.

"Do something like that again, and I'll take it to HR. We wouldn't want your face plastered across the tabloids as a playboy *and* for harassment."

The air leaves my chest in one brutal exhale.

"You wouldn't dare."

"Try me."

She walks out, leaving me standing there with blood roaring in my ears.

The door is still trembling from Mya's exit when a knuckle taps the glass.

Shaina slips in without waiting. "Everything okay?" Her tone is curious, nosey. Her eyes travel to the direction where Mya just vanished, then back to me. "You look... tense."

The blinds are closed, so I'm not concerned that she saw anything, but I'm sure she saw Mya stomp her way back to her desk.

"I'm fine." I straighten the cuff of my shirt, like that can smooth the static running under my skin. "Close the door."

She does, but instead of leaving, she leans against it, crossing one ankle over the other. "You want coffee? A drink? Or"—her mouth tilts—"something stronger to take the edge off?"

"No." My pulse is still hammering from Mya's threat, the HR landmine glowing behind my ribs. "I said I'm fine, Shaina."

She takes a step in, her scent too sweet and suffocating. "Because if it's... stress," Shaina says, letting the word linger, "I could help. We used to be good at helping each other."

My jaw ticks. "Not right now."

"Is it because of *her*?"

I look up. "Excuse me?"

"You barely look at me anymore. You barely talk to me. I'm not blind."

My fingers drum once on the desk, then stop. "Mind your business, Ms. Reed."

"So it *is* her." There's a quick flash of triumph on her face, then something pettier. "You know this is how it starts, right? You get a crush on the new girl and blow up your whole—"

"That's enough, Shaina. Whatever this is, it's not a conversation I'm having with you."

Shaina flinches, then recovers, taking another two steps closer, testing the boundary. "I'm just saying I could help you relax. We were good, Worth. We *worked*."

I stand, palms flat on the desk. "We were a mistake I let run too long. That's on me."

Color climbs her neck. "So that's it."

"That should've been *it* a while ago." I keep my tone even. "And it has nothing to do with anyone else."

Her eyes rake my face, looking for a crack. "You're sure about that?"

No. "Yes."

She laughs once, humorless. "This is unbelievable."

"Shaina," I say, quieter, because I don't want to be cruel, just done, "go back to your desk. We're finished. Professionally, you'll keep doing your job. Personally, there is nothing here."

For a heartbeat, I think Shaina will argue. Instead, her mouth flattens. "Right. Got it."

She turns on her heel, yanks the door open, then leaves.

I sink back into my chair and stare at the ceiling, pressing my thumb against my throbbing temple.

HR disaster count: potentially two.

I spend Saturday in the shed, pretending banging on wood will solve things.

This project has been sitting half-started for months: a built-in cedar window bench for the breakfast nook, with hidden storage for Bri's art supplies. I told myself I'd finish it "when the schedule clears." The schedule never clears. But today I need my hands busy.

I clamp a board, measure it twice, and cut once. The miter saw whines and fresh cedar dust lifts like smoke. I run a palm along the edge, feel a burr, and reach for the block plane. Shavings curl to the floor as I refine the wood.

My phone buzzes on the workbench, skittering against a box of screws. Unknown number.

I don't need the contact info to know who it is. I let out a sigh. It vibrates once more, then I swipe.

"What do you want, Vanessa?"

"Don't hang up," she rushes out. "I want to see Brianna."

"I told you I'm not doing this."

"If you agree, I'll get on a flight back to the States right away."

So she's still in Asia. My PI said Tokyo, then Bangkok. I keep my voice flat. "Even more reason to say no. You're not even in the country."

Her composure thins. "I'm *trying*, Worth. I'm making an effort and you—"

"You call from different numbers and move time zones like apartments. That's not effort. That's chaos. And last time, Bri waited for you for hours. She was heartbroken."

"I was busy and I apologized. You can't keep her from me," she snaps. "You think a judge won't see what you're doing?"

"I think the court will see a pattern." I stare at the clean line of the joint I just sanded. "As I said, if you have an issue, call my lawyer."

"God, you're such a—"

I end the call and drop the phone face down. My pulse ticks in my wrist. Something in me has been off the last few days, and I've been trying to tamper it with busywork. Vanessa's calls don't help, nor does the fact that I'm struggling to concentrate at work; whenever Mya walks into a room, my brain goes full-on territorial, like I have any right.

I dust off my hands then head back to the house. Inside, it smells like whatever sweet thing Maggie baked earlier. Bri is at the kitchen island, hunched over her sketchpad, tongue peeking out the corner of her mouth. Colored pencils explode in a bright fan around her.

"Whatcha got there, Piglet?"

"Wolf," she says without looking up, shading the fur along the animal's neck. "But this time I'm trying moonlight. Like it's shining on one side."

My chest softens. It's her favorite animal. She's been obsessed with wolves ever since we watched a documentary about them some time ago. "Looks good."

Bri tilts the page towards the light, squints, then adds a darker line. "Can we put it in the frame near the stairs when I'm done?"

"Of course we can."

She smiles, pleased. "What were you doing in the shed? I heard the loud cutter."

"Window bench for the breakfast nook. Art-supply storage."

Bri perks. "For me?"

"Mostly you," I tease.

She grins and goes back to shading. I don't mention her mother's call. The guilt nips anyway, but I know how this goes. I'm not letting my kid get her hopes up only to see them come crashing down.

My phone rings a second later. This time it's my lawyer.

"Work call," I tell Bri, tapping the counter. "I'll be in my office."

"'Kay."

Once inside, I close the door and answer. "Ryan."

"Worth," he says, voice clipped. "You free?"

"I'm here."

"Just got a heads-up from opposing counsel." Paper rustles on his end. "Vanessa retained a new firm. They're filing a motion to modify custody."

"On what basis?"

"Allegations of withholding access, parental alienation, the usual garbage. They'll push for expanded visitation as a first step."

Heat flares behind my eyes. I cross to the bar cart, pour two fingers of Black Briar and knock it back.

"She called me from an unknown number twenty minutes ago," I say, setting the glass down hard. "Said she'd 'fly back' if I agreed to a meeting. She's in Asia. I told her to go through you."

"Good," Ryan says. "Don't engage further. Send me the number and any texts."

"She doesn't text. She calls, throws grenades and runs."

"Then we'll defuse them. I'll file a response with a proposed structure: supervised, incremental, contingent on consistency. We'll attach the school records, counseling notes, your documented attempts to arrange contact in the past."

My jaw ticks. "She didn't say goodbye to Bri when she left. You put that in bold."

"It will be in bold, underlined, and highlighted," Ryan assures me. "Breathe. We've got this."

I force air in and out. "Send me drafts tonight, if you can."

"You'll have them. But Worth, you need to prepare yourself," Ryan says slowly. "This isn't just about her sudden reappearance. It's about how the court is going to perceive you. Custody cases live and die on perception, not just facts."

I scowl. "Perception?"

"Yes. Your reputation. The way the media frames you. To the public eye—and therefore to a judge—you look like a man who rotates women like cufflinks. There are tabloid spreads, photos of you on yachts, gala after gala with different women. It paints a picture of... instability, even if that's not the truth."

My hand curls into a fist. "I've raised Brianna alone for ten years. Where the hell is the instability in that?"

"I know that. *You* know that. But a judge won't look at the day-to-day reality of your parenting. They'll hear Vanessa spin a narrative that you're distracted, unreliable, too busy parading women around to provide a steady home. And if she hires the right attorney, they'll use your public image to undercut you."

The words settle like stones in my gut. He's not wrong. I've seen the articles myself.

"If Vanessa pushes this, she'll argue that Brianna deserves the stability of her mother's home. Even if that mother abandoned her," Ryan adds.

I slam my hand against my desk, startling even myself. "She left us. She doesn't get to just waltz back in like it never happened."

"I agree. But the court cares about appearances. About what *looks* stable, predictable, family-friendly."

I drag a hand down my face, pulse pounding in my ears. "So what do you suggest? That I stop breathing until the paparazzi go away?"

Ryan lets out a long exhale. "I suggest you show the world that you're not what the tabloids say you are. That you're not a playboy—you're a partner. A father. A man with roots."

I snort bitterly. "And how the hell am I supposed to prove that?"

"Show that you're capable of a committed relationship. The court doesn't want to see a revolving door of women. They want to see stability. A partner who's been around, who knows your daughter. Someone who can testify to your home being a steady environment."

My stomach knots, instinct screaming at the absurdity of all this. I rub at the back of my neck, unsure what to say.

"Consider it, Worth. As your friend, I'd hate to see you lose Brianna."

The fear of losing my daughter squeezes me harder than

my pride. Before I can think twice of my next words, I blurt out, "I've actually been dating someone. We've kept it private."

Shit. What am I saying?

"That's great, then now's the time to make it official. Before Vanessa makes her move."

After Ryan and I hang up, I pour one more finger of liquor, stare at it, before leaving it on the cart.

Back in the kitchen, Bri looks up.

"Soup?" I ask, exhaling through my tight chest.

"Soup," she confirms as I reach for a pot. "And grilled cheese. With garlic butter."

"We must never forget the garlic butter," I say, dead serious.

Brianna laughs, bright enough to sand the edge off the day.

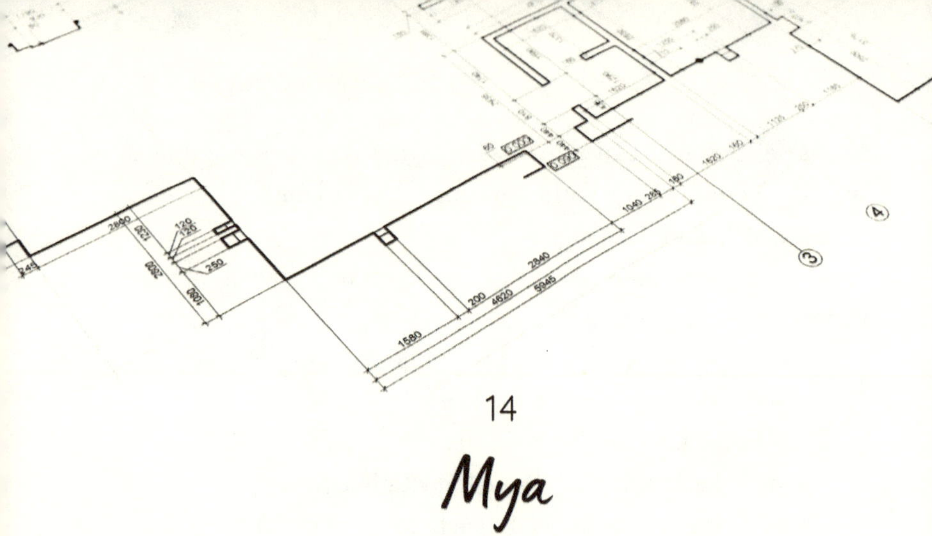

14

Mya

"You look great, MJ," Tiana says as I study myself in the mirror, patting down the dress she let me borrow for the evening.

The floor-length, deep emerald silk gown clings in all the right places and skims down to a slit at my thigh. The neckline dips just enough to hint at cleavage without being over the top, and the thin straps show off my shoulders. The fabric catches the light every time I move, making me look far more glamorous than I feel. Tiana insisted on lending it to me, swearing it was a crime to leave it hanging in her closet.

It's for the annual charity gala W.H.M. Construction hosts at the swanky Thompson Hotel—a fundraiser for women's shelters across Seattle. Every year, the event makes headlines. Paparazzi crowd the entrance, hungry for shots of celebrity guests and Seattle's elite dressed to the nines. Politicians, CEOs, actors, pro athletes—you name it. It's the kind of event that gets splashed across glossy magazine pages and gossip sites by morning.

All W.H.M. employees are invited and expected to attend,

which means I'll be rubbing elbows with people who practically invented the term "old money."

Demi whistles low. "Damn, Mya. Forget the celebrities, you're about to make headlines yourself."

I giggle, taking one last look in the mirror. For half a second, a ridiculous thought slips in.

What will Mr. Miller think when he sees me like this? I can almost picture him in one of his perfectly tailored suits, handsome enough to make the air shift when he walks into a room, his eyes dragging over me the way they did that day in his office.

Heat climbs up my neck. *Snap out of it, Mya.*

This is the same man who's spent weeks grunting at you like you're an inconvenience.

The same man who cornered me in his office, pressed too close, voice rough as he warned me not to test him. My pulse stumbles when I think back to how dangerous and intoxicating it felt, how a single second of weakness could've tipped me over an edge I'm not sure I'd come back from.

Fantasizing about my boss is beyond stupid.

By the time we're all finished getting ready, my bedroom looks like a tornado hit it. There are makeup brushes scattered across my vanity, bobby pins littering the floor, and three different curling irons cooling on the dresser.

Tiana and Demi insisted on coming over to my place so we could all get ready together. They're headed out for a girls' night on the town, while I attend the gala.

"Okay, before we go our separate ways, we're toasting," I announce, grabbing a bottle of cabernet and three glasses in the kitchen.

"Hell yes!" Demi cheers.

As I turn my back to them, I hear Tiana rummaging in the drawers. "Do you have a corkscrew?" Then, there's a startled sound that makes the hair on the back of my neck stand up.

"What the hell are these?"

My stomach drops. I know exactly what she's holding. I spin around and see her clutching the letters I hid away. Tiana's wide eyes lock on mine, as if I've just been caught committing a crime.

Shit.

I find the corkscrew and twist it into the wine bottle, pretending like this moment is perfectly normal.

"Mya." Her voice is panicked. "Tell me this isn't real."

Oh, it's very real. I've been pretending those letters didn't exist for weeks now, stacking them in drawers, telling myself I'd deal with them later.

But later kept getting pushed back.

First it was finishing my master's thesis. Then job applications. Then starting at W.H.M. I told myself that once I landed the position, everything would even out. That I'd catch up—but I just didn't.

Tiana opens one. "Collections?!" she all but shouts, waving the paper like a flag of shame.

Demi blinks. "Wait—what?"

Heat rushes to my cheeks, humiliation prickling under my skin. "It's not a big deal," I lie, reaching to snatch the letter, but Tiana yanks it out of reach. "I'll figure it out. I always do."

Tiana huffs, frustration lacing her words. "You should've told me. You should've told Mom. Anyone."

I force out a tight smile. "I don't need rescuing, okay? I'm handling it. I'm not working at the cafe anymore. I have a real job now, remember?"

The second the words leave my mouth, I wince. *Real job.* Willow's *is* a real job, and Tiana, Demi and I put in the hours there. My throat tightens. "Sorry, I didn't mean it like that."

They both wave me off, though Tiana's jaw ticks.

"Forget it," she says. "Anyway, I thought you had a scholarship for college."

"I did. A partial one."

"How partial?"

"Enough to get me in, not enough to keep me afloat." I shrug, forcing a brittle laugh. "I thought I could cover the rest, that I could keep up."

"But you couldn't," Demi says gently.

I shake my head. "Not really."

Tiana's eyes soften, but there's hurt there too. "You should've told us."

"I know, I'm sorry. Just—don't tell Mom. Please. I don't want her to worry about this."

She opens her mouth to argue, then closes it again, rubbing her forehead. "You're unbelievable."

"I prefer 'stubborn,'" I say with a tentative smile. "Look, I'll take care of it, just like I've been doing with my other debts."

Her brows snap together. "*Other* debts?"

Shit. Shouldn't have said that.

I shift my weight, gripping the back of a chair. "Nothing serious."

"Mya."

I sigh. "Okay, fine. My credit score isn't great."

Her eyes widen, and she throws her hands up. "Not great? Oh my God!"

"Please don't say anything to Mom, TJ," I beg.

She blows out an exasperated breath, crossing her arms. "Fine. Well, if you get evicted, I guess you could just move back home. We all miss having you there anyway."

I shake my head quickly. "The last thing I want to do is move back, Tiana. I do miss you guys, but I like having my own space and independence. That would be my literal last option. No offense."

Tiana rolls her eyes but doesn't argue.

Demi pipes up, sliding into the conversation with a softer tone. "You could always come stay with me. Put your stuff in storage until you find a new place." She rounds the island and loops an arm around my shoulders, giving me a quick squeeze. "Either way, we've got you, babe."

I smile at her, warmth tugging at my chest. "Thanks. What would I do without you two?"

"Live on the street, that's what," Tiana deadpans.

I shove her shoulder, laughing. "Fuck off."

We sip our wine, and Tiana and Demi start chatting animatedly about where they're headed tonight, while my mind drifts elsewhere.

How am I going to get out of this mess?

Maybe I can ask for an advance. HR might be able to help me out. It's worth a shot.

I set my glass down, pull up my email on my phone, and draft a message to Claire, head of HR.

I hit send and take another gulp of wine. *Here's to hoping.*

AN HOUR LATER, I'M IN FRONT OF THE THOMPSON HOTEL. The ride only took twenty minutes, but the moment we pulled up, it felt like stepping into another world.

People are everywhere. Cameras are flashing; traffic jammed at the curb as sleek cars drop off Seattle's elite; paparazzi swarm the front entrance, their shouts cutting through the night. The instructions in the employee packet had been clear: *use the side door if you want to avoid the chaos.*

Clutching my small black purse tighter, I maneuver around

the crowd, hugging the edge of the hotel until I spot the discreet staff entrance.

A black town car glides up then, and Worth steps out, broad shoulders filling his perfectly tailored tuxedo. My stomach does a traitorous flip.

A woman emerges after him. Tall. Leggy. A beautiful redhead in a black sparkly gown that probably cost more than my annual rent. Diamonds glitter around her throat, wrists, and ears, catching every camera flash. Her manicured hand slides into the crook of Worth's arm like it was designed to rest there.

She's elegance personified. Gorgeous. Exactly the kind of woman who belongs on his arm.

I scoff under my breath. Another night, another beauty. Another headline waiting to happen for the blue collar playboy.

Worth Miller rotates women like he rotates luxury watches.

He and his redheaded goddess pause at the curb, immediately swallowed by the frenzy of flashing bulbs. The cameras eat them alive. She tilts her chin, dazzling smile locked in place, while Worth stands steady beside her, jaw set, every inch the composed CEO. He doesn't look uncomfortable, but almost detached, like this is just another transaction.

Still, the sight of them posing together twists something in my stomach. They look perfect, fitting effortlessly into each other's worlds. I feel like a fraud in comparison, sneaking towards the staff door in my borrowed dress.

Just as I start to move again towards the side entrance, his head turns, as if pulled by some invisible thread and his gaze lands directly on me.

My breath catches, heat racing down my spine. For one impossible second, it's just Worth and me, locked across the crowd. His eyes narrow, like he's trying to read me from a distance, pin me in place.

Heart hammering, I duck my head and hurry inside, pushing into the quieter hallways of the hotel. The muffled beat of music and the hum of voices guide me toward the ballroom.

Only then do I let out a breath.

I shake off the memory of Worth's gaze on me and step deeper into the room, scanning the crowd for familiar faces from the office.

I'm about to head towards the bar when someone falls into step behind me.

"Jones."

I turn and blink. For a second, I don't even recognize him.

Griffin. In a tux.

The rugged, slightly scruffy architect I'm used to seeing in jeans and work boots is gone. In his place is a man in a perfectly fitted tuxedo, white shirt crisp, bowtie knotted just right. His copper hair is smoothed back, his jaw clean-shaven, and damn, he looks good, polished.

My lips tug into a smile. "Wow. You clean up nice, Hayes. I almost didn't recognize you without sawdust on your boots."

He chuckles, shaking his head. "Don't get used to it. Tuxedos aren't really my thing."

"Well, it suits you." I nudge him lightly with my elbow.

He grins but it fades almost instantly when he glances at his phone. His brows knit, thumb swiping the screen, before locking it again.

"You okay?"

"Yeah," he says quickly, but the tightness in his jaw betrays him.

I raise a brow, waiting.

Finally, he exhales. "Just a little nervous. My son is with a new babysitter tonight. His usual nanny—my neighbor—is getting older and can't keep up with him anymore. So her granddaughter is filling in."

"Oh, I'm sure it'll be fine," I say, trying to reassure him.

"Yeah," he murmurs.

"I don't know you that well yet, but I'm sure you're a good dad, Griff."

His eyes meet mine, something vulnerable flashing there before he looks away, forcing a smile. "Trying my best. He's a handful, but he's my world."

Something about the way he says it makes my chest ache. I clear my throat, deciding to nudge the conversation back into safer waters. "So... Did you bring a date tonight?"

Griffin gives me a deadpan look. "No. I don't have time for dates."

The bluntness makes me laugh.

"Fair enough. Guess you'll just have to put up with your coworkers as your dates for the evening."

That earns me a grin, brief yet genuine. He then checks his phone again with the same pinched expression as before. I bite back the urge to tease him. This isn't the same easygoing Griff from the office; this is *Dad Griff*, the one who's worried about his kid.

I reach out and rest a hand on his shoulder. "Hey. Try not to think the worst. He's probably running circles around that babysitter, charming the socks off her. You deserve to have fun tonight."

His mouth pulls into a reluctant half-smile. "Yeah. You're right."

"Of course I'm right. Now... Where is everyone else hiding, anyway?"

"Some are near the silent auction tables, others are hovering by the buffet like vultures. Dre's probably making her rounds to keep us in line."

I nod. "Perfect. I'll grab a drink and see if I can find them."

THE BAR IS CROWDED, BUT I MANAGE TO WEDGE MYSELF IN and get a glass of champagne. I've barely taken my first sip when the air shifts. That familiar prickle down my spine tells me who it is before I can even look.

Worth steps in beside me, his presence pressing in from all sides. "Ms. Jones. Enjoying the evening?" His voice is calm, professional.

My pulse kicks up. "Yes, Mr. Miller."

The muscle in his jaw ticks, subtle, though impossible to miss. It happens every time I use his last name, like the sound of it coming from me grates on him.

Worth's eyes flick briefly across the ballroom before landing back on me. "I've noticed you and Griffin have become quite close."

My breath hitches, and for a second, I can't tell if it's an observation or an accusation.

"So you *are* jealous, Mr. Miller." I angle my head, letting the challenge hang in the air. "All that talk about not fraternizing with other employees the other day, and yet..."

That twitch in his jaw again, and the faintest flare of his nostrils—like he's fighting to control a reaction.

Worth's mouth curves. "Careful with that word, Mya."

"Why? Did I hit a nerve?" I sip my champagne, feigning nonchalance even as heat coils low in my belly.

He leans in just slightly, lowering his voice so only I can hear. "Jealousy implies possession. And I don't make a habit of laying claim to my employees."

Something reckless sparks in me. "Good. Because I don't

make a habit of belonging to anyone. You don't get to *claim* me."

His eyes hold mine for a second too long. It's not professional or distant, like the front he usually puts up. "Then stop looking at me like you want me to."

My throat goes dry, but I force a smirk and push back. "Why don't you go back to your girlfriend?" I nod towards the redhead across the room.

"That's not my girlfriend."

"Go figure," I mutter under my breath.

His head tilts. "What was that?"

"Nothing," I answer quickly, pasting on another polite smile.

Worth studies me, his gaze lingering.

"I read your email to HR."

The champagne nearly goes down the wrong pipe. I cough, eyes wide. "What? How—"

"It's my company. I know everything."

Embarrassment creeps hot into my cheeks. Of course he does. And apparently that includes snooping through payroll requests.

I don't know why I assumed he wouldn't find out.

"Right. Well... Never mind about that. It was a mistake." I wave it off, even though inside I feel about two inches tall.

His tone shifts. "Is everything okay, Ms. Jones?"

"Yes," I lie too quickly, and I know he hears it. His eyes narrow, as if he's dissecting me on the spot. I give him a tight smile, willing him to drop it. *Please don't look at me like that.*

Like a charity case.

Worth nods and orders a drink. Then, he tips his glass in my direction and walks off, leaving me gripping my flute a little too hard.

I exhale slowly, trying to steady myself. I should feel relief that he's gone, but instead, my skin still burns with the remnants of his presence.

And that's a problem.

THE MUSIC SWELLS, COUPLES DRIFTING ONTO THE DANCE floor. I'm halfway through another sip of my drink when I hear a familiar voice, "Hey, Mya."

I turn to find Ethan, one of the project managers from design. He's been at W.H.M. for years, and knows everyone, remembers birthdays, and manages to charm even the prickliest clients.

"Ethan," I greet with a polite smile.

He grins, charming without trying too hard. "You look incredible tonight."

Heat creeps up my cheeks. "Thanks. You look nice, too."

His eyes stay on me a little too long, his smile softens a little too much. It's subtle enough to brush off, but I make a note of it.

I take him in quickly. Tall, lean build, sharp jawline, the kind of guy who probably runs marathons for fun. Always dressed neat without being showy.

He's... cute. Objectively.

And yet I've never really paid him much attention.

He tilts his head toward the dance floor. "Care to?"

Why not? I set my glass down, slip my hand into his, and let him lead me out. His touch is respectful. One hand at an appropriate height on my back, the other guiding me with ease. But his voice drops low when he leans in, murmuring something about how well I move, and it's impossible to miss the flirtation threading through.

I smile, playing it off, but as he twirls me back into his arms, my eyes catch on another couple across the floor.

Worth and his date move effortlessly, her body draped against his. To anyone else, he looks composed—exactly what you'd expect from a man used to being watched.

But his eyes aren't on her.

They're on *me*.

His stare burns hotter than Ethan's hand at my back. Anger simmers there, buried beneath a mask of indifference. No one else would see it. But I do.

My chest tightens, heat crawling up my throat. I force a laugh at something Ethan whispers in my ear, trying to pretend I'm unaffected. But with every twirl, I feel Worth's gaze like a tether pulling me across the room.

Then the microphone squeals, cutting through the music.

"Ladies and gentlemen, please welcome our host for the evening, Mr. Worth Miller."

The crowd applauds, couples slowing their steps. Worth guides his date off the floor, but before he heads for the stage, his gaze lingers on me for a moment longer.

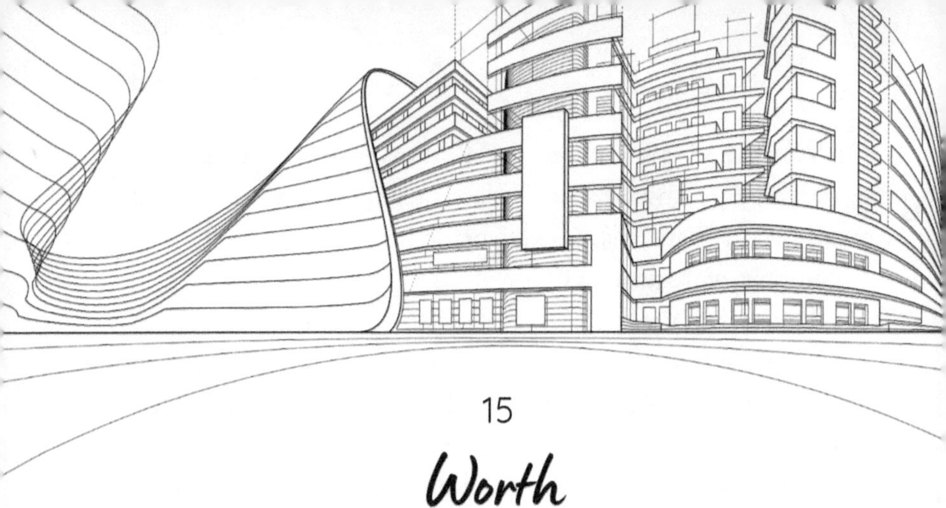

15

Worth

I adjust my cuffs and stride towards the stage. My gaze should be on the cameras flashing, on the donors waiting to be impressed. Instead, it catches on a swirl of green fabric in the crowd.

Jesus Christ—that dress. Emerald silk that clings to her in all the ways I shouldn't notice, a neckline that dares the eye lower, hair loose and tumbling over her shoulders, like it was made to be tangled in my fists. Mya doesn't look like my employee. She looks like temptation wrapped in satin.

Sliding up beside her earlier at the bar nearly undid me. The faint scent of her perfume, the brush of her arm on mine... Fuck.

And watching her laugh with Griffin like she's known him forever... It looked comfortable. Easy. The opposite of how she is around me. I hated how much it gnawed at me, even knowing Griffin's not interested in anyone like that.

And when Ethan-fucking-Chan put his hands on her, guiding her across the dance floor? I nearly saw red.

This is just an attraction. Maybe all I need is to get her out of my system and I'll stop feeling like I'm about to combust every time she walks into a room. But I refuse to cross that line and break my word to myself, to Griffin, to Henson, to Andrée. Not happening.

I take the podium, grip it tight until the wood bites into my palms.

"Thank you for joining us tonight. This marks the thirteenth year W.H.M. has had the privilege of hosting the gala for the Seattle Women's Network. Thirteen years of supporting a cause that uplifts, empowers, and advocates for women in our city."

Applause ripples, flashes go off. I keep talking. "Your generosity is what made this possible. Not just through donations, but through the friendships, connections, and partnerships formed here. We thrive when we work together. When we lift one another up."

My gaze slides back to Mya, her lips parted slightly like she's hanging on every word.

"And as important as friendship is," I continue, shifting my tone, "it's equally important to remember boundaries. Professional boundaries."

I watch her stiffen. Good. Let the message sink in. For both of us.

"At W.H.M., we value teamwork, respect, and collaboration. Those things can't thrive without professionalism. We must remember that no matter how tempting it may be, stepping outside those boundaries risks fueling the very kind of harassment this foundation is committed to ending."

The crowd nods, completely oblivious. To them, it's corporate policy. To Mya, it's a warning.

And to me? It's the closest I can get to saying what I really want.

I end my speech and step down from the stage, striding towards the redhead waiting for me off to the side.

I usually bring dates to these events as a buffer. But tonight, I almost didn't.

After I told Ryan I was seeing someone off the record, I spent days brainstorming who could carry the part. Sophia made sense on paper: we've been seen together, we've dated casually, and she's *very* eager to be the one to take Worth Miller off the market. She'd say yes even if it was fake.

But every time I tried to lock that plan, Mya muscled to the front of my mind and wouldn't move. So I brought the buffer anyway, hoping to drown out thoughts of the doe-eyed, tan-skinned beauty who's been plaguing my thoughts for weeks.

I haven't even kissed Mya and I crave her like a starving man craves his next meal. It's visceral. The defiance in her eyes when she calls me *Mr. Miller*, the sway of her hips in that emerald dress—it's enough to drive me wild.

I don't even recognize myself like this.

I've built an empire by staying in control. But when it comes to Mya, it's a thread unraveling in my hands.

Sophia hooks her arm through mine. "Shall we get seated, honey?"

I cringe. I'm not her damn *honey*.

We make our way to the dining area. As expected, I'm at the head table, Sophia glued to my side, flanked by the rest of the executives and higher management. The chatter is polite, full of forced laughter and networking bullshit, and I let my eyes scan the room.

Mya is seated at a table not too far away. And right next to her is *Ethan Chan*.

My fists curl under the tablecloth, knuckles straining against the linen. He leans towards her with a smile. My gut twists, territorial anger sparking hot in my veins.

I force myself to ignore it and focus on Sophia.

Except, before I look away, my gaze locks with Mya's.

She doesn't cower or lower her eyes. She holds my stare, her chin tilted ever so slightly in defiance.

My cock twitches.

She's such a brat. And God help me, I'd love nothing more than to bend her over and punish her for it.

I spend the entire dinner with my jaw locked, pretending Mya doesn't exist. Pretending the sound of her laugh doesn't slice through the chatter at the executives' table.

It works—barely—until dessert is cleared and the band shifts into something upbeat.

That's when I finally let myself glance her way again.

She leans toward Chan, says something I can't hear, then gets up from the table. A few seconds later, he follows.

Motherfucker.

Are they about to leave together?

Against every shred of better judgment I've ever had, I shove back my chair and follow.

Sophia calls out to me, but I ignore her.

Mya slips into the bathroom, while Ethan waits outside the door like some eager puppy. I linger to the side, brushing off a donor who tries to snag my attention, eyes locked on the scene unfolding across the hallway.

When Mya steps out, she startles at the sight of him, her brows pinching before she smooths it over with a polite smile. Interesting. She masks discomfort well, but I see it.

Ethan says something and leans in, brushing a strand of hair from her face.

Red floods my vision.

I stalk forward, every step heavy with the fury that's been simmering for weeks. "If you value your job, Mr. Chan, I suggest you get back to your table. Now," I seethe, teeth clenched.

He pales, mumbling some apology and scurrying off like the coward he is.

Mya looks at me with wide eyes.

I don't give either of us time to dwell on it and grab her wrist, pulling her away. I angle us in a shadowed alcove behind a bank of palms, away from any cameras. A couple slips past us toward the dance floor; a server glances over, then away.

Mya jerks slightly, protesting. "Worth, what the hell are you doing?"

"I have a business proposition."

Her eyes narrow. "A... proposition?"

Watching Ethan crowd her space, something in me went volcanic. That decided it. Not Sophia. Not anyone else. It has to be Mya. For Brianna, but also for me. I need her close, where I can control the story. I need to burn this out of my system, and a temporary arrangement is the cleanest way I can think of.

"Don't look so nervous." My mouth twitches, even though this isn't actually funny. "I need your help with something," I continue, my expression schooling into something more serious.

"Okay... what can I do?"

I choose my words carefully. "It's about my ex-wife."

I proceed to tell her what my lawyer advised. By the time I lay out my plan, Mya is blinking at me like I've lost my damn mind. Maybe I have.

"You can't be serious," she bites out. "You want me to *pretend* to be your girlfriend?"

"No... I mean yes, but no."

"What do you mean then?"

"I want you to pretend to be my girlfriend, then my fiancée, and then... my wife."

Her eyes widen like saucers. "Worth, that's nuts! *You're* nuts. Why would I ever agree to something like this?"

I drag a hand down my face. "What if I offer you something in return?"

Her arms cross instantly over her chest, protective. "Like what?"

I hesitate, choosing my words. "You've been... struggling financially. I could compensate you for helping me."

Her face hardens, cheeks blazing red. "Fuck you, Miller. I'm not a wife for hire!"

Shit. Wrong words. The last thing I meant was to make Mya feel like some escort I could purchase.

"That's not what I meant," I rush out. "I'm saying this could be mutually beneficial. You'd get a way out of the financial stress. And I'd get—" I stop myself before I say *you*. "I'd get to protect Brianna."

Mya shakes her head, curls bouncing, fury radiating off her. "Do you even hear yourself? Do you have any idea how condescending that sounds? I've worked for everything I have. I don't need to be rescued by a man."

I close the space between us even further, desperate for her to understand. "This isn't about saving you. It's about saving my daughter."

She exhales. "No one has ever even *seen* us together outside of work."

"That works in our favor," I counter. "We can say we kept it quiet for professional reasons. Discretion. It's believable."

"And what about the fraternization rule?"

"It's my company. I'll change it."

Her jaw drops. "You're crazy."

"Practical," I correct.

"No. People are going to think I'm fucking my boss to get ahead." Her voice trembles, equal parts anger and disbelief.

"They won't. Not if they believe the relationship is serious. And if anyone talks shit, I'll fire them."

"You can't just do that."

"Watch me."

She scoffs. "And what about my *age*? Won't it bother you, being married to someone so much younger than you?" Her lips curl, sarcasm sharp as glass.

"No, we're both adults."

Mya's brows lift, clearly unconvinced.

"Though I am aware of how much younger you are than me."

Mya glares at me like she wants to set me on fire. "There it is. You don't care because this is convenient for you."

I step closer, bracing my hands on the wall above her, lowering my voice. "Convenient or not, I don't have another option." I brace my hands on the wall above her and lean forward, lowering my voice. "Vanessa is coming after my daughter, and I'll do whatever the hell it takes to protect her. Please, Mya."

Her lips part, but no words come. For a moment, it's just her stare locked on mine—furious and conflicted. And beneath all of it, something that tells me she hasn't completely slammed the door shut.

"I can't marry you, Worth." Mya's chin tips up stubbornly. "What would I even tell my family? What will you tell your daughter? This is completely unbelievable."

"Then we'll work hard to make it believable. Sell the story. We'll be a whirlwind romance. And don't worry about Brianna, I'll handle her."

Her eyes flash. "*Handle* her? Worth, she's not a business deal. What if she hates me? You'd be forcing a stranger into your daughter's life. And me—" she presses her hand to her chest, voice breaking "—I'd have to move into your house. Be in her space. Oh my God, this is insane. I can't do it."

She pushes off the wall when a laughing couple squeezes by with two champagne flutes and a *sorry*.

"Mya—"

"I'm not a damn charity case. You want a rent-a-wife? Find someone else."

She storms off, but pauses, shoulders rising and falling with the weight of her breaths. When she finally speaks again, her voice is softer, but it cuts deeper. "I thought you respected me, Worth. Guess I was wrong."

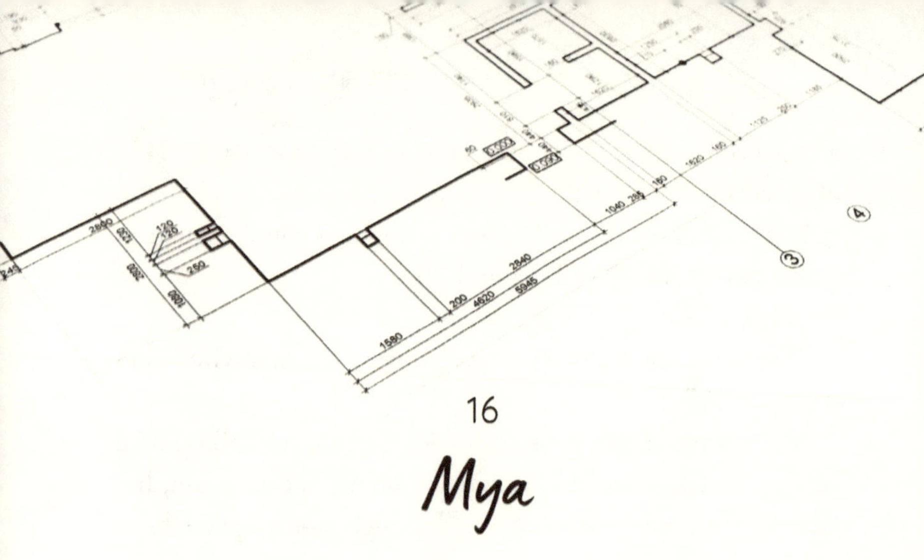

16

Mya

My pulse is still roaring in my ears as I stalk down the hall. By the time I reach the doors, my hands are shaking badly.

I can't believe him.

Asking me to be his fake wife? For compensation? Changing the HR policy like this is some kind of power play? The audacity. The arrogance. The *nerve* of that man.

I press the heel of my hand against my chest, willing my racing heart to slow. But it's not just anger making me this worked up—it's hurt. Disappointment. I actually thought Worth respected me, at least a little. That underneath all the growling and mixed signals, there was a man who... God, I don't even know. *Saw* me.

Instead, he wants to *use* me.

I can't believe I might have secretly wanted him to mean something else when he said he needed me.

No. No, I can't go there.

I push past the double doors and into the cool night air.

Relief—or maybe panic—rushes through me as I gulp down a huge inhale.

I head straight for the curb and throw up a hand. A cab screeches to a stop, and I slide inside.

Lights smear across the windows as we move. Only then do I finally let myself breathe.

I grab my phone and call Tiana. I don't expect her to pick up, but I desperately need to tell her what happened.

On the fifth ring, she answers.

"Mya?" I hear the fading sound of music and the faint pulse of bass in the background. "What's wrong?"

"Worth."

She exhales. "What did he do now?"

"He asked me to marry him."

Tiana chokes on the line. "Come again?"

"Not for real-real," I clarify quickly. "Some fake marriage arrangement to help with his custody case. He wants me to play wife so he doesn't look like a playboy in front of a judge." I lower my voice. "You have to swear, TJ, you cannot tell *anyone*. Not Mom, not Devon, not JJ."

She whistles. "Sworn to secrecy. But... That might not be the worst idea I've ever heard."

I gasp. "Are you well?"

"Think about it. You'd live in his mansion. Have you seen his article in Architectural Digest? That place is unreal. And you could set the rules and your own terms. Plus... You'd be shacking with a ridiculously hot billionaire. There are worse fates, MJ."

I throw my head back with a groan. "Oh my God, you're just as crazy as he is."

But even as I say it, a tiny, dangerous part of me wonders if she's right.

By the time Tiana is done working her persuasive magic on me, my head is spinning.

At home, I move on autopilot; keys in the dish, shoes by the door, kettle on. I don't even hear the water boil until it squeals. I pour a cup and stare at the steam like it might give me answers.

I fold onto the couch and press my palms over my eyes until little starbursts pop. The worst part isn't the logistics. It's the memory of the vulnerability and the pleading in Worth's voice.

It's how my heart answered before my head did.

IT'S BEEN A FEW DAYS SINCE MY HEATED ENCOUNTER WITH Worth at the gala, and everything has gone back to business as usual. Or at least, that's what it looks like on the surface.

Worth has been ignoring me, barely acknowledging my presence unless work requires it.

Today, Griffin is taking me on my very first site visit. We're checking out the community homes being built a few blocks over, and I've been buzzing about it all weekend. It'll be my first time slipping into steel-toe boots and a hard hat, and it makes me feel like I'm finally stepping into the real work, not just being stuck behind a desk drafting endless designs.

He stops by my desk just after nine, holding a cardboard box and grinning.

"Got your gear, newbie," he says, dropping it onto my desk with a thud.

Inside is a neon vest, a pair of heavy boots, and the brightest yellow hard hat I've ever seen. I bite back a smile as I pull the vest out.

"Please tell me I don't have to wear this in the office."

Griffin laughs. "Only if you want to be a fashion icon. We'll change before we head out."

We chat while I try the boots on for size and he runs me through the plan for the morning.

Then, as if on cue, the mood shifts.

Worth strides in late, coat in one hand, phone pressed to his ear. His voice is low, but the tension in his jaw says more than words ever could. He doesn't look in my direction, doesn't so much as glance at Griffin standing a foot away from me. He heads straight into his office and shuts the door.

"He's been even grumpier than usual. Which, you know, is saying a lot," Griffin says, rolling his eyes before turning back to the files on my desk.

I clear my throat. "Do you know why, by any chance? Has he said anything?"

Griffin chuckles. "Nope. Probably just stress. He's been picking up the slack while Henson's away."

"His brother," I say, nodding.

"Yeah, Henson's been up in Vancouver for weeks, leading a big project. He's coming back today. So Worth's been dealing with double the load."

That makes sense. Sort of.

I know one of the reasons why Worth has been acting even grumpier than usual, but I won't admit it has anything to do with me out loud.

I lean back in my chair, chewing the inside of my cheek. Henson left before I started, so I never got to introduce myself.

"I guess I'll finally get the chance to meet Henson."

Griffin grins. "You'll like him. He's the more charming Miller, if you ask me."

"Low bar," I mutter under my breath, and he laughs, loud enough to turn a few heads in the office.

My eyes glance to Worth's door, but it's shut. I guess he's still upset that I refused his proposal.

Good. Keep ignoring me. I'm mad that he propositioned me in the first place. I ought to tattle on him to HR for the way he's been treating me, but I always decide against it.

It's better for both of us if he stays away.

Although a tiny, traitorous part of me is disappointed.

BY THE TIME WE GET BACK FROM THE SITE VISIT, MY HAIR is a mess under the hard hat, my boots feel about ten pounds heavier than when I first laced them up, and my cheeks ache from grinning so much. It was everything I hoped it would be, and I can't wait to do it again.

When we step into the office, I spot broad shoulders, a navy suit, and easy laughter carrying across the room. The man is standing with a group of staff, fully engaged in conversation.

That must be Henson.

As we approach, he turns, eyes warm, and extends a hand before I even have a chance to introduce myself.

"You must be our new junior designer. Mya, right?"

I blink, momentarily thrown off. "Yes, that's me."

"Thought so." His handshake is firm, his smile friendly.

I feel a little flustered. I've never spoken to Henson before today, yet somehow he knows my name and my position. The contrast between him and his brother is immediate and impossible to ignore.

Where Worth is gruff and curt, Henson is warm and approachable. He's the kind of person who makes everyone in the room feel comfortable.

I still somehow find myself favoring Worth, despite all his rough edges and impossible moods. Maybe it's because he doesn't make things easy. Maybe it's because every time he looks at me, it's like standing too close to a fire.

But I can't let those thoughts consume me.

Henson asks about my first projects and if I've settled in with the team. He listens, nodding thoughtfully, as though he genuinely cares about my answers.

It's clear why everyone seems to like him. He's the type of leader who knows how to put people at ease.

Henson slips his hands into his pockets. "By the way, I had a look at the preliminary drawings you worked on for the Singapore project."

My heart skips. *He's seen them?*

"They were solid, Mya. You've got an eye for blending design and function."

Heat rushes to my cheeks. "Thank you. I really enjoyed working on them."

"How would you feel about seeing the project?"

It takes me a second to process the question. "In person?"

"Yes, in Singapore," he clarifies with a chuckle. "We're sending a small team down to check on progress, meet with Lau Construction, and make sure everything is running smoothly. I want you to be part of that team."

For a moment, I just stare at him, blinking like an idiot. My chest tightens with a mix of excitement and disbelief.

"Wow. Yes. Absolutely. I'd love that," I blurt, probably too eagerly, but I don't care.

Henson smiles. "Good. I'll speak with Dre to finalize the details. Consider this your official welcome to the big leagues."

He gives my shoulder a friendly pat before excusing himself to talk to someone else, leaving me standing there with my heart racing, mind already spinning with what this trip could mean for my career.

And yet, despite the exhilaration flooding through me, a single thought needles its way in.

If I'm going to Singapore that means I'll be traveling with Worth.

And I have no idea if that thrills me or terrifies me—or both.

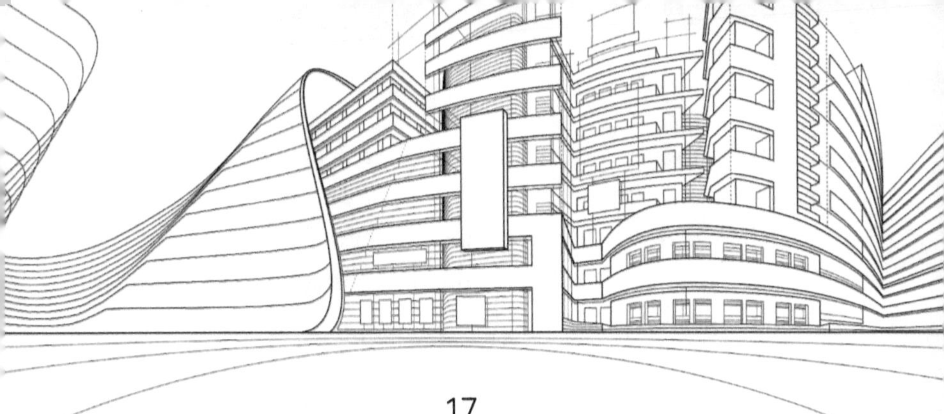

17

Worth

"You did what?" I practically roar, the sound bouncing off the glass walls of my office.

Henson just stands there, a stupid grin plastered across his face, like this is all some big joke. "I invited her to join the Singapore trip," he repeats, casual as hell. As if he didn't just light a match and toss it into gasoline.

I drag a hand down my face, trying to steady my breathing. My blood turns hot—I hate how easily my brother can get under my skin. "You had no right."

"She's working on the damn project, Worth. Why wouldn't she go? You should be thanking me. It'll be good for her."

Good for *her*. Not for me. Not for my sanity.

I start pacing. The thought of Mya in Singapore—on the plane, in the hotel, on job sites with me—is enough to make my brain short-circuit.

Henson wants to put us in the same city, the same fucking meetings, side by side?

Christ.

"She's not ready," I bite out. It's a weak excuse, and Henson knows it.

"She's more than ready," he fires back, crossing his arms. "I've seen her work. Mya is talented. Hungry. She should be getting exposure, not locked behind a desk."

I glare at him, but he doesn't flinch. He's always been the calm and reasonable brother. The one who doesn't let his cock dictate his decisions.

I shove my hands in my pockets to keep from balling them into fists. "You don't understand."

"I don't? You've been off your game for weeks, Worth. Snapping at Dre. Ignoring Griffin. Hell, even Brianna noticed. You think I don't know what's going on here?"

My nostrils flare. "Drop it."

He studies me for a beat, weighing whether to push. Finally, he shrugs. "Fine. But Mya is going. Deal with it."

He turns to leave, and I follow him to the door, trying one last time to convince him it isn't a good idea.

"I don't want Mya there, Henson."

And of course, that's when Mya passes by my office. Her head jerks up, eyes widening like I just stabbed her in the chest. She gives me a glare but doesn't stop, doesn't say a word, just all but bolts down the hall.

Goddamnit.

That's twice now she's overheard me talk about her.

I rub my forehead. If I'm not more careful, she'll have HR breathing down my neck, and honestly, she'd have every right.

I sure as hell gave her the ammo.

That's why I've been avoiding her. Because a small, ugly piece of me is ashamed at the way I cornered her at the gala.

How I propositioned her in a corridor as if I wasn't negotiating something that would rearrange her entire world.

Because if she looks me in the eye, I'll have to own it—I'll have to say I'm sorry. And I don't know how to do that without saying everything else I'm not ready to say.

Henson shakes his head, but I snap, "Don't fucking say a word."

I don't even think, just move. My legs carry me out of my office, after her. I've never run after a woman. Not once in my life. But here I am, following Mya through the office like a madman.

At the end of the hall, she darts left into the mail room. I glance behind me, then step inside after her, locking the door behind me.

She's facing the printer, her back rigid. She doesn't turn.

I clear my throat. "Mya—"

"Save it, Worth."

"I didn't mean what you heard."

She whirls on me. "Oh, no? Because this is the second time I've overheard you say you don't want me here. So what is it, Mr. Miller? Because you're giving me whiplash." Her tone drips with anger, but underneath it, I hear the hurt. "You literally asked me to *marry* you a few days ago."

I move towards her slowly, raking a hand through my hair. "I—fuck. I don't know, Mya."

She exhales hard, shoulders drooping. "I'm just trying to do my job, Worth." Her voice cracks, and it guts me. "I was actually even considering accepting your proposal. I'm such a fool."

My chest grows tight. "I'm sorry. For everything."

For a beat, neither of us speaks.

Her eyes search mine, wary. "Sorry doesn't justify why you keep making me feel like I don't belong here."

I grit my teeth, fighting the instinct to tell her the truth— that she doesn't just belong here, she's one of the best employees we've had, and the company is already better for it.

That she's lodged under my fucking skin, that I want her near me all the time, and I don't know what to do about it.

Instead, I step closer, close enough that I can smell the faint trace of her shampoo. My hand twitches at my side, aching to touch her, to prove the opposite of every cold word I've thrown at her.

"Mya..." I rasp, voice low. "You deserve to be here. More than most of them out there. That's the problem."

Her lips part, but I don't give her the chance to speak.

"You've invaded my mind these last couple of months. I can't fucking shake you. One second I want to push you away, the next I—" I break off, dragging a hand down my jaw. "I've been taking it out on you. It's cruel and I know it. I'm aware of every goddamn second of it."

Mya blinks at me, wide-eyed.

"I don't know how to act around you," I finish.

Her breath hitches, the smallest sound.

I close the distance and cup her face. When she doesn't move out of my grip, and starts to lean forward, it's enough to snap the last thread of my restraint, and I crash my mouth onto hers.

It's reckless. The one thing I told myself I wouldn't do. But the second Mya's soft lips meet mine, every ounce of logic I've been clinging to goes up in flames.

She gasps against me, and for a heartbeat I think she'll shove me away. But then she kisses me back.

Her mouth is sweet, her lips pliant, the kiss hungry.

My hand fists in her curly hair, tugging her closer until her body is flush against mine. The other finds her hip, sliding around to grip the curve of her ass. Mya fits against me like a glove, like she was meant to drive me fucking mad.

I groan into her mouth when her tongue brushes mine. My

cock hardens instantly, straining against my slacks, pressing into her stomach. Her sharp inhale tells me she feels it.

She doesn't pull away.

Instead, she grabs at my suit jacket, fingers digging into the lapels, tugging me closer.

I taste coffee and mint on her tongue, and it's addictive. My pulse pounds in my ears, drowning out everything but the feel of her. Her curves, the little whimper catching in her throat, her body arching into mine like she's just as desperate as I am.

My hands roam lower, memorizing every line, every curve. I want to bend her over the damn printer and sink into her until she's screaming my name. The image flashes through my mind so vividly I almost groan aloud.

But then—too soon—Mya tears her mouth from mine, panting. Her lips are swollen, her eyes wide, chest heaving.

Reality slams back into me like a freight train.

She stumbles back a step, shaking her head. "No. No, no... we can't—" Her voice cracks as she straightens her blouse. "We have to stop this."

I stand frozen, my cock painfully hard, the taste of her still lingering on my tongue.

Mya avoids my gaze as she rushes for the door, yanking it open. Before she slips out, she throws one last line over her shoulder:

"You're my boss, Worth. I can't lose this job. This can't happen again."

The door slams shut, leaving me alone with the echo of her words and the ache in my body.

I drag both hands down my face, muttering, "Fuck."

She's right.

But I know I'll never be able to keep my hands off her.

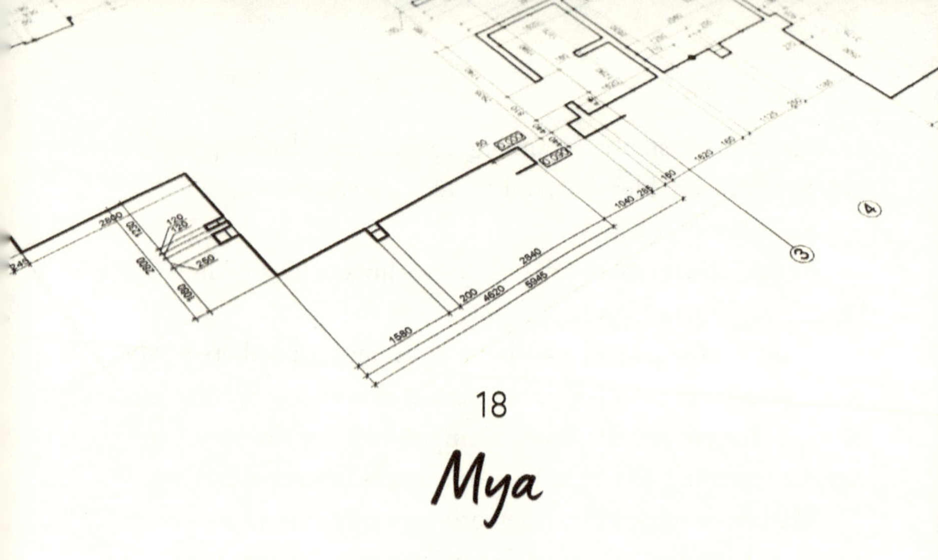

18

Mya

I don't stop moving until I'm back at my desk. My lips are tingling, my whole body thrumming like I just stepped off a rollercoaster.

What the hell just happened?

One second I was furious with Worth, ready to unleash every ounce of anger for making me feel unwanted again, and the next... his mouth was on mine. His hands on me. His body pressed against me so tight I could *feel* how much he wanted me.

And I wanted him back. *God*, I wanted him back.

The kiss was nothing like I expected it to be. It was rough, unyielding, all of the tension and fury spilling out at once.

For one reckless moment, I didn't give a damn that he's my boss.

His lips moved against mine as if he'd been starving for it, and the hunger was contagious.

I press trembling fingers to my lips, heat rushing through me.

Shame battles against the ache between my thighs. I'm an idiot.

Every warning bell in my head was screaming, but my heart was pounding so hard it felt like it was trying to crawl out of my chest just to get closer to him.

I shove the thoughts down and focus on breathing. On keeping my head above water. If I'm not careful, I'll drown in him.

I straighten my posture, force my hands to still, and plaster my best "everything's fine" face on. Because if anyone even suspects what just happened behind that locked door, I'm finished.

So I'm done with him.

But as much as I tell myself that last part... I don't believe it.

Instead of stopping at my desk, I push through the bathroom door and brace my hands on the cool edge of the sink.

My reflection is a dead giveaway: flushed cheeks, swollen lips, wide eyes, as if I've seen a ghost. Except it was Worth-fucking-Miller with his hands all over me, kissing me like he wanted to eat me alive.

I splash cold water on my face, trying to calm down, but it only makes my hands shake harder. My phone is already in my grip before I register unlocking it.

SOS.

I don't bother with context. Tiana will know it's bad.

I sink onto the little bench near the stalls, my head in my hands. I need to get it together.

My phone buzzes a second later.

TJ:

What happened???

> I have to quit my job.

A beat later:

TJ:

> ...

> Take a breath, drama queen, and start from the beginning.

I groan, sinking lower on the bench, but force myself to tell her.

> I kissed Worth.

> Well, Worth kissed me.

There's a three-dot bubble. Then another.

TJ:

> STFU! Tell me everything!!!

Of course this is her reaction.

> No, TJ. Don't enable this behavior. He's my BOSS.

TJ:

> Your really hot boss who wants you.

> He hates me.

TJ:

> Hate sex is the best!!!

> OMG. This is some forbidden workplace romance shit.

I bite back a hysterical laugh. My sister thinks this is hot and exciting. Meanwhile, my chest is growing tighter and my hands are still shaking.

TJ:

How did it happen???

Did he shove you on the desk? Press you
against the wall? Tell me.

I squeeze my eyes shut. She's not far off.

He kissed me like he hated that he
wanted me.

And I kissed him back.

TJ:

AHHHHHHH. THIS IS MY ROMANCE NOVEL
DREAM.

So??? How was it??

I chew on my lip, staring at the words. My fingers fly before
I can stop them.

Like I couldn't breathe but didn't want to
stop.

And it was a mistake. A HUGE mistake.

If anyone finds out, I'm done.

TJ:

Orrrrrrr you're about to be the main character
in the sexiest office romance of all time.

I let my head fall back against the wall, torn between
laughing and crying. Trust Tiana to make a potential scandal
feel like entertainment.

TJ:

But still, I agree that you need to be careful. I don't want you risking everything because some billionaire with perfect hair decided he's into you.

I know. I'll handle it.

TJ:

Promise?

Promise.

TJ:

Okay. Now text me back the exact way he kissed you before my imagination kills me.

Stop it! I'm serious, TJ. This can never happen again.

TJ:

Mhm. Keep telling yourself that.

I shove my phone back into my pocket, take one last steadying breath, and leave the bathroom. All I need to do is sit down at my desk, bury myself in work, and pretend like nothing happened.

"Hey, Mya."

I glance up to find Ethan heading my way, a stack of folders in one arm and a coffee in the other.

"Hi," I say, managing a smile.

He stops right in front of me, his easy grin in place. "I heard you're coming to Singapore with us."

I nod. "Just found out today."

"That's great. You'll love it. First time traveling for work?"

"First time traveling *anywhere*. So this feels big."

His laugh is warm. "Trust me, you'll kill it. I'll make sure you get the best crash course on international site visits. The locals are going to love you. They always appreciate a new face," he says with a wink. "I'm originally from there, so if you need someone to show you the ropes—or, you know, the best hawker stalls in Singapore..." He shrugs, the corner of his mouth quirking. "I'm your guy."

I open my mouth to reply, but then I feel a burning sensation on the side of my face.

I glance past Ethan and catch sight of Worth down the hall, just outside his office. He's standing still, his eyes locked on us, watching.

My stomach flips.

Ethan doesn't notice. He just gives me a final smile before heading off, leaving me standing in the middle of the hall like my pulse isn't going haywire.

When I look back, Worth is still there, and the intensity in his stare makes me almost trip over myself to get to my desk.

Only when I sit down and pretend to be busy with my computer does he finally turn and disappear into his office.

Singapore is going to be... interesting.

And I don't believe for a second that Worth Miller is going to leave me alone.

19

Worth

"And don't forget to call me if anything goes wrong while I'm away," I tell Brianna as I fold the last of my shirts and drop them into the suitcase.

I'm leaving for Singapore on a red eye tonight, and worry sits heavy on my chest.

A week away doesn't sound long, but when it comes to my daughter, it'll feel like forever. Maggie will be here the whole time, and I trust her more than anyone, but the thought of leaving makes my gut tighten.

"Yes, Dad," Brianna says with a dramatic eye roll. "We'll be fine."

I grunt. "I know you'll be fine. I'm worried about Maggie."

Sitting nearby with a notebook in her lap, she frowns. "Why?"

"Because she'll have to deal with a little menace like you for an entire week." I cross the room in two strides and dig my fingers into her armpits. Brianna squeals, laughter bubbling out of her as she shoves me away.

"What do you mean? I'm an angel!"

"The devil was once an angel, too, Brianna," I deadpan.

She gasps, clutching her chest in mock offense. "Dad!"

I chuckle. "I'm just kidding, Piglet. But in all seriousness, I programmed all of our emergency contacts into your phone, and Dre printed a copy for the fridge so you and Maggie have them handy. I also gave Uncle Henson and Uncle Griffin a spare key and the garage code. They'll be checking in, too."

"Such a helicopter dad," she teases.

Hell yeah, maybe I am. But I don't care. Bri is my whole world, and I'd rather smother her than ever let her feel unprotected.

"Come help me pack the rest," I say, handing her a pile of pants.

She sighs but joins me, folding with exaggerated slowness just to get under my skin. I let her.

As I watch her hands move, a thought cuts deep through me. Her mom is missing this. Every new piece of the young woman Brianna is becoming. And though I'll never forgive her for walking away, sometimes I wonder if Brianna feels that absence more than she lets on. It makes me wonder if I should give Vanessa another chance?

It's been incredible to watch my daughter grow, to see her find her voice and her confidence. I wouldn't trade a second of being a single dad to her. But there's always a sliver of fear gnawing at me—that I'm not enough. That one day she'll realize the gap her mom left and think I could never fill it.

I shove the thought away and zip up the suitcase. "See? We make a pretty good team."

Brianna smirks. "Obviously. You'd be lost without me."

And she's right.

The runway lights glow against the tarmac as I step out of the car and towards the company jet. Our plane isn't flashy, but it's large enough to hold the six members of our team comfortably.

I send a quick round of texts before boarding.

To Brianna: *Remember to call me if you need anything. Love you, Piglet.*

To Maggie: *Plane's here. I'll check in once we land in Singapore. Thanks, Mags.*

To Henson and Griffin: *Boarding now. Keep an eye out at the house. Appreciate it.*

When I climb the steps into the cabin, my eyes scan the rows automatically, not for my seat, but for *her*. Mya isn't here yet.

Disappointment settles in my chest, enough to irritate me. I brush it off. The last thing I need is to start my week-long trip with that particular feeling.

I sit in a leather seat near the front, rolling my shoulders back. I've already decided: no more pursuing her. Whatever the hell I feel when Mya looks at me—heat, hunger, that magnetic pull that makes me act reckless—it has to end. I don't beg. I don't chase women.

And if the whispers and headlines want to keep painting me as the blue collar playboy, so be it. I know who I am, and I know what I'm not. It gnaws at me sometimes, the idea that my daughter might one day believe the tabloids over the man who raised her, but that's my cross to bear.

I'll just have to figure out another way to convince the judge that I'm suitable to continue being Brianna's full-time parent.

I drag in a breath, grip the armrest, and close my eyes for a moment.

Her perfume hits me before I see her.

When I open my eyes, Mya is stepping onto the plane, curves wrapped in a business-casual outfit. My pulse betrays me instantly.

Her gaze doesn't land on me once. Not even a glance. She passes by, the faintest brush of air following her, and keeps walking until she's at the very back of the plane.

My jaw locks.

So that's how it's going to be.

I flag down the flight attendant with a clipped gesture. "Scotch. Neat. Make it a double."

She nods quickly, disappearing down the aisle, and I pinch the bridge of my nose. By the time the attendant sets the glass down on the tray beside me, my patience has already worn thin. I knock it back in one go, the liquor scorching a path down my throat.

The burn should ground me. It doesn't.

I pull out my phone, pretending to scroll through contracts, emails, zoning updates—anything to keep me focused. My thumb moves, but my brain doesn't register a single word. Instead, I'm straining to hear something else.

Her voice. Her laugh.

There's nothing.

Mya's silence irritates me more than it should. With a scowl, I tilt my head slightly, just enough to look over my shoulder.

She's all the way at the back, tucked into an aisle seat like she's trying to disappear. Her knuckles are white around the armrests, chest rising and falling fast. The fear written across her face is obvious.

For all her bravado, Mya is terrified of flying.

And I hate how much I want to get up, go back there and comfort her.

I debate it for all of ten seconds. Then I'm on my feet, striding down the aisle before I can talk myself out of it.

Mya doesn't look at me when I stop beside her row, just keeps her wide eyes locked on the seatback in front of her like it might save her life.

"What's wrong?"

No answer.

I lean closer. "Are you scared?"

Finally, Mya gives the smallest nod. Her shoulders bunch in tight, and for the first time, I notice how tiny she looks with me hovering over her. The sight sparks an irrational urge to scoop her up, hold her against me, and tell her nothing can touch her while she's in my arms.

"Have you ever been on a plane before?"

Another tiny shake of her head.

Something twists in my chest. Without thinking, I slide into the empty seat beside her. Her gaze snaps to mine at last.

"What are you doing?" she hisses, her voice shaky.

I buckle myself in, leaning over her before she can stop me. "Sitting next to you for takeoff." My hand brushes her hip as I tug her seatbelt across her lap and click it into place.

Her eyes dart towards the aisle, then back to me, panic flickering across her face like she's worried one of our colleagues will see us.

Her throat bobs as she swallows.

The seatbelt sign dings above us. The flight attendant's voice begins droning through the safety message, but all I hear is Mya's quick breathing.

I reach for her hand without giving myself time to reconsider. Her palm is cold, stiff as stone in mine. "Squeeze when you get scared," I murmur.

For a few seconds, she's rigid, like she might yank away. But then her fingers soften, fitting against mine.

Her hand is so damn small—and fuck if it doesn't feel like it belongs there.

The engines roar as the plane lurches forward. Beside me, Mya's back goes ramrod straight. Her nails dig into my hand, and the little squeezes shoot straight up my arm. She still won't look at me.

I don't say a word. Just keep my hand firm around hers, anchoring her.

When the nose tips up and the pressure shifts, she squeezes again, harder this time. My thumb drags over her knuckles in slow, grounding circles. The cabin rattles, the sky opening wide, and still I don't let go.

Finally, the hum evens out. The seatbelt light dings off, signaling we've leveled at cruising altitude.

And just like that, Mya yanks her hand free, leaving mine abruptly empty.

"Thanks," she mutters, still staring ahead. "You can go back to your seat now."

Dismissed. Just like that.

For a second, I consider staying put, forcing her to look at me. But her shoulders are stiff, her body angled away, a clear line drawn in the sand.

So I bite back the words burning in my chest, unbuckle my belt, and push to my feet.

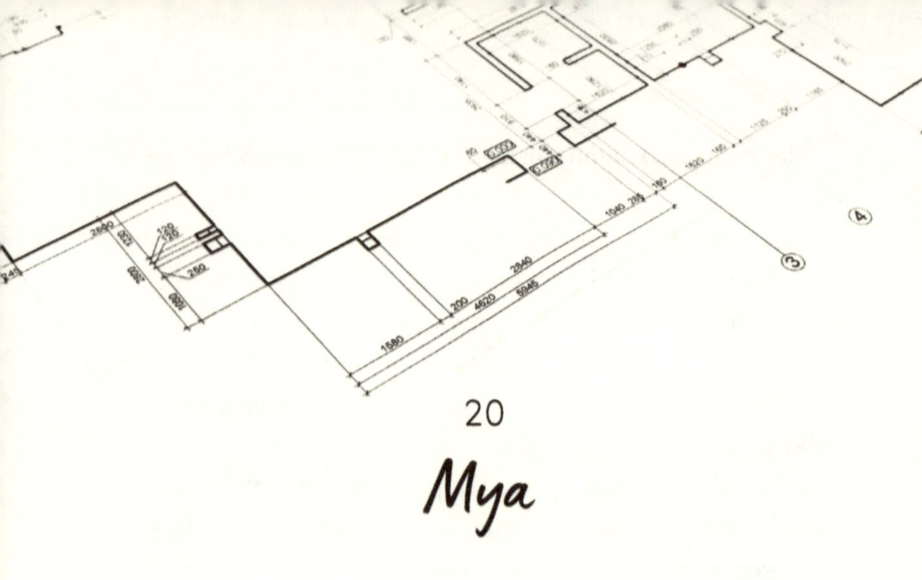

<h1 style="text-align:center">20</h1>

<h1 style="text-align:center">Mya</h1>

Worst sixteen hours of my life.

By the time my heels hit solid ground, my legs are jelly and my head feels like it's still floating somewhere above the clouds. For a split second, I'm tempted to drop to my knees and kiss the tarmac.

The hot Singapore air clings to my skin, and I drag in a shaky breath.

I glance back as my colleagues exit the plane together. Worth is the last to step out, immaculate in his tailored trousers, suit jacket draped over one arm and not a hair out of place. He doesn't look like he's just spent sixteen hours in the air. Damn him.

Ethan slides next to me. He was kind on the flight, even after I nearly snapped his head off mid-panic. I apologized, blaming nerves, and he'd laughed it off, handing me two little pills that knocked me out cold for hours.

"How was your sleep?"

"Fine," I answer with a smile. "Thanks again for the help, and sorry for almost biting your head off."

His laugh is loud, and it carries back to where Worth trails behind us. The grunt that rumbles from him is audible, even at this distance. My eyes roll so hard it's a miracle they don't stick. Ethan doesn't notice, still chatting, still smiling like nothing is amiss.

After clearing customs, we pile into two town cars; I'm buzzing with nerves and awe. When we finally pull up to the hotel—a massive glass tower glittering against the skyline—I nearly forget how exhausted I am. Inside, it's all marble floors, golden chandeliers that look straight out of a luxury magazine. W.H.M. really didn't spare any expenses.

I follow the others to reception. Out of the corner of my eye, I catch Worth moving towards the elevators with his usual unbothered stride, phone still pressed to his ear. He doesn't even glance at me.

After we've all checked in, the others gather in the lobby and start tossing around dinner plans.

"You coming with us?" Ethan asks, sounding hopeful.

I hesitate. My first instinct is to decline. I'm running on fumes, and all I want is a hot shower and twelve hours of uninterrupted sleep, even though it's not nighttime yet. My eyelids feel like sandpaper, and every muscle aches from the flight. Jetlag sucks. My lips part to give him a polite *"maybe next time"* when Seraya—our lead-technical-engineer-turned-friend —chimes in from across the group.

"Mr. Miller said he'll join us later. He always comes out with the team the first night of a trip," she says, slinging her bag over her shoulder like it's nothing.

My pulse gives a tiny, traitorous kick. Damn it.

"Yeah. Sure. I'll come," I answer Ethan. *Not because of Worth. Obviously.* "I'll see you in a bit then."

I barely make it to my hotel room before I'm peeling myself out of my clothes. The bathroom fills with steam, and the hot water works away some of the stiffness in my legs and back. I close my eyes under the spray, but the second I do, images of Worth on the plane creep back in—his broad frame beside me, his steady hand wrapped around mine, the way his presence made the fear disappear.

My brain takes me back to the kiss we shared in the mail room and my fingers go straight to my lips where the memory of Worth's mouth on me won't stop running in a loop.

I press my hands flat to the slick tile, trying to will the images away, but instead they multiply. His scent, his low, raspy voice in my ear, the thumb that traced lazy circles on my palm like it was his right. My chest heaves, and the water cascades over me, hotter, harder, as though it could wash him out of my system.

My fingers drift lower, slipping between my thighs until they find the heat of my center. A jolt rushes through me at the first brush, stealing my breath. I circle my clit in slow strokes, pretending it's *Worth's* hands on me, *his* body surrounding me.

Every droplet feels like him. His touch ghosting down my spine, his mouth branding the curve of my neck. God—why does thinking of him feel so good when it should feel like the worst idea in the world?

My rhythm quickens, urgency clawing at every nerve. I tip my head back beneath the spray, teeth sinking into my lip to stifle the needy sound building in my throat. Pleasure coils tight, threatening to unravel me at the seams. A few more desperate strokes and it snaps, light bursting behind my eyes as a moan tears free, loud and unrestrained.

I stay there, caught between the scalding water and the ache he left behind, knowing I'll never scrub Worth Miller off me, no matter how hard I try.

Freshly showered and wrapped in the hotel's plush robe, I flop onto the bed and FaceTime Tiana. She picks up almost instantly, her face filling my screen, hair piled on top of her head and a mischievous grin tugging at her lips.

"I didn't think you'd pick up," I say, returning her smile. It's 1 a.m. on a Sunday in Seattle, so I was expecting my call to go to voicemail.

"Yeah, well... I'm catching up on episodes of Grey's Anatomy. Might regret it in the morning."

"Just make sure not to miss opening Willow's. Mr. Patel might have a panic attack."

Tiana gasps. "I could never be the reason for that poor man's stress," she says, feigning all innocence. We both know that she's a thorn in Aravind's side. But he would never replace Tiana, regardless of how crazy she is at times.

"How was the flight? Singapore already looks good on you," she teases.

I groan. "Sixteen hours of hell. I thought I was going to die during takeoff. And don't even get me started on the turbulence. I was able to sleep for most of the flight, though."

"And Worth? How's *he* been acting with you?"

I chew on my bottom lip.

Tiana's eyes narrow. "Spill it, sister."

"I was panicking—you know, since I've never been on a plane before—and he noticed. He came over, buckled my seatbelt, and told me to squeeze his hand if I was scared."

Her jaw drops. "Hold on. You held his hand for sixteen hours?!"

"God, no. Just for takeoff," I snap, cheeks heating. "Still. It actually helped."

Tiana smirks. "MJ, do you hear yourself?"

I bury my face in the pillow and mumble, "It wasn't like that."

"Sure. Just like kissing him at the office wasn't *like that* either."

I groan, louder this time. "Why did I even call you?"

"Because you're obsessed with your boss and need someone to keep your secrets."

I roll my eyes, though a reluctant smile tugs at my lips. "Am not."

"Are too!"

We both fall into a giggling fit, and it reminds me of when we were younger and used to tease each other like this all the time.

My phone buzzes, a new message lighting up the screen.

WORTH:

Check outside your door.

My breath stutters.

"TJ, I'll talk to you later," I rush out, hanging up before she can protest. I'm still in my robe, hair damp, but I scramble to the door anyway, curiosity winning over.

I glance up and down the hall before spotting a black-and-gold package perched neatly on the floor. My pulse trips as I crouch to pick it up. The box alone screams expensive.

Inside is a silk kimono-style robe in midnight blue with delicate embroidery at the hem. It looks like something plucked straight from a luxury boutique. I don't even want to imagine the price.

A small envelope sits on top. My fingers tremble as I open it.

Mya,

You looked like you were about to collapse getting off the plane. A massage therapist will come by your room in an hour. Wear this.

—W.

I press the card to my chest, heart racing. A mix of outrage and... something warmer coils low in my stomach.

Why is he making this more difficult than it already is?

I stomp back into the room, silk robe draped over my arm, and snatch my phone off the bed.

> I can't accept this.

WORTH:

Why not?

Is he serious right now?

> Worth. Bosses don't give their employees robes and massages!!!

WORTH:

I've definitely gifted employees and clients spa gift certificates.

I scoff out loud.

> This is different and you know it.

WORTH:

How so?

I growl under my breath. He's playing dumb, and it's infuriating.

> You're kidding, right? You just gifted me a silk robe that probably cost more than my entire suitcase and its contents, and you're sending a massage therapist to my room. And you asked me to marry you just days ago. This is a clear line crossing, Mr. Miller.

WORTH:

If the robe is worth more than your clothes, then we need to take you shopping, Ms. Jones.

I bury my face into the pillow and groan.

Besides the point.

WORTH:

Just enjoy it, Mya. You were stressed the entire plane ride. I feel bad that you suffered at our expense.

I pause. That's... almost sweet. Almost.

It's fine, really. Ethan gave me sleeping pills so I was able to snooze for a few hours.

His next reply takes longer, and when it comes, my stomach drops.

WORTH:

He's fired.

Shit. No, no, no.

I jab at the screen and press his number. He answers on the first ring, irritation already lacing his voice.

"Ms. Jones."

"Don't fire him."

"I do what I want. And right now, I want to fire his punk ass."

I scoff. "What did he ever do to you? From what I know, he's a great employee."

"Yeah, well he's overstepping."

"Just like you are?"

The line goes silent, and it stretches so long I almost think he hung up.

"Worth?"

His voice comes back low. "Watch it, Mya."

I grip the phone tighter, pulse fluttering. "Why? Because I pointed out the hypocrisy? Or because I'm right?"

Another pause. I imagine him sitting somewhere in his perfectly pressed shirt, jaw tight, eyes narrowed the way they do when he's seconds from snapping.

"You don't get to compare me to him. Ethan doesn't get to put his hands where they don't belong."

Heat rushes up my neck. "Neither do you." Though the memory of his hand on mine—of his *lips* on mine—flashes through me like lightning.

There's a sharp inhale on the other end of the line. I just poked the dragon.

"I shouldn't have kissed you," he says after a beat, voice rougher now. "I know that. But don't make the mistake of thinking I regret it, Mya."

My stomach flips violently, my mind torn between indignation and the hot, treacherous pulse low in my belly.

"Enjoy the massage, Ms. Jones. I'll see you at dinner," he adds abruptly, as if cutting himself off before he can say more.

The line goes dead.

I lower the phone, staring at the screen.

The massage appointment is still a half hour away, my muscles wound even tighter than before.

What the hell is Worth doing to me?

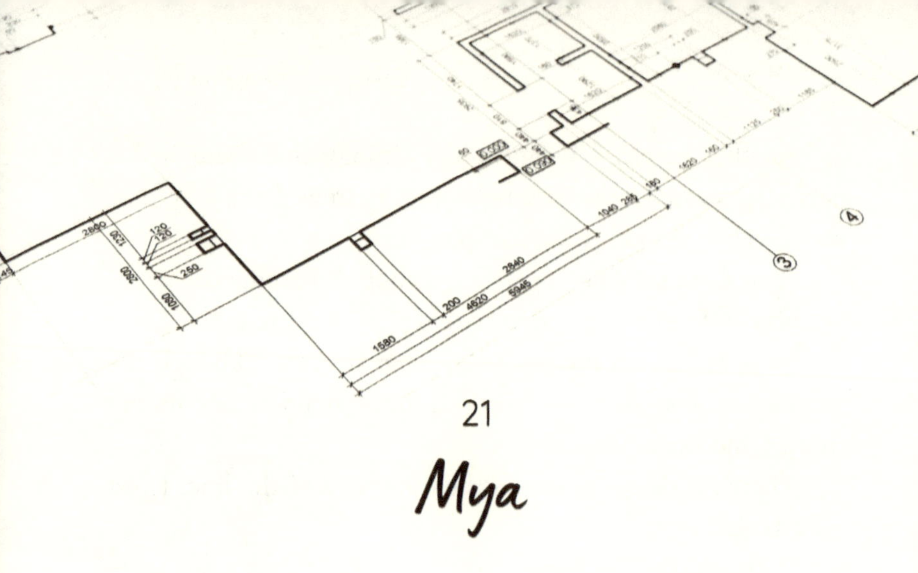

21

Mya

The massage leaves me relaxed, loose-limbed—and annoyed.

Annoyed because I actually enjoyed it, and I don't want to be grateful to Worth Miller. I should be furious at him for constantly crossing lines.

As I get ready for dinner, I decide to channel that irritation into my outfit: something provocative but still classy. A black dress with a low back, a slit that teases mid-thigh, paired with strappy heels that make my legs look longer than they are. If Worth is going to mess with my head, I may as well return the favor.

I exchange a quick text with Seraya confirming the meet-up time, swipe on a final coat of lipstick, and head downstairs. The others are in the lobby. Worth waits near the others, in a dark suit tailored to perfection.

He doesn't say a word, but the way his eyes drag down my body and then back up makes my stomach flip. His face smooths out into that unreadable mask he always wears, but I feel the tension, thick as a barbed wire.

We don't speak. Just exchange a curt nod.

Then Ethan lets out a low whistle. "Damn, Jones."

Heat crawls up my neck; before I can respond, Seraya chimes in, grinning as she gives me a once-over. "You'll be turning all the guys' heads tonight."

Out of the corner of my eye, I catch the tiniest twitch at Worth's temple, and I stifle a smug smile.

When we arrive at the restaurant—an upscale spot tucked against the bay, glowing with candlelight—we're promptly seated at a long table near the glass walls showcasing the skyline.

Worth takes the chair beside me without hesitation. Out of all the empty options, he chose the one next to me.

The waiter hands out menus, but all I register is him so close. Heat radiates off his body, and when he leans in, his addictive cologne invades me at once.

His lips brush dangerously near my ear as he whispers, "You look pliable tonight, Ms. Jones. I gather the massage went well."

My throat goes dry, and I curl my fingers around the stem of my wineglass to hide the way they tremble.

Pliable. Who even says stuff like that—and at a work dinner? My boss, apparently. My infuriatingly magnetic boss who knows damn well what his words do to me.

I force a scoff, tilting the glass toward my lips so I don't have to meet his eyes. "Are you flirting with me, Mr. Miller?"

The corner of his mouth tugs upward. "What if I said yes?" he murmurs, before leaning back in his chair as if he didn't just set my entire bloodstream on fire.

My pulse hammers against my ribs. I will the heat in my cheeks to fade as I focus hard on the menu, on the conversations swirling around me, on literally anything but the man beside me.

Because if I don't, I'll forget where I am. And that this is supposed to be *professional*.

"I told you to stop, Worth," I say, though it comes out thin, weak.

He leans in closer again. My gaze darts nervously around the table, worried one of my colleagues will catch him in the act, but everyone is too distracted by conversation and wine to notice.

"Do you really want me to?" he whispers, breath tickling my skin.

Worth's eyes travel down to my arm where goosebumps have risen, then lower to my chest, where my nipples peak traitorously against the fabric of my dress. Damn me for skipping a bra tonight.

"I guess I have my answer." His tone drips with arrogance. The bubble of heat I was suspended in pops, and irritation surges.

The blue collar playboy is back.

"Yes, I mean it," I snap under my breath. "So, if you'll excuse me, I'd like to enjoy dinner without you breathing down my neck."

Worth chuckles before lifting his glass. He takes a slow sip of amber liquor, watching me over the rim. "As you wish."

I force myself to focus on the people around me as dinner continues. On the surface, everything is fine. But I feel Worth's gaze brushing over me the entire time, even when he converses with the others. It's unnerving, and yet, deep down, a shameful part of me thrills at it.

When the last plates are cleared, Seraya leans towards me with a grin. "We're heading to a club. You in?"

My body is heavy with exhaustion, but the thought of going back to the hotel alone, replaying every charged second with Worth, sounds dreadful. "Yeah, I'll come."

Across the table, another colleague pipes up, smirking at Worth. "Guess we'll see you tomorrow then, Mr. Miller. We know clubs aren't really your thing."

Worth sets his glass down. "Not tonight," he says smoothly. "I'll join you."

A chorus of surprised sounds follows, but everyone quickly grows excited at the idea of their CEO coming along for a night out.

Several minutes later, we're making our way through the neon-lit streets of Singapore. We arrive at our destination where a long line snakes outside the poshest club I've ever seen. Worth pulls out his phone and fires off a quick text. Within seconds, the doorman says something into his earpiece, his gaze shifting to our group, and he waves us forward.

My coworkers erupt in cheers and high fives, grinning like kids who just snuck into the world's best amusement park.

Worth shrugs. "I know the owner," he says simply, holding the door open for us to pass. "W.H.M. built this building."

When we step inside, Seraya immediately grabs my arm, her voice raised over the music. "This place is insane!" She's practically glowing, her sequined dress catching every shard of light.

I smile, letting her energy fuel me.

The rest of the team scatters—some heading for the bar, others for the dance floor. Worth lingers near the entrance, scanning the room.

"Come on," Seraya says, tugging me towards the bar.

Ethan materializes on my other side, leaning in close so I can hear him. "First round's on me."

I laugh, shaking my head. "You don't have to—"

But he's already ordering. Three shots of tequila are slid in front of us moments later, salt and lime on the side. Ethan raises his glass in a toast. "To surviving W.H.M. Construction."

I snort and clink my glass against his. "Barely."

The tequila burns, but it loosens something in me. Warmth unfurls in my chest, enough to drown out Worth's earlier words at dinner.

Still, I feel him across the room. His gaze, hot and unrelenting, finds me through the throng of bodies. Even with distance, it feels like static sparking between us, my skin too aware of him.

I turn back to Ethan, who's already asking me if I want to dance. Seraya wiggles her brows and nudges me forward. "Go. Live a little."

I let Ethan lead me to the dance floor. The music is loud, bodies packed tight.

Worth is at the edge of the room now, tall and immovable, a drink in his hand. He doesn't look like he belongs in a place like this. But his eyes are locked on me. Angry. Possessive. Like I'm committing some crime by dancing with a colleague.

My pulse stutters. I'm allowed to dance. I'm allowed to breathe. He has no right to be jealous. I don't belong to him.

Worth's gaze doesn't falter. It pins me in place even as I spin and Ethan's hand steadies me.

After a while, I excuse myself to go to the bathroom for a breather, leaving Ethan abruptly on the dance floor.

The second I'm inside, I sag against the sink, dragging in a shaky breath.

I splash cool water on my wrist but it does nothing to calm me, especially when I can still feel Worth's eyes burning into my back.

The heavy door opens behind me, and I whirl around just as he steps inside. "What are you doing? Are you out of your mind? This is the women's bathroom!"

Worth chuckles low. "No. You wandered into the employee

bathroom." He tips his head towards the sign I missed, smirk curling his lips. "Convenient, isn't it?"

I glance under the stalls, heart battering against my ribs. Empty. Relief tangles with dread. "You can't be in here," I babble, stepping back. "We can't—"

But Worth is already moving. His presence swallows up the tiled space until my spine hits cool metal. He nudges me backwards into a large stall, and before I can form another protest, the lock clicks shut behind him.

"Worth—"

He cuts me off with his mouth. Hard. His lips crush mine, and my gasp is swallowed whole. The taste of him explodes across my tongue.

His palm slides into my hair, fingers tangling deep. He tugs, angling my head back, and his mouth trails fire along my jaw, down my neck. My knees weaken.

"We have to stop," I breathe, words stumbling between frantic kisses. "We can't do this. It's a disaster waiting to happen."

But my body betrays me, arching as his lips drag lower, grazing the swell of my chest where the neckline of my dress dips scandalously low. My nipples tighten against the thin fabric, shameless proof of how badly I'm unraveling.

His mouth sears down my neck, and I can barely think. My hands push weakly at his chest, but it only presses me deeper against the wall.

"Worth, we can't—" My voice shakes. "This is... this is wrong. You're my boss. You literally sign my paychecks. If someone finds us in here, it's not just my job on the line, it's my whole career—"

His lips graze the dip of my collarbone and my knees buckle. I grip his shoulders, desperate to keep myself standing, pulling him closer.

"I'm serious," I rush out, breathless. "This is reckless and stupid, and people like you don't get caught, but women like me? We're the ones who get chewed up and spit out, and—"

His teeth nip at my skin, wrenching a gasp from me.

"You're... you're making it impossible to think straight—"

His fingers tighten in my hair, tugging my head back to expose more of my throat. Heat floods me, shame and need colliding in a dizzy mess.

"And if this keeps going, I don't even know what I'll do, because I can't stop wanting it, even though I know it'll ruin everything, and—"

"God, you talk too fucking much, Mya," he growls against my mouth, cutting off my ramble with a kiss that leaves no space for air, no space for protest, just the furious clash of lips.

His other hand grips my hip, thumb pressing into bare skin where my dress has ridden up.

Then, Worth drops to his knees.

The sight knocks the air from my lungs. Worth Miller, CEO, on the grimy bathroom tile, looking up at me with hunger. His hands skim up my legs, gripping, possessive, as if he could hold me in place by sheer will.

"I can't bear another second not touching you, Kitten," he rasps, voice guttural. "I need to get this out of my system—for both our sakes. Just this once." His fingers curl against the hem of my dress, inching it higher, pleading with his touch as much as with his words.

His mouth scorches a path up my thighs.

"Let me do this," he rasps. "Just once. Let me have this. Please."

My head shakes, even as I arch towards him. I should say no. I should shove him away. Instead, the words tumble out. "Okay. Yes."

In the next breath, my thong is torn away, and then his

mouth is on me. Heat explodes through my body as his lips seal around my clit, sucking hard. A cry rips from my throat. My fingers dive into his hair, gripping tight, and my eyes roll back.

"Fuck, Worth," I moan, my voice breaking as his tongue traces relentless circles, lapping me up like he's starved.

His groan rumbles against my core, sending shivers through me, amplifying everything. One hand clamps around my ass, holding me firm, while the other slides between my thighs, thick fingers pressing into my entrance.

A whimper escapes me when he thrusts and curls them just right, dragging another raw sound from my lips.

"You're so goddamn tight around my fingers, Mya," he grits out, voice muffled against me. "Fuck. I can't wait to feel you gripping my cock."

I feel my climax perched right at the edge. "Shit. Yes. I'm going to come. Don't stop."

But suddenly, Worth's mouth pulls away. My hips buck in protest, a growl ripping out of me. "No. Get back."

"Ask nicely, Mya," he says, his voice commanding.

I roll my eyes, frustrated and desperate all at once. He nips at my clit, sharp enough to make me squeal.

"Ask. Nicely. Mya."

Goddamn him. My pride is burning, but the throbbing between my legs wins. "Please, Mr. Miller. Put your mouth back on my pussy."

The sound that leaves him is feral, like he's losing control. His lips crush back against my sex, tongue working me over in long, rough strokes, while his fingers continue their relentless beckoning inside me.

The pressure builds fast, and before I can stop myself, I'm moving against him, riding his hand, his mouth—chasing the orgasm I've been teetering on.

A white-hot eruption detonates inside me. My body bows, trembling as wave after wave crashes through me.

Worth groans into my core, drinking down every sound, every shake, holding me steady like I'm his to unravel.

When I finally come back down to earth, he rises, dragging me into a fierce kiss. I taste myself on his tongue, and the filth of it only makes heat rush all over again.

As his mouth claims mine, I fumble at his belt, my desperation matching his. The metal clinks as I shove my hand down the front of his pants, needing to feel him.

His cock is thick, hot, and so much heavier against my palm than I imagined. My pulse races at the thought of tasting him.

I sink down and drag my tongue across the swollen head.

"Mya..." Just my name. Nothing else. But the way he says it brands me. His fist tangles in my hair, guiding himself into my mouth like he's seconds from breaking apart.

How the hell are we supposed to do this only once?

But we have to. We both know it.

It's the only way to survive each other.

The second I wrap my lips around Worth and look up, the world narrows to nothing but his breathless stare on me.

"That's it, pretty girl. Open wider."

His hungry stare makes heat pool low in my stomach, and I moan around him.

"Yes, Mr. Miller."

The words slip out on instinct. I say his name every day at work—but this time, it feels different.

Worth's hips tense, a groan scraping from his throat. I hollow my cheeks and take him deeper, loving how his head thumps against the stall.

He's trying so hard not to lose control. I can sense how he's holding back, in the way his fingers twitch like he wants to grab my hair and give in to every filthy thought passing behind his eyes.

If we weren't in a club bathroom, I know he'd already have me bent over and ruined.

But right now, all I want is to make him fall apart.

I drag my tongue along his length, easing him further down my throat, feeling him throb against my lips.

Worth's breathing stutters.

"Fuck," he grits out.

His release hits the back of my throat, hot and sudden, my core clenching hard at the sound he makes. He looks unraveled and breathless.

Staring down at me, eyes dark, he says, "Don't swallow just yet."

I freeze, obeying without thinking. He pulls me up, tilting my chin with his fingers.

"Open your mouth."

I do, heat flushing across my cheeks while he looks at me like I'm the most beautiful thing he's ever seen.

"Swallow half."

I gulp down.

Then, his lips are on mine.

The kiss is messy, consuming and filthy in a way that feels like worship. His taste mixes with mine, and his groan vibrates through my lips, into my bloodstream.

The bathroom door suddenly creaks open.

I jolt, panic flaring hot. Before I can breathe, Worth presses a steady hand over my mouth. I hold still, heart hammering against my ribs.

"Have you seen Mya anywhere?"

Seraya.

Another woman laughs. "No, but Worth is missing too."

Shit.

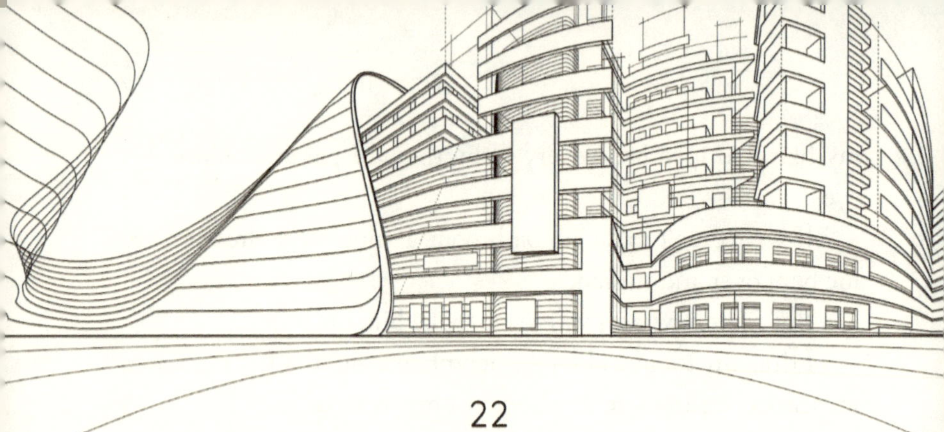

22

Worth

Mya's eyes widen even further, horror written all over her face and she shifts in my grip. I tighten my palm against her lips, lowering my head.

"Quiet," I murmur, low enough that only she can hear.

Her lashes flutter, breath hot against my hand. My cock stirs again despite the situation—*because* of the situation. Having her caged against me, both of us forced into silence while her colleagues speculate outside the door...

The women move toward the sinks. "I'm just gonna fix my lipstick before I start looking like a melted wax figure."

Jovana, the junior architect on our team, snorts. "Honestly, same. My mascara is probably halfway down my cheeks by now."

A pause, then she lowers her voice conspiratorially. "Still... Mya disappearing at the same time as Worth? Suspicious."

"Oh, stop," Seraya whispers back, laughing. "She probably stepped out for air. God knows I would if I were working that closely with *him* every day."

"True," Jovana replies, water running briefly. "Okay, I'm good. Let's find the others."

Their footsteps fade toward the exit and the door swings shut behind them.

Only then do I ease my hand away, dragging my thumb slowly from Mya's bottom lip. Her breath shudders out.

"See what you do to me, Mya?" I whisper, taking her hand and putting it on my hardening crotch. "Even the thought of someone finding us isn't enough to make me stop wanting you."

That molten, sultry look that had me ready to lose control suddenly hardens into something distant, and a wall slams down between us.

"We said just this once, Worth." Mya's voice is steady despite her body still trembling against mine. "Please... Keep your word."

For a second, my jaw locks so tight I'm sure I'll crack a tooth. I'm angry. Not at her, but at myself. Because she's right. I promised one time.

Still, it doesn't stop the sting. Doesn't stop the need clawing at me to pull her back in, to remind her that what we just shared was anything but forgettable.

Instead, I nod once, shoving every ounce of fury and desire back down.

Mya slips out of the stall, straightening her dress with shaking hands, leaving me in the wreckage of my own restraint.

When I make it back to the main area of the club, my employees are clustered by the bar, drinks in hand. It's time for me to go. I stride over, ready to say my goodbyes.

Ethan spots me first. He slaps a hand on my shoulder, and irritation flares hot in my chest.

I really want to fire this little fucker.

"What's up, Mr. Mills. You missed all the fun," he slurs, words barely coherent.

Mr. *Mills*. My jaw ticks. He's going to get an earful tomorrow when he's sober.

"I was at the back talking to Mr. Tan," I say casually. "I'm calling it a night. I better not see any of you hungover tomorrow."

They all groan, laugh, and promise they'll be fine. I nod. My gaze skims over them and lands on Mya. She's trying very hard not to meet my eyes.

Just as I turn to leave, movement behind the bar snags my attention. A flash of short, glossy black hair. Familiar features that freeze me in place.

No, it can't be.

But when the person lifts their head and our eyes meet, I know it's her. Her gaze widens for the briefest second before she masks it with that million-dollar smile. The one she always used like a weapon.

She leans into the man beside her, murmurs something, then slips away. And then she's rounding the bar, coming straight for me.

No. Fuck no.

But it's too late for me to walk out without making a scene.

"Worth, darling. Long time no see!"

"Vanessa," I bite out. She steps into my space, arms open, and hugs me. I stand stiff, not returning it.

Her smile doesn't falter, even though my eyes are shooting daggers.

"How have you been? How's Brianna?" she asks, as if she didn't threaten to take me to court only a few weeks ago.

"Leave, Vanessa."

She tilts her head, feigning a pout. "Come on, Worth. It's been years. We need to catch up. *Properly.*"

My teeth grind so hard my temples ache. She's talking to me like nothing happened.

Rage churns hot in my veins until my eyes catch Mya's. Concern is etched all over her face. She tilts her head, silently asking if I'm okay.

Just like that, the fury eases. The storm inside me dulls, replaced with the memory of her lips, her laugh, the way she tastes. Like an anchor.

"I didn't know you were in Singapore," I say flatly, glancing at the man she was with. "What brings you here?"

"Oh, just an Asian tour with my business partner." She smiles sweetly.

Business partner, my ass.

Her eyes look past me, lingering deliberately on Mya who's moved closer, then drifting to my colleagues, and the women around me, her smile morphing into a sneer.

"Funny seeing you all the way out here, in another country, surrounded by beautiful women." Her eyes return to mine. "Staying true to your blue collar playboy ways, I see."

The implication hangs between us—poisonous, and intentional. And I know, with absolute clarity, that she said it hoping it would trigger me.

"Left our daughter at home while you're out here trying out the country's *delicacies?*"

I'm ready to explode when Mya steps forward, cutting through the tension. My employees are too occupied to even notice the conversation over the music and chaos.

"Brianna is doing great and is with her nanny right now. We're on a business trip," she says crisply, extending her hand. "I'm Mya. Worth's girlfriend."

The world tilts. I see the shock on Vanessa's face—which mirrors how I feel. But I keep my face unreadable.

Girlfriend? When minutes ago she was worried about colleagues speculating? I look at her, brow furrowed. But Mya just nods, mouthing *trust me.*

And I do.

"Well, tell my daughter I'll be seeing her soon," Vanessa says to me, ignoring Mya's hand.

"No, you won't," I snap.

"Worth, I'm her mo—"

"Enough, Vanessa." My voice is steel. "I already told you that if you want to talk about Brianna, you can contact my lawyer."

Vanessa huffs, venom flashing in her eyes. "Fine."

She stalks off, leaving me staring after her, Mya's hand in mine.

I release it and step back. "I have to go." Before she can answer, I'm already walking away.

"Worth—" Her voice catches, but I don't stop.

The air outside slams into me like a wall, hot and humid, though still easier to breathe than the suffocating tension back inside. I wave at our driver, and he immediately pulls the car around. My pulse is hammering when I sink into the leather seat.

"Hotel," I order.

The car eases forward, and I glance back at the glowing club doors.

Mya bursts through them, curls bouncing as she scans the street. She looks small under the neon lights, shoulders tight. For a second, I almost tell the driver to stop and let me out.

But I can't. I want to be with her, but I also need to be alone.

The last person I expected to see tonight was Vanessa.

The fact that she's in Singapore feels like some cruel joke. I knew she was in Asia—my PI had last reported her in Tokyo months ago—but what are the odds she'd be *here*, of all places, the same time as me?

After years of nothing but absence, she dares to ask about our daughter like she didn't abandon her?

I glance out the tinted window again. Mya is still standing there, eyes locked on the car as it drives farther away. A second later, Seraya comes out and joins her, leading her to the other town car.

I rest my head back, a bitter laugh rumbling low in my throat.

When I finally reach the hotel, I don't linger in the lobby. I head straight to my suite.

The second the door clicks shut behind me, I lean back against it, dragging a hand down my face. I need a goddamn minute to breathe.

My phone vibrates in my pocket and I'm about to throw it onto the bed when I see the message.

MYA:

I'll do it.

My heart rate races.

Do what?

MYA:

Your arrangement. I'm in.

Are you serious?

You don't have to, Mya. It was stupid and entitled of me to ask.

MYA:

I want to help.

I don't know what to say.

Her reply is instant.

MYA:

You can start by saying thank you.

Words aren't enough to express how much this means to me, but I do as she says.

Something in my chest starts to loosen as I let out a rough exhale.

MYA:

Are you okay?

I hesitate. My instinct is to brush her off, keep the armor intact.

I'm fine.

MYA:

It's okay not to be okay, Worth.

My jaw clenches. She's right, but I've spent my entire adult life pretending I was made of steel—for Brianna, for myself, for this company. Weakness has never been an option.

I just can't believe she's going to barge back into Brianna's life just like that. I don't want her near my daughter, she's already hurt her enough.

I stare at the words after I send them. I shouldn't be admitting this shit to her.

MYA:

I don't know how it feels to be a single parent, but from what I've seen, you're doing great, Worth. And I'm sure anyone can see that.

I let out a low breath, sinking onto the bed. Her response is like a balm I didn't ask for but need anyway.

> Thanks for the kind words, Ms. Jones. If I didn't know any better, I'd think you were complimenting me.

MYA:

Complimenting your parenting, not you. Don't get it twisted, Mr. Miller.

A smirk tugs at my mouth despite myself.

> I like it when you call me that...

MYA:

I know...

That makes me pause.

> How?

MYA:

Your face does this thing where it looks like you're holding yourself back, and your breathing stutters.

Christ. She's been watching me that closely?

> Seems like you've been observing me quite a lot.

MYA:

Maybe. It does help that I have to see your annoying face every day.

> You're free to quit, Ms. Jones.

MYA:

And leave Griffin and Ethan? I could never 😜

That smirking wink makes jealousy coil in my chest.

> Mya.

MYA:

Worth.

> Where are you?

There's a pause this time. Long enough that I feel my pulse spike.

MYA:

In Ethan's room.

The world tilts.

> What the fuck, Mya?

> What are you doing there?

> That's it. He's getting fired after this trip.

My grip on the phone is white-knuckled.

MYA:

I'M JUST KIDDING!!!!!!!!!!!!!!!

I growl low in my throat, scrubbing a hand over my face.

> Not fucking funny.

> I'm still firing him for putting me through distress.

MYA:

A playboy AND a drama queen? Wow.

My cock twitches at the bratty tone I can practically hear in her texts.

I ought to punish you for the way you talk to me.

MYA:

I'd like to see you try.

I'll take that as a challenge.

23

Worth

The next morning, I call Brianna.

It's seven a.m. in Singapore, which means it should be right around the time she'll be getting home from school back in Seattle. I haven't spoken to her since I landed yesterday, and I'm itching to hear her voice.

She picks up on the second ring.

"Dad!"

Just like that, the tension in my shoulders eases. No matter how much stress I carry, hearing her voice always cuts it in half.

"Hi, Piglet. How's my girl?"

"Good! I just got home from school. Guess what? Kennedy slipped up and told us that his mom is seeing our teacher—"

And she's off, recounting every piece of high school gossip like it's headline news. I lean back in the desk chair, smiling.

Moments like this remind me just how lucky I am. Our relationship isn't just father-daughter. Bri trusts me with every-thing, and so do I. She's my best friend.

By the time she's finished dragging half the town, I'm

laughing so hard my chest aches. "Alright, alright. Enough dirt. What are your plans tonight?"

"Maggie said Uncle Henny, Uncle Griff and Sylas are coming over for dinner. Apparently they insisted when she told them she was making lasagna."

I chuckle.

Henson has always been there, from day one. When Vanessa walked out, he stepped in even more. He's Brianna's anchor as much as mine. She respects my brother deeply. And Griffin—and his boy, Sylas—are family in all but blood. We've been through the trenches together—two men left standing with kids to raise. Though, unlike me, Griffin lost his first love to death. He's stronger than I'll ever be.

"Say hi to the boys for me, and make sure you save me an extra piece of lasagna," I say, smiling.

Bri laughs, and we say our goodbyes, ending the call.

I drag myself into the bathroom and turn the water on hot, steam filling the space as I step into the shower.

I scrub a hand over my face under the spray. Last night flashes back. The teasing texts with Mya knocked me off balance, and her bratty jokes actually managed to make me forget the issues with Vanessa for a while. And the moments in the bathroom at the club—Mya's mouth, her taste, her sounds...

I was sure I'd toss and turn all night, eaten alive by rage over my ex-wife resurfacing. Instead, I slept deeply. Because of Mya. Somehow she makes me feel at ease, even though she's also the source of half my fucking turmoil.

My cock throbs, insistent, and I give in. Wrapping my hand around the thick length, I stroke it, slowly at first, water pounding against my shoulders.

I close my eyes—and it's Mya kneeling in front of me again, eyes wide, lips slick and swollen, calling me *Mr. Miller*. My hips jerk, hand pumping harder, chasing the edge like I'm chasing her.

A guttural sound tears out of me as release takes over, scalding water and the memory of her taste tangling into one sweet high.

When I finally come down, I brace both palms against the tile, panting.

Mya is dangerous. But she's the only thing keeping me steady.

As soon as we step out of the last client meeting, I'm craving a stiff drink.

Hours of presentations, back-and-forth negotiations, and pretending not to notice the way Mya kept sneaking glances at me, drained me dry.

It's early evening in Singapore, but with the jet lag and the long day, it feels closer to three in the morning. Everyone is tired, but instead of dispersing, Seraya—ever the social butterfly—pipes up.

"Dinner, everyone?" she asks, dropping her portfolio onto a nearby armchair. "We deserve something after that marathon."

A chorus of agreement follows. Ethan throws out the name of a seafood place he knows, another colleague suggests something more upscale. But my mind is already drifting to the quiet solitude of my hotel room.

I don't join in the conversation. I hang back, scrolling on my phone, listening.

Because what I'm really waiting for... is Mya's answer.

"You in, Mya?" Seraya asks her.

Mya hesitates, and for a second I think she'll say yes. But

then she shakes her head. "Thanks, I think I'll pass tonight. Room service and an early night sound better."

The group groans, Ethan calling her a party pooper, and she laughs along, like it's no big deal.

I slide my phone into my pocket.

"Enjoy yourselves," I say smoothly to the group, stepping past them. They nod, already caught up in a debate over crab curry versus cocktails. None of them notice the way my gaze drags over Mya as I head for the elevators.

Back in my room, I toss my jacket onto the chair and loosen my tie. I grab the hotel phone off the nightstand and punch in the number for room service.

Then, I pour two fingers of scotch into a glass and wander to the window. Singapore's skyline glitters. I should feel good about solidifying a new project, but all I can think about is Mya.

Her saying yes to the arrangement should've settled things. I thought I'd feel relief. Instead, there's something about her that strips me down in ways I don't want to admit. That makes me think of something I swore off years ago: permanence.

And that scares the shit out of me.

I take a long swallow, the burn scorching down my throat, hoping it'll kill the thought. It doesn't.

Then reality crowds in. Mya's so much younger. She's still figuring herself out, chasing her career, building her life. Meanwhile, I've got Brianna. My daughter is my whole world, and the last thing she needs is someone walking in half-prepared to play a role they're not ready for. Mya doesn't deserve that pressure, and Brianna doesn't deserve the risk.

The bubble bursts. Maybe it's better off this way—keeping her at arm's length.

I down the rest of my drink, strip off my clothes, and step into the shower.

By the time I'm out, towel slung low on my hips, I hear the vibration of my phone on the counter.

MYA:

picture attachment

Worth Miller!!!

I swipe the photo open and a smile tugs at my mouth.

I see you got the food.

It takes her only seconds to reply.

MYA:

The food??? You mean the FEAST? How am I supposed to eat all of this?

I huff out a laugh, shaking my head.

I didn't know what you liked, so I ordered the entire menu.

The three dots bounce.

MYA:

This is absurd, Worth.

Absurd? Maybe. But I picture her face lighting up in surprise when she opened the door, and I don't regret it.

You're welcome.

MYA:

Thank you, but I didn't ask for this.

Her resistance is so predictable.

You didn't have to ask. I wanted to.

MYA:

Why?

I rub the back of my neck. Hell if I know why.

I'm not sure. It felt right. Enjoy it.

Silence stretches long enough for me to check the time. Then—

MYA:

I can't eat all of this alone… Maybe I should call Ethan to come join me.

The phone nearly cracks in my grip.

That brat.

My jaw grinds. She's doing this on purpose, dangling his name like bait. She wants to see me react.

I yank a shirt over my head, jump into sweatpants, and shove my feet into shoes without bothering with socks. She might be teasing, but I'm not giving her a chance to follow through.

Because even the idea of her alone in that room with *him?* Unacceptable.

I step out of the room. The elevator ride feels like a slow descent into hell. My pulse hammers against my throat, hands fisting and flexing at my sides like I'm heading into a fight. Maybe I am—Ethan might already be in her room, and I can't promise that I won't punch the kid at first sight.

I stalk down the hallway, counting the numbers until I reach Mya's room. I pound on the door.

When it opens, every rational thought I had is obliterated.

Mya stands there barefoot, drowning in the soft light from

the lamp behind her. Her pajamas—if you can call them that—are nothing but a thin, silky camisole that hugs the curve of her breasts, and shorts that barely cover the swell of her ass.

My throat dries.

Fuck.

Her hair is loose, curls tumbling over her shoulders like something out of a fantasy I shouldn't be having.

I drag my gaze back up to her face. Her lips are parted, her cheeks flushed.

"Worth," she breathes, clutching the doorframe for support.

I should say something reasonable, but reason is hanging by a thread, and professionalism went out the window the moment she joked about Ethan.

All I can manage is a low growl. "You were going to call Ethan?"

Mya blinks, and that tiny pause is all it takes to tip me over the edge. I step forward, forcing her back until I'm inside her room and the door clicks shut behind me.

I can feel the heat coming off her body, her chest rising and falling under that sinful scrap of silk.

Her throat works as she swallows. "I was joking."

My lips twitch into a wicked smile. "You think I don't see what you're doing? You dangle his name just to get a rise out of me."

Her chin tips up, defiant. "Maybe because it works."

For a second, I simply stare at her. She's right. It does work. Too damn well.

I close the distance, stopping just shy of pressing against her. My fingers battle the urge to reach for her. "Do you know what you're doing to me, Mya? You walk around in little scraps of silk, talk back like you own the place, mention other guys' names in your room, and then you act surprised when I can't fucking think straight around you."

Her lips part, a shaky breath slipping out. "Ethan isn't—"

"Say Ethan's name again, and I'll lose it."

The silence between us burns. Her gaze darts to my mouth, then back up. I see the crack in her wall, the tremor in her body.

My hand shoots up, tangling in her curls, angling her head back just enough. I capture her mouth with mine, devouring, taking—because I can't fucking help myself.

Mya gasps into me, and I swallow it whole, my other hand gripping her hip, pulling her flush against the hardness straining at my sweatpants.

Too soon, she pushes at my chest. "Worth. Enough."

The sound that rumbles out of me is a growl of frustration. I step back and swipe a hand down my face, trying to rein myself back in. My body wants more—*so* much more—but I know the wall is back up.

"You can stay," Mya says, voice softer now, though resolute. "Help me eat the food. But no more kissing. Or touching. Promise me, Worth."

Every muscle in me resists. The thought of keeping my hands off her when she's sitting there in barely-there silk borders on torture. But I'd rather have her like this, than not at all. If this is the only way she'll let me near, then I'll take it.

"Fine," I grit out, forcing myself to relent.

I drop onto the edge of her bed, while she spins her desk chair to face me.

"We need to talk."

My head tilts, interest sparked. "I'm listening."

Mya takes a steadying breath. "I know that I've technically accepted this," she gestures her hands between us, "arrangement. But I have a few conditions."

"Okay."

"You pay off my school loans and the rest of my debts. If

I'm agreeing to upend my life, I won't do it while drowning in bills."

I don't even flinch. I expected that, so I just give her a curt nod.

"I'll move in," she continues, "but I want my own room. My space. That's non-negotiable."

"Sure." I ignore the disappointment flaring in my chest.

"And I want to meet Brianna a few times before we tell her anything. No surprises. No blindsiding her by suddenly appearing in her life as her dad's new girlfriend." Mya's voice wavers slightly, but she holds my gaze. "She deserves better than that."

I study her in silence, and she presses on.

"Finally, I get to tell people at work before it hits the tabloids. I won't have my colleagues—or anyone else—thinking I slept my way into this job. Or your fortune."

My jaw works as I nod.

"Agreed. You'll be able to meet Brianna a few times. I don't want to upend her life any more than necessary."

I push off the bed and straighten to my full height. "But if we're doing this, Mya... we're doing it my way too."

She looks up at me, waiting.

"You'll be expected to attend every public appearance with me," I say, steady as stone. "Fundraisers, galas, charity dinners, board events—if my presence is required, so is yours. Unless you're sick or there's an emergency, I won't accept excuses. We have to look seamless."

"I'll agree to separate rooms," I continue, and Mya sags in relief—until the other shoe drops. "But Brianna can't see that. She can't think we sleep apart. We'll tell her you're using the other room as a closet. Clothes. Shoes. Whatever story works."

Even though Mya initially refused my proposal, I'd already thought this through in excruciating detail to make sure none of it affected Brianna. But I can't tell if that's reassuring or terrifying Mya.

"And finally, I'll have a prenup drawn up. It will state clearly that I'll cover your school loans and any debt you've accumulated up until the marriage. But anything you rack up after is on you. I don't want to be responsible for any reckless spending."

Mya crosses her arms. "Wow. You really know how to romance a girl, Mr. Miller. I'm surprised you didn't have Dre draw up a PowerPoint presentation."

I smile, amused by Mya's annoyance.

"When the whole fiasco with my ex-wife is over, we'll annul the marriage quietly and go our separate ways."

Mya nods; my heart lurches in my chest, and I can't for the life of me explain why. *This is just an attraction.*

"Okay, agreed. Though I have one more condition," she adds. "In public, I'll play the part. I'll hold your hand, kiss you, if it sells the illusion. But behind closed doors, we're back to being just colleagues—friends. No touching. No kissing. No sex. "

My jaw ticks, the muscle pulsing, but I don't let my expression crack. "Fine."

"Then it's a deal."

Mya extends her hand. I look at it for a long moment, before finally wrapping my palm around hers. The heat of her skin sears me instantly, sending a shock wave up my arm.

Damn this effect she has on me.

The next few months are going to be brutal.

We settle down, quietly, a tray cart overflowing with enough food for ten people between us. We dig in, and slowly, conversation replaces the silence.

She tells me about her family—her mom, stepdad, siblings. Her eyes light up when she talks about Tiana, her step-sister, and the chaos they grew up in together. When Mya mentions her little brother, her smile softens, and I can already see how protective she is of him. She admits she's a die-hard Cowboys fan, courtesy of her late father, and there's a flash of pain there that she quickly hides with practiced ease.

Then she drops something else, almost shyly. "I've always had this thing for old vinyl records. I've been slowly building a collection, when I can afford it. There's just something about the sound, you know? Imperfect but real."

When it's my turn, I tell her about Brianna—her quirks, sass, the way she's grown into her own too fast for my liking. I talk about Henson and how we built W.H.M. from nothing, and about Griffin, who's been with us since day one. Mya listens intently, as if she's genuinely interested, and it disarms me more than I want to admit.

The conversation is easy, almost too easy. I laugh more than I should. She teases me, rolls her eyes, calls me out when I dodge a question. For a while, it feels like we're not CEO and employee, just two people eating takeout in a hotel room.

And it's... nice.

But beneath it, a dangerous truth hums: my attraction to her isn't just physical. It's in the way she looks at me, the way she listens, the way her laugh pulls me apart and puts me back together again.

And that terrifies me.

Because I can't allow myself the luxury of falling for someone. Not when my company is scaling faster than ever. Not when Brianna is a teenager who needs every ounce of me. Even more now with Vanessa trying to claw her way back into our lives.

So I shove it down, drowning the thought. But no matter how hard I try, Mya lingers like a fingerprint I can't scrub off.

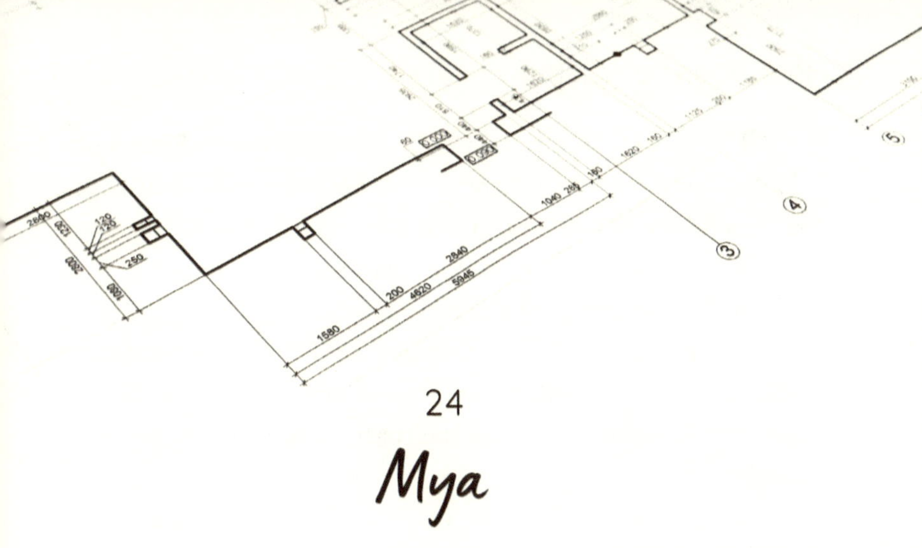

24

Mya

T he week flies by, and before I know it, we're back at the airport, waiting for the company jet to be ready for boarding.

After that night Worth ordered room service for me, no lines were crossed beyond that one kiss I baited out of him by dropping Ethan's name. Since then, nothing. No stolen touches, no testing my boundaries.

A part of me is relieved. The other part aches, like something is missing.

But it's better this way.

Until I've told my colleagues, family and friends about our "relationship," I'd rather keep him at arm's length.

Ethan appears at my side, holding out a paper cup.

"Here's your latte, Mya. Oat milk, no sugar."

Just how I like it. If I were even a little interested in him, this would've been a winning move. Ethan has been kind, thoughtful, and always circling just close enough to make his intentions obvious. Eventually, I'll have to tell him I'm not interested before he gets the wrong idea.

"Thanks, E," I say, taking a sip. The warm bitterness blooms across my tongue and I can't help the moan that slips out around the rim of the cup.

Ethan grins, but my gaze shifts across the terminal.

Worth is watching, as always.

At this point, I'm convinced Worth Miller missed his calling as a professional stalker. One of these days, I'm going to start charging him rent for all the space he occupies in my line of sight.

He's standing with Seraya and one of the project leads, his broad shoulders framed by his suit jacket, phone in hand, only half-listening to whoever's speaking. And his eyes are locked on me.

My stomach flips. That unreadable mask of his makes it impossible to tell what he's thinking, though I know one thing for sure: he noticed Ethan's nice gesture.

I tear my gaze away, pretending to be fascinated with the coffee lid. Ethan starts talking about the meetings we wrapped up yesterday, but the words blur. Worth's stare is like static over my skin.

When I finally glance back, he's typing something into his phone.

My phone buzzes against my palm, and I glance down.

WORTH:

> If you take another sip of that coffee, I'm going to march over there and dump it over the fucker's head.

My brows shoot up. *Jealous much?* Though for some reason, I kinda like it.

I dart a glance at Ethan, who's still chatting and smiling beside me, completely oblivious. I can't believe he's still hovering after Worth practically threatened him at the gala.

Either he was too drunk to remember or he's got a death wish.

Heat creeps up the back of my neck.

You wouldn't.

WORTH:

Oh, I would, Mya. I dare you.

I suck in a sharp breath. Is he serious? My hand tightens around the paper cup, pulse racing. Slowly, I raise it to my mouth, testing him.

Worth takes one deliberate step forward from across the waiting area, eyes locked on me like a predator.

Oh my God. He *is* serious.

Panic flares, and I quickly toss the cup into the trash behind me. Ethan doesn't notice.

My hands tremble as I type furiously.

You're crazy.

His reply comes instantly.

WORTH:

I don't make a habit of lying, Ms. Jones.

I press my lips together to keep from smiling.

You have no right to tell me what to do.

WORTH:

You have the option not to listen, but you'll face the consequences.

My thighs clench together at the word *consequences,* damn it.

> That's strong-arming, Mr. Miller. I didn't know you to be so cunning.

WORTH:

> You're the cunning one, Mya.

A shiver slides down my spine at the way he turns everything back on me.

> Maybe a little.

WORTH:

> For someone who claims to not want anything to do with me, you sure know how to contradict yourself with your actions.

Touché. My cheeks burn.

> Whatever.

We finally get the call to board the plane, and I tuck my phone into my pocket as I head toward the jetway with the group.

But the closer I get to the plane, the heavier my chest feels. The memory of being trapped in the sky for sixteen hours rushes back.

By the time I reach my seat in the back, my palms have gone clammy as I grip the armrests, legs locking in place, unable to move.

You got this. Just breathe.

"Ms. Jones."

The sound of his deep voice rolls over me.

Slowly, I turn. Worth is watching me with soft eyes.

"Yes, Mr. Miller?" I manage, though my voice wobbles.

"Please sit next to me on the flight. I need to go over the final drawings for the Singapore project."

I blink. He's giving me an excuse. A shield. And he's dressing it up as work so no one else will question it.

My heart squeezes so tight I almost forget how to breathe.

I grab my stuff and sit next to Worth.

THE SIXTEEN HOURS BACK FEEL SHORTER THIS TIME. Maybe because I kept my eyes glued to the window. Maybe because I slept in uneven stretches, conscious of the man sitting beside me. After going over the drawings for the project, we barely exchanged words, but he stayed lodged under my skin.

When the plane touches down in Seattle, relief floods me. I'm bone-tired, but grateful to breathe familiar air again. The others gather their things and we file down the steps.

"Great trip, guys," Ethan says, giving me a little wave before jogging towards the rideshare queue. Seraya hugs me quickly, promising to catch up on Monday. Everyone disperses, dragging their suitcases behind them, until the only ones left are Worth and me.

Tiana is waiting at the curb, sunglasses perched on her head like a crown. The second she spots me, she waves both arms, grinning. Then her eyes shift and land on my boss.

Her smile drops and she actually gawks at him. "Oh. My. God." Her voice is barely above a whisper, but I catch it all the same when I reach her.

I want to sink into the pavement. "TJ," I hiss under my breath. "Stop staring."

But she doesn't. Her gaze tracks Worth like he's walking straight out of a billionaire bachelor magazine spread, because —well, he kind of is.

Worth offers her a polite nod, then winks at me before heading off.

Tiana blinks three times fast, then leans towards me. "That's your boss? That's *your* Worth Miller? He's even hotter in person."

Heat prickles across my cheeks. "Get in the car."

She smirks, and I roll my eyes at her, shoving my bag into the trunk before she can embarrass me further.

Tiana sneaks another glance at him in the rearview mirror as we drive off. "Tell me everything."

I sigh, leaning my head against the cool window. "There's not much to tell. It was work. Meetings, site visits, more meetings, and..." I pick at a loose thread on my sleeve, then just rip the Band-Aid. "I took your advice."

"Which advice? The 'say yes to the hot billionaire's insane plan' advice?"

I swallow. "Yes."

Tiana slams a palm against the steering wheel, letting out a victory gasp. "MJ! You actually did it."

"Don't make it a thing," I warn, though I can't stop the tiny smile pulling at my mouth. "The terms are clear. We set boundaries—and it's only temporary."

"Uh huh. Temporary with a man who looks like *that*." She wiggles her brows.

"I'm serious, TJ." I lace my fingers together to still them. "This is mutually beneficial. It's not—"

"Romance," she supplies in a sing-song. "Got it. Totally not romance. Purely contractual. Absolutely nothing to do with the way you look when you talk about him."

I groan into my hands. "Drive."

Tiana laughs. "We'll circle back to the *real* details later. But right now, I need to swing by Willow's to grab the weekend schedule."

Soon enough, after the detour, we're pulling into our

parents' driveway. My chest warms at the thought of seeing them. I didn't realize how much I missed home until now.

Dinner is loud. Mom fusses over me, Devon teases, and JJ fills us in on middle school drama.

Later, Tiana and I collapse on her bed. I curl up against her pillows while she flips through her planner.

After catching her up on what happened in Singapore, I ask, "So, how's Willow's been holding up without me?"

Her lips curve though her shoulders sag. "It's been tough. Aravind asked me to find a replacement for you, but everyone I've tried either flakes or just isn't good enough. You left big shoes, MJ. We miss you."

My chest pinches. Before I can reply, she adds, "And I talked to him again about me buying the place. But he wants to sell soon, and I don't have the down payment, and there's no way I can work a second job right now."

I sit up straighter, suddenly remembering how worried Griffin was at the gala. "Wait. What if you tried nannying?"

Tiana snorts. "Me? A nanny?"

"Why not?" I grin. "You're amazing with kids. You used to babysit the whole neighborhood; you even made those business cards Devon helped you design. Griffin, one of my bosses, has been looking for someone reliable to watch his son. It could be perfect. Especially if it's live-in. You'd have mornings and evenings with the kid, and you'd still be able to work at Willow's during the day while he's at school."

She blinks, chewing it over. "Huh. That actually... doesn't sound terrible."

"See? Perfect fit."

Before I can push more, my phone buzzes on the nightstand. Worth's name lights up the screen. My heart kicks.

WORTH:

Great work this week, Ms. Jones.

I bite back a smile, warmth spreading through me as I lock my phone without replying. It's safer that way.

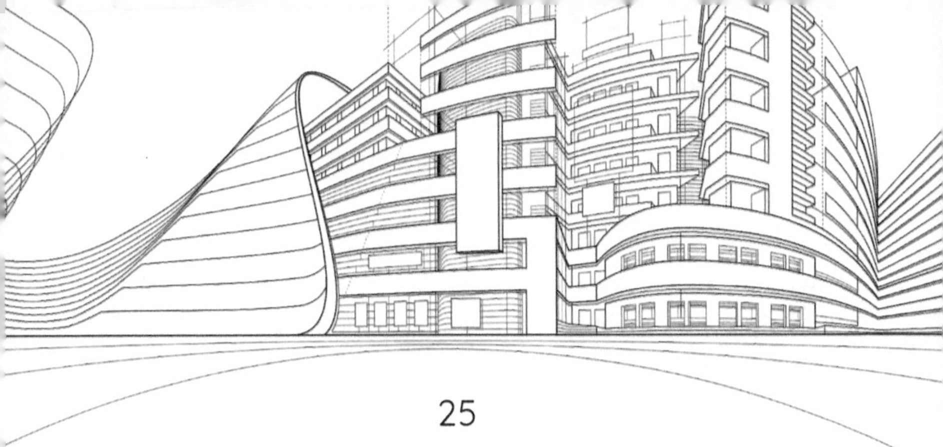

25

Worth

W hen I step through the door, Brianna barrels towards me with a wide grin on her face. I drop my bags and catch her, lifting her off the ground like I used to when she was small. She's taller now, lankier, but I don't care. I hug her tight and kiss the top of her head, breathing her in. God, I missed her.

"Dad!" she squeals, squeezing my neck. "You're back!"

"Always, Piglet," I murmur, setting her down but keeping my arm slung over her shoulders. "You look happy to see me."

"Duh!"

I bark a laugh. "I missed you, little one."

She grins, a wicked little thing. "Me too!"

Before I can get another word in, Bri starts yapping about her week. I let her talk, the sound of her voice untangling the stress in my chest as we head towards the kitchen together.

Maggie is at the stove, wooden spoon in hand, stirring something that smells delicious. At the island, Henson sits with a glass of something green. His face says it all. He catches my eye, then points at the drink, mouthing *help me*.

I chuckle under my breath and raise both hands. *You're on your own, brother.*

It's probably one of Maggie's so-called miracle juices. She swears her concoctions can cure everything from headaches to heartbreak. Judging by Henson's grimace, he must've complained about something earlier and got stuck being the guinea pig.

I circle the counter and press a quick kiss to Maggie's cheek. "Smells good in here."

"Welcome home." She gives me a side hug before turning back to the pot.

Then, casually, she asks, "So... Are you boys going home to Nantucket for the holidays this year?"

"Yes," I respond without hesitation at the exact same time that Henson says, "No."

We both turn to each other, and Maggie's brow shoots up.

"Mom is going to be upset," I tell him flatly.

He shrugs, sipping the juice like it's poison. "You know how I get at functions where there are too many people. She'll understand."

Crowds trigger Henson's anxiety, and pushing him into a situation like that usually ends badly. I've been there, seen it firsthand. But this is family. And if there's one thing our mother loves, it's gathering every last one of us under the same roof for the holidays.

"Hen, this isn't some gala or fundraiser. Mom needs you there."

He gives me a look as if he wants to argue, but I see the unease in his eyes. Panic lingers under the surface, even when he tries to mask it.

I sigh and sit on one of the barstools across from him. "I get it. I do. But maybe we figure out a compromise, because Mom will never let you live it down if you don't show up at all."

Henson scowls at me like I've just betrayed him. I take it as a win.

Maggie shoos us out of the kitchen to give her space, so I pull my laptop from my bag and settle at the dining table.

Henson drops into the chair across from me, setting his own laptop down with a sigh. We work for a while, the only sound the clacking of keys and Maggie humming faintly to herself.

Then, out of nowhere, Henson says, "So... how was the trip?"

I don't bother looking up. "Fine."

"Fine?" He draws the word out. "That's all you've got?"

"Yes." Besides the fact that I'm getting married to my employee.

A beat of silence, then: "How's Mya?"

My jaw clenches. I shut the lid of my laptop harder than necessary and level him with a look.

He smirks, unbothered. "Your silence tells me all I need to know."

"It tells you nothing."

"Please. You're my brother. I've known you my whole life. You shut down whenever something hits too close." He leans back, arms crossing over his chest. "You like her."

I exhale sharply, shaking my head. "Even if I did, it doesn't matter."

"Why not?"

My throat tightens, but I push through it. "Mya is not interested in me like that. She thinks I'm some fucking playboy —and let's face it, I've given her plenty of reasons to think that."

Henson's gaze softens. "You don't help your image, I'll give you that. But if she knew the real you, the one I know? She'd think differently."

I shrug, leaning back in my chair. "Doesn't matter. She's my employee. And she made it clear she doesn't want to be entangled with her boss."

Henson smirks again. "So fire her. Then ask her on a date."

I bark out a laugh. "Right. Like she wouldn't hate my guts after that."

His grin fades when I lower my voice. "Something else happened. It's to do with Vanessa…"

"What about her?"

I fill him in on everything. About Vanessa contacting me twice to see Brianna, running into her in Singapore, and the threat to take me to court for custody. My hands fist as I talk, the words tasting like poison.

Henson's expression sours. "Shit. Have you spoken to Ryan?"

"Yes. Last week."

"Good. Don't let her get one inch past the line. Not after what she did."

"I won't." But the truth is, I'm not sure I can stop her. If Vanessa really pushes, the law will be on her side.

That thought alone makes my stomach twist.

Before my nerves can get the best of me, I tell him about my plan to marry Mya.

"Holy shit!" Henson whisper-shouts. "We have to call Griffin, right now."

"No, don't—"

But it's too late: my brother already has my best friend on a video call.

Griffin crosses his arms and pins us with a stare. "What's going on?"

Here we go.

After I'm done filling him in on the issue with my ex-wife, Griffin exhales. "Damn, Worth. I'm sorry, man."

I chuckle, but it's humorless.

"So, what's the plan?"

I don't bother sugarcoating it. "Mya is going to help me with the situation. We're getting married."

"Come again?" Griffin's head jerks back. "You're joking, right?"

"I wish I was."

His laugh is incredulous. "You said you'd never get married again. You've sworn that for years, Worth."

"True," I concede. "But this isn't a marriage of love. It's a means to an end. I need to prove to the judge that I'm a family man who can give Brianna a steady, stable household. Vanessa's sudden reappearance means I can't leave that to chance."

"And you think a whirlwind marriage to your employee is going to scream *stability*? Come on, Worth. Everyone saw you walk into the charity event with Sophia on your arm not long ago. Now you're telling people you've been secretly dating Mya? That's one hell of a pivot."

Griffin turns his gaze to Henson. "Hen, help me out here."

"Nothing happened with Sophia that night," I snap.

"Didn't have to. Optics, Worth. Optics," Griffin argues.

"She was just my companion for the event. We didn't touch. We didn't kiss. There's nothing to spin there."

Henson's smirk spreads slowly. "And why was that, Worth?"

I glare at him, teeth grinding. "Shut up."

"Uh huh. That's what I thought," he says, smug as hell. "In all seriousness, though. You think this is a good idea?"

"It's the only way."

Griffin leans forward on the screen, his stare cutting through me. "What if feelings get involved and you get hurt?"

I scoff. "You know me, Griff. I swore off relationships a long time ago."

He gives a dry laugh. "Yeah, you and me both, my friend.

But this is different. She's not some date you'll forget in the morning. She's going to be your *wife*, living in your house, brushing shoulders with you every day at work, entwining her life with yours and Brianna's. That's a very fine line to walk."

"I know," I admit, dragging a hand down my jaw. "But what other choice do I have?"

Griffin studies me for a long beat. "How did you even get Mya to agree to this insanity?"

"I spun it in a way that made it mutually beneficial. I'll help her out financially, and she'll help me look like the steady family man the court needs to see."

Henson brows climb. "Wait. You're *paying* her to be your wife?"

I glare at him. "No. Not like that. I offered a solution that works for both of us."

Griff shakes his head slowly. "I just hope you know what you're doing, Worth."

I lean back, exhaling through my nose. *I hope so too.*

My mind keeps coming back to the same thing.

How the hell am I supposed to bring this up to Brianna?

The prenup will be ready tomorrow. But if my daughter reacts badly to the idea of me dating—let alone marrying—I'll have to pivot. Bri comes first, always.

After ending the call with Griffin, Brianna—having finished her homework—joins us at the table, laughter and teasing floating through the air as Maggie serves us delicious food, and for a while, I let myself forget the storm brewing outside these walls.

When dinner is finished, Henson says his goodbyes, and Brianna scoops up her books and heads back upstairs, announcing something about a FaceTime with Kennedy. I make a mental note to ask her about him. She's been talking about him a whole lot lately.

While part of me wants to shrug it off as harmless school chatter, the dad part wants to know exactly who this boy is, and why my daughter's eyes light up every time his name slips from her lips.

I glance at Maggie, who's busy stacking dishes. "Can I talk to you about something?"

She tilts her head, curious. "Of course."

I clear my throat. "There's... someone. A woman I've been seeing."

Her eyes widen, surprise turning into a smile. "Worth. That's wonderful."

"Thank you," I say, trying to sound genuine. "I'd like your advice on how to bring it up to Brianna. I don't want to blind-side her."

"You're right to be careful. She's old enough to understand, but still young enough to take it hard. The key is honesty. Let her see how important this woman is to you. If you're steady, Brianna will follow your lead."

Steady.

That's the word that keeps circling me like a hawk. With Mya, steady is the last thing I feel.

Maggie dries her hands on a dish towel and gives me a look that says she's about to dig even if I don't want her to.

"So... Who is she?"

I pause mid-sip of my drink, pulse ticking a little faster. "Just someone from work. Her name is Mya."

Her brows lift. "Wow. Someone from work who has you smiling to yourself while you're pretending not to?"

I grunt, shaking my head. "Busted."

She softens, leaning her hip against the counter. "Worth... I've known you for years. I've seen you at your worst and at your best. You don't let people in easily. This woman matters to you. I can tell."

I don't respond. Not because she's wrong, but because she's too damn close to the truth. Instead, I thank her for the advice and kiss her cheek, muttering something about checking on Brianna.

Upstairs, I knock on my daughter's door and hear muffled giggles before the sound cuts off.

"Come in!"

I push the door open and find her sprawled across her bed, phone still in hand. Her cheeks are pink, eyes bright. She looks so grown up it makes my chest ache.

"Hey, Piglet," I say, leaning on the doorframe. "Can we chat?"

"Of course."

I walk over to sit on the edge of her bed. "So... Kennedy?"

Brianna groans and hides her face behind a pillow. "He's just a friend."

"Uh huh." I tug the pillow down, meeting her eyes. "Listen, I don't care if he's just a friend or something more one day. What I care about is that he treats you with respect. You know what I mean?"

"I know, Dad. You don't have to give me the whole lecture."

"Yeah, I do. It's in the Dad Handbook."

That earns me a laugh, and I tuck a stray curl behind her ear. "Just remember, if Ken gives me a reason, I'll show him exactly how scary a protective dad can be."

She rolls her eyes, but I catch the small smile tugging at her lips.

"Speaking of friends," I start, resting my forearms on my knees. "There's someone I'd like to talk to you about."

Brianna practically springs upright, her eyes shining. "Oh my God. Do you have a girlfriend?"

I blink. "Why do you sound so excited about it?"

"Because lately you've had that... thing. The thing in your steps."

"The *thing*?"

"The... pep?" She squints. "The pep-up step?"

I shake my head, laughing. "Pep in your step, Peanut."

"Whatever. You have it." She huffs, tossing her hair over her shoulder like it's the most obvious thing in the world. "Dad. Don't think I haven't noticed how lonely you've been."

"That's not true. I have you and Maggie."

"Yes, but me and Maggie aren't going to warm your bed at night, Dad."

I choke, gasping. "Brianna! How do you even know to say something like that?"

She bursts out laughing, covering her mouth with one hand. "I'm young, but not stupid."

"You're growing up way too fast. It's terrifying. Please don't ever say that again. And for the record, you're not allowed to have anyone warming your bed until you're thirty-five."

Bri rolls her eyes again. "So dramatic. That's not the point." Her expression turns more serious. "I just want you to have someone other than me. It's a lot of pressure, you know, to be the only reason you're happy."

Her words knock the air out of me. I never thought about it that way—that my daughter might feel responsible for filling a space in my life that no kid should have to fill. I swallow, guilt prickling at the back of my throat.

"I'm sorry, sweetheart," I murmur, reaching out to squeeze her hand. "I never wanted to make you feel like you had to carry that weight."

"No, it's not like that. I just don't want you to be forever alone. I want you to be happy, Papa."

My chest clenches so tight it hurts. *Papa.* She hasn't called me that since she was little, and the sound of it now nearly undoes me. I have to clear my throat to keep my voice steady.

"Tell me about her," Bri then says, almost shyly.

"Okay, well..." I take a deep breath. "Do you remember that woman we saw working at Willow's months ago?"

Her eyes light up instantly. "Yes! I knew there was something there. I could immediately tell."

I squint at her. "How?"

"The way you both tensed up when she came up to our table. And you were kind of nice with her about the whole grief thing. That's when I realized you were lonely, Dad. I knew you were really talking about losing Mom."

I brush my hand gently through her hair, heart aching. "You know I'd never want to replace her, right?"

"I know. And honestly, I haven't seen much of her, so... there's nothing to really replace."

Anger coils inside me at Vanessa again for disappearing and leaving Brianna with nothing but fragments and me to pick up the pieces. This is exactly why I don't want her barging back in.

"Would you want to see her?"

"Your new girlfriend?"

"Your mom."

Brianna shrugs, eyes looking away. "I guess."

"I can make that happen if you want. I'm sure she'd be open to it."

Her brows knit. "How do you know?"

I exhale, deciding she deserves the truth. "Because she called me, and I saw her in Singapore. She told me she wanted to see you."

Shock ripples across her face. "You saw her?"

"I did—but I don't want you to get your hopes up, okay,

Piglet? We'll see if she actually comes through. I don't want you to get hurt again if she doesn't."

Brianna nods. "Thanks, Dad."

I press a kiss to her forehead, hugging her close. "I will introduce you to Mya soon."

Her eyes brighten again. "I'd like that."

"Great." I force a smile, even as my chest tightens.

I stand, ruffling her hair. "Now get ready for bed. Don't stay up too late—and no talking to boys on the phone past nine."

She groans. "Yes, Dad."

I step out of the room with a laugh, though my mind won't stop racing.

THE DOOR TO MY OFFICE SHUTS BEHIND ME AS I HEAD straight for the decanter. I pour two fingers of scotch, and sink into the leather chair behind my desk. The amber burn steadies me, but not enough. My mind is still tangled in Brianna's words.

I pull out my phone and scroll to the contact I haven't used nearly enough these last few weeks.

She answers on the second ring. "Worth, sweetheart."

"Hi, Mom." I let out a rough breath. "I wanted to hear your voice."

Her chuckle is warm. "Well, that's a lovely surprise. What's on your mind?"

I hesitate. The truth would be messy, complicated, and I'm not ready to dump it on her. So I take the easy way out. "I'm seeing someone."

Silence, then a sharp inhale. "Oh, Worth. That's amazing. Tell me about her."

I smile despite the flicker of guilt at lying to my mother, leaning back in the chair. "Her name is Mya. She's... beautiful. Smart. Sharp-tongued. And doesn't put up with any of my shit."

"That's exactly the kind of woman you need," Mom says, and I can hear the grin in her voice. "I just want you to be happy, sweetheart. After everything with Vanessa, you deserve that."

The mention of Vanessa twists something in my chest. I swirl the scotch in my glass, debating whether to tell her. But she's my mother, and I can't keep it from her.

"I saw her in Singapore."

There's a pause, then her voice drops. "Vanessa?"

"Yeah. She says she wants to see Brianna."

I don't mention the impending custody battle because I don't want to worry her.

Mom doesn't skip a beat. "And what does *Brianna* want?"

"She's not sure, she might be up to seeing her. I just don't want Bri to get her hopes up. I don't want her hurt again."

"I understand," Mom says softly. "Whatever you decide, I'm here. We'll handle it together, like we always do."

The knot in my chest loosens a fraction. "Thanks, Mom. I miss you."

"I miss you too, baby. We'll see each other soon for the holidays."

I smile. "How's dad?"

"Grumpy as ever, of course. Just like you."

I chuckle, the sound easing some of the tension. "Still keeping everyone on their toes?"

"Oh, you know him," she sighs. "He asks about you all the time. He's proud, even if he won't say it the way I do."

The warmth in her tone wraps around me like a hug. For a

moment, it feels like I'm a teenager again, sitting at the kitchen counter while she fussed over me.

We talk a little longer about Mya, Brianna, work, and about nothing at all before we say goodnight. When I finally hang up, my heart feels a little lighter.

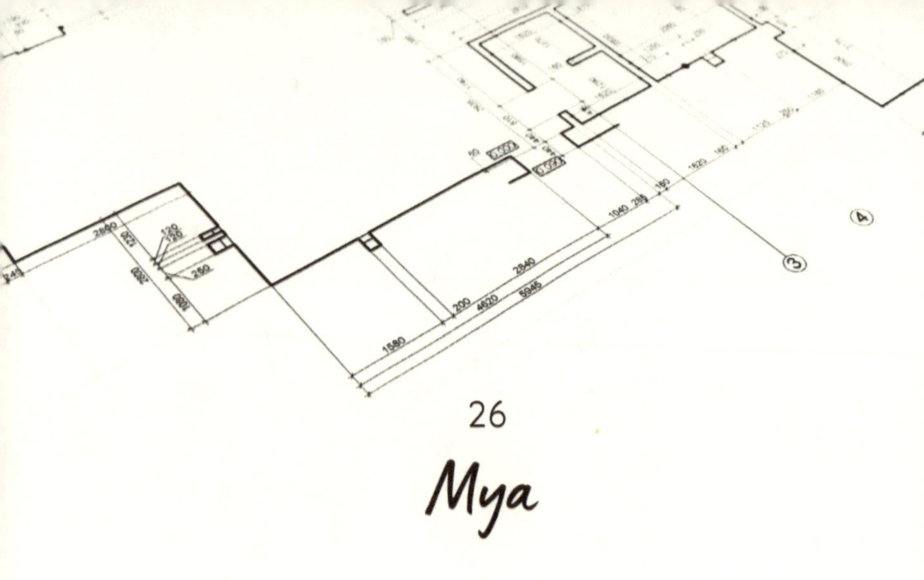

26

Mya

I t's late afternoon, and I'm buried in notes and projects when Worth's voice hits me like a command.

"Ms. Jones."

My head snaps up and I find him leaning against his office's doorframe. "Yes, Mr. Miller?" I push my glasses up the bridge of my nose, instantly aware I never wear them to the office.

"In here, please."

My brows knit, but I stand anyway. The walk to his office feels longer than it is. Worth closes the door behind me and, for a second, I brace myself, half expecting a lecture.

"Have a seat." He gestures to the chair opposite his desk, though he doesn't retreat behind it. He leans his hip against the edge, watching me. I adjust the frames again and cross my legs to keep my knee from bouncing.

"You don't usually wear glasses," he says, voice lower than it needs to be. "I like them."

My breath stutters and heat pricks the back of my neck as I push the frames higher.

"I told Brianna about us," he adds before I can respond. "I'd like you to come to dinner on Friday."

My stomach flips. *He told her about me already?*

"That was fast. How did she take it?"

"Really well, actually. She said she doesn't want me to be "forever alone.""

A laugh bursts out of me. "Sounds like a typical teenager. I like her already."

Worth smiles.

"I'm glad she's open to it, though. I can't wait to officially meet her, though it's a little nerve-racking."

"Just be yourself. Bri will like you, just like everyone else does," he replies.

That last part makes something warm uncoil inside me. I should ignore it. Instead, I say: "Including you?"

I hold my breath, regretting it instantly. Did I just *flirt* with him when I specifically told him to respect the boundaries between us?

"Yes."

My throat dries up.

"I got the prenup ready," he adds.

I wince.

His mouth twitches. "Sorry. This is uncharted territory for me. I've never had to do this."

"A fake marriage? Or you didn't have a prenup with your ex-wife?" I ask, leaning back in the chair.

"Both. Vanessa and I got married before all this." He gestures around him. "I was able to get out of the divorce almost scot-free because she forfeited custody of Brianna."

There's a tug in my chest, but I keep my tone even. "Well, I have no interest in your money outside of our agreement, Mr. Miller. Pen?"

He slides one across the desk, and I take my time. I go over the documents twice, making sure every stipulation we agreed on is there.

My stomach knots as I scrawl my name at the bottom. This is really happening.

Am I crazy for agreeing to this?

"There." I cap the pen with a click. "Done."

His gaze holds mine. "Thank you."

The sincerity in his voice nearly undoes me. I nod once, forcing a small smile. "You're welcome."

I stand, pushing the chair back, ready to escape, but before I make it to the door, Worth grabs me by the waist, pulling me flush against him. My breath stutters.

"What are you doing, Worth?"

He doesn't budge at my half-hearted push at his chest.

"You're like a kitten when you're cornered," he murmurs, voice low and sinful. "All hiss... no bite. And I know you'll purr if I keep touching you."

Heat floods my cheeks, my body betraying me as his thumb grazes slow circles into my side. My pulse thrums like a warning bell, but instead of shoving him away, I stay put.

"Worth," I whisper sharply, tilting my head towards the door. "People will see us."

He leans closer, his mouth brushing my ear, sending shivers racing down my spine. "Let them see," he growls softly. "You're going to be my wife soon, anyway."

"I said no touching, remember?"

"Yes," Worth answers, his lips curving in a smirk. "But you also said *behind closed doors*. Right now, we're in public. Which means we keep up appearances."

My jaw drops. "Appearances? No one even knows we're dating yet."

His gaze burns into mine, hot enough to make me forget we're standing in plain sight. "Well, this will get them talking. And then you can tell your co-workers the news."

I glare at him. "You're insufferable, Mr. Miller."

His smirk deepens, eyes glinting. "Just wait until you become *Mrs.* Miller."

Dre walks into the office, clutching a stack of files, and her eyes narrow.

"Oh, uh—" My voice trips over itself. I slip quickly out of Worth's hold, straightening my blouse like it had been out of place. "We were just, um... talking about an upcoming project."

Worth doesn't even flinch. He stays exactly where he is, composed as ever, not a shred of guilt in his expression.

Before the silence can crush me, Griffin walks in, holding a coffee and looking at us with curious eyes. "Did we interrupt something?"

"No," I blurt too fast, shaking my head. "Not at all."

Griffin's brows lift, a knowing smirk curling his lips. He doesn't press, but the way his gaze lingers on me and Worth makes my cheeks burn.

I grab the nearest documents off the desk and hug the file to my chest like a shield. "I should, uh... get back."

I don't wait for permission. My heels click rapidly against the floor as I bolt out of the office, heart hammering, knowing that if I look back, Worth would still be watching me like I belong to him.

I'm barely five steps down the hall when Shaina's voice stops me.

"Mya."

She's standing behind the reception desk, tablet in hand.

"Yes?" I ask, trying to keep my tone neutral.

The moment I saw Shaina walk out of Worth's office on my

first day, I knew exactly what kind of woman she was. Since then, she hasn't missed a single opportunity to make it clear she's not a fan of mine.

But if Shaina had no haters, I'd be dead. Not that I have any claim over what Worth does—or did—but that doesn't stop the jealousy from curling tight in my chest at the thought of them together.

She glances at the screen, then up at me.

"Mr. Miller usually schedules meetings," she says coolly. The implication lands exactly where she wants it to.

"Mr. Miller asked me to come by, Shaina."

Her gaze flicks to the closed office door behind me. "I see." There's a pause. "Next time, I'll need advance notice if you're planning to... drop by his office."

My brow furrow.

"Mr. Miller's time is carefully managed. Drop-ins can disrupt his day."

I hold her stare. "Then I'm sure he wouldn't have requested one."

Shaina forces a polite smile. "Fair. But try not to keep him too long," she says lightly. "Some of us actually *work* with him."

"We were discussing work," I reply evenly.

Her lips press into a thin smile. "Of course you were."

I don't dignify that with a response.

"Last time I checked, Andrée was in charge of Mr. Miller's schedule. So, if there's an issue, I'd be happy to discuss it with *her*. Now, if you'll excuse me." I turn and walk away, refusing to let her see how much she rattled me.

By the time I reach my desk, my pulse is still racing.

Seraya's head pops up over my cubicle wall almost immediately. "Okay. What was *that*?"

I drop into my chair, exhaling. "Nothing."

She gives me a look. "You just came from Worth's office, Shaina looks like she's plotting your murder, and you're pissed."

I huff out a laugh. "We just don't like each other."

Seraya's lips curl. "Yeah. I noticed." Then she brightens. "I know what'll take your mind off that heathen: drinks tonight?"

Technically, I have final tweaks due on a work proposal, but a distraction sounds medicinal right now.

"Come on, Mya. You've been promising me for weeks!"

She's right.

"You know what? Why the hell not."

"Yay!" She throws both hands up. "I'll go tell Jo. The Copper Finch at six?"

"Perfect."

Excitement buzzes under my skin. But my stomach does this nervous little swoop at the thought of telling them about... whatever Worth and I are.

Seraya saunters off to tell Jovana, and I shake off the nerves and dive back into my doc.

By late afternoon, my phone pings.

TJ:

Mya, are you free tonight? We're going out for drinks after work.

Sorry! I already promised I'd go out with Seraya and Jovana.

DEMI:

Gasp. Are we being replaced?

ERIC:

She could never find other friends like us, Dem. Be serious.

LOL. Never replacing my originals. They're my work friends. Actually... want to join us? I'm sure they won't mind.

I pop my head over my desk. "Hey, is it cool if my sister and two friends meet us?"

Seraya grins. "The more the merrier!"

I sink back into my chair and type:

> They're down! Meet us at The Copper Finch at 6.

TJ:

> Can't wait!

DEMI:

> Sounds great!!

ERIC:

> Do you work with any hot boys?

> I do, but none of them are coming tonight.

ERIC:

> Bummer.

Tiana and Demi react with a laughing emoji to his message, and I just chuckle.

> I have to finish this deck. See you later, gremlins.

HOURS LATER, WE WALK INTO THE COPPER FINCH, AND Seraya waves me over to a round table near the window. Jovana is already there, hair slicked into a perfect low bun, flipping a cocktail menu with clinical focus.

"You're late," Jo says without looking up.

"You're the one who's early," I protest, sliding into the seat.

Seraya grins. "We all know 'Jovana time' runs ten minutes before the clock."

A server appears with water and a small dish of Castelve-trano olives. I scan the menu, my nerves doing hopping-jacks. "Something light," I say. "Not too sweet."

"Ginger-lime spritz?" the server offers.

"Perfect."

"Negroni," Jo says. "And the burrata."

"Paloma, please," Seraya chirps. "And those parmesan truffle fries before I eat my own knuckles."

By the time our drinks land, the door swings open and Tiana beelines toward us, dragging Demi and Eric in her wake.

"There she is!" Tiana sings, squeezing me in a hug. "You look hot."

"She's right," Demi says. "Very 'girl boss' energy."

Eric kisses the air beside my cheek. "And curls that could murder a man."

I laugh, already feeling looser. "Please sit before you keep complimenting me to death."

Introductions fly. Seraya and Jo charm my friends instantly, earning real-friend badges in under three minutes.

Conversation ricochets from office gossip to Demi's customer-from-hell to the time Eric accidentally sent a thirst trap to his professor (cropped, thank God).

My phone buzzes under the table. I ignore it. It buzzes again. Tiana cocks a brow.

"Work?" she asks, teasing but soft.

"Probably." I risk a glance.

WORTH:

You're not at the office.

Great observation, Mr. Miller.

WORTH:

Where are you?

I'm at The Copper Finch with friends.

WORTH:

Does that include Ethan by any chance?

I roll my eyes.

Oh my God. Are you ever going to let it go?

WORTH:

If you let me fire him, then yes.

For the umpteenth time, you are not firing Ethan.

WORTH:

You're not the boss, Ms. Jones.

Fair point. I'm off the clock. Do you need anything, sir?

WORTH:

I thought we agreed on Worth after 6 p.m.

Did we? Must've missed that memo.

WORTH:

Your smart mouth will get you in trouble one day, Mya.

I'm counting on it...

WORTH:

Brat.

Have you eaten?

WORTH:

Do you care about me, Ms. Jones?

> Don't flatter yourself. You've been holed up in your office all day. I'm just protecting my assets.

WORTH:

> You wound me.

> Get over yourself and answer the question.

WORTH:

> Yes… wife.

Smiling, I place my phone face down on the table.

Seraya leans forward first, eyes sharp and amused. "Okay. No. You don't just smile like that at your phone for five minutes and *not* explain yourself."

Jovana hums in agreement. "That was not a work smile. That was a *someone-has-you-on-a-leash* smile."

"I do *not* smile like that."

"Yes, you do," Demi says immediately.

Eric points at my phone. "So. Who was it?"

I lift my glass and take a slow sip, buying myself time. "No one."

Tiana scoffs. "Mya."

I lower the glass. "Fine. It was Worth."

The table goes quiet.

Then—

"*Worth* Worth?" Seraya asks.

Jovana blinks. "Our *boss* Worth?"

Eric lets out a low whistle. "Mr. Blue collar billionaire himself?"

Demi's eyes widen. "You were texting your *boss* like that?"

I grimace.

"That is not an answer," Tiana says, leaning back in her chair, grinning. She's the only one who knows the truth of my relationship with Worth and she's clearly loving every second of this.

I exhale slowly, fingers tightening around my glass. "We're... dating."

A gasp. More silence. And I can't tell if they're shocked, excited or mad.

Jovana breaks the quiet first. "I called it."

I blink. "Called what?"

She glances at Seraya, who's already smirking. "Singapore."

My stomach dips. "What about it?"

Jovana nods. "You disappeared from the dancefloor at the same time Worth Miller went completely MIA."

Eric's eyebrows shoot up. "Wait, you *both* vanished?"

"No goodbye. No 'bathroom break.' Just—poof," Seraya adds. "I knew something was up!"

Demi lets out a slow, impressed "Oh."

I groan, dropping my head into my hand. "You guys are unbelievable."

"Am I wrong?" Jovana asks sweetly. "Because I distinctly remember saying, *either she left with him or she got kidnapped.*"

Tiana and Eric laugh.

"You were glowing when you reappeared," Seraya continues.

I lift my head. "I was not!"

Eric points at me. "So Singapore was the beginning."

I hesitate just long enough for them to notice.

Demi grins. "Oh my God. It *wasn't?*"

I exhale. "Fine. Yes. Something was already happening."

Tiana studies me, acting clueless. "And now?"

I glance at my phone, still face down on the table. "Now, it's real."

Seraya grins. "Is it serious?"

I can't help it—I smile.

"Very."

Even though our relationship is fake, I have to sell it. And yet, there is a part of me that is genuinely excited to start this journey. My life has always been carefully planned, every step measured. This is so far outside my comfort zone it almost makes my skin itch. But for once, I'm doing something for *me*—without overanalyzing the fallout—while still helping someone else in the process.

"How do you think people at your work are going to take it?" Demi asks, resting her chin in her palm.

I grimace, swirling the ice in my glass. "That's the only part I'm worried about. But Worth says he has it under control."

"Hell yeah, he does!" Eric beams, leaning back in his chair. "I can't believe you bagged a fucking billionaire, MJ." He wiggles his brows. "Does he have any friends? Brothers?"

Eric is *always* hunting for his next hookup.

I laugh and swat his shoulder. "He does, but I'm not opening that door for you. Find your own rich man to shag."

The table erupts in laughter, and for the first time since this whole thing began, the knot in my chest loosens just a little. Having my friend's support makes this a tad easier. Though I wish I could tell them the truth.

Seraya reaches across the table first, squeezing my hand. "I'm really happy for you, Mya. You deserve something exciting."

Tiana nods, her smile soft. "As long as you're okay with it—and it's what *you* want—that's what matters."

"I am. I think. I just didn't expect it to feel... right."

Eric lifts his glass. "To MJ, patron saint of accidentally landing billionaires."

I laugh, clinking my glass against my friends'.

The conversation drifts to travel plans, work gossip, and Jovana's latest dating horror story. Eric disappears to flirt with the bartender and comes back far too pleased with himself. At some point, someone orders another round, and the music gets louder.

I catch myself laughing more than usual, leaning into the warmth of the table, the easy comfort of people who really know me.

Tonight, I stay exactly where I am, surrounded by friends, letting the night unfold without worrying about where it's all going next.

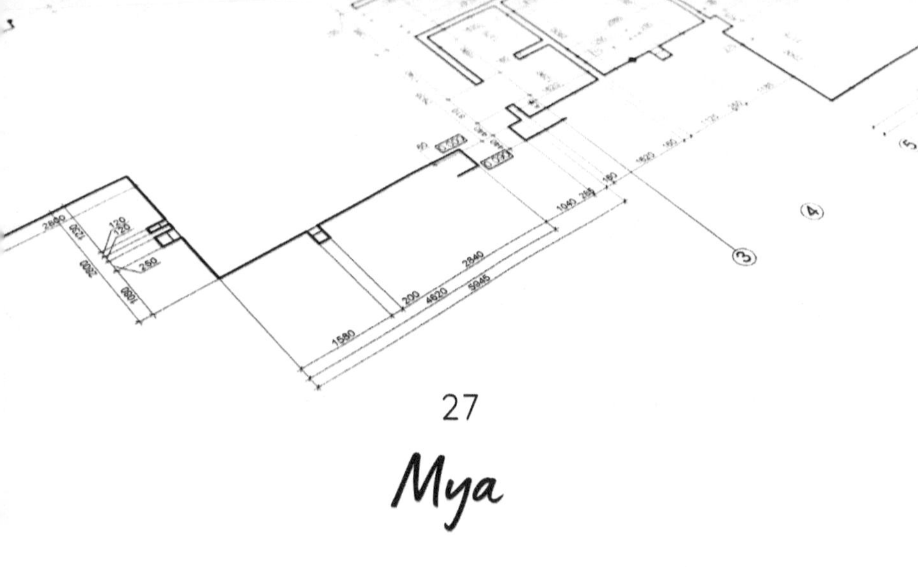

27

Mya

I t's Friday, and I'm a goddamn wreck.

Tonight, Mya is supposed to come over for dinner and officially meet Brianna. As my *girlfriend*.

The word feels foreign on my tongue. And yet, I've caught myself repeating it in my head all week.

We've been not-so careful at the office, sneaking moments where someone might catch us close enough to stir suspicion. Her bent over my desk while I "point out corrections," my hand brushing her back a second too long in the breakroom, our heads tipped together over blueprints. Subtle enough to be deniable, suggestive enough to fuel gossip.

It worked.

On Wednesday, HR rolled out the revised fraternization rules, and within hours, three other couples came forward like roaches under light. Turns out I wasn't the only one breaking my own damn policy.

Now, I'd bet my last dollar people are whispering about me and Mya.

I grab my phone and shoot my *girlfriend* a text.

Minutes later, there's a knock, and then Mya slips inside my office, shutting the door behind her. She's in wide-leg slacks, blouse tucked in, glasses perched on her nose. Christ. Every time she wears those glasses, my blood runs hotter. Like I want to ruin her in the filthiest ways and then straighten them back on her face after.

I nod at the chair opposite my desk, but she doesn't sit. She plants a hand on her hip instead.

"What is it, Worth?"

No pleasantries, straight to the point. "Did you tell Ethan?"

Her brows knit. "Tell Ethan what?"

"That you and I are dating."

"No." Her answer comes quickly, clipped. She crosses her arms. "Why would I? He's been avoiding me, so he's probably heard, anyway."

"Good," I say. "Better off that way."

The thought of Ethan anywhere near her grates in ways I don't understand. Jealousy isn't an emotion I've ever entertained, but with Mya, it's instinct. It doesn't matter that what we have is staged, signed, and bound by circumstance.

Her eyes roll. She's perfected that move with me. And god help me, it makes me want to pin her against the wall every damn time.

"Tread lightly, Ms. Jones," I murmur, leaning back in my chair, deliberately letting my gaze drag over her face. "One of these days, I'm going to make sure those pretty eyes stay rolled back for an entirely different reason."

Her lips part, color blooming across her cheeks, but she doesn't fire back right away. Which means she's thinking about it—imagining what it would be like. Exactly the reaction I want.

I smirk, satisfied. "Back to work. I'll see you tonight."

She turns on her heel with a muttered, "You're the worst,"

and storms out, but not before I catch the way her fingers tighten around the doorknob, as if she's holding herself together.

It's evening, and I'm pacing the kitchen like a caged animal. Maggie swats me away from the stove for the third time.

"Shoo, Worth. You're making me nervous. Since when do *you* get jittery?"

I grunt, pretending to check the oven. She's right, I'm never nervous. But tonight is different.

Brianna is perched at the island, chipper as always. She keeps sneaking glances at me, like she's been waiting her whole life for this moment.

I check the time again. Almost eight. Which means—

The doorbell rings.

My pulse spikes.

I stride to the door and open it.

Mya is standing on the porch, bundled against the Seattle chill, curls escaping her scarf. She holds out a bottle of wine in one hand, and in the other, a sketchbook and a pack of fine-tip markers by the exact brand Brianna's been doodling with.

Thoughtful. I had mentioned to her that Bri was into art quite a while ago.

She really listens.

"Hi," Mya says softly, offering a tentative smile.

For a second, I just stare at her.

The porch light glows against her skin, and I can't stop my eyes from dragging over her outfit. A simple dress, nothing ostentatious, but on her it looks like it belongs in a magazine spread. She's beautiful.

"You look great, Mya." My voice is rougher than intended and I try to clear my throat.

She smiles shyly. "Thank you."

I step aside. "Come in. They're waiting."

We head to the kitchen, where Maggie is fussing over the final touches of dinner. She wipes her hands on a dish towel, then surprises me by wrapping Mya in a hug.

"Oh, it's so nice to finally meet you." Maggie's smile is kind and genuine.

Mya returns the hug and inhales deeply. "Likewise. It smells amazing in here!"

Maggie beams, clearly pleased.

We settle around the table, plates soon filled, and Mya makes a deliberate effort to keep Brianna engaged. She asks about school, friends, and even compliments the doodles scattered on the table beside Bri's plate. My daughter lights up like a Christmas tree, soaking up every ounce of attention as she pulls her tablet closer.

"Look," Brianna says, showing off a half-finished sketch of a wolf. "I'm still working on the shading."

Mya leans closer. "This is incredible, Brianna. You have such a good sense of proportion. Do you draw every day?"

Bri nods eagerly. "Pretty much. Dad says I leave drawings everywhere."

I hide a smile behind my glass.

Mya laughs softly. "I used to do the same thing, though what I draw isn't nearly as fun. Mostly boring stuff, like buildings and interiors."

"You draw *buildings*?"

"Mhmm. Floor plans, elevations, the kinds of sketches that eventually turn into real spaces. It's not exactly artistic, but it's how I learned to see details." Mya picks up one of Bri's markers, spinning it between her fingers. "That's what makes your art so good. You already see the balance."

Brianna blushes under the compliment. "Really?"

"Really," Mya says warmly. "You've got an artist's brain. I'd love to see all your sketches one day."

My daughter's smile grows shy. "There's a lot."

"I've got time," Mya teases. "Maybe when I come over next, you can teach me how to draw something that isn't a building."

Bri lights up. "We could draw together! Like a collab!"

"Exactly." Mya leans in conspiratorially. "But you'll have to promise not to laugh at my attempts at drawing animals."

Brianna giggles. "Deal."

The two of them fall into easy conversation, swapping stories about their favorite colors, tools, and how frustrating it is when ink bleeds through the page. They even start sketching quick little doodles on the back of Bri's napkin, side by side. Mya's lines are sharp and clean; Brianna's are full of energy and imagination. Together, they look like something I'd frame.

Watching them, I feel something loosen in my chest. Relief —maybe even hope.

Across the table, Maggie catches my eye. She winks and mouths *I like her.*

I can't help the smirk that tugs at my mouth, even as something drops in my stomach. My carefully-rehearsed plan is already unraveling at the edges. Mya looks like she belongs here, and that scares the hell out of me.

By the time we've cleared the table, Brianna's practically attached to Mya's side.

"You have to come back soon," she insists, holding up her pinky. "Promise?"

Mya hooks her little finger with Brianna's, smiling. "Promise."

Satisfied, my daughter disappears upstairs, calling over her shoulder, "Goodnight, Dad! Night, Maggie! Night, Mya!"

Mya chuckles, watching her go. "She's special."

"She is. Her mom and I did one thing right together."

Her smile falters just slightly, but she nods. "You're doing better than you think."

Maggie gathers her things and says her own goodbyes, slipping out with one last smile at me.

And then it's just me, Mya, and the remnants of the wine.

I tilt the bottle toward her glass. "Another?"

Mya hesitates, then nods. "One more. But that's it. I have to drive home."

I pour, and the sound of wine spilling into the glass fills the quiet kitchen. We both take our stools again.

"Tell me something," I say, leaning my forearms on the counter. "Something I don't know about you."

Her lips curve. "Like what?"

"Anything."

"Hmm." She takes a sip. "Well, my favorite band of all time is Queen."

I arch a brow. "Classic. I approve."

"I've been dying to get my hands on a signed copy of *A Night at the Opera* record on vinyl," she adds. "But it's rare. Like... ridiculously rare. I've looked everywhere, and no luck."

"Why that one?"

Her smile softens. "My dad used to play it all the time when I was little. Saturday mornings, he'd put it on while making pancakes. The whole house smelled like syrup and butter, and Queen would be blasting in the background. I think that's when I first started falling in love with music." She lets out a quiet laugh, then shakes her head. "It's funny, the things that stick with you."

Her eyes dim a little. "It feels like one minute we were

arguing over who got the last pancake, and the next, he was just... gone. I think that's why I love that album so much. It's the last sound that reminds me of him before everything changed."

I don't say anything, simply listen.

Mya traces her thumb along the base of her glass. "I used to think grief was something you got over. But I don't think it works that way. It's more like a scar under your skin. You stop noticing it every day, but it's still there when you press hard enough."

I nod. "You just learn how to live around it."

Her gaze meets mine across the island. She's not hiding behind sarcasm or control or all the walls she usually builds this time. Mya is just *here*, open and human. And somehow, that makes me feel seen in a way I haven't in years.

"Sorry," she says after a beat, forcing a small smile. "That got dark fast."

"Don't apologize. I'm glad you trust me enough to talk about him."

Her expression shifts. "I guess I do," she admits quietly.

That simple confession settles somewhere deep in my chest, in a dangerous territory I've spent years avoiding.

For a moment, we sit in silence, and I ignore the fact that this already feels like more than a fake marriage arrangement. More than a business deal.

"So," I start, swirling what's left in my glass, "we need to talk about next steps."

Mya sets her glass down slowly, her lashes flicking up to meet my gaze. There's a hint of apprehension in her eyes.

"On Sunday, we'll make our relationship public. The gala is the perfect stage."

She shifts in her seat, chewing her bottom lip. She looks

nervous. I almost tell her we can delay, but she straightens her spine and nods. "Okay."

"After that, I'll propose. Nothing too dramatic, but showy enough to make it official. Do you want me to tell you when it'll happen? Or would you rather be surprised?"

Her lips part, and for a moment she just stares at me. Then, softly, "Surprise me. That way, my reaction will be genuine." She tilts her head. "Is this weird?"

"Yes," I admit. No point in pretending.

Mya exhales a short laugh, shaking her head. "I pictured my marriage differently. I imagined real love, a cute engagement filled with little hints of my relationship with my future husband. Dress shopping trip with Tiana. My dad walking me down the aisle. None of this..." Her hand gestures between us. "Was in the script."

Guilt claws at me. I rake a hand through my hair. "I'm sorry, Mya. I didn't mean to take that from you."

"Don't apologize. I knew what I was getting into when I said yes. I made the choice, and I'll stick to it."

We lapse into silence again. I drain the last of my wine, wishing it would burn hotter, dull the twist in my chest.

Mya pushes back from the stool and stands. "I should get going."

Every instinct screams at me to tell her to stay. To offer her the guest room, the couch, anything. But I only nod, because wanting more doesn't change the rules we set.

"Thanks by the way," she adds as I walk her to the entrance.

"For what?"

"Approving the advance," she says sheepishly. "I was able to get my landlord off my back."

"Of course, Mya. I would've approved it even if we weren't in this together."

She nods.

I grab her coat and slip it around her shoulders, my fingertips grazing her skin, and she shudders.

"Drive safe."

"Goodnight, Worth. See you on Sunday."

I watch her walk out, and the hollow ache in my chest settles in deep.

"Do I hear seventy-five thousand?" the auctioneer booms, voice cracking like a whip across the room as he surveys the bidders.

"Eighty!" a man calls from the back.

"Eighty-five. Ninety. Ninety-five!" The numbers climb, each one stoking the room's energy.

I sit perfectly still, paddle balanced on my knee. I could walk out right now, let someone else take it, but I don't. I need this one.

The auctioneer's gaze scans the crowd. "Do I hear one hundred thousand?"

The room stills, tension snapping tight. I raise my paddle. "One hundred."

A ripple of whispers cuts through the crowd. No one else lifts a hand.

The auctioneer slams the gavel. "Sold! One hundred thousand dollars, bidder number twenty-seven!"

Polite applause trickles around me, but I'm already rising. I barely notice the champagne trays circling.

Outside, cool air cuts against my skin as I slide into the back of the town car. The driver nods once, pulling us into traffic.

I lean back, closing my eyes briefly, a smile tugging at my mouth.

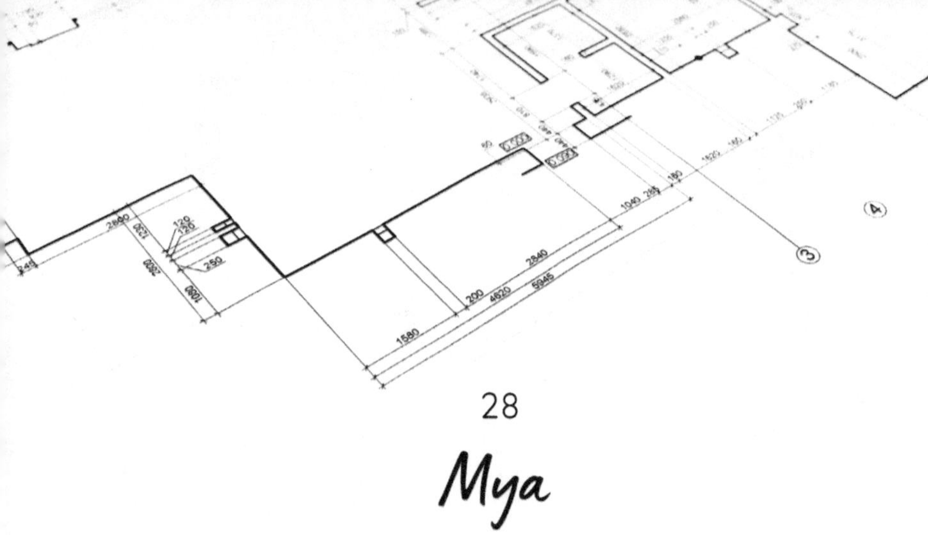

28

Mya

I t's Sunday morning, the day Worth and I are supposed to announce to the world that we're a couple.

My gaze sweeps around the living room of my tiny apartment. I grab my phone and message him.

> You shouldn't have done this.

It only takes him a few seconds to reply.

> WORTH:
>
> I don't know what you're talking about.

That little shit.

It's laughable. My small couch is pushed against the wall, and in the middle of it all are two rolling racks crammed with couture gowns worth more than a year's rent. A stylist, sent by my *boyfriend*—God, I still can't get used to calling him that—showed up at my door this morning with garment bags and boxes, a personal assistant in tow.

I fire a text back.

> I shouldn't have told you I needed a new dress.

WORTH:

Just say thank you, you stubborn woman.

I can almost hear the smugness. I roll my eyes and type back.

> Thank you, Mr. Miller. 😳

WORTH:

10.

> 10, what?

WORTH:

10 spankings for every eye roll you've given me.

His reply makes me choke on air.

Heat slams into my cheeks, rushing straight down between my thighs. I refuse to dignify that with an answer. Damn him for knowing exactly how to get under my skin.

He's fully aware nothing sexual is going to happen again, so why the hell would he even tally the number of spankings he thinks he owes me?

Typical Worth Miller.

And yet, despite myself, a thrill shoots down my spine at the thought of his large hands on me, rough and commanding, teaching me a lesson I secretly wouldn't mind learning.

Nope. Absolutely not.

I shake my head hard, as if I can physically rattle the image away. I cannot—*will not*—succumb to his antics. Not again.

"Um... why do you look like you just got caught doing something illegal?" Tiana narrows her eyes at me over the rim of her champagne glass.

I whip my head towards her. "What? Nothing. I'm fine."

She smirks. "Mhm. You're flushed, fidgety, and holding your phone like it just whispered dirty secrets in your ear. Spill, MJ."

"I said it's nothing." I busy myself tugging at the zipper of a dress on the rack, pretending to examine it.

Tiana lets out a laugh. "Girl, if that man's texts got you looking like *this*, you're in deep."

I shoot her a glare, which only makes her laugh harder. "Shut up and help me pick a dress."

Tiana leans back on the couch, drink in hand. "Damn. A girl could really get used to this. Do you think he'll notice if I sneak a dress?" She gestures to the rows of gowns shimmering under the light, sequins and silks in every shade.

"It's *way* too much." I pick up a Tom Ford black cocktail dress. "I could've just worn something from my closet. Or bought something affordable." The lie tastes bitter. I don't own a single thing that could pass for gala attire, and we both know it.

"Affordable is overrated when you've got a billionaire boyfriend."

I pin her with a stare. "Don't start."

"Oh, I'm starting. You'd better try on every damn one of those dresses, sis. If I'm your audience, I demand a show." Tiana tops off our glasses, offering some to the stylist and assistant.

Rolling my shoulders, I take another sip of champagne, nerves tangling in my chest. Fine—if Worth wants me to look the part, then I'll look the damn part.

I head to the bedroom to change. This is just another performance. A role I've agreed to play. So why does part of me already wonder which dress will make Worth lose his composure first?

After trying on what feels like a hundred gowns, I finally settle on a Marchesa Notte floor-length dress in deep blue with delicate beadwork embroidered across the bodice. The neckline dips just enough to be daring without forfeiting elegance, and the silk chiffon skirt flows around my legs like liquid air. Against my will, the stylist forces me to take five other dresses too, carefully folded into garment bags. Apparently, Mr. Miller told him to make sure I had "enough options." I try to argue, but apparently Worth has everyone on a damn leash.

A few hours later, Tiana is gone, and my hair and makeup are done. The stylist pinned my curls into a soft updo, leaving a few tendrils to frame my face, while the smoky bronze shadow makes my eyes almost *smolder*. A swipe of nude gloss completes the look.

At seven sharp, my phone buzzes with a message from Worth telling me he's outside.

I grab my clutch, take a breath, and head downstairs.

A sleek black town car waits at the curb. When the driver opens the door, Worth steps out, and for a split second, I forget how to breathe. He's in a black suit, with a dark blue tie that matches my gown exactly. Even the subtle square in his pocket is the same shade.

This man.

Broad shoulders, commanding stance, and that salt-and-pepper beard perfectly trimmed. The sight of him alone sends my pulse skittering.

Worth's eyes rake over me, head to toe—and for once, the unshakable CEO falters. His Adam's apple bobs, his jaw ticks, and his hands flex at his sides, like he's fighting the urge to touch me.

"Jesus Christ, Mya," he mutters. "You're breathtaking."

The compliment lands straight in my chest, setting my whole body alight.

I swallow the flutter in my chest. "Thank you. You don't look so bad yourself."

Worth smirks at the understatement.

"How did you know what color I was wearing?"

"Deshawn told me what you picked," he says, adjusting his cuff. "So I made sure to coordinate. And for the record—" his gaze drags down the length of me again, slow and searing— "blue has never looked so damn good on anyone."

Heat creeps up my neck, and I have to look away before I combust on the spot.

He offers his arm, the perfect gentleman. "After you."

Once inside the car, my nerves finally rear their ugly head and I start twisting my hands in my lap. Worth notices instantly. He takes one of them in his, his thumb tracing lazy circles against my palm. The small, steady motion calms me more than I want to admit.

"It'll be fine, Kitten. Don't worry about the cameras or the questions. I'll handle it."

I exhale. For all the ways he drives me insane with his bossiness, it's nice to let someone else take the reins for once.

He reaches into the inside pocket of his jacket and pulls out a slim velvet case. When he flips it open, my eyes nearly fall out of my head. Nestled inside is a diamond necklace so brilliant it looks like it could blind the whole damn city. The stones catch every bit of light, glittering like fire, delicate yet undeniably worth more than my entire student debt ten times over.

"Worth..." My voice is barely a whisper as he takes the necklace out of the case. "I can't take this. It looks like it belongs in a museum."

His eyes lock on mine, burning right through me. "Turn around."

"Worth—?"

"Turn." His tone brooks no argument, and before I can

protest again, I find myself shifting in my seat, my spine straightening, as though obeying him is instinct.

The case snaps shut, and cold diamonds brush against my skin when he drapes them around my neck. His fingers graze my nape as he fastens the clasp, and the contact sends a hot shiver through my body I pray he can't see.

I catch my reflection in the darkened car window—the necklace glitters like starlight against my collarbone, transforming me into someone I barely recognize. Someone elegant. Someone who looks like she belongs at Worth Miller's side.

My lips part. "I don't know what to say."

Worth leans back into his seat, a smile forming at his lips. "It's nothing, really. To keep up appearances."

The words slice clean through the haze, dousing the spark in my chest with ice water. Of course—nothing more than appearances.

I nod stiffly, forcing my hands to rest in my lap, even though every part of me wants to rip the necklace off before it sears me. "Thank you," I manage, the words dry and brittle.

Beside me, Worth studies me for too long, like he knows exactly what just shifted inside me.

The rest of the ride stretches in silence.

When we finally arrive at the venue, the car has barely stopped before the flashes start. Bright white light explodes in every direction, disorienting me.

"Mr. Miller, is this your new girlfriend?"

"Worth! Over here—can we get a smile?"

"Who's the mystery woman? Name, please!"

The barrage of questions fires like bullets, and my chest tightens. Worth slips out first, then offers his hand to me. The second I take it, his arm sweeps around my waist, firmly tugging me flush to his side.

Security closes in, ushering us forward, but the photographers keep pressing, voices overlapping, camera shutters stuttering like machine guns.

Worth lowers his mouth to my ear. "Relax, baby. I'm right here. I got you."

The word 'baby' almost makes me stumble. Just minutes ago in the car, he made sure I understood this was only for appearances. Now he's sweet-talking me like he means it? My pulse spikes at the contradiction, and I force a smile so wide it aches as we pause for the cameras.

He holds me steady, anchoring me with the pressure of his hand at my hip. I mimic his composed stance, angling slightly towards him while cameras flash in a relentless storm.

Once inside the building, my lungs expand for the first time in what feels like forever.

The night passes in a haze of introductions and fake smiles. Worth doesn't leave my side. His hand is either splayed across the small of my back, curled around my fingers, or guiding me through the crowd.

When he introduces me, it's never just "Mya" or "my girlfriend." It's always: *"This is my woman."*

At one point, I finally whisper, "Why not just say girlfriend?"

"Sounds too juvenile for what this is, Kitten."

Whiplash. Again.

The more the night goes on, the more confused I become. Every protective gesture, every whispered word in my ear, every lingering glance feels too real—too much like something a man in a real relationship would do.

And yet, I can't forget. This is business. A performance. Nothing more.

So why is my heart not getting the memo?

The gala finally winds down, and I can breathe again. My cheeks ache from smiling, my feet are screaming in these heels, and if I have to shake one more hand and engage in any more small talk, I might combust.

When we slip out the back exit, the night air hits my overheated skin. The driver is waiting by the curb. Worth's hand finds my back once more.

The door opens and I slide inside, exhaling in relief. The moment Worth follows me in, the door thuds shut. He signals for the driver to move with a clipped nod, then reaches forward and slides the privacy partition up in one smooth motion.

Before I can ask what he's doing, he pivots suddenly, capturing my mouth in a bruising kiss.

I squeak in shock, but it's swallowed immediately by the hungry drag of his tongue. His kiss is rough, unyielding, as if he's been starving for me all night.

My stomach free-falls like I've just stepped off the edge of a cliff.

"Worth—" I try, breaking the kiss, breathless. "We shouldn't."

My protest sounds pitiful even to my own ears, especially when my hands are fisted in his jacket, pulling him closer instead of pushing him away.

The next thing I know, he's sliding off the seat and onto his knees.

Onto his knees in his goddamn car.

"Worth," I hiss, looking towards the tinted windows. "What are you doing? We're going to get caught."

But he doesn't stop. His big hands are already curling under my dress, dragging me forward until my ass is at the very edge of the leather seat. His eyes lift to mine, blazing and hungry, and my entire body trembles.

"Say the word and I'll stop," he rasps, lips brushing over my throat, along my collarbone, scorching everywhere they touch. "But don't lie to me, Mya. You want this as much as I do."

My nails scrape over his shoulders as he leans down, desperate for an anchor. "I don't—"

Worth's teeth nip my thigh and I jolt, a sharp gasp ripping from my mouth.

"Don't lie to me, Kitten."

"This is a bad idea, Worth," I babble, my head tipping back against the seat as his mouth moves, hot and wet against the inside of my thigh. "We'll regret this. We have an agreement. This is—*oh God*—this is only a recipe for disaster."

A whimper escapes me, humiliatingly loud in the enclosed space. My thighs clench and my chest heaves.

"I've been craving you since Singapore," he growls, voice muffled against my skin. "Couldn't get the sound of you falling apart out of my head. Couldn't get your taste off my tongue."

His hands grip me tighter, keeping me in place—one spreading my thighs wider, the other pressed firmly on my hip. My arguments tangle in my throat, dissolving into incoherence the second his hot breath fans over where I need him.

And then his mouth is on me.

"Worth—" My protest splinters into a scream as he sucks my clit, hard, pulling it between his lips and flicking with maddening precision. My back bows off the leather seat, fingers clawing for purchase in his hair as pleasure detonates low in my belly.

This feels so wrong. It shouldn't be happening. *God, maybe that's why it feels so good.*

I've been craving him too, even when I told myself I shouldn't. Even when I tried to shove every thought of him into the farthest corner of my mind. Because what happens if I fall? If I let feelings get tangled in this mess and end up heartbroken? Would I even survive the humiliation of seeing him every day at the office after that? No. I'd have to quit. Pack my life up. Move across the damn country just to get away.

He must notice my head spinning, my chest rising too fast, because his voice cuts through the chaos.

"Mya." His lips brush my folds. "Baby. Focus on me. Let me make you feel good."

His tongue alternates between soft, lazy swirls that make me melt, and greedy strokes that have me on the edge of madness. He sucks me like he wants to own me, devour me whole, and each drag of his mouth makes my body shake harder.

"You were so beautiful tonight," he murmurs between licks, his words hot against my soaked flesh. "Having you on my arm... introducing you as *my* woman..." He groans like the memory alone is enough to wreck him. "It did something to me, Mya."

Those words—*my woman*. I tried to tell myself it was all just part of the act. But here, with his tongue buried inside me and his voice laced with hunger, it feels like the most dangerous truth I've ever heard.

The pleasure is unbearable in the best way, each lick and suck a punishment and reward all at once. My thighs tremble, but Worth just grips me harder, spreading me wider, as if he wants to consume every last bit of me.

"Worth." I gasp his name for the umpteenth time, fingers twisting in his hair. "I—God, I can't—"

"Yes, you can. Give it to me, baby. Come for me."

He doubles down, tongue pressing in deep while his lips close over my clit, sucking with merciless precision. The combination shatters me. My body bows off the seat, a scream tearing from my throat.

I ride it out on his mouth, his groans sending aftershocks through my overstimulated nerves until I collapse back against the leather, panting and boneless. Still, he doesn't move, licking me softly, savoring every last drop.

Finally, he pulls back, his mouth glistening. He wipes the back of his hand over his lips but doesn't look away from me—like I'm the only thing in the world worth seeing.

"Fuck, Mya. You taste like sin."

Heat floods my face. My heart is pounding so loud I'm sure he hears it.

When he climbs back onto the seat beside me, he kisses me, letting me taste myself on his tongue.

It's filthy, but I kiss him back anyway, like I don't care that we're crossing a line that's already been crossed a hundred times in my head.

Worth leans back and slips a hand into his jacket, pulling out his pocket square. He glances at the seat between my thighs.

"You made a mess, Kitten."

I follow his gaze to the evidence pooling on the leather. Mortified, I shift, but he presses a hand on my thigh, stopping me.

"Don't." He crouches slightly, dragging the square of fabric over the wet patch until it's soaked. Then, without shame, he lifts it to his face and inhales.

My mortification spikes. "Oh my God—"

He cuts me off with a groan, eyes closing. "Goddamn, you smell so good. Do you know what this does to me?" His gaze pins me, raw and unflinching. "I'm keeping this. Forever. I'll never wash it. Every time I wake up, I want to breathe you in. Remind myself that you're mine."

And he might be right.

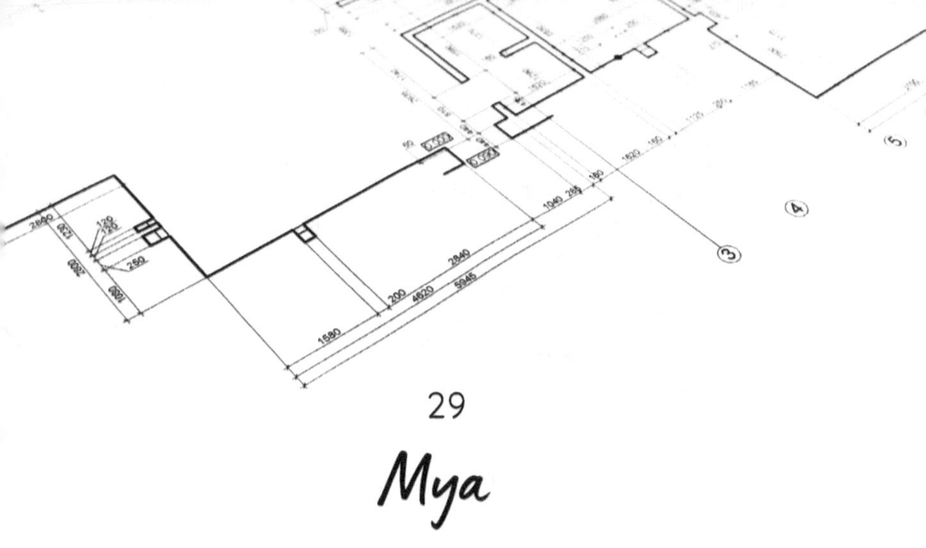

29

Mya

"**W**olves are among the most socially intelligent animals on the planet. They share information constantly through posture, sound, and subtle shifts in movement."

Onscreen, a pack moves through the forest in quiet formation, each member aware of the others without needing to look.

"*They don't just hunt together,*" the narrator continues. "*They raise their young collectively. Protect the vulnerable. The survival of one depends on the awareness of all.*"

Brianna leans closer to the television, eyes bright. "See? That one's the leader. But he still waits for the others."

I smile, nudging her gently. "Because leaders don't go alone."

"They're a pack," she says simply, like that explains everything.

A gray wolf lifts its head, ears twitching, and the others respond instantly, changing direction as one.

"They talk without talking," Brianna adds. "That's why they're so smart."

I nod. "They trust each other."

The front door opens.

Moments later, Worth steps into the living room, jacket draped over one arm, pausing when he takes in the sight of us on the floor—pencils scattered, a half-finished wolf sketch laying between us.

"Did I interrupt something important?" he teases.

Brianna looks up at him, grinning. "We're learning about wolves."

Worth looks at the screen, then back to us. "That explains the serious atmosphere."

I smile. "Brianna is very invested."

"She's been talking about this documentary for weeks," he says, setting his jacket aside. "I assumed it was a cartoon."

Brianna scoffs. "Cartoons are for kids, Dad."

A chuckle escapes him. "Noted."

I lean back on my hands, watching the two of them—how naturally Brianna gravitates toward her father, how easily he softens around her. It's been a few weeks since the gala—and even though nothing sexual has happened again between me and him, everything has shifted.

I've been here every day. Just... here. Some days we just sit on the floor, drawing wolves, as Brianna explains—in great detail —why they're better than dogs and how one day she wants to see them in the wild. Sometimes it's just the two of us, sometimes Maggie is there too, and Worth joins us for dinner when he can.

Bri and I have grown fond of each other quickly. Faster than I expected. Faster than I probably should have.

Worth watches us now with a smile.

"How about I take my girls out for dinner when the doc is done?"

My girls.

My stomach flips, tiny dancers somersaulting in my chest.

Even though I keep reminding myself that this is just for the sake of the arrangement, my heart can't help but react to Worth's softness. In front of the world, he's this big bad wolf, a man people fear crossing. But in front of Brianna, he's something else entirely. Gentle in a way that feels almost guarded, like softness is a language he only speaks at home.

I could get used to this life. I can picture it too easily, which is exactly why I can't let my mind drift there.

The only part that truly breaks my heart is losing this connection with Brianna. She's such a strong girl, and I've loved getting to know her—the way she thinks, how deeply she feels, how fiercely she loves the things that matter to her. It's going to hurt when I have to cut ties.

But maybe I won't have to.

I'm sure Worth wouldn't mind if Bri and I stayed friends.

After the documentary ends, we head out to a small Greek restaurant Worth has been raving about.

The moment we step inside, the owners greet Worth like family, ushering us toward a private table near the back, close to the open kitchen where the cooks move with ease.

"Kalispera, Worth!" the cook calls out with a grin.

"Kalispera, fílos mou!"

I blink. "You speak Greek?"

Worth laughs, shaking his head. "Don't get too excited. That's about the extent of it. Greetings, thank you, and whatever helps me get fed faster."

Brianna giggles, and I grin.

We order mezze to share—warm pita, tzatziki, dolmades, grilled halloumi—followed by souvlaki for Brianna and lamb for Worth. I let him order for me, something I don't usually do, and I don't miss the satisfaction in his expression when I ask him.

Midway through dinner, Brianna launches into an excited explanation about her school hosting an art show next month.

"I'm showing one of my wolf drawings," she says proudly. "I really want you both to come."

Worth looks at me. "Are you in Mya?"

"I'd love to come," I say without hesitation.

Brianna beams, practically vibrating in her seat.

The rest of the evening blurs into easy conversation and laughter.

When we're finishing up, one of the owners comes by.

"Dessert is on us." He ignores Worth's protests, as a waiter brings out loukoumades—golden and warm, drizzled with honey and dusted with cinnamon.

Later, Worth excuses himself to use the restroom, and the moment he's gone, Brianna turns to me, her expression suddenly serious.

"I've never seen my dad this happy. I'm really glad that you're in our life."

Emotion swells in my chest, sharp and sweet all at once. I reach for her hand, squeezing gently. "I'm really glad too."

And I am. Which makes it hurt all the more knowing it's temporary.

Does it have to be? my mind wonders.

In the privacy of Worth's home, we fit effortlessly.

Out there, though? Worth is the blue collar playboy.

And I'm just... Mya.

A nobody.

I shake off the intrusive thoughts just as Worth reappears, and somehow, he immediately senses the shift.

"Are you okay, Kitten?"

"EW!" Brianna exclaims. "Why would you call her *that*?"

I burst out laughing. Worth's expression doesn't falter, though I know he's fighting a smile.

"Because she's—"

Brianna holds up a hand. "Please spare me the explanation. I might gag."

That finally does it—Worth chuckles. "I just love getting you riled up, Piglet."

She groans dramatically, but she's smiling.

After a good fifteen minutes of lingering goodbyes with the owner, we head back to Worth's place.

When we pull into his driveway, I hug Brianna tightly, promising to see her tomorrow. She heads inside to get ready for bed, then I turn toward my car.

"Leaving already?" Worth calls after me.

"Yeah. It's a work night. I shouldn't be out late," I joke.

He joins me beside my car, eyeing it critically. "We need to get you something new."

"We absolutely do not," I protest. "My car is fine."

Worth circles the vehicle. "You sure about that?"

He nudges a loose piece of metal with his shoe. It clatters to the ground, rusted clean through.

I gape at it. "Well, if you didn't go around kicking my precious vehicle, maybe!"

Unbothered, he reaches into his pocket and presses a button on one of his key fobs. The garage door rolls open, and my jaw practically hits the pavement.

Inside sits a fleet of cars. Four of them. Plus two motorcycles.

"You've got to be kidding me."

"Take your pick. Although I'm guessing you don't ride bikes, so maybe steer clear of those."

I drift closer, still stunned. "Who needs this many cars, Worth?"

He shrugs. "I used to have more. Sold a few. Figured six sports cars was excessive."

"I am not taking one of your cars."

"Why not?"

"Because it's too much. And like I said: I'm not a charity case."

He stops in front of me, expression serious now. "Mya. Just borrow one of the cars."

"I don't want to."

"I can't sleep comfortably at night knowing you're driving that monstrosity. Please."

I sigh. "Fine. Which one is the most normal?"

Worth lets out a low laugh. "*Normal* might be a stretch."

He steps closer, coming up behind me, and his scent wraps around me. I inhale deeply.

"How about the least flashy one?"

His chest brushes my back, close enough that I can feel the steady rise and fall of his breath. His mouth hovers near the shell of my ear, grazing it, and my skin prickles in anticipation.

"That one," he says, nodding toward the sleek black car. "Porsche 911. Fast. Loud. Fun. But it attracts attention. And you don't strike me as someone who enjoys being watched."

My pulse skips as his knuckles skim my hip, goosebumps erupting all over my body.

Worth chuckles, darkly. "Unless you do. And I've been missing out," he whispers.

"The red one over there," he continues, voice lower now, "is the Ferrari Portofino. Beautiful, but impractical. You'd freeze half the year, and I don't like the idea of you being uncomfortable."

I swallow.

"And that one?" he adds, nodding toward the polished Audi. "Smooth. Controlled. Looks innocent enough until you push the gas." His body shifts, pressing into mine. "Just like a certain kitten I know," he breathes into my ear, his hand settling at my waist as he leads me to the last vehicle. Wetness pools at my center, and I muffle a moan, pushing my ass against his crotch. Worth groans in response, turning me around and pressing me against the car, successfully trapping me in between him and the large SUV. Hiding us in plain sight.

His expert hands travel up my thighs. "Fuck. I love when you wear skirts and dresses around me, like a filthy little tease." I gasp and my body tenses.

"This is the one," he decides, eyes settling on the Range Rover behind me. "It's spacious. Solid. You could fit your whole life in there if you needed to." His lips close enough now that I feel the warmth of his words against my mouth, "and safe, because I need to know you're protected."

He leans closer, as if about to kiss me and my breath hitches. Just as soon, he pulls away. The loss is abrupt and unfair.

I huff in protest, heat still throbbing beneath my skin, my body desperate for what my brain knows I shouldn't want.

Even though I know it's better for us not to engage in anything sexual, deep down, I still wish Worth would use his expert hands to make me come.

We've been dancing around the tension like it might bite if we get too close. It's almost as if something opened between us, but also built a higher wall neither of us has dared to climb. Maybe because we're both afraid of what is waiting on the other side. Of how far we'd fall if we let ourselves step over it.

At least, that's why I haven't.

But to say I don't crave him would be a lie. Every brush of his hand, every look that lasts a moment too long, chips away at whatever's left of my restraint.

I try to avert my gaze, shame and want wiring violently inside me. I know this is the right decision. I know stopping is smarter.

It doesn't stop the ugly sting of disappointment.

Worth pinches my chin between two fingers, bringing my eyes back to his. "Hey. Don't do that. Don't shut down."

"All of this is a bad idea, Worth," I whisper. "We keep saying we'll respect the lines and then we end up here again."

His face falls. "I'm sorry. I got carried away."

Worth takes a step back. He drags a hand through his hair, as if he's just as frustrated and he hates that he can't do a damn thing about it.

He walks toward the far end of the garage and retrieves a set of keys. Then presses them into my palm.

I'm still leaning against the Range Rover, trying to wrap my head around my conflicting feelings but coming up short.

Worth leans over and kisses my forehead.

"Get home safe, Mya."

"Yeah," I breathe, not trusting myself to look at him. "Okay."

I climb into the SUV, fingers trembling on the steering wheel. Then, I drive away.

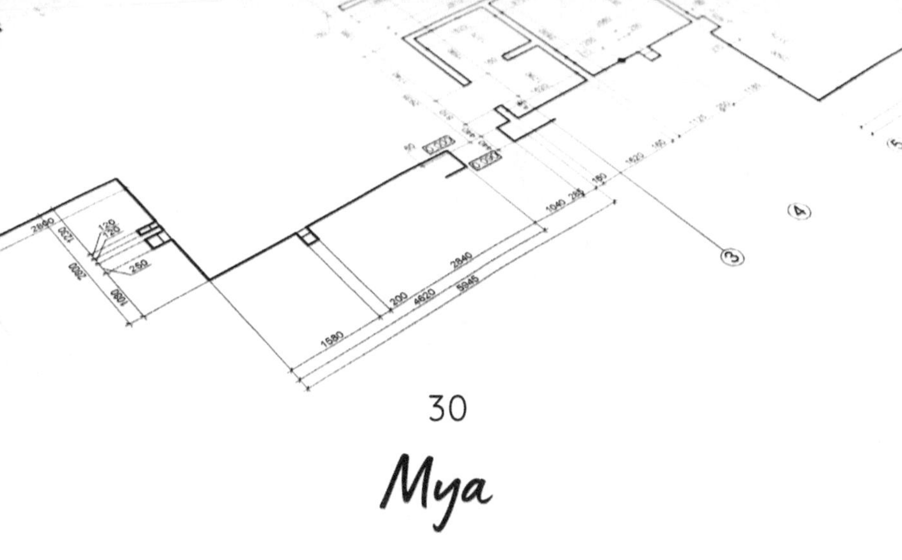

30

Mya

It's been weeks and my face is still on gossip sites.

Today's headline screams at me in bold letters: ***BLUE COLLAR BILLIONAIRE'S NEW ARM CANDY: WHO'S THIS MYSTERY WOMAN?***

There's a photo of me and Worth at the gala, his hand at my waist, his mouth tilted in that smug almost-smile that makes women swoon. Except the focus isn't on him. It's on me—my dress, my hair, my nervous smile.

I scroll, stomach sinking as words blur together. Some tabloids speculate about my background. Others pick apart the dress I wore. A few wonder if I'm just another notch in Worth Miller's expensive belt.

My cheeks flame. I want to slam my laptop shut, but I can't stop reading.

An unfamiliar voice makes me freeze.

"You can't stop me! I'm going in."

I snap my gaze to the front desk, where Shaina is half-standing, palms braced on the counter, trying to block someone from bulldozing through.

"I'm sorry, ma'am, you can't go in without an appoint—"

Shaina's words become muffled in my head.

Because I recognize the woman standing in front of her.

It's Worth's ex-wife, Vanessa.

My lungs lock up. Instinct tells me to duck behind my monitor and disappear before she sees me.

But Vanessa doesn't even glance my way. She storms straight through reception like she owns the place. Shaina throws her arms in the air, but doesn't dare follow her.

The glass walls of Worth's office don't hide much. I can't hear every word, though I don't need to. His expression says it all.

Worth looks livid. Jaw tight. Shoulders stiff. His voice rising and falling in muffled waves.

I hug my arms to my chest, torn between running as far away as possible or barging in to defend him. But what right do I have?

So I sit there, heart hammering, watching the storm unfold.

Vanessa doesn't back down until Henson appears, stepping into Worth's office without knocking. His presence alone seems to force her hand. They exchange heated words I can't make out, but finally, with a huff of frustration, Vanessa yanks open the glass door and stalks out.

For a split second, I think I'm safe.

Until her eyes land on me.

She freezes, and her perfectly lined lips curl into a scowl sharp enough to slice me in half. The message is clear in the venom of her glare.

Then she storms away, Henson on her tail.

My knees are shaky, but my feet move on their own, carrying me to Worth's office. I slip inside and close the door behind me.

I barely make it two steps before Shaina appears, planted firmly in front of his door.

"No," she says flatly.

I stop short. "Excuse me?"

"Mr. Miller isn't taking visitors," she replies, chin lifting. "You'll need to come back later."

"I'm not a visitor," I say, keeping my voice even. "I'm his *girlfriend.*"

She scoffs. "Yeah, sure."

I step close, lowering my voice. "Listen, Shaina. I don't know what transpired between you and Worth before, or how things ended—it's none of my business. But what you're not going to do is disrespect my relationship. So think twice before you say something you might regret."

"You don't get to just walk into his office whenever you feel like it, Mya," she retorts, standing her ground.

The use of my name feels intentional, and it's taking everything in me not to slap her audacious face.

"I'll take my chances," I spit, turning to enter Worth's office.

He's pacing. His tie is loose, jacket discarded on a chair, and his fists clench and unclench like he's one second away from exploding. On his desk sits a thick envelope, its contents spilling. Legal papers.

"She served me," he grinds out. "Court papers. She's filing for custody, like she said she would."

My chest tightens. "Oh my God, Worth…"

He drags both hands through his hair, then spins to face me, eyes blazing. "We need to speed up the marriage."

The air leaves my lungs. I knew this was coming, but hearing it—seeing the desperation in his eyes—makes the whole thing feel terrifyingly real.

Worth stalks to his desk, yanks open a drawer, and pulls out a small black box.

He flips the lid open and pushes it toward me, like it's a line item on a to-do list instead of a life-altering moment.

I stare at the ring, heat crawling up my neck. Not because it's ugly—of course it's not. It's massive, sparkling. But the way he presented it...

Wow. *So* romantic. Truly, every girl's dream.

"This is how you propose?" I'm unable to keep the bite from my voice. "Out of a desk drawer, as if you're handing me a stapler?"

Worth's jaw ticks. For a moment, I think he'll snap back, but instead he says, "Do you think I don't know how this looks? That this isn't how a man should ask a woman to marry him?" He exhales hard through his nose. "I don't have the luxury of romance right now, Mya. I have a daughter to protect. And if I have to look like an asshole to do so, then so be it."

The words hit me square in the chest, deflating my sarcasm.

Damn him for using the Brianna card right now.

My hand hovers over the ring, and I slowly lift it from the box. The diamond catches the office light, scattering it across the glass walls. For a second, I let myself imagine this is real.

I slide it onto my finger, almost tentatively; it fits perfectly. How did he know my ring size?

When I glance back at Worth, his eyes are locked on me.

I clear my throat, suddenly unsure what to do with the air between us. "Okay. So... what's next?"

He exhales, then straightens, like he's already building the plan in his head.

"We're going to Paris."

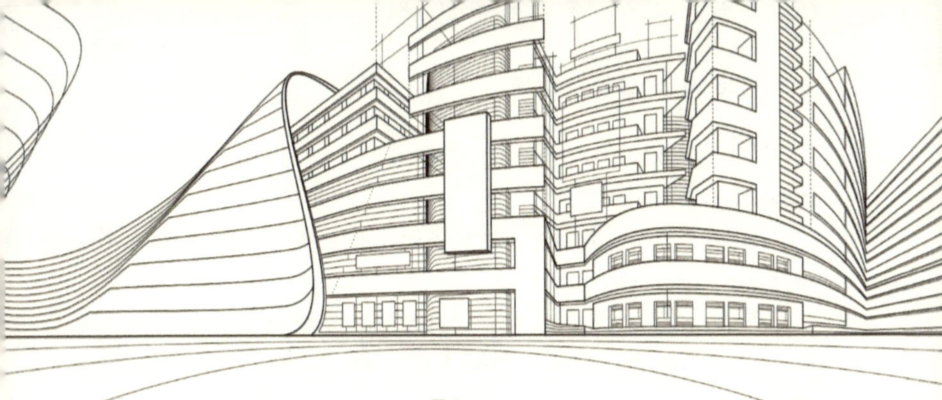

31

Worth

The words leave my mouth as calmly as if I'd just said we were going for coffee.

Mya blinks at me, mouth parting, brow furrowing. "What?"

I steeple my fingers. "Paris. The city of love. We leave Friday."

She's still staring at me like I've lost my damn mind. "I—what do you mean *we're* going to Paris?"

I can't help the smirk tugging at my lips. "Exactly what it sounds like. A weekend trip. You, me, a few staged photos. And... our wedding."

She jerks back. "Our *what?*"

I push off my desk and walk toward her, slowly. "Think about it. People know about us now. The tabloids are circling. The headlines are everywhere. If we play this like it was a spur-of-the-moment decision—two people madly in love, swept away by the magic of Paris—it sells the story. No one will question it."

Mya shakes her head, curls bouncing around her face. "No one just runs off to Paris to get married, Worth."

"They do when they're rich and in love. And that's exactly what they'll believe."

I can see the battle waging in her eyes—logic versus the reality of what we've already set into motion. "This is crazy."

"Crazy," I agree, taking her hand, my thumb brushing her knuckles, "but believable. And believable is what we need right now."

Mya finally exhales, like she's given in to a battle. "Fine. Paris it is. But right now, I need to get back to work before Seraya hunts me down."

I nod once, watching her walk out of my office with her head held high.

The second the door clicks shut, I pull my phone from my pocket.

"Dre," I say when she picks up. "Clear my schedule Friday through Monday."

There's a beat of silence. "You're taking a long weekend?"

"Not just me. Ms. Jones, too. Tell the pilot we're heading to Paris."

"France?" Dre's voice hikes up an octave. "As in... *Paris, France?*"

"Yes, Dre. The other Paris doesn't quite cut it for what I need."

Another pause. "Done. I'll adjust the schedule and inform the pilot."

I hang up and lean back in my chair, texting the boys.

Going to Paris on Friday.

HENSON:

Thanks for the invite, bro.

I shake my head, smiling.

I actually need one of you to tag along.

GRIFFIN:

What for?

I drag a hand down my jaw, knowing this is going to land like a damn bomb.

My wedding.

HENSON:

What?

GRIFFIN:

???

Mya and I decided to elope in Paris, but I need a witness. Who's free?

HENSON:

Damnit. I could've gone for a good croissant this weekend, but no can do. I promised Amira I'd help her with an event.

I smirk. My brother, turning down Paris for a woman. He's been hooked ever since the holidays in Nantucket. I've never seen him like this, not even with his ex. Amira is an event planner, and after pulling off our family's New Year's Eve party flawlessly, she caught the attention of half the city's elite. Her calendar has been packed with high-profile events ever since. They make a good match. He's smitten.

Griff?

There's a long pause before his reply.

GRIFFIN:

What am I supposed to do with my boy,
Worth?

Maggie can watch Sylas and Brianna for the
weekend.

GRIFFIN:

Sigh Fine.

I push off my desk and pace to the window. I switch threads and fire off a message to Mya.

You'll need a witness.

MYA:

Uhhh, okay. I'll see if my sister can take the
weekend off. This is pretty last minute,
after all.

I smirk, already typing.

I'm sure she won't mind an all-expenses paid
trip to Paris.

MYA:

Don't be such a rich douche.

I chuckle under my breath.

You like it.

MYA:

I don't like anything about you, Mr. Miller.

Liar.

I'VE CLOSED BILLION-DOLLAR DEALS WITHOUT BLINKING, but telling my daughter I'm getting married feels like walking a tightrope blindfolded.

Brianna's curled up on the couch, legs tucked under her, half-watching some baking competition. She's growing up so fast, but right now she still looks like my little girl: barefoot, hair in a messy bun, and focused on frosting techniques like it's life or death.

I clear my throat. "Piglet."

She hums in response, eyes still on the screen.

"Can I talk to you for a second?"

That gets her attention. She pauses the TV and turns to me, brows raised. "You sound serious."

"I am." I take a breath, my palms damp against my jeans. "It's about Mya."

"Okay... what about her?"

"I'm going to marry her."

The words hang there between us for a few moments.

Brianna blinks. "Wait... like, *marry* marry?"

"Yeah. In Paris."

Her jaw drops slightly. "Wow. That's... fast."

I nod, a faint smile tugging at my lips. "It is. But sometimes when you know, you know."

She tilts her head, studying me with a gaze that's too perceptive for her age. "Do you?"

I look down at my hands, pretending to brush invisible lint from my jeans. "I do. I know Mya is good for us. She makes things easier, and I haven't felt that in a long time."

My gut twists, because it's a lie, or at least, it's supposed to be.

Brianna is quiet for a moment, as if turning the words over in her mind. "I like her," she finally admits. "She's nice, and she actually listens to me."

"That's good to hear."

"But..." Bri hesitates, frowning slightly. "Be careful, Dad. I don't want you to get hurt again."

"Hey." I reach over and take her hand. "I appreciate that, Piglet, but I promise, I know what I'm doing. I just need you to trust me."

She squeezes my hand back, her eyes softer now. "I do trust you, Dad. If you're happy, then I'm happy."

I pull my daughter into my arms, pressing a kiss to the top of her head. "You have no idea how much that means to me."

She groans against my shoulder. "Okay, okay, you're crushing me."

I laugh, releasing her. "You'll live."

Brianna rolls her eyes but smiles. "I just hope she says yes."

I let out a soft laugh. "Yeah. Me too." I ruffle her hair and add, "You won't be upset about not being there, right?"

"Not as long as you promise to have another party here. Soon."

I grin. "Deal."

The word barely leaves my mouth before guilt starts to eat at me. Because there won't be another party. The marriage won't last long enough for a promise like that to mean anything.

Brianna beams, leaning into my side, already picturing something I know I won't be able to give her.

The worst part about all this is letting her believe in a future that I'm already planning on taking away.

But I convince myself that it's the best thing to do in order to protect her.

I STAND IN THE FOYER, MY BAG SLUNG OVER MY SHOULDER, the car waiting outside.

"I'll call you when we land, Piglet."

"Okay. Be safe." Her arms squeeze me tight, and when she lets go, Maggie steps forward to hug me too.

"Don't worry about a thing here," she assures. "We'll be fine."

I nod, but worry is second nature to me when it comes to my daughter, especially now. I give Bri one last look before I step out the door.

Right then, a car pulls up to the house. It's Griffin.

As soon as he exits the vehicle with Sylas in tow, he fixes me with an unimpressed glare.

"What?" I ask.

Griffin ignores my question at first, ushering his son inside. He pulls Sylas into a quick hug, presses a kiss to his hair, and promises to call as soon as he lands. Only then does he turn back to me. Once the door is shut, he finally responds.

"Don't 'what' me. We need to talk about this Paris bullshit."

I rub a hand over my jaw. "Which part?"

"The part where your girl's sister is tagging along."

I arch a brow. "Since when do you give a damn?"

Griffin snaps, "Since Sylas won't shut up about her."

I bite back a smirk. I've known my best friend my whole life. And if I've ever seen him off his game, it's now. "Tiana does a good job with him. Admit it."

Silence. Then, through gritted teeth, "That's not the point."

But it *is*. Because for a man who's built his reputation on not giving a damn about women, Griffin seems rattled. And that makes me suspicious.

"You sound pissed. You sure this isn't about something else?"

His growl is answer enough, and I exhale a laugh through my nose. Paris is already complicated, and we haven't even left yet.

When we all arrive on the private tarmac, the driver opens my door, and the cool wind cuts across my face.

Mya emerges from another car, clutching her bag, hair whipping around her cheeks. She looks up at me as we start walking toward the plane.

Griffin strides ahead, all long legs and bad attitude, barking something into his phone before snapping it shut. He's muttering by the time he climbs the stairs, and I know exactly why.

When I board after my future wife, Tiana is already curled into one of the wide leather seats, legs crossed, phone lifted at just the right angle to catch the cabin light.

The first thing out of Griffin's mouth is a grumble. "You've got to be kidding me."

Tiana doesn't bother looking up. She just rolls her eyes and turns her chin to catch the light better.

I bite back a laugh. *Apparently, the dramatic eye roll is a family thing.*

Griffin drops into the seat opposite her with a scowl. "You here to witness or to pose?"

Tiana turns her gaze over him, unimpressed. "Can't it be both?" She flashes a grin and goes right back to her phone.

His grunt is low, venomous. She hums to herself like she doesn't hear it.

I shake my head, amused, before guiding Mya toward the seats on the other side. "Sit here."

She arches a brow. "Why?"

"In case anyone on staff decides to gossip later." I let my hand hover at her back, not quite touching. "Better they see us together. Let them carry the right story."

Her mouth opens, as if wanting to argue, but then she sits. Our thighs brush, though neither of us moves away.

The attendant brings champagne. I take two glasses,

handing Mya one. She tries to refuse, but I press it into her hand. "Get used to it. You're about to be my wife. Paris won't be the last time you're spoiled."

Her eyes narrow, though she sips anyway, muttering something about me being insufferable. I smirk into my own glass.

Across the aisle, Griffin finally snaps, "So this is it? Drag me halfway across the world to watch you play house?"

"Not play." I swirl the champagne lazily in my glass. "Marry."

Griffin's jaw ticks and Tiana's brows lift in amusement. He shoots her a glare that only makes her grin wider.

I open my briefcase and slide a folder onto the table. "Here's the plan."

Mya blinks at me. "You actually wrote out a fake proposal presentation?"

"Optics matter," I say. My eyes trace her mouth, not the papers. "And no one questions a man who puts a ring on the woman he can't keep his hands off."

Her blush deepens.

After going through the plan a couple times, exhaustion wins and Mya leans back, shoulders softening.

"Rest," I murmur, tugging a blanket over her lap. "We've got hours to Paris."

She hesitates, then lets her head fall against my shoulder. I shift, adjusting to make her more comfortable, my fingers brushing her arm. Not for the staff. Not for show. For her.

For *me*.

PARIS GREETS US WITH SOFT GRAY SKIES AND THE FAINT shimmer of rain on cobblestones. Even after all the years of business trips here, the city still carries that air of romance and mystery and 'je ne sais quoi.' Exactly the kind of place where lies can masquerade as truth.

The car winds through narrow streets, until we pull up to the hotel I chose—one with suites that look straight out at the Eiffel Tower. The staff is already lined up at the entrance, ready to usher us inside.

I step out first, adjusting my jacket, then offer a hand to Mya. She takes it, reluctantly at first, but doesn't let go.

Griffin emerges from the car behind us, looking as sour as he did when we left. Tiana follows, phone already in hand as she takes pictures. His glare follows her every move.

Inside the lobby, I pause, issuing orders before either of them can complain. "Mya. Tiana. I'm sending you both shopping."

Tiana's brows arch above her sunglasses. "Shopping?"

"For dresses." My gaze cuts to Mya, holding hers steady. "You'll need something for tomorrow."

Her lips part, caught between shock and protest, but she doesn't get a word out before Tiana clasps her arm with sudden enthusiasm. "Wedding dresses *in Paris*? Don't mind if I do."

"You'll have a driver. Charge whatever you need to my card," I say, giving them my black Amex card.

Mya swallows, eyes widening, and I know she must be overwhelmed. Paris. Wedding dress shopping. The façade is becoming more real by the minute.

Tiana throws a quick, smug smile over her shoulder as she pulls Mya along, and the car door shuts with a snap.

By the time Griffin and I step into the penthouse suite, he looks one comment away from combusting.

I toss my jacket onto a chair, and take in the sweep of the room—the velvet furniture, the champagne chilling on ice, the glass wall framing the Eiffel Tower like a painting. Paris knows how to dress for the part.

Griffin doesn't move, just prowls to the window, jaw tight.

"So, you want to tell me what your problem is?"

He snorts. "Take a look around. You dragged me across the ocean to play witness to your fake wedding, Worth. That's problem enough."

I study him a long beat. "No. This is about Tiana."

His shoulders stiffen. "I don't know what—"

"Don't waste my time. You've been seething since we boarded the jet—hell, before we even left the house. So what is it with her?"

Griffin exhales hard, raking a hand through his hair. "You really want to know?"

"Wouldn't ask otherwise."

He turns, pacing for a few moments before blurting out, "I knew who she was before I even met her."

I blink. "How?"

"Instagram."

Confusion knots in my chest. "Instagram? You *hate* social media."

"I know," he snaps, glaring at me as if I forced the confession out with a knife. "But one night I was scrolling. Don't ask me why—I couldn't sleep—and I stumbled across her profile."

I arch a brow.

"She was... Fuck, Worth. She was captivating. I couldn't look away. So I kept watching. Her videos, her stories." He shakes his head, almost disgusted with himself. "Imagine my surprise when I show up to Willow's and find out she's Mya's *sister*. I had no fucking idea."

I lean forward, arms crossed. "Okay. What's the big deal?"

His laugh is bitter. "What's the big deal? She's a beautiful twenty-one-year-old influencer with the body of a goddess. She has no business being around me or my son. How the hell am I supposed to focus while she's parading through my life? I can't function when she's around. She's—" Griffin cuts himself off. "Forget it."

For a moment, I just stare. And then a laugh rips out of me.

Griffin's eyes narrow. "What the hell is so funny?"

"This is karma."

His scowl deepens. "Karma?"

"Yeah. For every time you mocked me about hiring Mya. For every time you called me whipped, distracted, unprofessional... Look at you." I gesture at him. "A gorgeous twenty-something smiled your way and suddenly you're spiraling."

His glare could cut glass. "It's not the same thing."

"It's *exactly* the same thing. *And* you stalked her social media." I pour myself a drink, shaking my head. "Welcome to my world, brother. Tiana got under your skin, and now you can't shake her off. "

Griffin mutters something obscene and stalks toward the second bedroom, slamming the door behind him.

I take a sip of scotch, still grinning, the Eiffel Tower glittering beyond the window. Paris is going to be fun.

LATER THAT EVENING, WHILE THE GIRLS ARE STILL roaming Parisian boutiques, Griffin and I slip away to meet one of his brothers, Adrian—who now lives in France to run his Formula 1 team—for dinner.

The driver drops us at Le Petit Lutetia, a tucked-away bistro near Saint-Germain-des-Prés.

Adrian is already seated near the back, one arm slung casually over the chair beside him. His cane is tucked neatly between the table and his seat—close enough to reach, but not on display.

"About time," he says when he notices us, a grin breaking across his face.

Griffin reaches him first, clasping his shoulder before pulling him into a careful hug. "It's good to see you, little brother."

When Adrian first lost mobility, watching him move slower, get frustrated, and go from world-class race driver to man-relearning-steps gutted all of us. But he's been working hard, and with his new physical therapist (the one he's totally, absolutely, completely *not* in love with), he's damn near himself again. He still needs a cane and a wheelchair sometimes, but his swagger is back.

Once we're settled, the waiter takes our orders, setting down our drinks when my phone vibrates on the table.

I pick up. "Worth Miller."

"Good evening, sir. Apologies for the interruption, but we need authorization before processing some charges to your Black Card."

I lean back in my chair, already shaking my head. "Go on."

"First, Dior for €500,000."

My brows tick upward, but I keep my face neutral.

Half a million at Dior. Jesus, Mya.

"Second, Cartier for €325,000."

I drag a hand across my mouth, forcing my expression to stay flat.

"And lastly, a private opera singer and an entire string quartet booked for tomorrow evening. €150,000."

My eyes widen, and I stifle a laugh. *Is Mya serious? Why stop at the clothes and jewels when you can bring half the Paris Philharmonic along too?*

I exhale slowly through my nose. "Run it."

"Yes, sir. "

The line disconnects.

"What was that?" Griffin asks.

I take a sip of wine, unbothered. "Just my fiancée putting my Black Card to use."

Adrian barks out a laugh. "What'd she do, buy out all of Paris?"

"Something like that."

I grab my phone again.

> A million euros in one shopping trip. Really, Mya?

I spear a bite of sea bass.

MYA:

> You said it yourself that I should get used to being spoiled.

A smirk tugs at my mouth. I take another sip of wine to hide it.

> You're right. If that's the case, try harder next time.

MYA:

> I wasn't trying anything. I just couldn't pass up on the diamonds. They were so shiny!

I shift in my chair, leg bouncing under the tablecloth, picturing her in that dress and those jewels.

> Well, I'm not sure what'll shine brighter tomorrow… those diamonds, or your face when you'll be screaming my name after I take you out of them.

I set the phone down just long enough to cut my fish. Griffin glances up at me, brow furrowing. I give him nothing. Inside, I'm burning, every thought hijacked by Mya. That brat lives to get under my skin.

The screen lights up again.

MYA:

...

I huff a quiet laugh, covering it with a cough.

Cat got your tongue?

MYA:

We are not having sex, Worth.

A newly-married couple should consummate their marriage, Mya.

MYA:

Jesus. Do you hear yourself?

I think you want it as much as I do, wife.

MYA:

I'm not your wife yet. And you sound like those mafia men I read about.

I smirk to myself.

Maybe they're onto something.

MYA:

Too bad I'm not a virgin.

A sudden stab of jealousy cuts through me, uninvited. My grip on my fork tightens.

If I could erase all the men you've been with before, I would.

MYA:

Erase??? You're unhinged, Mr. Miller.

I fucking love it when she calls me that. My smile darkens.

Guilty, when it comes to you.

MYA:

Stop giving me mixed signals. This marriage
is fake.

Whatever you say, Mrs. Miller.

MYA:

It's Ms. Jones.

Not for much longer.

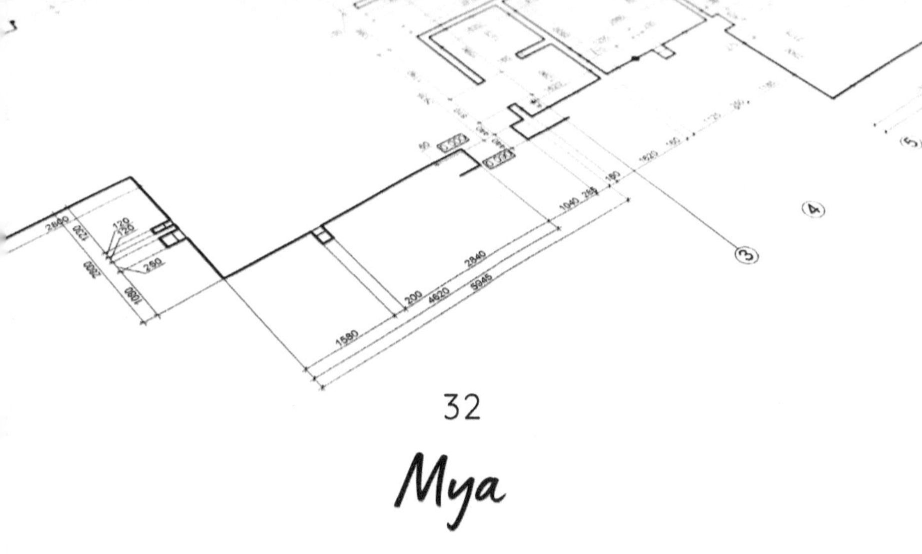

32

Mya

My phone screen goes dark, but the last message burns hotter than the champagne in my veins.

My insides twist, heat curling low in my belly. Worth is so damn possessive, so bossy—and the worst part is, I kind of love it. He talks like I already belong to him, like this all isn't just for show. Even if it's fake and temporary, tomorrow, I'll be his *wife*. The word feels dangerous on my tongue, and my chest tightens at the thought of being tethered to him in any way.

"Okay, spill," Tiana says, sliding a stack of shopping bags across the seat of the car. "What did Worth say?"

I bite down a smile and shrug, playing it cool. "He approved everything. Our plan to piss him off didn't work."

Tiana smirks. "It didn't work because he's down bad."

"He is *not* down bad. He's just playing the part."

Her grin widens. "Uh huh. Sure. 'Playing the part' while dropping a million euros on you without blinking."

I roll my eyes, but my cheeks heat. "You're delusional."

"You're in denial."

I open my mouth to argue, but my sister waves me off, steering the conversation elsewhere. "Anyway, enough about your broody billionaire. Let's talk about me."

I perk up, curious. "Right. Your time as Sylas's new nanny. How is it?"

Her expression softens, surprising me. "It's good. Honestly. I love Sylas. He's such a good kid. Smart, sweet, funny. He's got this way of looking at you like you're the most important person in the room. Kind of breaks your heart, in the best way."

I smile at that.

"But Griffin?" She shakes her head, laughing under her breath. "He's like a volcano about to erupt every time I'm around him. One wrong look, one smart comment, and I swear he's seconds from exploding."

"Seriously?" I blink, surprised.

"Seriously, it makes no sense. I don't know what his deal is, but it's entertaining as hell, so I keep egging him on." Her grin is wicked. "He's so grumpy, it's like a challenge."

I laugh. "That's wild. He's the complete opposite with me at work."

Tiana tilts her head. "I guess I bring out his inner monster."

I shake my head, still laughing.

The Parisian night air is cool against my overheated skin through the window, and for a minute, I stare down the street in a daze.

I bought a ridiculously expensive wedding dress. One I'd sworn I wouldn't let myself want. And somehow, they're going to alter it by tomorrow.

The gown is breathtaking—*too* breathtaking for a fake elopement. It's the kind of dress I used to dream about when I was a teenager, scrolling Pinterest. The kind of dress you wear once in your life, if you're lucky. The second I saw it, I just couldn't help myself. I had to have it.

The Cartier diamonds and the opera singer and string quartet were just extras. Add-ons to push Worth's buttons. Except, judging from his texts, it didn't even work. If anything, he seemed happy that I was spending his money.

Tiana loops her arm through mine in the back seat, dragging me out of my spiraling thoughts. "Okay, Mrs. Black Card. We've shopped, we've conquered. Now it's time for dinner."

"Where?" I ask, still distracted by the vision of my dream dress.

Her grin is mischievous. "Remember that place we saw on *Emily in Paris?* The one with the glowing courtyard and the pink cocktails? I booked us a table."

"No way!"

"We're going to Café de Flore. We came all this way; it'd be a crime not to."

A smile pulls at my lips as the city blurs past us, glittering in the night. I can't decide what's more surreal: dinner at a famous bistro in Paris with my sister, or the fact that tomorrow I'll be getting married to my boss.

After a delicious and expensive dinner, the car drops us off at the hotel, and for once, I'm thankful for the quiet elevator ride up. My stomach is pleasantly full, my feet ache from traipsing around the city, and I'm more than ready to collapse into bed.

When Tiana and I step into the suite, Worth and Griffin are stretched across the modern couches in the living room, nursing tumblers of dark liquor like kings surveying their domain.

Worth looks perfectly at ease, long legs crossed, glass balanced loosely in his hand. Griffin mirrors him, at least until his eyes catch on Tiana.

The change is immediate. His shoulders go stiff, his easy

sprawl snapping rigid. His glass clinks against the table a little too hard as he puts it down.

I frown. *What is up with that?*

Tiana doesn't seem to notice, or maybe she does and just enjoys it. She tosses her hair, sauntering past him with a smile that makes his jaw tick. They both disappear into different rooms.

I turn to Worth, dropping my shopping bags onto the armchair. "Okay, so... I count three bedrooms."

He takes a lazy sip of his drink. "Correct."

"Is my stuff in Tiana's room?"

"No, in mine."

My stomach drops. "Don't tell me you expect us to sleep in the same room."

His cocky smirk is infuriating. "Of course I do."

"Worth." I cross my arms, glaring at him. "No."

"It's expected. You're my fiancée. We share a room."

I flounder for an argument, until a thought sparks. "It's bad luck to see the bride before the wedding, you know."

He doesn't even blink. "This isn't a typical wedding, Mya. And luck has nothing to do with it." He tips his glass toward me. "I expect you in my room tonight."

My jaw clenches, heat rushing to my face. "You are impossible."

"True." His eyes glitter over the rim of his glass. "But I usually get my way."

I huff, grabbing my bags and storming past him, slamming the bedroom door behind me.

The adjoining bathroom is a marble dream, and I peel off my clothes with jerky movements, my pulse racing far too fast. Steam curls around me as I twist on the shower, stepping under the hot spray.

The water beats against my skin, but it does nothing to wash away the frustration I feel about Worth's hot and cold behaviour.

Steam still clings to my skin when I step out of the bathroom, towel knotted around me. I stop dead in my tracks.

Worth is sitting in the chair tucked in the corner of the room near the loveseat, his glass of whiskey dangling from his hand, face half-hidden in the shadows. Watching me.

"Are you serious?" I snap, clutching the towel tighter. "Do you make a habit of lurking in women's bedrooms like a stalker?"

His mouth curves, that infuriatingly arrogant smirk catching in the dim light. "Only when the woman is my fiancée."

Warmth rushes to my cheeks, mostly in irritation. I march to my suitcase, snatch my pajamas, and storm back into the bathroom to change. When I reemerge, he's still there. Same chair. Same piercing stare that makes my skin prickle.

I grab a pillow off the bed and hug it to my chest. "Fine. You stay here and play sentry, I'll take the couch."

"No, you won't."

I blink. "Excuse me?"

"You'll be uncomfortable all night."

"I'll survive."

"You're not sleeping on the couch, Mya."

The air in the room feels heavy as he rises, stepping closer.

Words tangle in my throat. "I don't want to sleep next to you."

He sets the empty glass on the dresser and tilts his head slightly, the faintest crease forming between his brows.

"I'm not asking you to want it," he says evenly. "Just don't act like I'm the enemy."

"I'm not," I murmur, clutching the pillow tighter. I let out a sigh. "I just need space. That's all."

Worth moves even closer. "Funny. You didn't seem to mind my space that night after the gala."

Heat floods my cheeks. "That was different."

"Was it?" His voice dips. He takes another step closer, enough that I can smell the faint trace of whiskey and his cologne. "You can have space. Even in the same bed."

"Worth—"

He cuts me off, his eyes never leaving mine. "You'll still end up right where I want you, Mya."

"Keep talking and *you'll* be sleeping on the couch."

His mouth quirks, still infuriatingly calm. "I'm going in the shower. When I come out, you'll be in the bed, where you belong."

"Don't count on it," I snap, but my pulse is already racing.

Worth chuckles, brushing past me. "We'll see who ends up where, Kitten."

He grabs a towel and disappears into the bathroom.

The second I hear the water running, I move. I toss the pillow onto the loveseat, snatch the spare blanket from the closet, and make myself a makeshift bed on the couch. It's not exactly comfortable, but it's the principle of the matter.

I'm busy arranging the blanket when the bathroom door opens with a hiss of steam.

For a heartbeat, I forget how to breathe.

Worth's hair is wet, strands of dark and silver slicked back from his face. Water glints in his salt-and-pepper beard, dripping down the column of his throat and his chest. His broad shoulders taper to a hard stomach, abs cut deep enough to make my mouth go dry. I've felt his body pressed against mine before, but always through clothes.

His eyes narrow. "You're on the couch."

I lift my chin. "I told you I'm not sleeping in the bed."

He scowls, jaw tightening, then walks to his bag and pulls out a pair of grey sweats. Without hesitation, he turns his back to me and drops the towel.

I gasp out loud before I can stop myself.

The muscles of his back ripple as he moves, water still sliding over his skin. His ass is firm, sculpted, like it's been carved. Heat blooms low in my belly, completely against my will.

He pulls the sweats up slowly, then turns, eyes locking on me with a look of pure determination.

In three strides, he's on me, and before I can scramble away, he hauls me up like I weigh nothing and tosses me over his shoulder.

"Worth! Put me down!" I pound at his back, kicking. It's useless; he's all muscle and has an unshakable grip.

He carries me to the bed and throws me onto it like a caveman staking a claim.

"My. Bed."

I push up on my elbows, glaring. "I swear, I will end you in your sleep."

His mouth curves into a dark smile as he braces his palms on either side of me. "Make sure to suffocate me with your perfect pussy. That would be my preferred way to die."

I huff, shoving a pillow lengthwise between us, creating a makeshift wall of cotton and stubbornness. "There. Touch that barrier and you're dead."

Worth's low chuckle rumbles across the dark room. He doesn't seem fazed. Instead, he just slips into the bed, settling on his side with his back to me.

"Goodnight, Kitten," he murmurs.

WORTH

I wake up in a haze, the room still dark, the city lights a faint glow against the curtains. Heat rolls through me, clinging to my skin, making me sweat. For a second, I think it's the sheets or the liquor in my veins.

Then I realize it's Mya.

Her back is pressed flush against my chest, the barrier pillow lost somewhere at our feet.

A laugh slips out, quietly. She went through all the trouble to build a fort, and here she is glued to me anyway.

When I shift slightly, Mya stirs. Her breath deepens, hitching softly as she wiggles in her sleep, her ass pressing back against my cock. It hardens instantly.

I should roll away and put space between us. But instead, my hand finds its way to her waist, fingers skimming up her torso until they reach her breast. Her hand moves, covering mine. She moans, still asleep, murmuring something when I squeeze gently.

I tug at the neckline of her pajama top, dragging it down just far enough to bare her breasts. Her nipples pebble instantly, and I pinch one between my fingers, watching the way her body twitches in response.

My cock throbs against her, my control fraying thread by thread.

I press my nose to the curve of her neck and inhale, dragging my fingers slowly back down her body, over her stomach.

A soft sound slips from Mya's lips. "Worth…"

For a second, I think she's awake, but her lashes simply flutter. *Is my kitten dreaming about me?*

I let my fingers drift lower, between her thighs, until I find her heat under her shorts. A guttural noise slips past my throat. She's not wearing panties and she's wet, already open to me, even in her sleep. I brush her entrance before sliding a finger inside. She twitches, a whimper caught in her throat. I stroke her slowly, in and out, feeling her growing slicker, her breathing growing uneven as her body yields to me without conscious thought.

This should feel wrong. But pressed against her like this, her softness giving way to my touch, it feels inevitable. If she were awake, she'd probably remind me that we shouldn't be doing this, but her body betrays her every time.

I ease a second finger inside, stretching her. Mya lets out a broken mewl that shoots straight to my cock, already hard against her ass.

"That's my good kitten," I murmur, curling my fingers.

Her body goes rigid as she starts to wake. "Worth... what are you doing?"

"Making you come."

Mya whispers a protest, but her pelvis presses into my hand.

I quicken my pace.

"Worth..." she moans.

Harder.

"Please..."

"Please what, Kitten?" My thumb finds her clit, circling slowly. "Do you want me to stop?"

She mumbles something incoherent, then lets out another low moan.

"Please... Make me come."

A growl rumbles from my chest as I lean in, teeth grazing her earlobe. "Your wish is my command, pretty girl."

I work her until she's trembling, breath splintering, moans

rising. When I feel her cresting, I curl my fingers upward and beckon, my palm grinding against her clit.

Mya gasps, arching hard, her thighs locking around my wrist. "Yes. Fuck, I'm coming."

It's the most beautiful sight I've ever seen.

Then, as if nothing happened, her body slackens, her breathing evening out as she slips back into sleep.

I bring my fingers to my face, inhaling her scent. One I never want to forget.

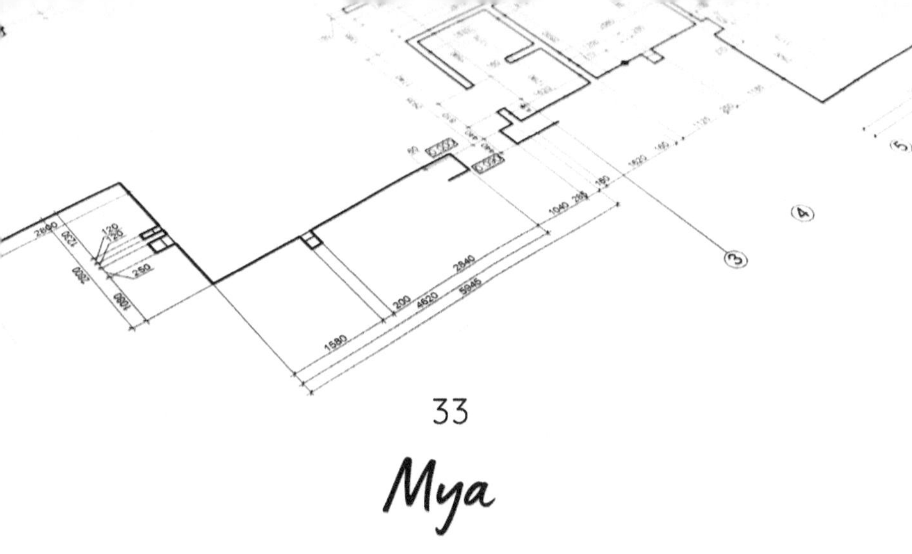

33

Mya

It's my wedding day.

The words loop in my head as sunlight spills across the penthouse suite and Tiana tugs at my hair for the third time.

"Hold still," she scolds, a brush clenched between her teeth while she pins another curl in place.

"I am still," I mutter. "You're just aggressive."

"It's not my fault you keep flinching. You need to look perfect. It has to look real."

"It's not real," I grumble, but my heart skips anyway. My stomach has been twisting itself in knots since dawn. Real or not, I'm about to walk down an aisle in Paris for my wedding. To Worth.

Tiana hums under her breath. "So... Did you tell Mom and Dad?"

I freeze. "About the wedding?"

"Yeah." She arches a brow at me in the mirror. "It'll be kind of hard to hide the whole *getting married in Paris* thing."

I let out a nervous laugh. "No, I didn't. I honestly didn't know how to bring it up without sounding completely unhinged. 'Hey, Mom, I'm marrying my boss in Paris tomorrow, but don't worry—it's just for business!'"

Tiana snorts, shaking her head. "Good point."

"I'll tell them the truth eventually." I smooth the silk of my robe over my knees. "Once we're back and things settle. I just want to be able to explain it properly, you know? Mom's going to be shocked. Devon, too. But once they hear everything, I think they'll understand."

Tiana's expression softens. "They will."

I nod, but the reassurance doesn't stop the ache building in my chest.

I stare at my reflection while Tiana works, and the woman looking back at me almost fools me, too.

When I first opened my eyes this morning, the pillow fort I built last night was a heap on the floor. I don't remember when it fell, only the heavy warmth of Worth beside me, the faint trace of his cologne still clinging to the sheets.

And Worth's fingers giving me the best orgasm I've ever had. The fact that he was touching me while I was asleep should freak me out, but when I woke to his strong hand between my thighs, his hot breath on my shoulder, and his hard cock pressing against me—I don't know what I would've done if he had stopped.

A blush creeps up my neck even now. I shouldn't like how easily he gets under my skin, how every move of his body rewires something inside mine. But I do.

Worth was already gone when I got up. No trace of him, except a folded note.

Went to the gym with Griffin. We'll get ready in the other suite so you and Tiana have privacy.

"Stop smiling like that," my sister says, snapping me out of it. "You're just supposed to be nervous, not lovestruck."

I roll my eyes, though she isn't wrong about the nerves. My palms are damp, my pulse uneven.

Tiana dusts a shimmer across my cheekbones. "Worth is going to lose his mind when he sees you."

A strange ache blooms in my chest. I look away, exhaling slowly as Paris hums beyond the windows. The dress hangs near the door, waiting. It feels too beautiful, too sincere for a pretend wedding, but it's mine now, just like this day.

It's almost time to leave, and I hear low male voices drifting in from the other side of the suite. Worth and Griffin are back. Tiana perks up instantly, abandoning the last of the makeup brushes on the vanity.

"They're here!" she whispers, eyes sparkling with excitement. "Okay, don't move. I'm going to wait outside so I can record Worth's face when he sees you."

Before I can protest, she's gone, heels clicking down the hall, and I'm left alone in the bedroom with my racing pulse.

For some reason, this part—the reveal—feels like the most nerve-racking one of the entire day. Even more than the ceremony. *What if he thinks the dress is too much? What if he doesn't like what he sees?*

I glance at my reflection one last time, reminding myself I shouldn't care—that it's not real.

The gown hugs me perfectly. I lift the Cartier earrings from their velvet box and fasten them through my lobes, then adjust the matching necklace until it sits neatly at my collarbone. My fingers smooth over the front of my dress again, pressing down invisible creases I've already fixed many times.

My stomach does a slow, traitorous flip as I finally step into the hallway.

When I round the corner, there's a shift in the air. Tiana's already got tears in her eyes, clutching her phone, while Griffin lets out a low whistle.

"Wow, Jones," he says, shaking his head with an impressed grin.

My sister lifts her phone to record. "Do a little twirl, I need this for posterity."

Griffin groans. "She's not a debutante, Tiana."

But I can't help laughing, spinning just enough for the dress to flare around my legs.

And when I steady myself again, my eyes finally find Worth.

He hasn't said a word, though the look on his face says everything. It makes my breath catch.

He swallows hard, throat flexing, then takes a few slow, hesitant steps toward me. I'm aware of Tiana sniffling somewhere off to the side, Griffin muttering something I can't make out, but all I can see is *him*.

When Worth stops in front of me, his fingers find mine. He leans in close, his breath brushing my ear, voice a low rasp.

"You look devastatingly beautiful, Kitten. Like every dream I didn't know I had."

The words steal the air from my lungs. Worth Miller doesn't say things like that.

I can't find anything to say back. All I can do is look at him —really look—and I realize that for once, there's no mask.

He lifts my hand to press a kiss to my knuckles. His mouth lingers there a second too long, as if memorizing the feel of my skin. My cheeks burn, and I can't stop the smile that tugs at my lips. For the first time today, I forget that any of this is supposed to be pretend.

Finally on our way, I watch the city from the window, silently. To me, the world feels suspended, like it knows what's about to happen.

When we stop, I blink up at the small chapel tucked at the corner of a cobblestone square. It's nothing extravagant—old limestone walls, ivy curling up its sides, and a single bell tower rising above it. The heavy wooden doors creak as Griffin pushes them open, revealing rows of worn pews and sunlight spilling through stained glass in shades of gold and rose.

It's quiet inside. Sacred, in a way that makes my skin prickle.

Worth offers me a hand to help me step over the threshold. I take it, but I let go the second we're inside.

The officiant, a small man with kind eyes and a French accent, waits near the front. "Monsieur Miller, Mademoiselle Jones. Everything is ready."

Tiana squeezes my hand before taking her place beside Griffin, who looks far too grumpy for a best man. Worth stands beside me, tall and composed in his black suit.

I shouldn't stare, but I do.

It's not just how handsome he looks. It's how he makes me *feel*.

Safe. Seen. Alive in a way that's both thrilling and terrifying.

And it hits me all at once how unfair this is. Because if things had been different, if this wasn't all for show, maybe we could've made it here for real. Maybe I wouldn't be standing beside him *pretending*.

The thought aches, like something pulled too tight in my chest, and I force my gaze back to the officiant before it can swallow me whole.

The words wash over me, blurring together, muffled beneath the rapid beats of my heart. My dress feels too heavy, my pulse too loud.

When the officiant turns to Worth and says, "Do you, Worth Miller, take this woman to be your lawfully wedded wife?" Worth's answer is immediate. "I do."

I swallow, my mouth suddenly dry.

"And do you, Mya Jones, take this man to be your lawfully wedded husband?"

There's a heartbeat of silence. Then I lift my chin, steadying my voice. "I do."

The officiant nods, smiling. "By the power vested in me, I now pronounce you husband and wife."

Worth reaches for my hand again, his thumb brushing over my knuckles, and the touch sends a tremor through me. The moment our eyes meet, he leans in and kisses me.

It's soft, brief, almost chaste, yet it still leaves me breathless. When he pulls back, I force a small smile, because that's what a new bride would do.

He keeps hold of my hand, and I somehow can't tell where the act ends and the truth begins.

And that's when it hits me. I think I'm falling for my fake husband.

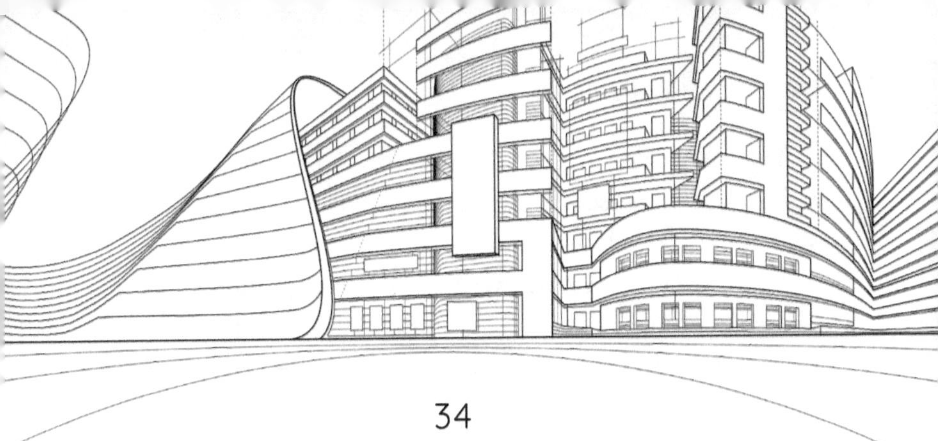

34

Worth

I'm married.

Again.

And it's to the most beautiful woman I've ever laid eyes on.

Mya is sitting beside me now, her flawless skin gleaming under the restaurant's candlelight, the silk of her dress catching every shimmer in the room. Her lips curve into a smile as she listens to Tiana, completely unaware of how undone she makes me just by existing.

My wife.

The words don't feel real. Mya might've married me out of obligation, to help me save face, but that doesn't change the fact that she wears my ring now. That she signed my name beside hers. That she's mine in ways I can't quite define.

We share a last name. Soon, we'll share my home.

And maybe, if the universe ever stops toying with me, we could even share more.

I glance around the private dining room. Half the restaurant is closed off for us—a ridiculous display of wealth and indulgence, if I say so myself. Still, I went through with it, because Mya deserves it. And we need privacy. Anyway, it worked out, because she hired a damn opera singer to entertain the four of us for the evening.

A string quartet plays softly in the background while the opera singer takes a break before the next piece. It's excessive, over-the-top, and entirely *Mya,* to try and get a reaction out of me.

I'm slouched casually in my seat, sipping from my glass, as if the night means nothing. But deep down, I care *too* much.

Dinner passes in waves of laughter, wine, and conversation. It should feel like any other night, except it doesn't. Not when Mya is close enough that her perfume teases me every time she moves. Not when I can feel the warmth of her thigh through the layers of fabric between us.

She laughs at something Griffin says. I look at her, and all I can think about is the faint tremor in her breath when I touched her last night. The way her body fit so perfectly against mine, like it's meant to.

I drag in a breath and rake a hand through my hair, trying to ignore the heat crawling under my skin.

"Worth!"

Griffin's deep voice pulls me back. He's watching me with a knowing look in his eyes that makes me want to wipe it off his face.

"You good, man?" His eyebrows are raised. "You've been staring into the void for a solid minute."

I blink. "Just thinking," I mutter, clearing my throat.

"About?"

"Business," I lie easily, lifting my glass.

After dinner, we make our way back to the penthouse suite. Mya's quiet beside me, her hands folded neatly in her lap, her eyes trained outside the window.

When we reach the hotel, Griffin and Tiana barely say a

word and just exchange quick goodnights and disappear into their rooms.

That leaves the two of us standing in the living room, alone.

Mya starts down the hallway, her steps hesitant. I follow, watching the way her shoulders tense with every move closer to our door.

I move up behind her, close enough that my breath stirs a strand of hair near her ear.

"Are you nervous?" I murmur.

She doesn't answer, but I see goosebumps rise along her bare arms. Her breathing stutters, and I have to resist the urge to smile.

When we reach the door, I scoop her up in one motion.

"Worth!" she yelps, clutching at my shoulders. "What are you doing?"

"Carrying my wife to bed," I say simply.

Mya squirms, but she doesn't tell me to stop.

I walk over the threshold and set her down on the edge of the bed. "Stay there and don't move."

Her brows knit. "What are you—"

"Just wait."

I step into the walk-in closet, unzip my suitcase, and pull out a neatly-wrapped package. When I return, Mya's still sitting where I left her, eyes wide with curiosity.

"Here."

She looks between me and the gift. "What is this?"

"Open it and see."

Mya's fingers work carefully at the paper, unfolding it layer by layer until the album cover appears. *Queen – A Night at the Opera.*

Her mouth parts in shock. When she removes the record, she sees it's signed by the entire band. "No. No way. Worth... How did you even get this? It's impossible to find."

I shrug. "Had an old friend track it down. Turns out it was being auctioned."

Her eyes widen. "*Auctioned?* How much did you pay for it?"

I tilt my head, considering how she'll react. "A hundred."

She blinks. "Dollars?"

"Thousand, Mya."

"You're joking."

I meet her gaze, dead serious. "I don't joke about Freddie Mercury."

"Worth!" she gasps, clutching the record to her chest. "Take it back. That's too much. I can't accept this."

I shake my head, stepping closer until I'm standing in front of her. "I can't. That's not how auctions work. And I want you to have it."

Mya looks up at me, eyes shining. "Why?"

"Because you said you wanted it."

"So?" Her voice cracks, somewhere between a laugh and a plea. "You don't have to buy me stuff, Worth."

I shrug again, but my voice is softer this time. "Maybe I like giving you things."

"You really shouldn't."

"Probably not. But I did anyway."

She just looks at me, like she's trying to convince herself this means nothing.

And I let her, because if she realized how much it actually means, I'm not sure either of us could pretend anymore.

Mya runs her fingers lightly over the sleeve of the record, as if afraid it might disappear.

"Thank you," she whispers, staring at it like it's the most precious thing she owns, like the designer dress she's wearing and the diamonds at her throat don't even register.

"My dad would freak if he saw this." A tiny smile tugs at her lips. "He's probably dancing in his grave right now."

Something tender twists in my chest. "I hope it makes you feel closer to him when you listen to it," I murmur.

She looks up again, and for a moment, the world goes quiet.

I shrug off my tux jacket, draping it over the armchair. Then I tug loose the bow tie at my throat, the silk slipping through my fingers before I undo the top buttons of my collar. When I turn back, she's still sitting there, unsure what to do next. I reach out and gently take the vinyl from her hands, setting it on the nightstand beside the bed.

"Come here," I say quietly.

When Mya hesitates, I lift her by the hand until she's standing in front of me, and I turn her around.

My fingers find the first button at the back of her dress. The silence between us grows heavier with each one that slips free. Only the sound of fabric and unsteady breathing fills the room.

I shouldn't want her this fiercely. As much as I keep telling myself that I'm closed off to feelings, every inch of her tests my control.

When the last button loosens, the gown slips off her shoulders and slides soundlessly to the floor. Her arms twitch, as if she's unsure whether to cover herself or let me look.

"Mya," I whisper. It's half prayer, half warning.

She turns slowly to face me, her head tilting up, breaths shallow. I let my hands linger at her waist, fighting the urge to pull her closer.

"You should know, I'm trying very hard to be a gentleman right now."

Her lips curve. "Then you're doing a terrible job."

I laugh. "You're such a brat, you know?" I step closer and let my hands roam down her body, past the curves of her breasts, the soft skin on her stomach.

"Tell me you don't want this."

When I reach her waist, I guide her gently back onto the bed, drawing her toward the edge of the mattress, and part her legs. Mya lets out a breath that trembles through the quiet.

"Mya, tell me you don't want this, and I'll stop."

I lower myself to my knees before her, hands braced on either side of her thighs. And I wait.

"I want this, don't stop," she breathes out and relief floods me as I let out a rough exhale.

For a moment, I admire what's mine, what I can't seem to get enough of. The sight of her like this, flushed and waiting, makes my cock stand at attention. Neither of us mentions that we shouldn't be doing this, that it's all pretend, that it'll hurt more when it's over. Because in this moment, it's *real*.

I slip my hand under her thong, finding her wet heat. Mya arches her back and lets out a small moan, squirming beneath my touch. She's so warm and ready for me, and I can't help the smugness I feel at being the one to make her writhe for me.

"Ready to beg already, Kitten?"

Her response is nothing more than a shiver.

The pad of my thumb circles her clit and she lets out a big exhale.

That's when I give in, leaning closer, tasting her with hunger, taking my time until she's shaking.

I suck and lick Mya's clit, humming from pure ecstasy as I get drunk on her taste.

Every sound she makes shreds what's left of my control. It's chaos disguised as pleasure. Each time I touch her, I lose myself in her completely.

It's *sick*.

"You're even more irresistible as Mrs. Miller." I ease two digits inside her pussy, pulling my mouth away to watch her come undone.

"God, Worth," she breathes, and pride coils low in my chest, possession igniting inside me.

I meet her dazed eyes. "I'm the only man who can touch you like this. From now on, this pussy belongs to *me*. You are *my* wife. You wear *my* ring. You share *my* name. You sleep in *my* bed. And whenever you start to forget that, remember the way you feel when *I* make you come."

She lifts her chin, meeting my gaze head-on despite the tremor in her voice. "Those things might be yours now, Mr. Miller. But my heart still belongs to me."

I don't dignify her comment with a response—because she's right. And I don't want to admit that some selfish part of me *does* want to claim that too. Even though what's left of my heart isn't something I can give.

So instead, I let my thoughts drown in her, focusing on every breath and tremor that gives her away. I savor each reaction until her body tenses beneath my hands.

"Fuck, *yes*," Mya screams as she climaxes hard on my tongue.

Making my wife come with my mouth has officially become my favourite pastime.

When Mya's breathing steadies, I rise slowly, straightening from where I'd been kneeling. My pulse is still hammering, my skin hot. I start to undo the buttons of my shirt, one by one, until the fabric slides from my shoulders.

Mya doesn't look away. Her eyes follow my every movement, dazed, lips parted like she's forgotten how to breathe.

"I want to fuck you now, Mya. Will you let me?"

For the first time, I see no hesitation in her eyes. She nods slowly.

"Get on your hands and knees, Kitten."

She obeys.

Her delectable ass is now on display for me.

"I can't wait to make this mine, too," I say, rubbing her ass cheek with my palm.

She squirms at the touch, but settles into it quickly, as I rub up from her entrance to the tight hole.

"But tonight, I'm going to fuck your perfect cunt, wife, and you're going to take every single inch."

I pull myself out of my briefs. I'm so hard, it aches. I need to feel the inside of Mya right now.

I let the tip glide over Mya's clit, teasing her and myself as I get her ready to accept my cock. She moans and writhes.

Just as I'm about to slide in, my phone starts vibrating on the nightstand. I ignore it.

Mya wiggles her ass, begging me to get inside. "Please, Worth."

I doubt I'll ever get tired of hearing her plead for my cock.

"Say it again."

With a frustrated sigh, she repeats. "Please, Worth."

"Please what?"

"*Fuck* me." The attitude is clear in her voice.

I growl, grabbing my length and slapping her on the clit with it. She yelps.

My phone begins vibrating again. *For God's sake.* Who could be calling me right now, when I'm about to fuck my wife for the first time? I ignore it again. Mya doesn't even notice the sound, too entranced in my teasing to care.

She's so wet, her arousal is leaking down her thighs. The vision is to fucking die for.

"Please, Worth. Fuck me. Please."

"That's more like it, Kitten."

I start pushing inside her as my phone buzzes with a call for the third time.

I growl out loud. "What the fuck?"

Mya, still breathless, finally notices the ringing. "Maybe important."

Reluctantly, I push off the bed, leaving her on her hands and knees as I grab my phone off the nightstand.

It's Brianna.

Fuck.

Fuck, fuck, fuck.

I answer immediately, my pulse slamming through my chest. "Brianna, sweetheart. Is everything okay?"

Her voice trembles. "Mom came by the house. She just left."

I freeze. "What do you mean she came by?"

"She just showed up, knocked on the door, and demanded to see me. Maggie wouldn't let her in."

My heart threatens to claw its way out of my chest. "Put Maggie on the phone."

There's a faint rustle, then Maggie's steady voice comes through. "Hi, Worth. Don't worry, I sent her off."

"How dare she show up unannounced," I snap, pacing the room. "How's Brianna?"

"She's fine. A little shaken, but you know your daughter—she's stronger than we think."

I drag a hand over my face, anger and guilt churning in my gut. I should've been there. I *promised* I'd protect her.

Mya approaches quietly, her hand coming to rest on my back. The slow motion of her fingers calms me instantly, pulling me back from the edge.

"Let me talk to Brianna again," I manage.

There's a pause before I hear her small voice. "Hi, Dad."

"I'm coming home, Piglet. I'm so sorry that happened and I wasn't there."

"Don't worry, Dad," she sighs. "I'll be fine. Please don't ruin your plans for me."

"The only thing I care about is you, Bri," I tell her firmly. "I'm coming home."

When we hang up, I'm already reaching for my suitcase, pulling on the first pair of pants that I find.

Mya's watching me, concerned. "What happened?"

I tell her everything, the anger that hasn't left my chest since I heard Brianna's voice comes roaring back.

"We should leave right now, then," she says.

I nod, dialing my pilot. "We're leaving within the hour."

Mya disappears down the hall to wake Griffin and Tiana while I wait for the call to connect. My reflection stares back at me from the dark window.

This night was supposed to end with my wife in my arms. Instead, it ends with the reminder of the one person who still holds the power to ruin my happiness and take my daughter away.

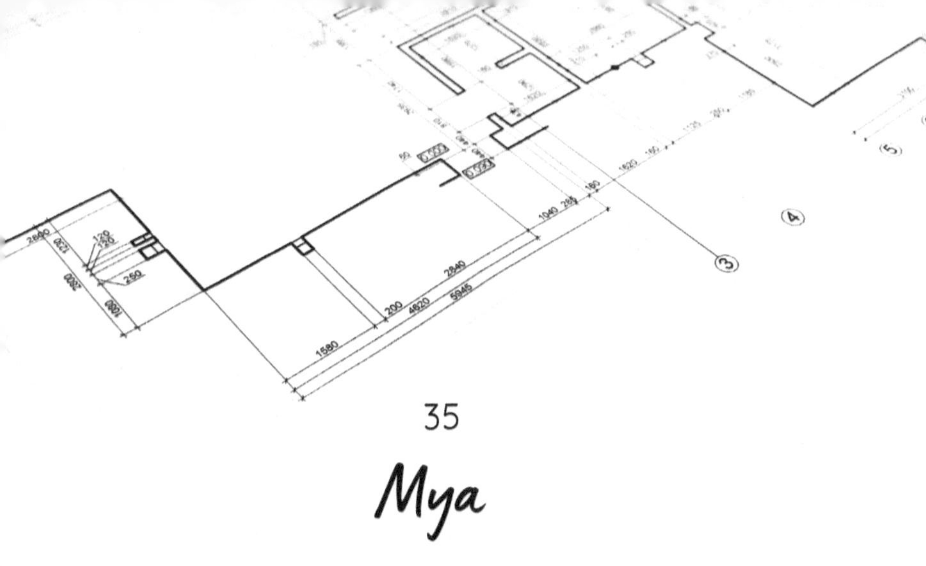

35

Mya

My mind is still spinning from what Worth just told me. His ex-wife showed up at his house, and I can tell he's already blaming himself for not being there, for not protecting Brianna the way he thinks he should've. The guilt was written all over his face.

And now we're packing up to leave Paris barely a few hours after saying *I do.*

I feel like I'm running on fumes. My legs are shaky, breath uneven, skin hot. If those calls hadn't come through when they did, I would've let Worth do whatever he wanted to me, no hesitation; he had me completely entranced. His voice, his hands, the way he said my name—it was like my body forgot everything but him.

Now that the spell is broken, reality slams back twice as hard. It was a bad idea. *A really bad idea.*

I might be reckless enough to let Worth kiss me, to lose myself when his mouth is on me, but anything more than that is asking for trouble I can't come back from.

I shove my phone into my pocket and hurry out of the

bedroom. The hallway is dim and quiet until I spot movement a few doors down.

Tiana is tiptoeing out of Griffin's room like a cat burglar, hair tousled, eyes wide. She freezes the moment she sees me.

"Uh..." I blink, stopping mid-step. "Hello?"

Tiana awkwardly laughs. "I was just... uh... checking to see if Sylas was okay; I overheard Griffin talking to him on the phone."

Her tone is too chipper and she looks *way* too guilty.

I narrow my eyes. "How did you even know he was on the phone?"

Tiana hesitates, eyes darting to anywhere but me.

"You would've had to be standing at his door to hear that," I add slowly. And then it clicks. "Were you eavesdropping?"

She exhales, caught, looking relieved. "Fine, you got me."

I cross my arms, fighting a grin.

"I went to get some water and heard a noise coming from his room, so I may or may not have put my ear to the door."

A laugh bubbles up before I can stop it. "You *may or may not have?*"

She glares. "Don't start. My phone slipped out of my hand, and he heard it and opened the door so..."

I can't help the chuckle that slips out.

"Whatever you say, TJ," I say, brushing past her toward Griffin's door. "Go pack. We're leaving in less than an hour."

"What? Why?"

"Worth's ex showed up at his house. Brianna's fine, but we're heading back home now."

I knock on Griffin's door. "Rise and shine, Mr. Hayes. Family emergency. Pack your things."

We arrive at the private hangar in record time. No one says much. All you can hear are the sounds of rolling luggage, murmured instructions from the staff, and Worth's clipped responses.

He didn't look at me once on the drive there. Didn't speak. He just stared down at his phone, scrolling, checking, refreshing, as if sheer willpower could keep Brianna safe through a screen. Every muscle in his body was coiled tight, like he was ready to spring into action but had nowhere to go.

By the time we board the jet, the weight of it all sits thick in the air. Griffin and Tiana take seats across from us, speaking quietly. I settle beside Worth, who's still silent, somewhere far away inside his head.

When the plane begins to taxi down the runway and my heartrate picks up, he reaches for me. His hand finds mine, his thumb brushing over my knuckles, like he's done it a thousand times before.

My heart leaps, but this time, it's not from the plane.

Even now, while he's fighting some invisible war behind those stormy eyes, he still remembers I hate flying.

And that's what messes me up the most.

The attraction is undeniable—has been since the start—but it's moments like this that make everything harder to compartmentalize. Because for every cold stare, every clipped word, there's this version of him who's gentle, thoughtful, and protective in ways he probably doesn't even realize.

It's as if he can't decide which side of himself he wants to be when he's around me: the guarded CEO who keeps the world at arm's length, or the man whose touch already feels like coming home.

I balance the phone between my ear and shoulder while wrestling an armful of clothes into a suitcase that's embarrassingly too small for my life.

"Mom," I say for the third time. "Please breathe."

There's a beat of silence on the line. In the background, I can hear the distant hush of waves and the faint cry of gulls—sounds that tell me she's probably standing on the balcony of their retirement rental in Florida, the ocean air doing absolutely nothing to calm her down.

"I *am* breathing!" my mother replies, except she absolutely is not. "I'm just... processing. Mya, you got *married*. In Paris. *Without telling us*. That's not like you. You told us you were seeing your boss a few weeks ago. Are you—are you okay?"

My stomach twists out of guilt for blindsiding her like this.

"I'm okay," I say softly. "I promise."

There's a shuffle and then a deeper voice joins in. "Mya?"

"Hi, Devon," I exhale, dropping a handful of folded shirts into the open box on my coffee table.

"Did he pressure you?" he asks immediately. "Was this forced? Was there a prenup? Your mother is pacing a hole in the carpet and I—"

"I wasn't coerced," I cut in gently. "No one forced me. Nothing bad happened. Yes, we have a prenup. No, I'm not in danger or being manipulated or secretly blinking SOS through the phone."

My mom lets out a strangled half-laugh that still sounds suspiciously like panic. "Well, excuse us for being alarmed. Our daughter disappeared to Paris with her billionaire boss and came back with a *husband*. That's not exactly a normal life progression, sweetheart."

I sit back on my heels and glance around my apartment.

"Mom, I'm okay."

"Why didn't you tell us it was this serious?" she demands,

gentler now. "We didn't even get to know him, be mad about him properly, interrogate him at the dinner table, threaten him like normal parents."

A puff of laughter slips out of me. "Trust me, Worth would probably survive the interrogation."

Devon clears his throat. "Still wouldn't mind having my turn."

I tape a box shut. "You'll get it. I promise."

There's another pause, as if they're both trying to read between the lines.

Mom's voice softens. "Are you happy?"

I look at the suitcase.

"Yes," I admit. "It's... complicated. But I don't regret it."

My step-father exhales into the phone. "Okay. That's something we can live with."

I push myself to my feet and carry the suitcase toward the door, then stop and rest my hand against the frame. My throat tightens unexpectedly.

"You're moving today?" Mom asks.

"Yeah. I'm packing now." I glance around again.

"So," Devon says, "what's happening with your apartment?"

"I'm keeping it."

Both of them say at once, "Why?"

I laugh, because I knew this was coming. "It just makes sense. For now. I worked hard for it, so I'm not ready to let it go."

"But you're married," Mom says, confusion threading with concern. "You have a home with your husband. Why would you need this place?"

"It's... insurance," I say instead. "A safety net. Just something that still belongs entirely to me."

Devon speaks gently. "Okay, that's reason enough."

My parents are quiet for a moment.

Then, Devon adds, "And Brianna? You mentioned his little girl."

A smile rises immediately. "She's everything. Smart. Funny. She already has me wrapped around her little finger."

Mom lets out a happy sigh. "You sound fond of her."

"I am."

"We trust you, MJ. We just love you and want to make sure you're not making a mistake."

My throat tightens. "I know," I whisper. "I love you too."

When I finally hang up, the apartment feels impossibly quiet.

One chapter closing.

Another one opening right beneath my feet.

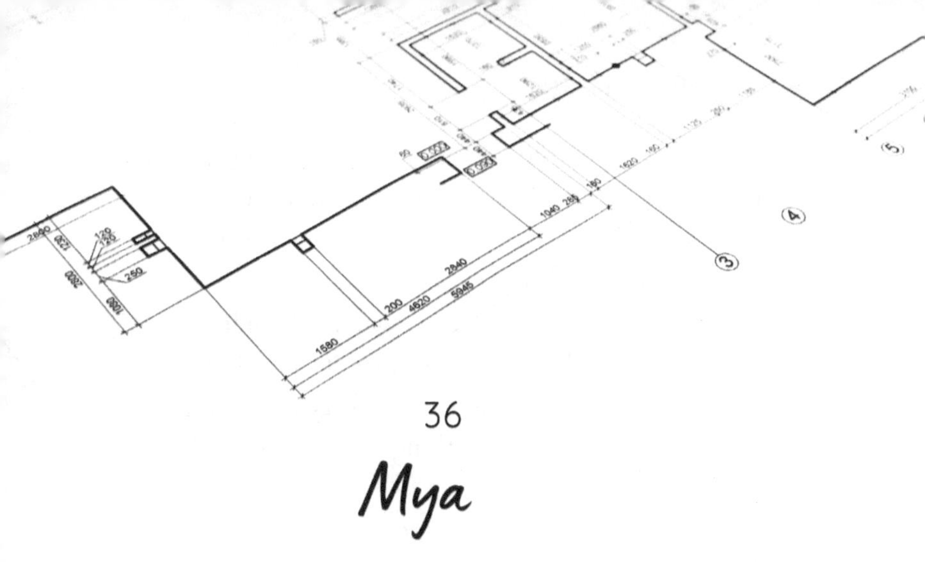

36

Mya

I t's been a month since Worth and I got married in Paris.

And the tabloids have still not had enough of the news.

Every few days, there's a new headline waiting for me before I've even had my first cup of coffee: **SEATTLE'S MOST ELIGIBLE BACHELOR FINALLY OFF THE MARKET; MYSTERY BRIDE CAPTURES BILLION-AIRE'S HEART; FROM OFFICE TO ALTAR: THE MILLER MARRIAGE NO ONE SAW COMING.**

Some articles are flattering, spinning our story into a modern-day fairytale. Others aren't as kind. The gossip blogs love to remind the world that I used to serve coffee at Willow's, that I'm "the ordinary girl who caught the boss's eye."

I told myself I wouldn't look. That what people say doesn't matter. But before I know it, I'm scrolling through comment sections like I'm searching for a reason to hate myself.

Worth says to ignore it. He doesn't even blink when he's asked about us. He's calm, composed, and effortlessly convincing. Meanwhile, I feel like I'm living someone else's life.

For the first few days after we came back, Worth was in full helicopter-dad mode, hovering, calling, checking in with Bri every hour like he could somehow make up for not being there when his ex-wife showed up. Brianna kept insisting she was fine, but I could tell he didn't believe her.

Vanessa hasn't come by again, thankfully. Worth mentioned it to his lawyer, who made it crystal clear to hers that if she tried pulling a stunt like that again, they'd file for a restraining order. The whole thing seemed to put her in her place—for now, at least.

Still, it's strange, sharing a home with my *husband*.

And even stranger knowing that, on paper, I'm someone's stepmom.

Brianna has handled everything surprisingly well.

We've found a small routine. Every evening, we spend an hour together sketching at the kitchen table. I can't draw to save my life, but Brianna doesn't seem to mind. It's when she's most relaxed, when she actually talks. That's when I hear about her friends, her classes, the things she won't tell Worth because she thinks he worries too much. And maybe he does. But in those quiet moments, I catch glimpses of Brianna's vulnerability.

This strange, new version of my life is starting to feel... not normal exactly, but something close to it.

By midafternoon, I'm at the office, buried in my submission proposal for the creative division. It's my dream project. The one that's been sitting in the back of my mind since college. *Project Rebuild:* a mixed-use community initiative that combines affordable housing with creative public spaces. My concept sketches show old industrial lots transformed into modern live-work studios, gardens built from reclaimed steel, and open plazas lined with art installations made by local youth programs. It's ambitious and bold, and it's exactly the kind of thing I've been dying to pitch to Worth's board, whether they think it's profitable or not.

Seraya sits across from me in the glass meeting room, her messy bun half-collapsing while she glances at her phone for the tenth time in five minutes.

"You're gonna burn a hole in the screen if you keep glaring at it like that."

She groans, setting her phone face down on the table. "Sorry. My new landlord is driving me insane."

I arch a brow. "Again?"

"Yes," she says, exasperated. "The man texts me about everything. *Everything.* This morning he messaged me to ask if I'd noticed the new mulch he put by the building entrance. Who texts about mulch?"

I laugh. "Maybe he's just... being neighborly?"

"He's being *weirdly attentive,*" she mutters, rubbing her temples. "Ever since I moved in, he's been popping up for the most random reasons. I swear, if he 'accidentally' locks himself out again and asks me to let him in, I might commit arson."

"Please don't," I say, smiling. "You just got that apartment."

"Yeah, well. I'm one text away from throwing my phone into the river."

My chest tugs. Seraya has been holding it together, but I can tell she's tired. Juggling a full-time job and a toddler is no small feat. I reach across the table and nudge her notebook. "Okay, no more landlord drama for ten minutes. We're finishing our presentations today, yeah?"

"Yeah." She nods, exhaling hard.

I catch a glimpse of a few coworkers passing by the glass wall, whispering to each other. One throws a glance my way before turning back around.

Ever since I came back as *Mrs. Miller,* the atmosphere around here has shifted. I knew it would, but knowing doesn't make it easier. Ethan barely looks at me now. He keeps a ten-foot pole between us at all times, which I'm sure makes Worth happy.

Others haven't been as subtle. I've caught whispers in the hallway, and conversations die when I walk into a room. Last week, I overheard two people from my department saying I'd probably get "preferential treatment" now that I'm married to the CEO.

When Worth found out, he offered—no, *threatened*—to handle it. But the idea of him scolding people on my behalf like some corporate knight in shining armor? Yeah, no thanks.

I told him I'd rather eat nails.

He didn't think that was funny.

Seraya notices my silence. "You okay?"

"Yeah," I lie. "Just thinking about the presentation."

She hums, unconvinced, and opens her laptop again. "You'll nail it, *Mrs.* CEO."

I groan. "Don't start."

She smirks. "What? It's true. You're practically the office legend now."

"More like the office cautionary tale."

Deep down, I can't help the fear that runs through me if *Project Rebuild* actually gets approved. I don't want it to be because of my new last name. I want it to be because of me.

I need that win for myself, and not for the man whose ring I wear.

When Seraya steps out to take a call, I head back to my desk to grab my sketch pad. I'm halfway down the hallway when a voice stops me cold.

Shaina is leaning against the copy room doorway, one manicured hand on her hip, talking to one of the HR clerks from the tenth floor. I wouldn't have paid her any attention until I heard Worth's name.

"So I was in Worth's office earlier," she says, lowering her voice just enough to make it sound scandalous. "And he asked me to get on my knees, for old time's sake. If you know what I me"

The clerk gasps. "You're kidding."

Shaina smirks, flipping her hair. "Please. Like he'd ever forget me. Men like Worth don't settle for... boring. And trust me, what he has now?" She lets out a pitying laugh. "Temporary."

The clerk glances around nervously. "You really think so?"

"Oh, honey." Shaina leans in conspiratorially. "This little 'marriage' of his has to be strategic. He must be getting something out of it. And Mya is definitely getting a bigger pay check." She shrugs. "He'll soon remember he prefers women who can actually keep up with him—in and out of the office."

My blood pressure spikes so fast I feel it in my ears. I can practically *taste* my irritation.

"And the way she walks around like she owns the place now?" Shaina adds. "It's so embarrassing. Poor girl doesn't realize she's just a placeholder."

That's it.

I stride straight toward them before my brain can talk me out of it.

I have no idea why I'm this angry. It's not like Worth and I are a real couple. I'm the one who insists this whole thing is just business, but hearing someone talk about our relationship like that does something sharp and ugly to me.

"Wow, Shaina," I say, my voice too calm to be anything but dangerous. "You sure you want to be spreading rumors like that in a building full of your colleagues and superiors?"

Both women stiffen. Shaina turns, startled for half a second before she recovers with a smirk. "Relax, *Mrs. Miller*. We were just talking."

"Right," I say flatly. "Because every innocent conversation

ends with a comment about your boss's and *my* husband's anatomy."

The HR clerk flushes scarlet and mumbles something about having to get back downstairs before basically sprinting away.

Shaina crosses her arms. "Don't take it personally, Mya. You're new at this whole wife thing. But some of us have *history* with Worth."

I bite the inside of my cheek so hard it almost hurts. "Funny. He didn't mention you in any of his stories."

Shaina's chin lifts. "Believe me, he wouldn't have had to. I was just in his office, remember?"

Something inside me snaps.

"Were you? Let's go confirm that, then."

Before she can respond, I turn on my heel and march toward Worth's office.

I don't knock and just push the door open, hard, only to find him mid-meeting with Henson and two suited clients.

Every head turns in my direction.

Worth blinks. "Mya?"

The silence stretches. My pulse thunders in my ears.

I glance back at Shaina, who's frozen in the doorway, eyes wide as saucers.

Perfect. Let her squirm.

Worth's jaw tightens, his authoritative tone sliding back into place. "Is there something you need, Mrs. Miller?"

The clients glance at each other, clearly entertained by the sudden domestic drama unfolding in real time.

I swallow hard, realizing just how bad this looks, but pride won't let me back down. "We need to talk."

I'm still standing at the door, heat rushing up my neck. Worth's brows lift, but the moment his gaze takes in my expression, that surprise twists into amusement.

Oh, he's enjoying this.

"Gentlemen," he says smoothly, "please give me and my wife a moment."

I want the floor to open up and swallow me.

Henson glances between us, clearly fighting back a grin. "Of course," he says, clearing his throat. "Let's continue this in the boardroom."

The clients gather their notes, shaking Worth's hand before exiting. Shaina is still frozen outside, as if watching a train wreck she caused. Worth shuts the door behind them.

The amused look hasn't left his face.

And I'm about two seconds away from throwing something at it.

"Are you still fooling around with Shaina?" I demand, crossing my arms so tight it hurts.

He leans on his desk, calm as ever, one brow arched. "Why would you think that, Kitten?"

"Don't call me *Kitten* right now," I snap. "This is serious. Do you have any idea what'll happen if anyone finds out you're cheating on your new wife?"

"No one will find out anything."

"She's going around telling people she was in your office, *on her knees,* Worth." The words feel vile coming out of my mouth, and my voice rises before I can stop it.

Worth chuckles. *Chuckles.*

"I'll take care of it," he says simply, like this is a scheduling issue and not a full-blown PR nightmare.

"Why aren't you more upset? This could ruin your entire plan, your reputation, the company, everything! I'll have married you for nothing!"

That gets his attention. He straightens, amusement morphing into something darker for a heartbeat, but then it's gone, replaced by that infuriating smirk that makes me want to both slap and kiss him senseless.

I scowl. "Are you still fucking her, Worth?"

He studies me, like he's trying to decide whether to laugh or drag me closer. Part of me wants him to do the latter.

Nothing has happened since our wedding night in Paris, and I don't know if I'm relieved or if I want to break the sexual tension between us once and for all—even if it might be the worst idea.

"Are you jealous, Mrs. Miller?"

"Absolutely not. I'm *concerned*."

"Right," he says, the ghost of a grin still on his lips. "Because that sounded a lot like jealousy to me."

"I'm not," I bite out. "I couldn't care less who you sleep with."

"Is that so?"

"Yes." The word comes out weaker than I mean it to.

"I think you're lying, Mrs. Miller." He tilts his head. "You're jealous of Shaina, and you don't want to admit it."

"Fuck off, Worth. I don't care."

He moves toward me, and I can feel the heat radiating off him.

My breath stutters when he slides his hand up my nape and grabs hold of my hair in a fist.

His voice drops to a whisper, right against my ear. "Then what's this attitude about, Mya?"

37

Worth

Sometimes a woman just needs to be grabbed by the throat, spun around, bent over, and punished for being a *fucking brat.*

And right now, I'm a millisecond away from shoving Mya's face into my desk and penetrating her so deeply, she'll have to admit that she's jealous.

Her sharp tongue and that unwarranted attitude need to be dealt with.

I spin her around and press her onto the table, my body crowding hers until her palms grab onto the polished wood. My cock grinds against the curve of her ass, and she lets out a soft, helpless moan that goes straight to my core.

Then awareness flashes across her face as she remembers the glass walls. "Worth," she hisses. "The blinds are open."

I turn to see Shaina still standing there, her mouth agape as she watches us.

"Good," I murmur against Mya's ear, my voice low and rough. She squirms, testing my hold.

"I want everyone to see who you belong to, Mya. Let them remove any doubt that I have eyes on anyone but *you*."

She writhes beneath me, her voice trembling. "I told you, I don't belong to anyone," she spits, fighting for composure more than freedom.

"I beg to fucking differ, *wife*," I growl. "You became mine the moment you signed those papers and changed your name."

"It's only temporary. Just for now," Mya snaps back.

"Just for now," I echo darkly, my grip tightening on her hip, "is still *now*. Until we go our separate ways, you're my wife, Mya, and you're going to start acting like it."

"No."

My pulse spikes. The sound of that word cuts through me like a dare. My hand flexes against her hip, the muscle in my jaw ticking as I lean closer until my breath fans her neck.

"No? You really want to test me right now?"

Movement beyond the glass catches my eye. A few people have stopped to gawk, Dre among them, wide-eyed and horrified as she frantically waves everyone away from the corridor.

I release my hold on Mya's neck, sliding my palm down her spine, tracing the soft curve of her dress until I reach the hem. I lift the fabric just enough to expose one perfect cheek hidden from view.

Mya gasps, her body going still beneath my touch.

My hand roams her thigh, savoring the tremor that runs through her before I bring my palm down in a controlled slap against her ass. The sound cracks through the office, echoing off the glass walls like a warning shot.

"One," I count.

Her eyes snap up. "One?"

I tilt my head, a smirk tugging at my mouth. "You think I've forgotten how many times you've given me attitude? A slap for every bratty comment you've made."

"Worth," she breathes. "We can't do this here."

"I can do whatever I want," I murmur, pressing closer until she can feel the weight of my control in every word. "My company. My building. My office."

She rolls her eyes, still defiant even now. "So humble."

I chuckle darkly. My palm comes down again. "Two." Then I lean in close, my lips brushing her ear. "Bold of you to keep mouthing off while I'm punishing you. Though let's be honest..." I drag in a slow breath, letting it fan across her neck. "I doubt this even feels like punishment. Not when I can smell how fucking turned on you are, Kitten."

My hand comes down again, sharper this time. "Three."

Mya lets out a small, startled sound that becomes breathier. I rub the spot with my palm, coaxing her to breathe through it.

Then another slap. "Four."

She moans, and my control wavers, a dark thrill crawling through my veins.

"That's it. Good girl."

Her shoulders rise and fall in quick bursts, the tension between us tightening until the silence feels heavy enough to break.

"I've given you time to settle into your new role, Mya. Now, you have to understand exactly what it means."

I can feel her pulse fluttering beneath my touch.

"Tell me," I whisper, the words more command than question. "Tell me you want this."

Mya nods, breath catching in her throat.

"Words, Kitten."

Her eyes meet mine. "Yes," she breathes. "I want this."

That's all I need to hear.

The outside world falls away until it's just her and me, locked in a current neither of us can escape. I reach past her for the remote on my desk and, with one click, the blinds slide shut, cutting off the curious stares and flooding the office with darkness.

"No one gets to see this side of you. Only me." I rest my hands on the desk on either side of her, caging her in. "You almost made me forget where we were."

Mya's lips part like she wants to argue, but she doesn't. Instead, she surrenders, and I know I have her attention completely.

I loosen my belt and unbuckle my pants, reaching down my briefs to pull out my aching cock. I need to finally feel Mya wrapped around me.

After almost having her on our wedding night, I've been a restless, desperate mess, caught somewhere between restraint and need. I've been waiting for her to be ready, refusing to push past the line she keeps drawing between us.

There haven't been any kisses or touches outside of the ones we fake for the cameras, and it's driving me insane. Every time she walks past me, every time she laughs—it's another test of how far I can stretch my self-control before it snaps.

Now, watching her on my desk, breath unsteady, squirming beneath me, I know there's no coming back from this.

I pull her head up by the strands of her hair and bring her mouth to mine, tasting defiance on her lips. God, it does something to me. Lights me up from the inside out.

I slip two fingers past the string of Mya's thong, right above her wet heat, and pull, snapping the fabric in half.

Her breath comes faster, a sound caught somewhere between a gasp and a moan.

With the pad of my thumb, I roll the bead of precum around the head of my dick, and bring my length to her entrance, teasing her with small strokes.

"Worth," she whimpers.

"Yes, pretty girl?"

"Please."

I've spent weeks fighting this, keeping distance, pretending that we're nothing but business, when every cell in me knows otherwise.

"Tell me what you need, baby."

Mya says my name again, voice breaking, and the sound settles in my chest, like a prayer I don't deserve.

"I need you to fuck me. Please."

I grab onto her hair tighter, pressing her face back onto the desk while I push inside her to the hilt. A broken shout escapes her.

"Worth. You're so big. I can't—"

"You fucking can," I growl. "Your pussy was made for me, Kitten, and you'll take every inch."

"Slow... down..." she tries to say, but she chokes on her words when I smack her ass.

Smack. Five.

"Ah, fuck!" Mya screams, her back arching.

"You're doing good, baby. Just breathe. If you need me to stop, tap on my leg. Okay?"

Mya nods.

Then, I fuck my wife with fast, punishing thrusts, the tension finally lifting from my chest.

Mya's hands clutch at the edge of my desk; mine tighten on her hips.

Thrust.

Smack. Smack. Six. Seven.

Mya yelps, her knuckles whitening against the polished wood.

"Good fucking girl," I whisper against her temple. I can feel how close she is from the way her pussy is clenching around my cock.

Thrust.

Smack. Eight.

Mya is trembling, tears slipping down her cheeks.

"I'm sorry, baby. Can you give me two more?" I lift her to me and lick them away, rough and reverent all at once.

She nods, and I move again, fucking her into oblivion, my own release building fast, threatening to drag me under.

Smack. Nine.

"Come for me, pretty girl."

Mya's voice breaks. "Oh, God... I'm right there. Don't stop."

The words motivate me like a spark to tinder. One last slap tears through the air, echoing off the glass walls, and I know anyone passing by can hear. But at this moment, I don't care.

The world narrows to her moans, and when the cord finally breaks, Mya orgasms and I follow, everything in me unspooling at once until all that's left is the sound of our ragged breathing and the wild rhythm of my pulse.

When it's over, everything is quiet again.

I steady myself, brushing a damp strand of hair from Mya's face. Her eyes are glassy, cheeks flushed. She looks both wrecked and radiant.

"Are you okay?"

She nods, still trying to catch her breath.

I press my forehead to her back. "You did so good for me, Kitten."

I pull away, adjusting my tie like that might somehow fix the chaos between us.

"We should... clean up," Mya mutters, exhaling a shaky laugh, tugging her dress back into place. "Before Dre passes out in the hallway."

The faint humor cracks something open in my chest. She's closed herself off again.

But as she turns toward the door, there is a truth that slams into me like a sucker punch.

Mya is mine—*but only for now.*
I shove the thought away before it can root too deep.

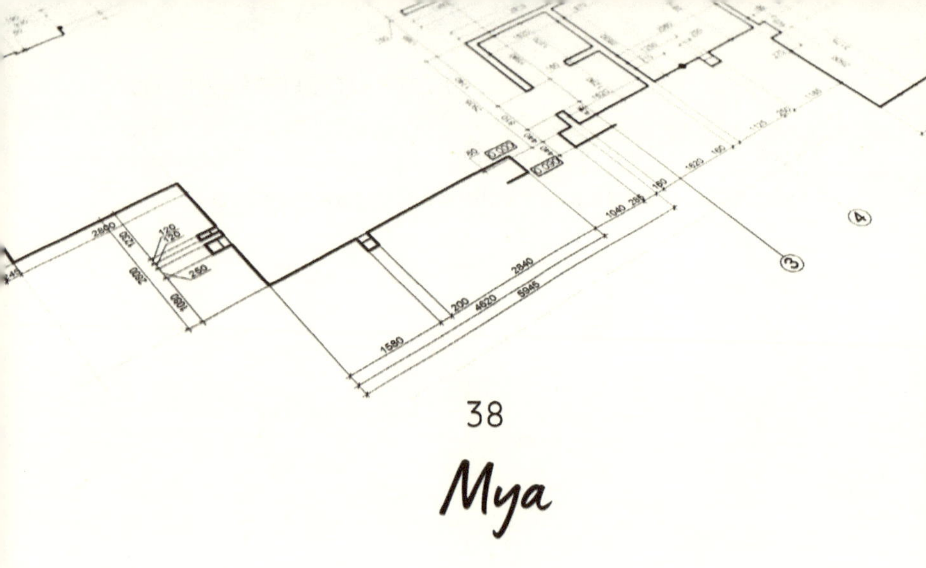

38

Mya

I t's Brianna's fourteenth birthday, and Worth's house is a cacophony of noise.

And every passing minute brings me closer to the moment where my worlds collide.

It's now been four months since Worth and I got married—four months of settling into this strange, beautiful in-between where nothing feels entirely real and everything feels deeply personal all at once. My parents, however, have been snowbirding out of the state since before the wedding, and have been spared from the immediate chaos of my very unexpected life choices.

But they're back and are coming over today. They want to see with their own eyes that I'm okay. That I'm happy, and that marrying my boss wasn't a spectacular lapse in judgment.

I've been pretending I'm calm about it, but my stomach has felt like a shaken soda can all morning.

Tiana's playlist is blasting from the kitchen speakers, balloons are taped to every available surface, and I'm holding a tray of pastel cupcakes that look like they belong in a bakery window instead of Worth's kitchen.

"Careful!" Tiana yells from the living room, where she's helping Brianna test out a foot bath. "Don't you dare ruin the frosting before the guests arrive!"

"I'm not even touching it!" I retort.

"You're breathing too close to it." Tiana turns to Brianna who is messing with the green clay mask covering her face. TJ swats her hand away.

"Beauty requires discipline, young padawan."

I laugh, setting the cupcakes down beside the mountain of pink towels and nail polish bottles. "Please don't turn Bri into a skincare Jedi."

Tiana winks at me. "Hey, she asked for a spa day. I'm just delivering luxury. Do you know how hard it was to get the Glow Haus estheticians here for free?"

When I first told Tiana about Brianna, I should've known they'd hit it off instantly. My sister has this uncanny ability to charm kids on sight. Within ten minutes of meeting, she'd made Bri her honorary little sister and had her giggling like they'd known each other for years.

"You didn't have to do that, TJ. Worth could've paid."

She waves me off like I've just insulted her religion. "Please. Exposure is currency. They should be thanking me."

Brianna bounces in her seat, beaming. "This is the best birthday ever! Thank you, Tiana and Mya!"

My chest warms. Bri looks so happy—and seeing that smile almost makes me forget that this is temporary.

Almost.

Worth's deep voice cuts through the noise. "You two really outdid yourselves."

I turn and nearly forget how to breathe.

He's leaning against the doorway, wearing a navy Henley that clings in all the right places, sleeves pushed up his forearms, and light-wash jeans dusted with a layer of sawdust. He must've been in his workshop again, finishing up Brianna's gift.

I'll never get used to seeing him like this.

Worth Miller is the picture of perfection in tailored suits, cufflinks, and that CEO polish that makes everyone else shrink a little when he walks into a room. But this version of him? All rugged and effortless and impossibly *male* is dangerous for my libido.

The first time I found him dressed casually, coffee mug in hand, barefoot, hair still damp from the shower, I nearly choked on my own drink. It's been months, and the effect hasn't worn off—if anything, it's worse now.

He looks relaxed in a way that feels intimate, as if only the people closest to him get to see him like this. And my body has the audacity to respond like it's never seen a man before.

Worth chuckles faintly, like he can read every thought running through my head.

"Don't look so surprised," I say, crossing my arms. "Did you not think we were capable of turning our house into a teenage girl's dream?"

He steps closer, lowering his voice. "That's not what surprises me."

"What, then?"

"The way you're looking at me, pretty girl."

Before I can respond, he bends and presses a light kiss to my forehead. The gesture steals the air from my lungs. It's so gentle, so... *married.*

For a second, I let myself pretend this is real.

"You're worried about your parents," he states, leaning against the kitchen counter.

"Worried is... a word," I mutter. "They trust me. But they also think you're either Prince Charming or a walking red flag."

A hint of amusement warms his eyes. "Let them decide. I'm just going to show up as myself."

"That's what I'm afraid of," I tease weakly, but the truth is: that's what comforts me most. He won't perform. He'll just be Worth.

He reaches over then, brushing his fingers over mine. "We're okay," he says simply. And somehow, I believe him.

"Worth," I whisper in protest when his lips brush the side of my neck, acutely aware of Tiana and Brianna close by.

Worth smirks against my skin. "Also, don't think I didn't notice how you said *our* house."

Shit. I didn't even realize it. "I didn't mean—"

"Yes, you did." He cuts me off with a nibble to my ear.

"There will be six teenage girls in this house any minute. And my parents. We can't."

His grin melts and infuriates me all at once. "Can't what, exactly?" He takes my hand, his thumb stroking slow circles against my palm, and pulls me gently toward the kitchen. My heart pounds as he opens the pantry door.

We've been dancing around the tension like it might bite if we get too close. It's almost as if something opened between us, but also built a higher wall neither of us has dared to climb. Maybe because we're both afraid of what is waiting on the other side. Of how far we'd fall if we let ourselves step over it.

At least, that's why I haven't.

But to say I don't crave him would be a lie. Every brush of his hand, every look that lasts a moment too long, chips away at whatever's left of my restraint. And now, seeing him like this— casual, dusted with sawdust, eyes dark with hunger—I know I'm not going to last much longer.

Worth hushes me with a look, his eyes dark. "Five minutes. Then I'll let you go play hostess."

He pulls me into the pantry and shuts the door behind us. The quiet swallows us whole.

Before I can speak, his mouth finds mine, and I press against him instantly. The taste of him, the rough slide of his hands, and the faint scrape of calluses against my skin is too good.

My fingers find the back of his neck, then his hair, tugging him closer until I can feel his pounding heartbeat and the hard ridges of his body against mine. The kiss deepens, turning wild, until I forget where I end and he begins.

Worth's hand slides to my throat and squeezes lightly, eliciting a moan out of me.

A low growl rumbles from his chest as he lifts me effortlessly, my back meeting the door. Instinct takes over, and I wrap myself around his waist and start grinding on his erection.

"That's my pretty girl," he groans against my lips, still squeezing on my neck.

When he breaks the kiss, we're both breathing hard, foreheads pressed together.

"It's almost like you knew I'd be fucking you today, wearing a skirt that makes you look just like a slutty wife," he whispers.

He reaches under and rips my panties off.

I gasp, still trying to catch my breath. "You owe me underwear, panty thief."

He smiles sinfully. "Fuck your panties, Mya. If it were up to me, you'd never wear them again."

Then Worth kisses me—harder this time.

He unbuckles his jeans and pulls them down, freeing himself from his briefs. His cock is hard, glistening, ready to take me. And I almost salivate at the sight.

His breath ghosts against my ear. "Like what you see?"

I bite my lip and nod. "Fuck me, please?"

"I thought you'd never ask." He plunges deep inside me in one rough thrust, placing a palm over my mouth. "Quiet, Kitten. We wouldn't want anyone hearing how good your husband fucks you."

Whenever Worth uses the word 'husband,' my body answers before my brain can catch up, betraying every line I've tried to draw between us.

He continues to fuck me against the pantry door, hard and fast, as I moan under his hand, feeling the fast climb of my orgasm swell inside me.

"Tell me you're close, baby. I don't know if I can hold it any longer," he mumbles, kissing down my neck.

"Yes, I am," I breathe, throwing my head back.

Worth creates some space between us, and spits down where we are joined, using his thumb to swirl his saliva on my clit.

"Fuck, Mya," he groans, working me until I can barely make a coherent thought. "You don't know what you do to me." Worth picks up the speed, causing an inhale to get stuck in my throat. "This pussy is mine. *You're* mine."

And just like that, my climax erupts, almost blinding me. A scream tears from my throat, but Worth brings his hand back to my mouth, muffling the sound.

Seconds later, I feel his cock swell inside me, his own release filling me up.

I'm still struggling to catch my breath when Worth sets me on my feet.

"Stand still," he says, right as I'm about to pull my skirt down.

He gently kicks my legs open and gets on his knees in front of me.

"Worth, what are you doing?"

"Making sure you don't waste a damn drop," he replies, just as his cum starts trickling down my thigh. He runs his fingers up my leg to scoop up the mess, before shoving them inside me.

"Oh, God."

Then he lifts himself up. "Open wide, pretty girl."

I oblige, and he shoves the sticky digits into my mouth.

"Now suck."

And I do, really well, sucking them dry.

Worth groans. "If you do that a second longer, I'm going to shove my cock back inside, baby."

"Your five minutes are up," I say, swatting him away, even though I don't really want them to be.

He laughs. "Then I guess I'm out of time." He kisses me once more, quickly, before we slip out of the pantry, and it leaves my knees a little weak. I smooth down my skirt, trying to look composed, but I know my lips are swollen, cheeks flushed, and that I don't look remotely innocent.

And of course, that's exactly when Brianna rounds the corner.

She stops dead in her tracks, a soda can in her hand, blinking between us. "What were you two doing in the pantry?"

I freeze like a guilty teenager caught sneaking in after curfew. Worth, on the other hand, looks very unbothered. His mouth twitches like he's fighting a grin.

"I—uh—we were just—" I stammer, searching for words that don't exist.

Brianna's face twists as realization dawns. "Oh my *God*." She points at us with the drama of someone announcing a scandal. "Ew. Gross. Get a room. And preferably *not in this house*."

She makes a gagging sound and spins on her heel, muttering something about needing therapy.

Worth loses it. He laughs, a deep, unrestrained sound that makes my face heat even more.

"It's not funny!" I smack his arm, mortified.

"It's hilarious. You should see your face."

I huff and elbow him in the ribs before stalking out of the kitchen, doing everything in my power not to smile. "I hope you get sawdust in your eyes!" I shout and that finally wipes the grin off his face. *Win.*

Just then, the doorbell rings.

In minutes, the house transforms into a blur of teenage shrieks. Glitter-covered gift bags pile by the door, pop music spills from the speaker, and Brianna's face lights up brighter than the candles that'll be decorating her cake.

Tiana is in full event-planner mode. She somehow manages to keep the spa stations running smoothly while joking with the girls and snapping photos for her Instagram story.

Brianna giggles as one of the aestheticians paints her nails a shade of metallic blue.

My heart jumps to my throat when the doorbell rings again. When I open it, my mother nearly knocks the air from my lungs with a hug.

"Mya." She cups my face, as if needing proof I'm real. Devon stands behind her, next to Jackson, carrying a brightly wrapped gift bag, his expression soft.

"You made it," I say, laughing shakily.

"You think we'd miss meeting our son–in–law and the girl who stole your heart?" Mom scoffs.

Worth appears beside me like he's been summoned, offering a warm but cautious smile.

"Mr. and Mrs. Jones," he says, extending a hand to my mother first. "Thank you for coming." he places a kiss on her knuckles and she blushes.

"Devon," Worth says, greeting my stepdad with a brief nod

before turning to my little brother, giving him a pat on the back. "Jackson. I've heard a lot about that mean left throw of yours. You'll have to show me your ways one day."

My mom exchanges a smile with Devon before her eyes drift past us, softening when they land on Brianna across the room.

"That must be the birthday girl."

Brianna joins us, smiling brightly with glitter on her face. "Hi."

My mom melts instantly. "Happy birthday, Sunshine."

After the last introductions are made, we all gather to eat from the food table Tiana managed to have catered from Willow's. Then comes the cake: pink frosting, gold candles, and Brianna's name piped across the top.

Worth stays mostly out of the way during the festivities, which I understand. This many teenagers in one room could make anyone want to hide, but I catch glimpses of him now and then, watching from the hallway with that smile he reserves only for Brianna.

My parents linger near the kitchen, chatting quietly with Worth. I hover around the entrance, pretending I'm not listening.

"Thank you for inviting us," my stepdad says. "We wanted to see things for ourselves."

My mother's brows soften as she studies him. "We adore our daughter. We just want to make sure she's in good hands."

Worth nods. "I can assure you that I'd do anything to keep your daughter happy. I don't take that lightly. Mya means a lot to us."

Devon's gaze drifts past my husband toward the noise of the party. "And your daughter?"

Worth glances that way, warmth bleeding into his expression. "Brianna is everything to me. And she loves Mya. This family may look unconventional from the outside, but it's real."

My mother finally exhales. "Okay, good. Then we're happy to be here."

Worth smiles, looking relieved. "Let me show you around. And please, make yourselves at home."

Something eases in me as I watch the interaction.

Hours later, the party begins to wind down, and once the last of the girls are gone, my parents and Tiana say their good-byes, promising to invite us to dinner soon.

Brianna and I begin to tidy the kitchen when Worth appears in the doorway, looking exhausted but content. "Hey, birthday girl. Got a minute?"

Brianna perks up immediately. "Yeah!"

"Come with me. There's something I want to show you."

Curiosity flares in her eyes, and she bounces to her feet. Worth gives me a smile and I follow them down the hall, stopping in front of the double doors to his workshop. When he pushes the doors open, Brianna gasps.

Inside, the faint scent of wood and varnish fills the air. The space glows under the overhead lights and, right in the center, stands a custom-built sketching desk in polished oak, with adjustable angles, and drawers lined neatly with pencils and brushes.

"For me?" Bri whispers, her hands flying to her mouth.

Worth's smile is wide. "Happy birthday, sweetheart."

She rushes forward, running her hands over the smooth surface, inspecting every detail like it's made of gold. "Dad, it's perfect!"

Something soft blooms in my chest. This isn't just a gift. It's hours of effort and thought poured into something just for his daughter.

He ruffles her hair gently. "You deserved a proper place to draw. No more using the kitchen table."

She spins around and hugs him tight. "Thank you, Dad. I love it."

Worth's arms circle her, and I swear I catch a glimmer in his eyes before he blinks it away.

I can't help my smile. Even though sadness fills me. Because in this moment, I realize I truly love being a part of this family. And I don't want to let them go.

39

Worth

When I wake, the first thing I feel is warmth.

Mya's arm is draped across my chest, her leg hooked over mine, hair a dark tangle on the pillow beside me. She's out cold.

I laugh quietly to myself.

This is the same woman who made a *huge* deal about needing her own room before she moved in, who didn't want to confuse boundaries. Yet every night since, she's ended up right here, in my bed and in my arms.

I guess boundaries only apply until the lights go out.

Slowly, I wrap an arm over her waist and pull her closer. Mya makes a sleepy sound, her body instinctively curling into mine. Her ass rubs against my hardening cock.

I bury my nose in her neck, inhaling that soft, warm scent that's become so familiar. My fingers find the curve of her hip, tracing lazy circles along the skin beneath the hem of her sleep shirt.

Mya stirs, body twitching, her leg shifting against me.

"Worth," she mumbles, voice thick with sleep.

"Morning, pretty girl," I whisper.

She lets out a soft, drowsy sigh and squirms again, not fully awake but already responsive. I can feel the goosebumps rising beneath my touch, the way her breath hitches when my fingers drift up to her ribs.

I pinch her chin between my fingers, guiding her face back to mine. The kiss that follows is searing and full of everything I shouldn't want this much. Mya melts against me, kissing me back with the same need that's burning in my chest.

Her lashes lift slowly, and when her eyes finally meet mine, the air shifts. It's like the whole damn room forgets how to breathe.

"I could get used to this," I murmur against her lips.

"Don't," she says, catching my bottom lip between her teeth.

I hiss through a grin. "You brat."

Before she can answer, I grab her waist and pull her up, settling her over me until she's straddling my lap.

As soon as she's on me, I feel the warm heat of her pussy through my briefs.

"Are you not wearing anything under that shirt, Kitten?"

Mya bites on her lip and shakes her head. "I didn't want you to ruin yet another pair of panties," she says with a giggle. The sound hardens my dick even more, and I begin to grind against her.

"Did my dirty girl go to sleep with the intent of getting fucked this morning?" I bring my hands up to her breasts to tug on her nipples. Mya moans, throwing her head back, and starts rotating her hips in tune with my movements. I look down and see a patch of darkness on my crotch. "Look at the mess you're making, baby. Let me clean that up for you."

I flip her onto the bed, her surprised gasp turning into a laugh, then climb over her, bracing one hand beside her head. I press my mouth to the curve of her neck, the skin there warm and soft.

My lips trace a slow path down, over her collarbone, across her chest, until I reach her stomach. Every inch of Mya shivers beneath my mouth, every breath catching like she's trying not to fall apart too soon.

Once I'm settled between her legs, I let the tip of my nose ghost over her clit, and she arches off the bed.

"You're already squirming, waiting to be devoured," I taunt, teasing her with slow kisses over her mound, avoiding the place she wants me the most.

Mya writhes underneath me, making pleading noises.

"Tell me what you need, baby."

"You, please. Your mouth. On me," she says, struggling through the words.

"Such a good wife, always saying please for her husband," I praise, giving her sex one quick flick of my tongue.

Mya moans louder, and I finally put my mouth on her clit, sucking it and swirling my tongue just the way she likes it.

"Yes. Oh my God. That's so good, Worth."

I hum as I devour her. Mya's sounds and taste turn me on so much, I can barely keep it together.

I grind my cock into the mattress, chasing any type of friction I can get as I munch on her cunt like there's no tomorrow. Because soon enough, there won't *be* a tomorrow, and the thought of not having her—of losing this—drives me out of my fucking mind.

"Mine," I growl, the word tearing from my chest before I can stop it.

Mya's legs clamp around my head, squeezing my ears as she starts to ride the wave of her orgasm.

I take the opportunity to slip two fingers inside her, and her hips buck once more. She's so close and so am I, humping the bed like a goddamn teenager in heat. I can't remember the last time I felt this uncontrollable need to fuck something. The difference is that this time, Mya is the only thing I want to penetrate.

After a couple minutes of sucking on her clit and fingering her g-spot, Mya erupts, her climax hitting her hard enough to explode. Her pussy throbs against my tongue.

She screams, probably forgetting that we're not home alone, and as reckless as it may be, I don't give a shit right now. Brianna's room is at the other end of the hall, so I doubt she'd hear anything anyway.

Mya's walls clench around my fingers and when I pull them out, I draw a gush of liquid.

That's all it takes. I chase my own release, grinding against the sheets like a madman. Then, I come almost violently in my briefs without even being touched.

Holy fuck. I glance up at Mya with a wide grin.

"Baby. You just squirted all over me."

It takes her a few seconds to register what I said, and she jolts up. "I did *what?*"

I chuckle. "You just squirted."

Mya's cheeks redden. "Oh my God!" She looks down at the sheet where there is a massive round patch of wetness. "I'm so sorry!"

I scowl. "Don't ever apologize for that, Mya. It's a damn pleasure to be showered by you."

She lowers her head. "I've never done that before."

Pride swells in my chest. "You better not be lying to me."

Mya giggles. "I swear. Most men weren't even able to get me there, let alone make me squirt."

I groan and pull her back on top of me, needing her close again.

"Don't ever talk to me about other men when I'm still

covered in you," I grit out. "Actually, don't talk about other men, period."

The thought of anyone else's hands on her makes something dark coil low in my chest. It's irrational, I know that. But every day she's around me, the need to claim her and make her mine in every possible way only gets harder to fight.

Mya rolls her eyes. "Fine."

I pinch her nipple and she squeals. "What was that for?"

"For giving me attitude," I say, unable to hide my grin.

She narrows her eyes, her lips curving. "You wouldn't have it any other way."

"Maybe not. But that doesn't mean I'll let it slide."

She settles over me again, her breath catching. "Your briefs are all wet." Her eyes widen like saucers at the realization. "Wait. Did you? In your pants? While you were eating me out?" Her shock is comical, and I can't help but laugh.

"Yes, pretty girl. I came in my pants while your pussy was in my face. That's how good you taste."

"Really?"

"Yes. And I'm not close to being done with you yet."

I hoist myself up to remove my briefs, then I grab Mya's waist.

"Sit down, baby."

She shakes her head. "I decide when, playboy."

I can't help the chuckle that rumbles out of me. "Oh, yeah? Is that so?"

"Yup. It's my turn to tease you."

"Careful what you start, Mya. You might not like how it ends."

She tilts her head, watching me with a devilish grin.

"I just think you can't handle it, Mr. Miller." She lowers herself on my cock though she doesn't put it inside her yet. It's still soft, but the way Mya moves on top of me has it hardening by the second.

She slides her wet pussy over my length at a torturing pace, moaning each time her clit meets the head. Fuck. Am I going to come from friction alone—*again?*

Reel it the fuck in, Worth.

"I'm not above begging, Kitten. Please put me out of my misery and sit on me."

But the brat decides to tease me some more; she grabs hold of my cock with a warm palm and puts the tip at her entrance, inching in and out without fully sitting down.

"Fuck. What will it take?" I groan. At this point, I'm squirming beneath her like a desperate man barely holding it together.

I drag a hand down my face, breath coming rough. "Mya."

"Yes?"

"I can't take it anymore." My voice is ragged, sweat beading at my brow.

Her lips curve. "But you're doing so well, *daddy.*"

My pulse spikes, and something between a growl and a laugh rumbles in my chest. *She has no idea who she's playing with.*

"That's it."

I grab Mya and slam her down onto my cock.

She screams while I suppress a whimper, and I begin to move underneath her. Every thrust steals the breath from Mya's lungs, but she smiles, like the wicked little vixen she is.

"Is this what you were planning all along?" I rasp. "You wanted me to lose control?"

"Y-yes."

"Brat." A smile tugs at my mouth. "You knew exactly what you were doing when you called me that."

"Maybe."

"What am I going to do with you, pretty girl?"

Keep you forever, my heart says.

But you can't, my mind snaps back.

Why the fuck not?

The argument is so loud inside me, it rips a sound from my throat. I growl—at her, at myself, at the impossible truth. That I can't seem to stop wanting Mya.

The push and pull between us is electric and neither of us is willing to surrender, both addicted to the game.

I continue to fuck her, letting out my frustration on her sweet cunt and she takes every damn thrust. Mya pushes my hands off her waist.

"Let me."

"Be my guest."

Then, she starts riding my cock like the sexiest professional bull rider.

"You're fucking trouble," I groan, watching her slam herself down on me while flicking her clit with one hand and pinching her nipple with the other. She closes her eyes and moans my name.

"I'm so close," she whimpers.

My voice quivers with my next inhale. "I'm right there with you, baby girl."

After a few more bounces, Mya brings her lips to mine in a searing kiss as she climaxes. She breathes my name like a confession, and I swallow her whimpers, letting them mix with the broken sounds that escape me when my orgasm hits me.

We both go quiet. Her head rests on my chest, skin warm against mine.

Out of nowhere, Mya says, "Do you want kids?"

I glance down at her, caught off guard. "Kids?"

Her cheeks flush. "I mean... more kids."

I take a slow breath, thinking it over. "Honestly? I didn't

think so. Not for a long time, at least." I pause. "But if I ever find the right person... yeah, probably." I tilt my head, meeting her eyes. "You?"

She nods softly. "Same. With the right person."

I grin. "Wait. Are you trying to tell me something? You pregnant, Mya?"

She smacks my chest, laughing. "No! But we've never actually talked about it, and we've been having unprotected sex."

I blink. "Damn. That's true." I rub a hand over my face, half-laughing. "Guess I've been too caught up in you to even think about that."

Mya shrugs, a small smile playing on her lips. "I'm on the patch, and I track my cycle pretty closely."

"Good to know," I murmur, pressing a kiss to her hair. "I wouldn't be mad, you know?"

"About what?"

"If you were pregnant."

"Worth..."

"I know," I say quickly, running a hand down her back. "I know our marriage isn't real. But you've seen how I am with Brianna." I meet her gaze. "I'd be the same with our kid too."

Her lips part, but she doesn't say anything. The silence that follows isn't awkward—it's heavy with so many unspoken things. And somewhere in the middle of it, I know.

I'm falling for her.

Somewhere between our fake vows and real disagreements, between every laugh Mya's pulled out of me, and every night she's spent in my arms, I stopped pretending.

The thought should terrify me. Hell, it *does*. Falling for her wasn't part of the plan. None of this was.

After a few minutes of quiet, Mya shifts beside me and sits up, the sheet sliding down her back. She glances over her shoulder, an almost shy smile curving her lips before she murmurs, "I'm gonna shower."

I nod, even though part of me wants to follow her. I want to keep her close a little longer.

But after what just passed between us—after everything I just realized—we both deserve a moment to breathe.

So I stay where I am, watching her disappear into the bathroom.

THE SMELL OF COFFEE REACHES ME BEFORE I EVEN MAKE it down the stairs.

Mya is already in the kitchen, hair tied up in one of those messy knots she somehow makes look intentional, wearing one of my old W.H.M. sweatshirts that practically swallows her whole.

For a second, I just stand there, one hand on the banister, watching her move around my kitchen like she's been doing it for years. The light catches her curls, her bare legs, the soft curve of her smile when she hums under her breath.

"Hi," I say finally, coming up behind her.

She startles. "Hey! You scared me."

"Sorry, baby. Didn't mean to." I kiss her forehead before moving toward the coffee pot and pour a cup.

"You don't have to call me 'baby' when we're home. No one's watching."

I try to mask the tug in my chest. "I know. I just figured if I keep saying it, it'll start to feel natural. More believable."

It's a lie.

The truth is, I like calling her that. I like the way her cheeks flush every damn time I do. But I can't tell her that, not when she still reminds herself this thing between us is pretend.

Mya nods, looking down, her fingers fidgeting with the edge of the counter. "You're right. Appearances."

I catch the quick flash of disappointment before she hides it behind a smile.

And it hits me again just how deep I'm in, because the last thing I ever want to do is make her look like that.

"What are you doing in here, anyway?" I ask, glancing at the ingredients on the counter.

"Brianna has a field trip today," she says, reaching for a bowl of fruit. "I wanted to pack her lunch before she left."

"You don't have to do that. She's old enough to do it herself."

Mya shrugs, slicing an apple. "I wanted to."

I take a slow sip, watching her. "You're spoiling her."

She smirks. "Takes one to know one."

Since moving in, Mya has taken her role in Brianna's life seriously, more than I ever expected her to. She helps with homework, remembers the little things, listens when Bri talks about her friends or some show she's obsessed with. It's subtle, but I see the positive changes in my daughter, and it warms me in a way I don't have words for.

I just hope Bri doesn't get too attached, because when this arrangement ends, I don't know what it'll do to her—to either of us.

Still, as I watch Mya tuck the apple slices into a lunch container, humming under her breath, the hope I try to bury creeps up anyway.

I hope she doesn't leave.

I hope she falls for me the same way I've already fallen for her.

And that maybe, she'll decide to stay.

Brianna comes downstairs a few minutes later, backpack

slung over one shoulder and hair in a braid. She grabs the lunch from Mya, hugs her, and then hugs me. "Bye, guys!"

When the door closes behind her, Mya leans against the counter, holding her mug in both hands. "You've got a good kid."

"I know," I say softly. "Sometimes I still can't believe she's mine."

"She's a lot like you."

I lift a brow. "Stubborn?"

"Strong," she corrects. "And careful with her heart."

I swallow the lump that rises in my throat and set my mug down.

Knowing that Mya *sees* me does something to me I can't explain.

Mya must feel it too because she suddenly looks down, fiddling with the rim of her cup.

"You should eat something. You've got a long day ahead."

Instead of answering, I take a step closer. Then another.

Her breath catches, her back pressing lightly against the counter.

"Worth..."

"Hmm?"

"This is a bad idea," she whispers, though her voice betrays her.

"So you always say." My hand finds her jaw. "But we've had worse ones."

Her lips part, and I lower my head, close enough to feel the warmth of her breath.

Footsteps thunder on the porch just before the door swings open and Brianna's voice calls, "I forgot my phone!"

We jump apart like teenagers caught doing something we shouldn't.

Mya spins, pretending to wipe the counter while I grab my coffee as if it's suddenly the most interesting thing in the room.

Brianna darts in, grabs her phone, and eyes us suspiciously. "Why do you guys look so weird?"

Mya forces a laugh. "We don't!"

"Uh huh," Brianna says, grinning as she walks out again.

When the door shuts, Mya turns to me, cheeks pink. "See? Bad idea."

"Maybe," I say, unable to stop my smirk, "but it would've been a good one, right up until she walked in."

Mya rolls her eyes and tosses a napkin at me, but I see the small smile she's trying to hide.

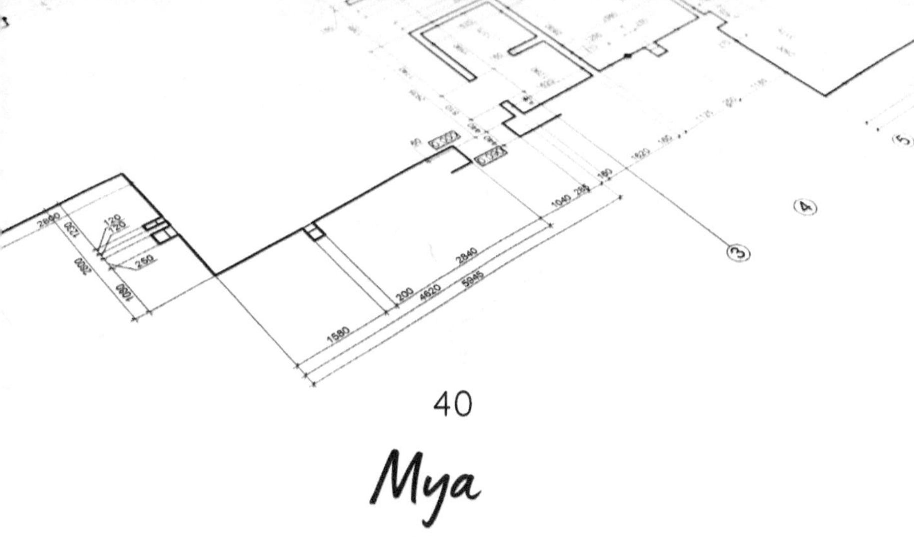

40

Mya

Today is the day I'll be pitching *Project Rebuild.*

Months of work, late nights, and second-guessing all boil down to a thirty-minute presentation in front of Worth's board.

The weight of it presses into my ribs until I can't breathe.

Beside me, Worth stirs. "You're awake," he murmurs.

I hum something noncommittal, staring up at the ceiling.

He props himself up on an elbow, eyes narrowing when he sees my expression. "You're nervous."

"Understatement. I'm *terrified,*" I admit, forcing out a laugh that sounds nothing like me.

"Hey. You've got this. You've been living and breathing this project for months. No one knows it better than you."

Worth shifts closer, his hand finding my waist, thumb brushing lazy circles on my skin.

Which would be a lot more comforting if I didn't feel like a fraud half the time. I told myself I'd go back to my own room every night to keep lines clean and my head straight, but I never make it past the doorway. I always end up here, tucked under his arm, stealing warmth I have no business wanting, and I can't even find the will to be mad about it.

How am I supposed to convince a board I know what I'm doing when I can't even convince myself to leave Worth's bed?

I bite the inside of my cheek. "Yeah, but it doesn't matter how much I know if the board has already made up their mind."

He frowns. "What do you mean?"

I finally look at him. "If they give me funding, it's only because I'm *Mrs. Miller.*" The title tastes bitter. "Not because I earned it or I'm good at what I do."

Worth sits up, rubbing a hand through his hair. "You're overthinking it. They wouldn't have asked for the presentation if they didn't believe in your work."

"That's easy for you to say." I sit up, too. "You walk into any room and people already respect you. I walk in, and they see the woman sleeping with the boss."

His jaw flexes. "Having an advantage isn't always a bad thing, Mya. Everyone uses what they've got."

My stomach drops. "You can't be serious."

"I'm saying it doesn't make your work less valuable. It's not like you *didn't* earn this."

I stare at him, disbelief clawing at my throat. "You just don't get it, do you?"

He blinks, thrown off. "How?"

"When all of this is over—" I gesture between us, "—you'll still be *Worth Miller,* billionaire mogul, CEO, whatever title you want. And I'll be the *ex-wife* who slept her way to success. The woman who got ahead because she played the part."

"Mya—"

"No," I snap, voice shaking. I press a hand to my chest, trying to keep my heart from breaking out of it. "We're not the same. And that's—that's why we can never be real."

Something dark flashes in Worth's eyes. "That's what you really think?"

I avoid his gaze, and stay silent.

He gets up to pace the room. "You know what? Maybe you're right. Maybe I *don't* get it. Because for once, I thought someone actually saw me for who I was. Not for the headlines or the bank account or the goddamn last name." He stops and looks at me, eyes full of fire. "But I guess I was wrong."

"Worth—"

"No. You're just like everyone else. You think I'm some guy who only cares about women and money, that this doesn't mean anything to me. Have I not shown you how much I care about you, Mya?"

The words slice through me. Guilt rises fast, but I force myself to hold my ground. "You're twisting my words. I'm being *realistic*. You need to stop living in this fantasy where we could ever actually work. We don't fit."

His laugh is humorless. "And who do you think would be the right fit for me then, huh? That redhead you saw me with at the gala?"

I cross my arms, refusing to flinch. "Someone like her makes more sense. Someone who belongs in your world."

His temper rises. *"You don't get to decide who I want, Mya!"*

The shout echoes through the room, and for a moment, neither of us moves.

His eyes burn. "You need to get out of your head and see what's right in front of you."

There's something desperate in his tone, almost pleading. It kills me, because a part of me *does* see it. All of it. Him. Us. What we could be if I weren't so damn afraid.

But fear wins. It always does.

I get up, heart pounding. "I need to get ready."

Before he can say another word, I storm into the bathroom. The sound of the shower masks the shaky breath I let out as the first tear falls.

By the time I'm out of the shower and dressed, the house is quiet. There's no sign of Worth or Brianna. Just Maggie in the kitchen, fussing with the coffee machine.

"May I?" I ask, coming around the island.

"Oh. Hi, dear. Yes, please do. Worth did something to it before he left."

"What do you mean?"

"He looked very angry and smacked the top of the machine with a curse when it wouldn't pour his coffee."

I sigh. Yes, the things I said were harsh but they needed to be said. Worth has to remember why we're doing this.

Maggie glances up at me. "What happened?"

"We got into an argument. It's no big deal."

She presses her lips together. "I beg to differ. Worth doesn't get rattled easily, and this morning he looked ready to erupt."

I swallow. "Yeah. I might've hit a nerve."

Maggie softens. "Don't let it follow you into today. Fix what you can before you walk into that boardroom."

I nod, even if my chest feels tight. "You're right."

I flip the machine off and on, reseat the portafilter, adjust the grind. It sputters, coughs, then finally pours a steady stream.

"Thank you," Maggie says softly.

"Of course." I slip on my blazer and check my phone. If I leave now, I can get to the office on time after a quick stop.

Twenty minutes later, I park in front of my parents' townhouse and let myself in.

My mom is curled up on the living room sofa, glasses low on her nose, a paperback splayed in her hand. Surprise skitters across her face when she looks up, then melts into a grin.

"Well, look who remembered she has a mother." She sets the book on the coffee table and opens her arms. "Ever since you got married to that hunk of yours, we've barely seen you."

It hasn't been that long since Brianna's birthday, but I can't remember the last time I visited my parents. I drop my tote by the armchair and throw myself onto the couch beside her. "Hi, Mama."

She studies me for half a breath. "What's wrong?"

I exhale. "I have the Project Rebuild presentation today."

"I know." Mom nods toward the mantel where my grad photo still sits crooked. "I lit a candle this morning."

"Thank you."

"But that's not why you came."

I lean back, staring at the ceiling like it might give me all the answers.

"I got into an argument with Worth," I say, picking around the edges. I'm not ready to uproot the whole truth. "About the project board... and me."

Her brows lift. "Go on."

"I told him I'm worried they'll fund the project because of my new last name, not my work. And that people will think I slept my way into an opportunity." The words taste ugly coming out. "He said an advantage isn't always bad. I said he doesn't understand. Then it got heated."

My mom is quiet for a moment. "When your father and I got together, people had opinions. He was older, had some money, and everyone said I only dated him because of that, including your grandparents."

I turn my head. "What did you do?"

"I worked twice as hard, so no one could make me feel like I didn't belong in the room I earned."

"That's the thing," I whisper. "I don't want anyone thinking—"

"Sweetheart." She reaches over and taps my knee. "People will think. That's what they do. Your job is to know who you are and what you've built. If a hand opens a door out of love or partnership, that doesn't erase your competence. It just means you're not walking alone."

I stare at our reflections on the black TV screen. "He said I don't see him and that I think he's just money and reputation."

"Do you?"

I shake my head. "No. I see how he is with Brianna. How he listens and remembers the small things, like how scared I am to fly, or when he checks to see if I've eaten when I've had long days. He cares deeply about his friends and family even though he comes off as rude and cold. He values his employees and their work, even if he rarely shows it. I see... more." The admission leaves me exposed.

"And he sees *you*. Which is why it stung when you threw his last name at him like a weapon."

I wince. "I didn't mean to hurt him."

"I know." She squeezes my hand. "But intention and impact aren't twins."

Silence again. The words I didn't say this morning cling to my skin like humidity. *I'm falling. This was never supposed to be real.*

"Here's my advice. Don't shrink yourself to prove you're not using anyone. And don't shrink Worth to prove you don't need him. If you want this project, claim it. If you love this man, tell him the truth—or at least stop lying to yourself."

I huff a laugh. "What's the truth?"

"That you're afraid." Her smile is a little sad. "Afraid that if you let your feelings sink in too deep, it will still end. Afraid that you'll lose him. Fear makes people pick fights they don't mean."

Something tightens in my chest. I've been afraid since the day we lost Dad and the world never went back to normal. I learned early that love can be a trapdoor; one minute you're standing on solid ground, the next you're falling, and there's no way to brace for impact.

Mom must see the thought cross my face. "When your father died, you started building walls and calling them plans. You needed to survive—and I understand that. But, Mya, not everyone who loves you is going to leave."

"What if it doesn't work? What if I open the door and it's just emptiness again?"

"It might not work. But you'll still be you. And the you I know is brave, even when she's shaking. Don't let old grief make all your new decisions for you. Let it teach you how precious it is when someone stays, and how to stay, too."

I breathe out, long and shaky. "I have to go. I still need to get to the office."

My mom stands and kisses my forehead, the same way she used to when I was little and needed comforting. "You will be brilliant. And if they give you anything because of a last name, take it and show them why the *first* name is what matters."

I grab my tote and step toward the door, then pivot back. "Mom?"

"Yes, love?"

"Thanks." I swallow. "For lighting the candle. And for the truth."

Her eyes shine. "Text me when it's done, okay?"

"Promise."

Outside, the air is crisp enough to make me stand a little

straighter. I unlock my car and sit with my phone in my hand for five seconds of courage. Then I type:

> I didn't mean what I said this morning. I'm sorry.

I don't wait for a reply. I start the engine, set the route, and pull into traffic.

I'm ready to stand in front of the board and make sure they remember *my* name.

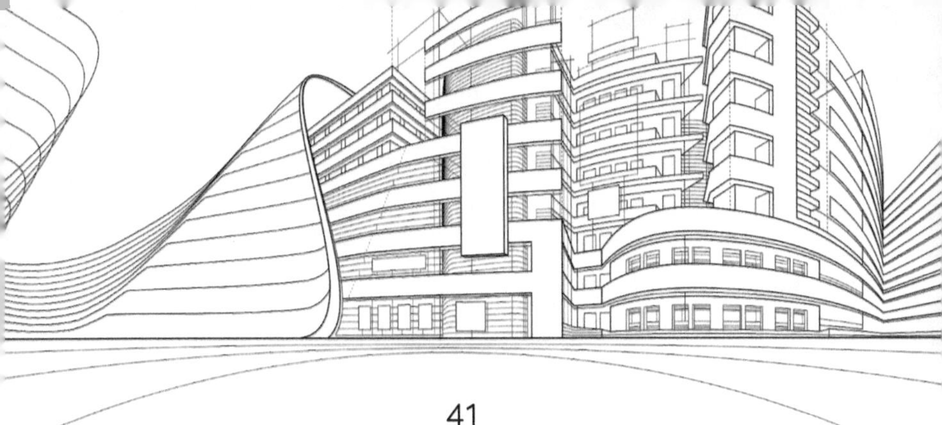

Worth

I close the door to the small conference room off my office and face the board of three internal directors, two externals, and the two I actually trust: Henson at the far end, Griffin beside him, arms folded.

"I'll be brief," I say, palms flat on the table. "Mya is presenting Project Rebuild this morning. She's my wife. You all know that. Here's what else you should know." I let my eyes cut across them. "She earned the slot. She ran the modeling. She built the partnerships. If her last name were anything else, I'd say the same thing I'm saying now."

One of the external directors shifts uncomfortably.

"You will evaluate the deck, the plan, and the numbers. Not the ring on her hand. You will not rubber-stamp it because she shares my address." I pause. "And you will not make her climb a steeper hill because of it either."

I can almost hear them doing PR calculus in their heads.

"She gets the same treatment as any candidate. No gentler. No harsher. That's the standard. We clear?"

Henson's mouth twitches. Griffin nods once.

A director clears his throat. "Mr. Miller, to avoid any perception issues, I assume you'll be recusing yourself?"

"I already signed the recusal," I say, sliding copies toward them. "I won't be in the room. The board coordinator will chair. You have what you need. You also have my expectations."

I hold each of their gazes in turn, then straighten. "That's all."

Chairs scrape and they file out, except Henson and Griffin.

When the door clicks shut behind the last director, my brother drags a hand through his hair. "All right, Worth. You want to tell us what's actually going on?"

"Nothing is 'actually' going on."

Griffin gives me a look I've known since we were kids. "What happened?"

"And don't give us the CEO version," Henson adds.

I exhale through my nose, staring at the grain of the table. "Mya and I fought this morning."

"About the board?" Griffin asks.

"About all of it." My jaw tightens. "She said she's worried the board will fund the project because she's Mrs. Miller, not because she deserves it. She also said when our arrangement ends, I'll still be me, and she'll be the ex who people think slept her way to the top. That we could never work outside of this."

Henson's brows lift. "And what did you say?"

"I told her she's wrong. I thought she saw *me* and not just this stupid fucking deal we made." I shake my head.

Henson and Griffin trade a look. Griff leans forward, forearms on his knees. "Be straight with us, Worth. Are you in love with her?"

The answer is so obvious, I barely have to think about it. "Yes."

Henson lets out a slow breath, like he'd been waiting to hear it out loud. "Okay."

"It doesn't matter," I add, before either of them can say anything else. I keep my voice even, because if I don't, I might lose my composure. "She doesn't feel the same. So I'm going to do what we agreed. I'm going to see this through, give her what we promised, and give her the out."

Griffin's mouth flattens. "You're out of your damn mind."

Henson nods, surprisingly fierce. "Mya cares about you. It's written all over her, man. You're the only one pretending not to see it."

A humorless laugh scrapes out of my throat. "If that's caring, she's got a funny way of showing it."

"She's scared," Henson says, as if it's the most obvious thing in the world.

Griffin agrees. "The woman moves into your house, takes your kid seriously, then fights you because she wants her work respected, not your name to carry her. That isn't indifference, Worth."

I rub the bridge of my nose. The room smells faintly of coffee and the lemon oil the cleaners use. The mix is giving me a damn headache. "I'm not going to argue feelings with you two."

"Then don't," Griffin says. "But don't lie to yourself either. You're still trying to control the situation, and you think honoring the deal means you have to pretend you don't want more."

I look at the closed door. "We made a promise. I keep promises."

"Keeping a promise and killing something good aren't the same thing," Henson murmurs quietly.

I cut my gaze back to him. "I'm not pushing. I'm not going to beg her to want me. I'll just keep pretending until it's over."

Griffin stands first, sliding his chair in with military precision. "You're like my brother, so I'll say this once: you're being a fucking idiot."

Henson nods in agreement and claps my shoulder before heading to the door.

They leave me alone in my office, and I stare at the table until the wood blurs.

I pick up my phone and open Mya's message from earlier.

MYA:

I didn't mean what I said this morning. I'm sorry.

I read it once. Twice. My thumb hovers over the keyboard uselessly.

I put the device facedown, the apology burning a hole on my desk. Then I stand, button my jacket, and step out of my office.

Mya is crossing the lobby with her folio, shoulders straight as she readies to face the board.

I don't go after her.

Instead, I take up my post in the hallway, pretending to scroll through emails.

I last ten minutes.

Then I find myself drifting down the corridor toward Conference B, and take a peek.

Mya stands at the head of the room, her back to me.

Slide light washes the wall: neighborhood heat maps, phased budgets, a tidy "Q3–Q4 ROI" in the corner. Her voice carries just enough through the door seam to reach me.

"As you can see, the risk is front-loaded, but so is the goodwill. The model compounds not just financially, but reputationally."

A director leans in. Even from out here, I can tell she's got them.

Then, as if she can *feel* me through the glass, she turns and her eyes find mine. I give her the smallest nod I've got.

Mya answers with a timid smile then pivots back to the board, clicking to the next slide as if she hasn't just knocked the air out of me with a look.

I step away from the window before the coordinator can scold me for hovering.

Damn, I'm proud of her.

My phone buzzes the second I turn the corner.

RYAN:

> Court just got advanced. The judge had an opening. Hearing is set for two days from today. I'll come by your office this afternoon to review the files and prep strategy.

Fuck. *Two days?* We weren't scheduled to see the judge for another two weeks.

My stomach flips. The case has been a drumbeat under everything, but now it's real.

I text Ryan my reply. Before slipping my phone back into my pocket, I consider texting Mya back, but I still can't find the right words.

Instead, I turn toward my office to pull the custody files. If I can't stand beside Mya in there, I'll damn well be ready to stand in front of Vanessa in court.

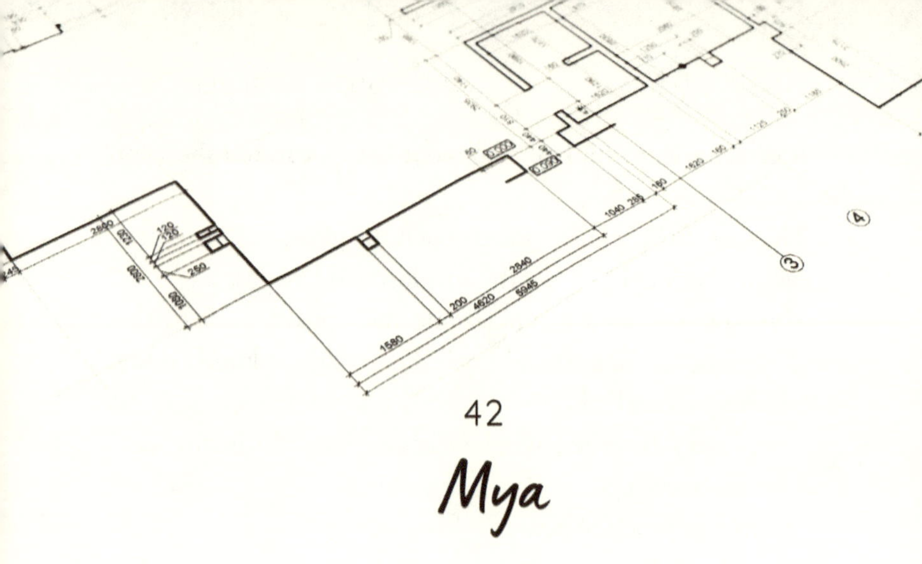

42

Mya

The door to the conference room clicks shut behind me, and the adrenaline that kept my spine straight for the last forty minutes drains out all the way down my body through to my heels, and my legs go a little watery.

Through the glass wall across the corridor, I catch a glimpse of Worth in his office—jacket off, sleeves rolled up, eyes glued to a stack of documents.

God, those forearms.

The way the fabric bites at his elbows, the veins standing out when he turns a page, do dangerous things to my pulse. It's infuriating how much I love any look on him.

For half a second I think about knocking, but I don't.

He never replied to my text. I tell myself he might need space, and that the smart thing is to give it to him. I adjust my blazer and head for my desk.

Seraya pops up the moment she sees me. "Well? How'd it go?"

I sag into my chair. "I didn't faint. Or cry. Or throw up."

"Low bar, babe, but I'll take it." She leans on the partition. "But Seriously?"

"It went good. They asked tough questions, but I had the answers. The board will reconvene and give everyone their decision in a month." Saying it out loud makes the waiting feel like an Olympic event.

"A month!" Seraya theatrically clutches at her chest.

I laugh. "I know, right?"

Her phone lights up on the edge of the desk. She grimaces when she sees the name. "Ugh. My landlord."

"Take it," I tell her. "I'll be here, breathing in and out like it's my full-time job."

She swipes to answer with a long-suffering sigh, pacing away. "Yes, Rafael?"

The office hums around me. Keyboards. Low conversation. The distant ping of the elevator. I stack my presentation notes into a neat pile I don't need to look at anymore and stare across the open floor to Dre's desk. If Worth needs space now, I can at least find out if he's available later.

I stand and make my way over. "Hey, Dre. Is he busy today?"

She glances toward the glass. "Ryan is coming by soon." Her voice dips. "They're going over case files."

My stomach tightens. The custody battle. "Right. Thanks."

I hover for a second, then move to the office and rap my knuckles lightly on Worth's door before easing it open.

He looks up.

"Bad time?"

Worth's expression is polite. Not cold, just... contained. "I've got a few minutes."

I close the door, suddenly aware of the way my pulse thumps in my wrists. "I, um... just wanted to let you know the presentation went well. They'll deliberate and get back to us in a month."

He nods once. "Good. I'm glad."

The space I created between us is yawning wide.

"Dre said you're meeting with Ryan. Everything okay?"

He leans back in his chair, fingers steepled. "The court moved our date." A beat. "It's in two days."

"Oh. That's... soon."

"Yeah." He looks past me, just for a second. When his gaze returns, it's all business. "We'll prep this afternoon and tomorrow. It's straightforward. It also means you'll be getting out of our arrangement sooner than planned."

Said so simply.

I nod because that's what I'm supposed to do. This is what I keep insisting I want. A clean end. Though my heart does not get the memo. It lurches, knocking into all the places I've been guarding.

"Okay," I manage. "If you need anything, just let me know."

"Ryan and I have it handled," he says, dismissive in the old Worth way, like when I first met him.

"Right." I nod again, not knowing what else to do with my hands, my voice, my face. "Then I'll, um, get back to work."

"Do that." He reaches for a folder. The conversation is over.

I turn for the door and pause with my hand on the handle. "Worth?"

He looks up.

"You'll do right by Bri."

For a moment, the control in his face cracks. I see the man who waited outside a conference room for me because he couldn't *not*. Then he nods once, the mask sliding back into place. "Thank you."

I step out before I do something stupid, like cry.

There's no one to blame for the cool edge in Worth's voice but the woman who sharpened it.

Back at my desk, Seraya is finishing her call, eyes stormy. She mouths *later* and I nod, sinking into my chair like it might hold me together.

I open my laptop and start typing up my post-mortem notes while I try to remember that I asked for lines, for rules, for endings.

I got them. Now I have to live with them.

At the end of the day, I pack up slowly. When I finally sling my tote over my shoulder and head for the elevator, the light is still on in Worth's office.

He doesn't usually stay past five-thirty. At least he hasn't in the past few months. He hates missing dinner with Bri.

Is it because of me? Logic says it's the custody prep and a day swallowed by his lawyer. But my chest says I'm part of the reason.

I stand there for a second, arguing with myself before I finally sigh and knock.

"Come in," he calls, voice rough.

He's at his desk, expression strained, papers spread around him. He barely looks up.

"You're still here," I say gently.

He signs something. "Looks like it."

"You should go home," I try again. "Eat. Rest. Be with Bri. Let your lawyer handle the rest tomorrow."

His pen stills.

"Mya, please don't do that."

"Do what?" I frown.

"Care," he says, sharper now. "Not like that. Not in that soft, worried tone that makes me think we're... something. Because five minutes later you'll remember you don't want that and suddenly I'm the asshole who didn't get the memo."

The words knock the breath out of me.

"That's not fair."

He finally looks up at me, eyes tired and frustrated. "Isn't it? Earlier you were the one pulling away. *Again.* Now, you're checking on me like you didn't just slam a door in my face." He shakes his head. "I don't know what you want from me anymore."

"I want you to be okay," I whisper.

Worth exhales, rubbing a hand over his face as if exhausted by himself and me and everything in between.

"Just go home, Mya. I'll be fine."

There's nothing left to say. So I nod and back away.

Instead of heading straight home, I drive across town to the community center gym, where cheer practice is wrapping up. The sun is dipping low, painting the parking lot in late-afternoon gold as kids spill out laughing.

Brianna spots the car, waves like she hasn't seen me in months, and jogs over. I told Maggie I'd pick Bri up today, and the sight of her is like a balm to the ache in my chest.

"Hey, Mya!" she grins as she climbs in, tossing her bag to the back. Her cheeks are flushed.

"Hey, superstar," I smile. "Good practice?"

She launches into a rundown of stunts, near disasters, and the girl who cried because someone messed up her TikTok, and somewhere between her dramatics and laughter, the heaviness of the day loosens.

Several minutes later, I pull into the driveway of Worth's estate.

Inside, Maggie is at the stove, spoon in hand, adding one last pinch of salt to something that smells delicious.

"Hi, lovelies," she chirps with a smile. "Perfect timing. Dinner's just done. Though I won't be staying tonight."

I set my tote on the bench and toe off my shoes. "Everything okay?"

"Oh, yes. I promised Worth's mother I'd call her and help with the banquet hall plans for her next event." She pats my arm as she passes. "You two will be fine."

Before I can answer, Brianna skids into the kitchen in socks. There's already a smudge of graphite on her fingers and a halo of baby hairs around her face from the ponytail she ditched after practice.

"It's just you and me tonight, babe." I lean down to bump her forehead to mine. "We're flying solo."

"How come?"

I keep my tone light. "Your dad is preparing for the custody case so he'll be late."

Bri nods once, eyes dropping to her socks. Her shoulders go a little square, and the skin at her throat tightens.

"Hey," I say softly. "It'll be okay."

She flicks her gaze up, then away. "Yeah. I know."

Maggie slips her cardigan over her shoulders and grabs her purse. "Call me if you need anything, girls."

"Thanks, Maggie." I see her out, then turn back to the kitchen. "All right, chef. Plates?"

While we eat dinner, I tell her about my coworkers' bad habits and Bri counters with a story about a girl in math class who keeps drawing male genitalia on her binder. After, we clear the table together and slide the dishes into the dishwasher. Then we draw for an hour at the dining table.

Bri's phone pings on the counter. She swipes it, reads, and chews her lip. "It's Dad. He says he's on his way home."

"Oh, okay." I aim for nonchalant, but the disappointment threads my voice before I can catch it.

Brianna looks up at me. "Did something happen?"

"No," I say too quickly, drying my hands on a towel. "It's—no."

"I'm not blind. Something is going on. Dad was acting like someone had pissed in his shoes this morning."

A laugh flies out of me.

I prop a hip against the counter and choose honesty, if not the whole of it. "We got into a little fight, but it's fine. We'll make up."

She studies me like a puzzle with one piece missing. "Okay."

We head upstairs together. At her door, Brianna starts to duck into her room, but I stop her. "Hey, can I come in for a minute?"

"Sure."

Bri drops onto the edge of her bed, fussing with the hem of her T-shirt. I sit beside her, leaving an inch of space.

"You got quiet earlier," I say. "When I told you about the case."

She shrugs, eyes on her fingers. "It's just... I don't know what I'm supposed to do about my mom." The last word comes out hesitant, like it doesn't fit right in her mouth. "Everyone has opinions. Grandma. Maggie. Dad."

"What about you? What do *you* want?"

"I don't know. I feel bad if I say I want to see her. Like I'm betraying Dad. But I feel weird if I say I don't. I keep thinking she'll get mad or—" She swallows. "Or leave again."

I reach over, palm up. Bri places her hand in mine, fingers tense. "You're not responsible for anyone else's feelings here. Not your dad's, not Vanessa's, not anyone else's. This is *your* choice. If you want to try seeing your mom, slowly, on your terms, that's okay. And if you need space, that's okay too."

She blinks fast. "Dad hates Mom."

"Dad is protective of you," I correct gently. "And he loves *you* more than he hates anything. If you decide you want a relationship with her, I know he'll respect that. You don't have to avoid your mother to prove you're loyal to him. That's not your job."

"But what if I try and it sucks?"

"Then we regroup. We set new boundaries. We make a different plan. You won't be alone in it. We'll be with you the whole way." I breathe, then add, "I don't talk about it much, but I know what it feels like to miss a parent. My dad died when I was little." The old ache wakes up, familiar and dull. "I remember that empty feeling, and the way it makes you scared to let people in—because what if they leave, too?"

Bri's chin trembles. "Yeah."

"We can't fix the past. But wanting connection doesn't make you weak. It makes you human."

Her face crumples. She tips sideways and presses her forehead to my shoulder. I wrap an arm around her and rub slow circles between her shoulder blades, letting her cry into my T-shirt.

"I don't want to hurt Dad if I want to see Mom sometimes," she says into the fabric. "I want to know why she left. And if she's really different now."

"That's honest and brave."

Brianna sniffs, pulls back, and I pass her a tissue from her nightstand. "How do I tell him?"

"Tell him exactly what you told me. That you want to try, on your terms. And if it ever stops feeling okay, you get to change your mind."

Her shoulders loosen a fraction. We sit there a minute more. Bri squeezes my hand, then releases it.

"Thanks, Mya," she says.

"Anytime." I brush a curl behind her ear and stand, smoothing the quilt on her bed before heading out into the hall.

Brianna stops me. "Mya?"

"Yeah?"

"I'm glad you're here."

The words land soft and fiercely in my chest at once. "Me too, Bri," I say. "Me too."

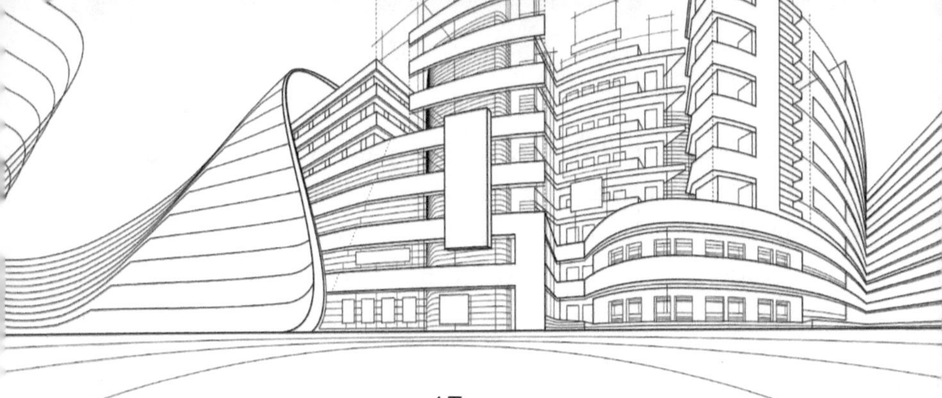

43

Worth

The house is quiet when I step inside.

I set my keys in the bowl by the door and listen. No Maggie humming, no footsteps thudding down the stairs, no Brianna watching a show at full volume.

The alarm panel blinks green and the place smells like roast chicken and lemon, so I know they're home.

I take off my shoes and head for the kitchen. The counters are wiped, the dishwasher is running and there are two glasses turned upside down on a dish towel to dry. Someone folded the dishcloth into a neat square—Mya's doing. She straightens small things when she's thinking too hard.

I check the family room. Empty, save for a wolf sketch that sits on the console with a half-moon penciled behind it.

All right. So either they're upstairs or in the theater. If it were a movie, I'd hear it by now. That leaves rooms.

I lean a hip against the island and rub a hand over my face. Today feels like three days stacked on top of each other. Ryan and I went page by page through the custody binders—attendance logs, school reports, witness statements, incident summaries. We flagged what the judge will care about and what Vanessa's attorney will throw against the wall hoping something sticks. It's all there in black and white: stability, education, medical, Bri's stated preferences. We're close. Two more letters from her counselor and the activity coordinator at her after-school program, and the file is as clean as it gets. We'll be ready.

I should feel lighter with the plan set. Instead, I feel scraped out.

I open the fridge for no reason, stare at a row of meal-prep containers, shut it again. I don't realize how long I've been standing there until the dishwasher changes cycles and I flinch like an idiot.

I think about the look on Mya's face in my office and guilt slides under my ribs in a dull ache. I don't like how I treated her today. It goes against every instinct I have around her. But I can't pretend I didn't hear her words this morning. She's said it a dozen ways since the day we signed papers: she expects nothing from this. No promises, no future, no mess beyond the one we were already in.

And why the hell would I keep pouring into a place that doesn't want more from me than a clean exit?

Because I want to, that's why.

Because being with Mya feels like a wire pulled tight in my chest.

Because I'm proud of her.

Because I care, no matter how I pretend.

I push off the counter and walk toward the stairs. I owe Mya better than the cold shoulder I put on today, but "better" keeps trying to turn into "more," and she drew a clear line. I'm not going to push her past it. Though I shouldn't punish her for it either.

I can't rewrite the rules alone, so I'll honor the deal. And I'll try to be the version of myself I'm not ashamed to look at in the mirror when it's over.

My phone buzzes. It's Ryan confirming that those last two letters are in motion for morning. I text back a thumbs up and a thank you, which feels inadequate for a man who's spent countless hours lining my life up so I can keep the most important part of it intact.

I stop and press a palm to the bannister. It's a stupid, steadying habit—touching something solid to remind myself I'm solid too.

From the landing, I can hear voices. I'm halfway to knocking on the door to my daughter's bedroom when something stops me.

Bri's voice is small. "Dad hates Mom."

I freeze, palm flat on the doorframe, holding my breath.

Mya's voice comes out steady like an anchor. "Dad is protective of you. And he loves *you* more than he hates anything. If you decide you want a relationship with your mother, I know he'll respect that. You don't have to avoid her to prove you're loyal to him. That's not your job."

My chest tightens as I listen to Mya comfort my daughter, reassuring her with a certainty I haven't been able to give. I've spent years telling myself it was enough to be both parent and safety net, that it was the two of us against the world.

But standing here, I realize that Brianna has been keeping her wishes secret, folding them away so she doesn't "betray" me. Protecting *me* when it should have been the other way around.

Hearing Mya wrap herself around my daughter's fear like it belongs to her too breaks me open in the best way. It shows me exactly where I've failed without ever making me feel accused.

I've been so focused on shielding Brianna from pain that I didn't notice she was learning to shrink herself for my comfort.

I just want to walk in, thank Mya, kiss her temple, and tell Bri she doesn't owe me her loyalty. But this is their moment, not mine, and I won't steal it by making it about me.

I back away on quiet feet, pulse loud in my ears, and head for the bedroom. Once inside, I sit on the edge of the bed and stare at my hands, knuckles nicked from the woodwork I did for Brianna's birthday gift.

I toe off my socks, stand, and start unbuttoning my shirt.

The bedroom door cracks open a few moments later and Mya steps in. She stops dead when she sees me halfway out of my shirt. Her eyes flick to my chest, then to the floor.

"Sorry," she says quickly, already backing out. "I didn't know you were here. I'll come back later."

"Mya." My voice comes out tighter than I mean it, and she freezes, hand on the knob. "Come back in here and close the door."

She hesitates for a fraction, then eases the door shut and turns around, chin up.

I hook my shirt off my shoulder and toss it onto the chair. I take a breath, reining in the parts of me that want to cross the space and pull her to me. "I heard some of your conversation with Bri."

Color touches her cheeks. "I didn't mean to overstep. She just needed to talk."

"I know." I take a step closer and stop. "And you said exactly what she needed to hear."

Her shoulders drop a notch. "She's scared of hurting you."

"I know," I repeat, quieter. "And I don't want that for her. I never have."

Silence stretches, full of the things I should have said earlier and didn't.

"I wasn't great today," I admit. "With you." I find the edge of the dresser, grip it. "I kept it cold. I'm sorry."

Mya studies my face, guarded. "We're fine. It's been a long day."

I shake my head. "I'm sorry for keeping you at arm's length. It's not how I want to treat you. I just—" I search for the cleanest version of the truth. "I don't know how to be near you without wanting more than you've said you want."

Her eyes soften. "Worth..."

"I'm not asking for anything," I say, raising my palms. "I just want to thank you for being there for Bri. For saying the exact right thing and making this house feel like a place she can bring the hard parts to."

Mya swallows, the barest nod. "She's brave. She just needed permission to be honest."

"I'm grateful for that, and I can see you care about her a lot."

"Bri is easy to care about."

"So are you." It slips out before I can stop it. Her breath hitches, and I let the admission hang there, simple and true.

Mya swallows. "You don't have to thank me for loving her."

That cracks me open all over again. I look away for a moment, then back.

I take another slow step toward her. "May I?"

She doesn't ask *what*. After a beat, she nods.

I lift a hand to her cheek, my thumb finding the faint damp track of a tear. Her skin is warm.

"I'm proud of you for today," I say, lower now. "And thank you, again. For putting up with me, even when I'm not at my best."

Her mouth tips, sad and small. "You were protecting yourself."

"Maybe. Doesn't make it right."

My hand moves to her jaw, thumb feathering just below her ear. Mya leans into it and I move forward. When she doesn't step away, I close the gap. The first touch of my mouth on hers is careful, testing the weight of this new shape we're taking. Mya exhales into the kiss, and something in my chest unclenches.

I kiss her again, a little surer this time. The tension of the day spills out of me and meets everything she's been holding onto. Her fingers gather at my nape.

When her lips part for me, I go slow. Deep.

We break just long enough to breathe, foreheads touching, noses brushing. She lets out a small, helpless sound, and I take it for what it is and find her mouth again.

The kiss changes, heat catching like a match. Between each breath, each brush of her mouth, the words tear loose before I can swallow them.

"I'll take whatever you give me," I murmur, lips skimming hers. "If 'just for now' is all I get, I'll take it."

Mya makes a sound, like a protest.

"I want to use the time we have," I whisper against her lower lip. "All of it. I want you, even if it's only—"

Her eyes go glossy, throat working like she's about to object. Instead, she surges up and kisses me harder, pulling me closer, as if proximity is the only thing that will keep her together. I answer in kind, but there's no mistaking the urgency threading through it, the plea to feel what's already true.

"Mya," I breathe, tasting the tremble of her inhale.

"Don't," she whispers back, shaking her head a fraction. "Not right now."

I turn us around and back her up against the bed, letting her fall onto the mattress.

"I need to taste you, Kitten. Please."

I've resorted to begging—because Mya-fucking-Dessen-Jones has me whipped.

And I'm in love with her.

Whether or not I get to keep her after doesn't change that fact.

Mya nods, and I pull on the hem of her pants, slipping them down her smooth, long legs, letting my fingers trail over her skin. She gasps as I kiss my way up her thighs. When I get to her mound, I bury my nose in her thong and breathe in long and deep.

Fuck.

This woman is my undoing.

"You smell like mine, Mya," I say, nipping at her clit through the fabric. "And I can't get enough."

"Worth, I-I... Ah!" She's unable to get the words out as I push her panties to the side and close my mouth around her delectable pussy.

I lap my tongue around her clit, enjoying the way each stroke elicits a whimper out of her, and decide I've had enough of her thong being in the way. I rip it in one pull.

Mya's upper body lifts off the bed. "Worth Miller!" she scolds, despite her voice trembling with need. "At this rate, I won't have any underwear left!"

I don't take my mouth off her as I reach into my back pocket, pulling out my wallet and fishing out my credit card. I throw it at her, just as I suck her clit into my mouth, and her back arches off the bed.

"2411," I mutter.

"What?"

"2411 is the pin."

Mya then notices the card lying next to her on the bed. "Why are you giving me this?"

"To buy new panties," I reply, inching two fingers into her entrance. "Buy the whole fucking store if you want. I don't care." I flick my tongue on her clit once more. She moans. "But

I'm not going to stop tearing those flimsy pieces of fabric off *my* pussy."

Mya rolls her eyes, and I clamp down on her, enough to make her yelp.

"Fuck!"

"A normal response would've been "Thank you, Mr. Miller"."

"No."

I bite down again.

"God! Fine, you crazy man. *Thank you, Mr. Miller,*" she drawls in a mocking tone.

"You're asking for it, pretty girl," I growl.

Mya bats her lashes, feigning innocence. "What ever do you mean, Mr. Miller."

I groan.

Hearing her call me Mr. Miller in bed feels exactly how I thought it would.

"Mya, baby. You need to come, and you need to come *now,* so I can shove my cock so deep up your tight cunt, you're choking on it for days."

"Then stop talking and make me."

Challenge accepted.

I dive right back in, showing no mercy, sucking and licking on her pussy like a man starved. After only a few seconds, I feel Mya's legs trembling, her body going taut.

"Keep going," she urges, and I don't slow down.

I stick my fingers back inside her and beckon on her sensitive spot.

She explodes, screaming. She grabs a pillow and shoves it over her face, her hips bucking against my mouth.

Mya squirted again.

I feel like a fucking champion.

This time, she doesn't cower at the sight of her arousal coating the sheets and my face. Instead, she smiles. *Good girl.*

"Turn around, pretty girl."

Mya obeys, getting on her hands and knees, her round ass on display for me. I ogle her as I unbuckle my pants to free my aching cock.

I drop them, followed by my briefs, and rub my length.

"Don't move," I instruct, walking over to my nightstand, pulling out the item I spontaneously bought with my wife in mind.

"Put a finger inside yourself."

Mya does, moaning and sliding her index and middle fingers in and out, as I take the object out of its packaging.

I then spread her ass cheeks apart. She gasps and attempts to wiggle away.

"I said don't move, Mya."

She stops.

I spit onto her tight hole and rub the butt plug around it.

"Do you trust me, Kitten?"

Mya nods, still fingering herself at a slow and steady pace.

"Pick a safeword."

Her body goes stiff. "What are you planning?"

"Nothing you won't enjoy. I promise."

She hesitates for a few seconds, then says, "Playboy."

"Good. Use it if you need me to stop, okay?"

"Okay."

I ease the plug into Mya's rimmed hole, and her entire body tenses. "Relax, baby. Let me in."

I bend over to pepper kisses all over her back and continue pushing the toy inside. It begins to slip in easier. "That's it. You're doing good. Keep fucking yourself."

Her moans get needier and louder as the plug finds its home.

"There you go. Such a good little wife. Soon, you'll be ready to take me there, but for now, I'm going to replace your hand with my cock, then fill you with my cum until it's leaking out of every hole."

Mya shivers at my words, squirming. I move her hand away, angling myself at her entrance. Then I push inside, easily this time—because of how wet and ready she is—but her tightness still sucks me in and keeps me hostage. I go still, needing a second to compose myself before I blow my load prematurely. Shit. I don't think I'll ever get used to this.

Mya lets out a guttural moan when I begin to move. "I feel so full. Oh, God."

I smack her ass, then grip it tight as I pound into her.

My pace is punishing, but Mya takes it, not complaining once. I've come to realize she likes it a bit rough, and I have no issues giving it to her exactly the way her body craves.

My wife is a closeted freak.

After countless thrusts and the many 'fucks' and curses that come out of our mouths, Mya tells me she's close.

"Whenever you're ready, baby. I'm right there with you," I tell her.

Within seconds, she goes silent, her body stiffening as she bites down on a pillow to avoid screaming again.

My wife is also a screamer.

I follow her, a loud groan erupting from my chest as I fill her cunt with my seed.

"Damn."

Mya giggles in response, breathless.

I turn her around, and climb atop her.

My mouth finds her in a searing kiss, our rapid breaths mingling together as we both come down from our highs.

We make out for a while and then I grab onto my semi-hard cock and rub it over her pussy, taking the cum that has started leaking out and pushing it back inside. The act is already making me hard again.

I've never been able to bounce back this fast, but there's something about Mya that I can't get enough of.

"How was that?" I ask, pointing down to the plug still inside her.

"Oh. I almost forgot it was in there," she says shyly. "Really good. I've never had anything in there before."

"Well, I'm honored to have been granted that first." I kiss her lips again. "Bring your knees up for me." She does, and I spread them apart. I reach over to my nightstand, grabbing a bottle of lube from the drawer and spreading a generous amount over my hardened length.

"Take a deep breath for me, Kitten."

She inhales. I pull out the plug, and she exhales a gasp.

"Another one."

Mya breathes in again as I place the tip of my cock at her asshole. She lets out the breath, and I push inside slowly.

MYA

"Oh, God," I moan, feeling Worth's thick cock penetrating my ass. It's not painful, but it's such a foreign feeling, I can't help but tense up.

"Keep breathing," Worth instructs, and I take in some air. "Good girl. I'm almost there."

I continue to draw in breaths as he inches in slowly. If I thought I felt full before, it's nothing compared to now. At first, I didn't think I'd be able to handle Worth's girth inside my pussy, let alone my asshole, but I trust him to make me feel good.

Once he's buried to the hilt, he starts to pull in and out, careful not to go too fast.

"Are you okay, baby?"

Baby. Kitten. Pretty girl. Wife.

Words that melt me and make me giddy at the same time. I'll never tire of hearing them from him. Worth may not be mine to keep, but I'll soak up everything he gives.

I nod. "Yes. I'm more than okay, *husband*."

His cock responds before his mouth does.

"Fuck, Mya. Say that again."

"Husband," I repeat, dropping my voice. He likes it; I can tell by the way his pace quickens.

He lowers his face and kisses me, sucking on my tongue and then nipping at my bottom lip.

"I can't wait to fill this hole too. Fuck,' he grunts, and I moan in response. "Flick your clit, Kitten. I want to see you touch yourself."

I do as he says, ever the obedient wife. I'm no pushover usually—least of all with Worth, who gets the brunt of my bite—but here, I *love* when he takes control.

I feel another orgasm cresting as Worth fucks my behind and I keep up the movement up with my fingers.

A surge of pure ecstasy seizes me and my release crashes through me like a storm.

"Yes, yes, yes," I chant. Worth goes still on top of me, bringing his face to the crook of my neck and letting out a muffled groan.

He pulls out slowly, and I immediately feel empty, and he disappears into the ensuite, leaving me naked against the sheets. A couple of minutes later he's back, wearing fresh briefs, a damp cloth in hand.

Worth cleans me gently, unhurried. We don't speak, though it isn't awkward.

Is this what it's like to have someone care for you?

I don't have exes worth mentioning, since I've never done serious or long-term, but this doesn't feel normal. Worth Miller is a phenomenon.

A really hot, really rich phenomenon who just fucked me six ways to Sunday.

Too bad it's temporary. *This is what you wanted,* I remind myself.

I squeeze my eyes shut, willing my tireless inner monologue to quiet down.

Later, we lie side by side, staring up at the ceiling. Our bodies almost touch—but not quite—like crossing that last inch would break some new rule. Ridiculous, given what we just did —yet somehow this feels more intimate. I let my pinky graze his hand. Worth catches the hint, draws my fingers into his, and rubs his thumb slowly over my palm.

Without looking at me, he asks, "Just for now?" His voice is low.

I nod. "Just for now."

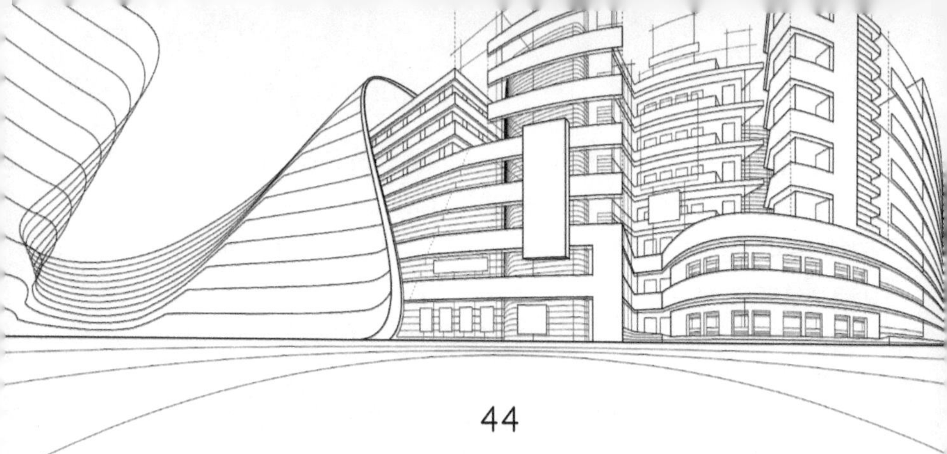

44

Worth

My stomach is in a fist.

Nerves buzz under my skin—but I'm ready.

Today, I walk in as Brianna's father. Everything else is noise.

First, I stop at work, because life doesn't pause for anything. The elevator doors slide open on the fifteenth floor, and I say good morning and nod to passing employees, then head down the glass corridor.

Shaina's desk sits empty. The day after she started spewing nonsense about being in my office, the HR clerk, scared of losing her job, went straight to Claire and told her everything. She handled it and terminated Shaina the next morning.

Good riddance.

I push through my door and set my briefcase on my desk. The new Paris project package is sitting atop of it: a three-inch block of paper with several tabs.

I sigh, shrugging out of my coat, rolling my shoulders once, and flip to the flagged pages. The terms are exactly as we nego-tiated—conservative on timeline, aggressive on quality control, plenty of outs if the market blinks. I uncap my pen and sign where the red arrows tell me to.

"Brother."

I glance up. Henson is leaning in the doorway.

"You look like you haven't slept," Henson says.

Translation: you look like shit.

"I'll sleep after the judge rules," I answer.

Griffin steps in behind him. "You've got this. The case is clean. You're the steady parent. Everybody can see it."

"Textbook," Henson adds. "And if it isn't, I'll file a textbook at the judge."

I huff something like a laugh. "Appreciate the confidence."

Henson sobers. "Seriously. Good luck in there today."

My throat works around the word. "Thanks."

We're silent for a second, then Henson slides a small wrapped candy across my desk. "For after," he says with a chuckle. "Because you'll forget to eat."

"Get out of my office," I tell him, pocketing the sweet with a smile.

He grins. "Text when you're done."

They peel off, and I'm alone again with the Paris file and the clock. I initial the last page, place the stack into the outbox, and breathe once, slowly.

It's time to go.

In the hall, Dre lifts a hand in a supportive, steadying wave. I answer with a nod I hope looks braver than I feel and step into the elevator. The doors close. For thirty seconds, it's just me and my reflection.

My phone buzzes in my pocket as I unlock the car.

MAGGIE:

Just picked up Bri from school. We'll meet you at the courthouse. She's got her sketchbook. She's okay.

The breath leaves me in a measured exhale.

I slide into the driver's seat and rest my hands on the wheel, knuckles white and veins up like they want to explode. I think about Bri and how scared she must be. I think about Mya's comforting words to her last night. And something in me cracks open again.

The drive is a blur. When I arrive at the courthouse, I kill the engine, and sit there a moment. The binder on the passenger seat is almost burning a hole in the leather. Inside, the life I built for my daughter is itemized and justified. It's absurd but necessary.

Ryan texts just as I step onto the curb.

RYAN:

I'm inside by security. Second-floor family court. We've got courtroom 2B. Vanessa is here with counsel.

He meets me at the base of the stairs, jaw set. "How we doing?"

"Ready." Because I am, even if my pulse disagrees. "Maggie is bringing Bri."

"Good. We're solid, Worth. Judge Martinez is efficient and thorough. We'll lead with stability and Bri's preferences, then education and medical continuity. Vanessa's counsel filed a late supplemental about 'maternal bond.' It's a throw, so don't bite."

"I won't."

Ryan starts walking, and I match his pace. We pass the bulletin board of schedules, the vending machines, a man in a too-big suit twisting a hat in his hands.

At the top of the stairs, the corridor opens to a row of benches. I check my phone once more, and there's a message from Mya.

MYA:

Be there in 10.

A weight is lifted off my chest.

I wasn't sure she'd show up today. Even after the moment we shared last night, guilt slips in over the distance I put between us. She drew those lines because she needed them. I respect that. But I won't beat myself up for feeling what I feel.

"Two letters arrived this morning," Ryan says, breaking me out of my thoughts. He flips his pad open. "Counselor and activity coordinator. Both are strong. I've got them tabbed and ready to hand them up if the judge wants them."

Across the hall, the courtroom door swings open and a clerk calls a name that isn't mine. I inhale, count to four, exhale, count to four. It's a trick a therapist taught me a lifetime ago. Sometimes I remember to use it.

My phone buzzes again.

MAGGIE:

We're here. Brianna wants to talk to you
before you go in.

I tuck the device away and tell Ryan I'll be right back. He nods. "Go. I'll hold our spot."

"Thanks."

Down the stairs, I spot Maggie in her blue cardigan, Bri with her sketchbook hugged to her chest, eyes brave. She smiles when she sees me.

I open my arms and my daughter steps into them like she always does. And my heart finds its rhythm.

"Hey, Piglet," I say into her hair. "You ready?"

Bri nods against my shirt. "Yes."

I ease back so I can see her face. She chews her lip, glances at Maggie, then up at me.

"Dad, can I tell you something before we go in?"

"Anything," I murmur, knowing what she's going to say. "Always."

"I think I want to try seeing Mom again. Not a lot. Not all at once. Just sometimes. With rules. And if it feels bad, I want to stop. I don't want you to be mad." She swallows.

"I'm not mad, sweetheart."

Her eyes flick to mine. "I don't want to hurt your feelings."

"You're not," I say, meaning it. "I'm glad you told me what you want. We'll do it your way. If it ever stops feeling right, we change it. I'll respect your wishes no matter what."

Bri's shoulders loosen a fraction. "Okay."

"We'll talk to the judge about what *you* want," I add. "You don't have to pick sides to love the people you love."

"Thanks, Dad."

I touch her cheek gently. "Thank *you* for being honest."

Maggie squeezes her shoulder. "We'll be right behind you."

I nod, pull Bri in for one more quick hug, then straighten. "All right, Piglet. Let's go."

Finally, we're called in.

Vanessa is already at the counsel table with her attorney, and turns when we enter, giving me a sly smirk, the kind that says she thinks she's going to win before the first word is even on the record.

My mouth is halfway to a reply I'll regret when Ryan's hand lands on my forearm. I clamp my jaw shut.

Vanessa shifts her attention to Brianna. For a second, I see the old softness in her eyes. Brianna feels the look, stiffens, and darts her gaze to the floor.

The clerk rattles through the preliminaries. Then Judge Martinez enters in her black robe and lays out the ground rules: time limits, order of presentation, what she'll consider, what she won't. It's brisk, clear, a map I can walk.

Mya isn't here yet, but just as the thought burrs under my skin, she slips in, quietly, eyes scanning the room until they find us.

Our gazes catch. She winces and mouths 'sorry.' I give her a small smile I don't have to try for. *She made it.* That's all that matters.

Counsel goes first. Vanessa's attorney paints a soft picture: maternal bond, renewed stability, earnest intent. Then he goes after me: tabloid clippings, gala photos, the "playboy CEO image" narrative he hopes will stick. He says *'image'* like it's evidence and tries to make headlines stand in for parenting.

Ryan doesn't bite. When it's our turn, he lays brick: school records, medical continuity, extracurriculars, Bri's stated preferences, a home that's been steady and safe for years. He adds that I'm now married, and that my wife has a strong, supportive relationship with Brianna that reinforces—not replaces—my role as her parent.

Questions follow. Judge Martinez to Ryan, to the other side, then to me. I keep my answers clean: Bri's routine, who gets her to school, who signs the forms, who meets with teachers. When Vanessa's lawyer prods at money and reputation—*your dating history, Mr. Miller? Frequent companions?* I refuse the bait.

"My personal life has never interfered with Brianna's care," I say. "Her needs come first. Always. And my marriage has only added extra stability to her day-to-day life."

When the judge asks about Bri's wishes, Ryan cites the counselor's letter and notes she prefers to speak through counsel. Martinez nods, satisfied.

It feels like hours and minutes at once. I grip the edge of the pew and keep breathing.

"I'm ready to rule," Judge Martinez says.

She acknowledges Vanessa's intent, notes the recent effort, then turns to the weight of evidence.

"On balance," she says, "it is in the best interest of the minor child that primary residency and decision-making remain with Mr. Miller."

My ears ring. I keep my face steady for Bri.

The judge continues. "Ms. Albright will have partial physical custody and visitation as follows: on the child's terms, to be scheduled in consultation with Mr. Miller and the child's counselor. The child's comfort and consent will guide frequency and duration. If at any point the child expresses discomfort, visits will pause and be re-evaluated. Parties will communicate through counsel as needed."

Ryan's pen moves on his pad. Behind me, Maggie exhales as if she's been underwater. Bri's fingers wrap around Mya's. Relief sweeps through me slowly and I finally feel like I can breathe.

The judge bangs the gavel once. "That is the order. We are adjourned."

Vanessa's attorney leans in to talk to her. She doesn't look at us as we stand.

I turn to Bri first. "You okay, Piglet?"

She nods, eyes bright. "Yeah."

Mya squeezes her hand, then meets my gaze over my daughter's shoulder. There's pride there, and something warmer. I give her a small, grateful nod. No words will cover how much she means to me.

Ryan joins us, already arranging next steps, but I let the moment be what it is: my kid is safe, the path is clear, and a weight shifts off a place in my chest I'd forgotten how to unclench.

Vanessa sweeps out first with her lawyer, without stopping to speak to Brianna.

So much for starting off the relationship with her daughter on the right foot.

Mya and Maggie follow a minute later. Mya puts a hand on Bri's shoulder as they pass, and says, "I'll be right outside." Brianna lingers with me while Ryan packs up the last of the files.

"Ready, Piglet?"

She nods. We step into the hall and stop.

Vanessa's voice carries around the corner. "... enjoy playing house while it lasts. You really think he'll keep you? You're a pretty stand-in with a borrowed last name. A glorified nanny who warms his bed."

Maggie's warning tone follows. "Ms. Albright, don't."

"This is neither the time nor place," Mya replies.

Vanessa laughs. "You don't get to set rules around *my* child. You slithered into a ring and think that makes you a wife and stepmom? Please. You were nobody before him, and you'll be nobody after."

"Enough," I hear Mya say. "Not here."

"You don't tell me where," Vanessa snaps. "You don't tell me anything, golddigger."

Heat climbs my spine. I hand Brianna my binder without looking away from the corridor. "Stay with Ryan," I murmur.

I find Mya standing straight, chin up, hands loose at her sides and Vanessa crowding her space.

"Back up, Vanessa," I seethe.

She doesn't. She tips her head, eyes raking over Mya. "Tell me. Do you cut the crusts off *my* daughter's sandwich because it looks good on camera? Or because you're practicing for when you have one of your own and he's already traded you in?"

Mya's jaw tightens, but her voice stays calm. "Brianna is not a prop. She's a child who needs *consistency*. I'm here to give her that because she deserves it."

Vanessa sneers. "Consistency? You've been here five minutes. I carried her. I bled for her. You don't get to step into my life and—"

"No one can *step into* being a mother," Mya grits out. "You show up for her or you don't. That's your choice. But you don't get to weaponize her to punish anyone."

Vanessa's face hardens. She jabs a finger toward Mya's chest. "You don't speak to me about motherhood. You slept your way into a house you didn't build."

My hand shoots out, catching Vanessa's wrist mid-jab. "That's enough."

Mya doesn't flinch. "I work with Bri on her math. I take notes at her counselor's request. I show up at pick-up, rain or shine. None of that replaces you. All of it supports *her*." She holds Vanessa's gaze. "If you want a relationship with your daughter, start by not attacking the people keeping her steady."

My ex-wife leans in, a whisper meant to bruise. "You're temporary. When he gets bored, you'll go back to whatever cubicle he plucked you from. Keep your hands off my daughter in the meantime."

I step between them, close enough that Vanessa has to tilt her chin to hold my gaze.

"Watch how you speak to my *wife*," I seethe, anger rolling off me. "Right now, and going forward."

She rolls her eyes, but I don't let her say another word.

"Here are the rules: you do not corner or harass my wife—here, at school, online, *anywhere*. You do not speak about her in front of Bri. You do not weaponize visitation. One more stunt like this, and I document it, and we ask Judge Martinez for restrictions you won't like. Control your damn self, Vanessa."

Her lawyer materializes from the corner. "Ms. Albright," he says carefully, touching her elbow. "This is not advisable."

Vanessa jerks once, eyes bright with spite. "Enjoy the ring

while it shines," she spits at Mya. "When he's done, you'll be a footnote."

Mya's expression doesn't falter. I'm so damn proud of her for standing her ground and not cowering. The way she defends herself, and Bri, pries my chest open wider.

I love that she's strong for herself.

I love that she's gentle with my daughter.

I love that she cares about me and my life.

I love *her*.

Vanessa's attorney steers her away down the corridor. She throws one last glare over her shoulder and disappears around the bend.

The air loosens.

I turn to Mya. "You okay, baby?"

She exhales slowly. "I'm fine."

Brianna joins us and looks from Mya to me, reading the room. I open an arm, and she steps in without hesitation, sketchbook thumping my side.

Over her head, Mya meets my eyes. "Let's go home."

MYA

I finally let out an exhale when we walk into the house.

Brianna heads upstairs early with her sketchbook, and I promise I'll come say goodnight.

After changing into comfier clothes, I find Worth in the kitchen, palms braced on the island.

"How's your heartbeat?" I ask, sitting on the bench.

He huffs. "Returning to human."

We stay silent for a minute, letting the quiet calm the storm of today.

"Thank you for showing up," he adds.

Heat presses under my sternum like an ache. "Of course. I'll always be there for you and Brianna."

His gaze flicks to my fingers on the counter, then to my wedding ring. Without thinking too hard about it, I turn my palm up. He sets his hand over mine, and I feel the tight coil inside me unwind a notch.

Bri pads down the stairs. "Goodnight," she mumbles, tipping her face to me first so we can bump heads. Worth presses his lips to her temple. She squeezes our hands together like she's fusing us and then disappears up the stairs again.

We don't move for a while after that. Eventually Worth says, "Tea?" and I nod. We drink it leaning hip to hip against the counter, and when the mugs are empty, I slide my hand into his. He threads our fingers together like he's been waiting to do it all day.

"Come upstairs with me," he says. Not a command—an invitation.

I hesitate just long enough to feel the line I drew, to choose it, or step over it with my eyes open. And then, "Okay."

In the bedroom, we don't flip on the overhead light, the lamps casting the room in a honeyed glow. I take off my slippers and Worth shrugs off his jacket. We meet at the foot of the bed as if our feet decided before our heads did.

"Can I?" he asks, palm hovering at my waist.

"Yes."

Worth draws me in, and the first kiss is the kind that lets everything from the day drain away. His mouth is careful; mine mirrors his.

We deepen the kiss, and I begin to unbutton Worth's shirt, then his trousers. When his clothes pool around him, I let my hands roam his body, my palms running over all of his edges. His Adam's apple, the muscles on his arms, the ripples on his stomach.

He hisses at my touch, eyes falling shut like he wants to savor all of it. When he meets my gaze again, there's so much I could say, but instead I breathe, "This feels real," into the small space between us.

"It is," he says, just as soft.

"Touch me, please?"

Worth doesn't respond with words. He nudges my arms up and slips off my shirt, then pushes down my leggings. He takes a step back to admire my almost naked form.

"You're so beautiful it hurts," he murmurs, toying with a loose curl at my temple. For a moment, we just look at each other.

Worth is sculpted like a damn statue. I can't take my eyes off him.

And I don't. I soak him in, memorizing every line like it might be the last time I get to see him like this. Because now that our arrangement has technically run its course, it means whatever this is between us is supposed to be over, too.

"Hey. Come back to me," Worth murmurs, pulling me out of my head.

I smile, eyes dropping to my feet. "Sorry."

He tips my chin up, and kisses me softly. "Don't be. Just be with me."

I know he means right now, in this moment, but we both know it carries more weight than that.

Worth wants me to stay.

But I don't know if I can.

Whatever is stopping me from believing this is real is louder than common sense, louder than how good he is to me and to Bri. It's fear—plain and simple. And I don't want to tell him that, because if I do, he'll move mountains to pull it out of me, and I know he'd succeed.

I just don't know if I'm ready for everything.

I don't know if *he's* ready for *me*.

He's lived a certain way for years—women, freedom, no explanations—and being thrown into this domestic bubble can mess with anyone's head. I don't want to be the woman he settles for, only to then realize later he doesn't want to be tied down. I don't want to hand him my whole heart and watch him remember he liked his life better when he didn't have to answer to anyone.

Worth notices I've drifted off again. "Talk to me, baby."

I can't.

I shake my head. "I don't want to talk. Just feel."

For once, I don't fight it. I allow the wanting to be uncomplicated. Tomorrow will bring logistics and every way life can test a choice.

Tonight, I let myself get lost in Worth.

45

Worth

Morning finds me with Mya in my bed and a knot in my chest.

She's asleep on her side, facing me, wearing my T-shirt and smelling like my soap, hair a loose halo on my pillow. If I were a smarter man, I'd just lie here and let this be what it is: a perfect, stupidly domestic moment I wasn't supposed to get. Instead, my brain does what it always does and skips ahead to endings.

Because the truth is, the arrangement is technically over. We did what we said we'd do. Mya could pack up and walk out tomorrow and no one could say she didn't hold up her side.

But last night didn't feel like two people wrapping up a deal. It felt like a couple coming down from a hard day together. It felt real. And I know that scares her.

I watch Mya breathe for a minute, my hand resting on the curve of her hip. I don't want to let this go. I don't want to go back to a house that's tidy and silent and doesn't have her laughter in the kitchen or her curls on my pillow. I don't want to see Brianna's face when she realizes Mya is no longer coming down for breakfast anymore.

So I tell myself maybe we don't have to rip the Band-Aid off in one clean pull. Maybe I can buy us a little time. Let her see more of my life and what it looks like when my family loves someone. Maybe if she sees she fits, she'll stop trying to outrun it.

I brush a piece of hair off her cheek. "Kitten," I murmur. "You awake?"

Her eyes flutter open. "Mmm. Barely."

I smile. "I need to ask you something."

"That sounds serious." Her voice is rough from sleep, and it does things to me I don't want to name. "What is it?"

"My mom's birthday is this weekend," I say. "We're going up to Nantucket. I want you to come."

Mya blinks once, twice. I see her guard go up as she pushes up on an elbow, T-shirt sliding off one shoulder. "I don't think that's a good idea."

I keep my face neutral, even though irritation flickers under my ribs. Of course she's pulling back. "Why not?"

"Because," she says, gesturing between us, "the arrangement is over. Meeting your family makes things... blurred."

"They think it's real," I remind her. "My parents have been asking to meet you for months. If I show up without my wife, they're going to have questions I don't want to answer yet."

Mya chews the inside of her cheek. "Then tell them I'm busy."

"That works once. Maybe twice. Not when it's my mother's birthday."

She sighs and falls back against the pillow. "It'll just cause more trouble. First they meet me, we get attached, then we separate, and I'm the villain."

"It doesn't have to cause trouble. We go, we celebrate, we come back. Simple."

"Nothing about this is simple, Worth..."

I lean on the piece I know she won't ignore. "Bri will ask why you're not coming."

That lands. I see it in the way her eyes soften, the way her shoulders sag. I don't love using Bri as leverage, but it's the truth. My daughter is attached. She's going to want Mya there. And if Mya suddenly isn't, she's going to be crushed.

I inch closer, prop my head on my hand. "Please come to Nantucket. Meet them. We'll keep it light. No heavy talks. No future stuff. Just living in the moment."

She stares at the ceiling for a few beats, jaw working. I can tell she wants to say no. I can also tell I've found the crack in her facade.

"Okay," Mya says finally, exhaling. "But we're counting this as my last contractual event obligation."

I bite back a smile. "Last one, huh?"

She narrows her eyes like she doesn't trust me. Fair. "Yes. After that, we go back to the plan."

After that, I think, *maybe you'll see what I see and the plan won't look so good anymore.*

Though I don't say it out loud. If I push, she runs.

"Deal," I say instead, brushing my knuckles over her arm. "They'll love you," I add before I can stop it.

"Don't say things like that."

"Why?"

"Because I'll believe you."

My chest squeezes. I smooth her hair back.

If I do this right, I won't have to convince her with words.

She'll convince herself.

THE WEEKEND COMES FAST.

By the time we pull up to the hangar, everyone's in good spirits—except Mya, who's doing that thing where she looks perfectly composed but her fingers won't stop fidgeting with the strap of her bag.

She loves the idea of traveling. She does *not* love being in the air.

I lean in. "You okay?"

"I'm fine." She shoots me a look that says *don't make a big deal out of it.* I don't. I just take her bag from her and keep a hand at the small of her back as we walk out to the plane.

Griffin and Sylas arrive almost at the same time, and Sylas immediately breaks free, barreling straight for me.

Then, Henson and his girlfriend, Amira, walk our way.

"You must be Mya! I'm Amira. I've heard a lot about you," Amira says with a warm smile.

Mya shakes her hand. "I hope it was good things."

"Oh, absolutely!"

Brianna launches herself at Henson. "Uncle Hen!"

He scoops her up, spinning her until she squeals. "Hey, trouble. Ready for sand and too many adults?"

"Yup!" she says, giggling.

On the plane, Mya sits beside me in the backseat, curls half-up, looking like she's fighting the impulse to scream *I shouldn't be here.*

"Stop overthinking," I murmur.

"I'm not."

I huff. "You're terrible at lying."

"Hey! I'm not."

Once the engines spin up and the plane starts taxiing, I feel Mya's whole body tense up. I take her hand. "Same as always," I say quietly. "Takeoff is the worst part. I've got you."

She exhales through her nose, squeezing back. "I hate that I'm this person."

"I don't. Means you need me for something."

That earns me a tiny smile.

I bring our joined hands to my thigh and cover them with my other one, caging hers there. When we lift off, Mya shuts her eyes and leans in, pretending to adjust her seat.

"You're okay," I whisper.

She nods against my shoulder, breathing in time with me. By the time we're level, some color has come back to her face. Mya opens her eyes, looking embarrassed. "Sorry. I know it's irrational."

"It's not. We're good. You're doing great."

Amira, who's been sitting across from us with Henson, nudges Mya. "Okay, quick Miller family download."

She gives Mya the rundown of my family members while Bri sprawls her legs across Mya's lap like this is the most normal thing in the world. Every now and then, when there's a little bump of turbulence, Mya squeezes my hand again, and every time I squeeze back.

By the time we land in Nantucket, she seems relaxed, laughing at something Sylas said. No one but me would know she was nervous. And I like it that way; her needing me for something only I'm aware of.

After we deplane, a second car waits to take Griffin and Sylas to the Kingston place on the other side of the island. "See you tomorrow night," Griffin calls.

Our driver takes us through town, then out toward my parents' place.

As soon as we pull up, the house's front door bursts open. My mother comes down the steps in a flowy linen dress, brown hair pinned back, arms already open. But she doesn't go for me or Henson.

She goes for Mya.

"Oh, *finally.*" Mom pulls her into a hug. "I have been waiting *ages* to meet you."

Mya stiffens a millisecond, then melts into her embrace. "Hi, Mrs. Miller."

"Oh, no. Call me Nadine." My mother holds her at arm's length to look at her. "You are even prettier in person."

Mya actually blushes.

Behind them, my dad steps onto the porch, hands in his pockets, and gives me a nod. Approval, so far.

"Come," Nadine says, looping her arm through Mya's. "I must show you the house. Worth never does it properly. He's always in a hurry."

I watch my mother whisk my fake-wife into the house, with a small smile on my face. *See? This is what I wanted you to see. This is why I brought you.*

Dinner that night is a breeze. Brianna sits between Mya and my mom, talking about art and school. Dad asks Mya about the project she presented to the board and she answers with confidence and just enough humility to make him like her even more. Amira jumps in with a joke and Henson steals potatoes from her plate, and her outraged expression makes everyone laugh.

Mya looks like she belongs here—as if that chair has had her name on it for years.

Let this convince you. Let this feel like home and make walking away harder than staying.

After dessert, everyone starts to head to their own rooms, a few people yawning. My mother hugs Mya again, kisses Bri goodnight, and squeezes my arm. "She's lovely," she whispers in my ear. "Don't mess it up."

I look at my wife across the room, smiling at my daughter. "I'm trying not to."

The next evening, we gather at a long farmhouse table on the back terrace; it's decorated with white linens, little glass vases of hydrangeas straight from Mom's garden, and candles in hurricane jars so the ocean breeze won't kill the flames. The sun's starting to drop, painting everything gold. You could even hear the waves if everyone stopped talking at the same time, which, with this crowd, never happens.

Mom sits at the head, radiant in pale blue, Dad beside her, looking proud. Mya is two seats down, between Amira and Bri, and the two women are laughing at something my daughter said.

Mya is in a simple dress, nothing flashy, and I keep sneaking looks at her like—*that's my wife.*

Halfway through appetizers, Griffin arrives with his son in tow, plus two of his brothers. Adrian is still in Paris with his racing team.

Damian goes right in for a hug with my mom. The other brother, Caleb—taller, darker, and quieter—follows, carrying a bottle of wine.

"Sorry we're late," Griffin says, kissing Mom's cheek. "Someone," he jerks his head toward Sylas, "needed chicken nuggets."

Sylas waves at Bri. She waves back with a huge grin, like she hasn't seen him in forever, even though it's only been a few days. He's like a little brother to her.

"Come in, come in," Mom says, delighted. "There's plenty."

Chairs scrape, places get added. Henson immediately launches into some story about Amira's uncle threatening him for not liking arak. Amira smacks his arm.

It's loud, warm, and exactly the kind of scene I wanted Mya to see.

Entrées come out: roast sea bass, summer vegetables, and risotto. Mya is talking to my dad about her project again, explaining the scope of the rehab project without sounding like she's showing off. He's impressed. I can tell. Bri keeps leaning into her, while showing Amira something on her phone. My mother watches it all, and it softens her whole face.

It's going well. *Too* well.

My phone buzzes in my pocket.

I ignore it. It's Saturday night. We're in Nantucket. Everyone I care about is here, and nobody from the office calls me on weekends.

It buzzes again.

I glance down and see Dre's name.

I frown. She knows I'm out of town. I let it roll to voicemail. A third time. Then a text.

DRE:

Call me back. It's an emergency.

My stomach tightens.

I dab my mouth with my napkin before pushing my chair back. "Excuse me. Work thing." I catch Mya's eye. She lifts a brow and mouths, "*Everything okay?*" I nod and head inside.

In the study, I close the door and call Dre back. She picks up on the first ring.

"Worth," she says, voice already in crisis mode, "look at your email."

"What is it?"

"Just look."

I pull it up on my phone. Top of the inbox: **FW: URGENT — have you seen this?** from PR. Another from Legal. Another from Dre.

I open the first one and my heart drops.

A big masthead I know too well. Headline in all-caps:

BILLIONAIRE WORTH MILLER'S "SECRET" MARRIAGE WAS A BUSINESS DEAL — INSIDER SAYS NEW WIFE IS "BROKE" AND "IN IT FOR THE MONEY."

There's a photo of me and Mya at the gala. Another of her leaving the office. A third of us at the courthouse yesterday. And under it is an entire speculative mess about our "sudden" wedding, the "convenient" timing before a custody hearing, and some trash quote from an "anonymous former employee" about "being in his office just last week."

Fucking Shaina.

"Worth? You still there?"

"Yeah," I manage to choke out.

"Is it true?" Dre asks, though her tone says she already knows the answer.

"I can't talk now. Call PR. Full response. Loop Ryan in. I need to talk to Mya before she sees it."

"It's already on socials," she answers quietly.

I end the call.

I take one breath. Two. Then I walk back out to the terrace, rolling my shoulders like that will make the world normal again.

The second I step outside, I know I'm too late.

Mya looks at me with eyes that are already glossy, phone clutched in her hand. Someone must've sent the article to her. Or she saw it herself. Either way, the damage is done.

"Mya—"

She stands so fast her chair scrapes on the ground. Tears well in her eyes. She shakes her head violently, and bolts, heading back into the house.

Amira is up a split second later. "I'll go."

"What's going on?" Henson asks, the easy-night vibe now gone.

I scrub a hand over my jaw. "The truth is out."

"Shit," Henson mutters.

Griffin swears under his breath too. His brothers and my parents look between us, confused.

"The truth?" My mother frowns. "Worth?"

I'm still staring at the door where Mya disappeared, wanting nothing more than to go after her, to tell her I'll handle it, that I will burn that magazine down. But I know she needs a second to be mad without me in her face. I force myself to sit back down, even though I feel like I'm vibrating out of my skin.

"Worth," my father says, sharper now. "Explain."

My fingers tighten around my napkin. "Mya and I... When we got married, it was part of an arrangement."

Silence.

"You... what?" Bri says, voice tiny and hurt.

My head snaps toward her, heart cracking right down the middle. Christ, I forgot she was still at the table.

"Bri. Piglet." I stand, reaching for her.

"I can't believe you two," she says, eyes filling with tears. "You *lied?*"

Then she's running past me and the house, and out to the back.

"Brianna!" my mother calls, rising.

I'm already moving. "I've got her."

I sprint across the lawn, the ocean wind slapping at us. I know exactly where Bri's going.

The old cottage sits at the edge of the property, tucked behind the main house. It used to be my childhood home. The one Henson and I paid off for my parents when we finally had the money. Bri loves it out here.

She reaches the porch, drops to her knees in front of the big blue pot, rummages under it, and pulls out the spare key. She jams it in the lock and slams the door behind her.

I catch it just before the latch flips.

"Bri," I say, breathing hard. "Let me explain."

"Leave me alone, Dad!"

She runs deeper into the cottage, and I follow her down the hall to the guest room on the left.

Brianna curls herself on the bed, her back to the door, knees pulled up, shoulders tight. She's angry.

I sit on the edge of the mattress, leaving some space between us. "Hey."

Nothing.

"Bri."

She sniffles. "You lied."

I close my eyes for a second. "Yeah, I did."

"You didn't have to," she fires back, whipping around. Her eyes are wet and furious. "You could've told me. I would've understood. I'm not a baby."

"I know you're not, Brianna. It wasn't because I thought you were a baby."

"Then why? Why did you pretend it was real and, like, romantic?" She grimaces like the word tastes bad. "You let me think we were a family."

"Because we *are* a family," I say instantly. "That part wasn't pretend."

Brianna blinks, thrown off. "But you started it for court."

"Yeah." I drag a hand over my face. "When we first did it, we were trying to make everything look clean for the judge. I wanted to make sure no one could say I wasn't giving you a stable home."

Bri is quiet, so I go on.

"But... If I'm being really honest, even at the start, in the back of my head, I didn't think it was fake. Not really. I liked having Mya with us. I liked how you two clicked. I think a part of me just grabbed onto it and didn't want to let go."

She studies me, eyes red. "So, it *was* real."

"It is real. For me."

"Then... are you and Mya gonna stay together?"

The question hits exactly where I knew it would. I breathe out. "No."

Her brows crash. "Why?"

"Because Mya wants to go her own way," I say quietly. "She didn't sign up for being dragged in magazines and judged by strangers. She didn't sign up for lying to you. She wanted to help. Now that it's done, she wants to leave."

Bri gapes at me like I've said the stupidest thing ever. "Really, Dad? Anyone can see she loves you."

A choked laugh slips out of me. "That seems to be the consensus. Henson and Griffin think so too. Her *words* don't match, though."

"Then make them match," Bri says, like it's obvious. "Convince her."

"I can't force her, Piglet. If she stays, it has to be because *she* chooses it, not because I boxed her in."

"You have to at least tell her how you feel," she says, jabbing at me with my own logic. "Mya can't choose if she doesn't know."

I look at my kid—my too-wise, too-soft kid—and something in my chest twists. "Yeah, you're right."

She sniffles again, wiping her nose with the back of her hand. "I'm still mad."

"That's okay. You're allowed to be. I'm sorry I didn't tell you sooner. I was trying to make it cleaner. Safer. I didn't want you dragged into a grown-up mess."

Her mouth trembles, but she nods. "Just don't lie next time."

"Deal." I squeeze her knee. "Can you come back to the house? Grandma will start worrying."

Bri hesitates, then sighs. "Yeah."

We walk back together, her hand in mine, the evening air cooler now. My head is already rehearsing what I'm going to say to Mya.

It was never fake for me. I should've told you. I should've protected you better. Stay.

I step into the house and call, "Mya?"

From down the hall, Amira appears. "She's gone."

I stop. "What?"

"She left," Amira says, wincing. "She packed her stuff and left for the airport while you were with Bri. I tried to talk her down, but she was crying and said she needed to go before it got worse. I'm sorry."

My stomach drops. "She left."

Mom comes up behind us and places a hand on my arm. "Don't worry about the party, sweetheart," she says softly. "Go."

From the dining room, Henson calls, "Man, what is it with us Millers ditching Mom's parties to chase women?"

Amira glares at him. "Not the time."

I flip him off over my shoulder. "Watch Brianna."

"Of course."

I'm already moving, grabbing my keys from the entry table, and shoving my phone in my pocket. On the way down the steps, I hit Mya's name.

It rings. And rings, until it reaches her voicemail.

I call again. Voicemail.

I text instead.

> Mya, wait. Please don't fly out yet.

I gun the car down the gravel drive, headlights cutting through the dark, jaw clenched so hard it aches. I hit her name again. Nothing.

She's running. And if I don't catch her, I might actually lose her for good.

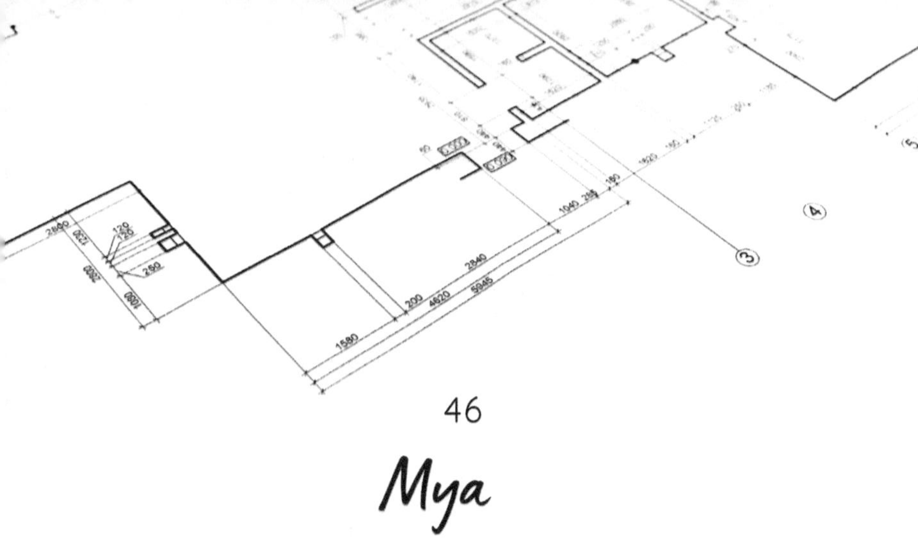

46

Mya

The office has mostly moved on, but I'm still stuck.

People stop talking when I walk into the kitchen. Someone on the marketing team sent me a "You're so strong" DM I didn't answer. And our new receptionist, bless her, pretends nothing happened and keeps telling me about the plane tickets to Cabo she's pricing out.

I hate the pity. It feels like confirmation of the headlines.

I haven't seen Worth since Nantucket either. He hasn't been back to the office—at least not when I'm here. At first, I thought it was a coincidence.

One day, I caved and asked Henson if Worth was okay, and he said, casual as ever, "Yeah, he's good. He's just working remotely for a bit."

Which is code for: *he's giving you space.*

Which is also code for: *he's avoiding you.*

That stings more than I want to admit.

Maybe because a tiny, traitorous part of me wanted him to show up anyway. To argue and ask me to stay. Even when I told him not to.

But Worth Miller is nothing if not a man of his word. I asked to end the deal, and he's... ending it.

I still remember exactly where I was sitting when the world tilted.

Nadine's terrace was glowing in candlelight, the ocean was humming behind us, Bri was stealing roasted potatoes off my plate, and I was thinking, *Okay. Maybe I was wrong. Maybe I can do this.* Then I got a text from Seraya saying, "Oh my God, is this real?"

My name. My face. *Broke gold digger. Business arrangement. Custody ploy.*

I saw Worth get up right before, phone to his ear, jaw tight. I knew something was wrong.

I didn't even read the whole thing. I didn't need to. The headline alone felt like someone cracked my rib cage open and poured salt straight into my insecurities.

I ran.

I ran choking on a sob, half blind from tears, Amira calling my name. I shoved clothes into my carry-on, grabbed my laptop, and booked the next flight out of Nantucket.

Worth called and called. But I couldn't answer.

Not because I didn't want to, but because if I had heard his voice, I would've stayed. And I couldn't stay. Not with his whole family looking at me like I was a fraud.

When I landed in Seattle, I drove straight to my parents' house, mascara streaking down my cheeks, hair in a sad bun, eyes swollen. My mom opened the door, and I broke. Knees-gave-out, ugly-sobbing broke.

She dragged me to the couch, wrapped me in a blanket, and made tea I didn't drink.

"Tell me," she said.

So I did. All of it. The fake marriage. The deal. The custody battle for Brianna. The way I fell in love with a man I wasn't supposed to. The article and the shame. The fear that everyone would think I was exactly what they wrote. That *he* would, too, even if he said he didn't.

Mom listened to the whole thing without interrupting. Then she did what she always does and pulled my grief up to the light.

"You're doing the same thing you've been doing since your father died," she said quietly. "You're leaving before you can be left."

I wiped at my face. "That's not it."

She gave me *that* look. "Mya."

"What was I supposed to do?" I snapped, the humiliation still raw. "Stand there while his whole family looked at me like I used their son? Let the Internet call me a gold digger? Let *Brianna* see that?"

"She saw you run, though, sweetheart," Mom said.

And that hurt worse than the article.

She smoothed my hair back. "This man didn't leave you. You left him because you wanted control over the ending."

"You don't understand," I whispered. "It started off fake."

"Lots of things start one way and become another," she said. "That doesn't make them less real."

I cried for hours. Since Dad died, I haven't cried like that— full-body, hiccuping, throat-burning crying. My mom just held me tighter.

We watched the sun come up. By morning, I'd decided on two things: 1) I wasn't going to hide, and 2) I wasn't going to stay in a marriage that started with a lie—even if somewhere along the way the lie turned into everything I wanted.

I sent Worth a text asking to start annulment proceedings that same day.

Now, I'm at my desk, weeks later, acting like my insides aren't shredded.

Which is why I asked Griffin to put me on the new Paris project W.H.M. acquired. I leave in two weeks—perfect timing. I get to disappear for a few months, pour myself into work, be an ocean away from the drama and from the man I love but can't choose yet. Paris can be my reset button.

I open my drawer for a pen and my fingers brush paper.

It's a wolf sketch that Bri drew for me the day we spent our first evening alone, the day we talked about her mom. There's a moon behind the animal and her crooked little signature at the bottom. *For Mya.*

My throat clenches.

I miss her so much it's a physical ache. I regret not saying goodbye face-to-face. I called her a few days after Nantucket, once things stopped spinning. She picked up right away.

"I'm not mad, just a bit sad," she told me. "But I get why you left."

"I hope I see you again," I said.

"You will," she answered, with way more confidence than I had.

I love you and your father, I wanted to add, but I didn't.

I press the sketch flat on my desk and blink back the sting in my eyes, right as Dre knocks on the cubicle wall.

"Hey." She looks tired. Her eyes drop to the sketch, then back to me. In her hand is a manila envelope.

"Special delivery," she says softly.

I already know what it is.

I straighten my shoulders. I asked for this. I'm the one who said we needed to end the deal before I could actually decide what I wanted.

Still. When Dre hands it to me, dread presses down on me.

"You okay?" she asks.

"I'm good," I lie, giving her my brightest *this is fine* smile. "Thanks, Dre."

She doesn't buy it. No one has bought it since I walked back in here with puffy eyes and a perfectly ironed blouse. But she nods, because she knows me.

"I'll be fine," I add, also trying to convince myself.

"Mm." Dre taps the cubicle once more and leaves.

I wait until she's gone to open it.

On top, there's a letter.

Mya,

As agreed, enclosed are the finalized dissolution documents. Everything has been executed on my end. Payment confirmations for your student loans and outstanding personal debts are attached for your records.

Thank you for everything.

—W.

Under the letter are the annulment papers.

We agreed we'd keep this quiet for now.

No public statements or legal filings made visible unless absolutely necessary, because the last thing Worth needs is for Vanessa to find any excuse to drag him back to court, waving "instability" and "failed marriage" like fresh ammunition.

I swallow hard.

This is what I wanted, I remind myself for the umpteenth time. So why does it feel like my world is officially ending?

I trace the edge of the wolf sketch with my thumb.

I love him.

But I need the deal to die before I can tell him that. Right now there are still too many people with opinions. Too many headlines. And I'm still trying to prove I'm not what they said.

I put the papers back in the envelope and slide it into my tote bag.

Then I square my shoulders, pick up my pen, and go back to work like my heart isn't sitting in my throat.

WORTH

Willow's is busy for a Thursday. I've got a black coffee going lukewarm in front of me and a clean line of sight to the counseling office across the street. Brianna is in there with Vanessa and the therapist for their "reconnection" session.

I still don't totally trust Vanessa. But since court, she's actually been showing up. On time, every week, no drama. She actually listens to Bri instead of talking *at* her. I don't know if it was the judge, the custody order, or her realizing she was about to lose her kid for real, but she's been serious about it. And if Bri's getting something good out of it, then I can live with not understanding why the change happened.

The door chimes.

"Worth."

I look up. "Tiana."

She's got a water bottle and a tote bag, looking like she stepped out of a lifestyle blog.

"May I?" she asks, nodding to the chair.

"Of course." I pull it out.

Tiana sits, studying me for a second. "You look tired."

"Thanks," I retort sarcastically.

"You're welcome," she says with a wink. Then, "How are you, though?"

"Surviving."

Her smile fades. "Why haven't you called her?"

I wrap my hand around my cup. "I didn't want her to feel cornered. She left for a reason. If I kept showing up, it would feel like I was making the choice for her."

"That's very considerate," Tiana says. We sit in silence for a few moments before she continues. "Mya misses you. She's not going to admit it, but I know my sister. I know when she's pretending she's fine."

My chest tightens. "I miss her, too. Every damn day, I pick up my phone to text her and put it back down. I call and hang up before it rings. But she wanted the deal over, so I'm trying to respect that."

Tiana tilts her head. "Respect is good. Silence... not always."

I take a breath. "I sent her the papers today."

Her brows lift. "You did?"

I nod, staring into my coffee. I've closed a lot of deals— never hated one like I hated this one.

"Mya told me she's going to Paris," Tiana says.

I exhale. "Yeah. Griff asked if he could move her onto the project. She was the best person for it, so I said yes."

"Reluctantly," she guesses.

"Yes."

Because it means I might not see Mya for months. That she is actually going to put an ocean between us.

"She's not running from you." Tiana's voice is softer now. "She's running from the noise and from what people are saying. From feeling like she was the problem."

"Mya was never a problem."

Before either of us can add anything, the door chimes again and Bri walks in, her backpack slung across one shoulder, hair a little frizzy from the wind. Vanessa is right behind her, coat over one arm, looking annoyingly put together.

"Hey, Piglet," I say, standing.

"Hi, Dad." She comes straight to me with a smile. "It was good."

"Yeah?" I glance at Vanessa.

My ex-wife nods and looks at Brianna. "Thank you for meeting with me."

"You're welcome," Bri says, happily.

Tiana gets up. "I'll leave you to it. Nice to see you, Worth." She gives Vanessa a tight smile. "Bri, want a snack?"

"Yes!" Brianna grins and follows Tiana to the coffee bar.

There's a brief moment of silence. Vanessa clears her throat. "Listen, Worth." Her eyes flick to me and away. "I, uh... I saw the article. About you and Mya."

My jaw tightens.

"I just wanted to say I'm sorry it blew up like that," she goes on, actually sounding sincere. "I know what it's like to have people think they know you. And she was good with Bri—despite what I said at court."

It's not much, but from Vanessa, that's practically a handwritten apology.

"Thanks." I nod once. "We're handling it."

I could leave it there, but something makes me push forward.

"A lot of what's out there isn't true," I add. "They twisted things. Ran with what they wanted. It's not what people think."

She lifts a hand, stopping me with a faint shake of her head. "You don't owe me an explanation. Regardless of what did or didn't happen, it sucks."

I study her. Once, all I saw when I looked at Vanessa was a

storm wearing lipstick and perfume. Right now, she just looks... human.

"Why do you care?" I ask before I can stop myself. "Why not use this against me?" I don't lace it with anger. Just the truth.

Vanessa exhales slowly. "Because I've had to sit with myself and with the part I played in how everything fell apart." Her eyes drift away, somewhere honest. "Every time I go after you, Brianna loses. She's the one who hurts. And I'm done letting my pride cost our daughter more pieces of stability."

"If I drag you back to court again," Vanessa continues, "if I try to punish you because I'm angry or scared... I risk losing her. I risk breaking whatever fragile trust she still has in me. And I won't do that again."

Silence stretches between us, but it isn't hostile this time.

Vanessa gives me a little smile. "And for the record, contrary to what you probably believe, I don't hate you, Worth."

I let that sit for a second.

"I don't hate you either."

She nods, a small breath escaping, like she's been holding it for years.

"Okay. Well. I'll see you next week."

She walks over to our daughter and places a hand on her shoulder, squeezing.

"Bye, Mom," Bri says, giving her a small wave.

Vanessa leaves, the bell jingling behind her.

Then, Brianna comes back to the table with bags of goodies and spots my empty cup. "You got the big one today."

I chuckle lightly. "Needed it."

She slides into the chair across from me and swings her feet. Then, almost as an afterthought, "Are you still sad about Mya?"

I nod. "But don't you worry about grown-up stuff."

Brianna rolls her eyes. "I'm not a baby. It must suck for you."

"It sucks for all of us."

"Yeah. It does," Brianna says quietly.

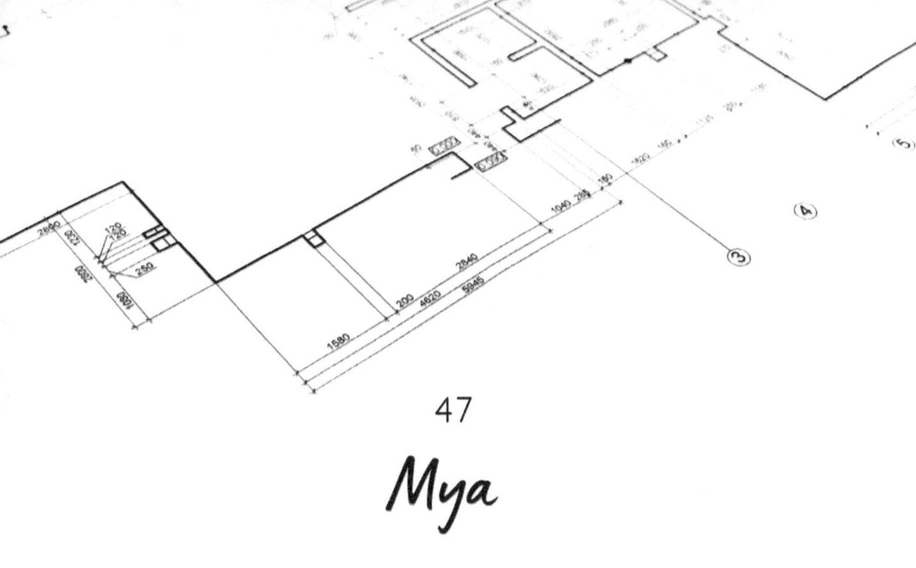

47

Mya

Paris fits me in ways I didn't expect.

I've been here for six months now, and the city has stopped feeling like a temporary escape and more like home.

I live in a shoebox of an apartment on Rue de Turenne, three blocks from the Paris office, with creaky wood floors, a slanted ceiling, and a balcony barely big enough for one chair and a mug of coffee. But when I open the French doors in the morning and watch the street waking up—boulangerie downstairs, scooters whining, someone yelling in French about deliveries—it feels like I did the right thing coming here.

We had our first official site visit today on the W.H.M. project, and everything was where it was supposed to be. The structural team showed, permits were cleared, and the local architect didn't pitch a fit about us Americans coming in to "modernize" history. We actually got compliments. On a European site? That never happens.

I'm high off it.

I rent one of those electric scooters on the way home just because it's sunny, and zip across the Seine, hair whipping behind me, grinning like an idiot. Paris glows at magic hour. It dares you to be sad.

I stop on the bridge and take a picture and send it to Seraya.

> Look at me being Parisian.

A second later, she sends a photo back.

It's a plant. A huge, ridiculous plant with a pink bow on it and a note.

SERAYA:

RAFAEL LEFT THIS AT MY DOOR.

It says "for your oxygen"

WHO SENDS OXYGEN AS A GIFT???

I burst out laughing right there on the bridge.

> Your landlord is in love with you and also unhinged.

SERAYA:

I told him I don't pay rent to date him then he said "we can negotiate"

COME BACK AND SAVE ME.

> Sorry. I live in France now. Au revoir 🐘

I tuck my phone away, still smiling, and ride back to my place.

In the stairwell, my phone buzzes again. I glance down.

WORTH:

Heard about the site visit. Congrats.

And my heart actually *aches*.

Worth and I have texted a handful of times since I got here. Always short and about work. Nothing more.

I stare at his message way too long.

I miss him.

I miss *them*.

But this time apart is doing what it was supposed to: I can breathe. The noise died down. People in Seattle moved on to the next scandal. I'm not "the gold digger" here; I'm just the project lead with good French and decent style.

I shove the phone into my pocket and climb the stairs.

That night, after a shower and leftover ratatouille out of a plastic container, I FaceTime Tiana.

We talk for a bit—about Paris, about how much lighter I look (her words), about how she's thinking of doing a floral workshop, about how Griffin actually has a nice side when he's not pretending to be made of cement. She asks about work; I tell her the site visit went well and that I haven't fallen off the scaffolding yet.

Then her face turns solemn. "And how's your heart?"

"Quieter."

"That's not the same as happy."

"It's getting there."

She studies me through the screen. "You talk to him?"

I shrug. "We've texted a couple times."

Tiana sighs like she wants to say more but also knows I need to figure this one out myself. "Okay. Check in again tomorrow?"

"Yeah."

After we hang up, I lie there for a second in the dark, Paris humming outside, the Eiffel Tower doing its sparkle far, far away, and I finally pick up my phone to respond to Worth.

> Thank you. Couldn't have done it without the team.

Three dots pop up immediately.

Then my phone rings.

I bolt upright, heart hammering. Part of me wants to let it go to voicemail. The bigger part wants to answer because I haven't heard his voice in weeks and I miss it so much my chest hurts.

I swipe.

"Hey," I say, breathless.

"Hi." And just like that, I could cry. God, I missed that voice. Low and warm and a little rough as if he's been talking all day.

I blink fast. "You called."

"Yeah," he says, and I can hear the faint clink of a glass. "Didn't really plan it. Saw your text and just hit call."

"What time is it there?"

"Middle of the day. You?"

"Past ten. I'm in bed."

"Yeah?" There's a smile in his voice now. "You decent, Mrs. Miller?"

I snort. "We're not married anymore, remember?"

He goes quiet. "I remember."

The silence after that one hurts.

I clear my throat. "Why'd you really call?"

He exhales, long. "I don't know. I just wanted to hear you. That okay?"

My eyes burn. "Yeah, it's okay."

"I miss you, Mya."

My throat closes. "I miss you too."

He's quiet for a second, like he's letting himself feel it. "How's Paris?"

"Pretty," I say, wiping under my eye with my thumb. "Loud. Smells like bread. Tiny apartments."

"You like it?"

"I do. I needed it."

"I know," he says, and I can tell he means it. "I'm proud of you."

"Thanks," I murmur. "How's Bri?"

"She's good. She misses you too."

I press the heel of my hand to my sternum like that will keep everything in. "When I'm ready to talk... about us, I will."

"I know. Ball is in your court, Kitten."

"Don't call me that." Though there's no heat in it.

"No." I can picture his smirk. "Not stopping."

I laugh. "You're annoying."

"Maybe." After a beat, he asks, "What are you wearing?"

I hesitate to reply because this can't lead anywhere good. But the way his tone went down an octave, and the way my body instantly reacted to his voice... I know I won't stop what's coming.

"One of your t-shirts. The one with Freddie Mercury's face on it."

"I was wondering where that went." Worth chuckles. "What's underneath?"

"Nothing, panty thief."

It's crazy how we're able to jump straight into our old ways, as if we haven't spent any time apart.

"Speaking of panties, I still have a pair." I hear him shuffling on the other side of the phone. "Right in my hand." I hear him take an inhale.

"Worth..."

"Mya..." he echoes. "Touch yourself for me, pretty girl. Let me hear how much you've missed me. Please. I need it."

Worth Miller begging will never get old.

I relent, knowing I can't deny this man anything when he says please.

Reaching down between my legs, I rub a circle on my clit and hiss into the phone. A few more strokes and I'm panting, my orgasm already coiling tight.

"Fuck, Mya. You sound so good," Worth says, groaning. "I'm rubbing my cock with your panties, thinking about how tight your cunt always feels around me."

His words sear through me, pleasure rippling down my spine. My whole body tingles, aching to actually feel Worth's hands on me.

Worth makes a low, whimpering sound. I can hear his hand rubbing up and down his shaft. It's downright filthy, and I'm loving every second.

"Slip a finger inside that sweet pussy, baby. No. Two. And let me hear how wet you are for me."

I do as I'm told, easing in my index and middle fingers, and crook them upwards to hit the perfect spot, using my other hand to continue flicking my clit. I can hear my arousal loud and clear.

"Oh, *God*. I'm getting close. I-I don't know if I can... hold it," I moan, struggling to get the words out. I'm frantic, rubbing my center as if it's a matter of life or death.

I've masturbated since the last time Worth and I were together, but nothing compares to touching myself with his voice guiding me in my ear.

"I'm right there too, pretty girl. I wish I could taste you," he growls. "Let go for me. Let me hear you scream my name."

After several seconds of working myself to the brink of explosion, I come, seeing stars and screaming Worth's name in a plea.

He follows suit, grunting loudly on the line, saying my name over and over like a prayer.

"Shit. I made a mess of your panties, baby," he chuckles. "Check your phone."

I take the phone off my ear and see a notification. When I open it, my eyes almost bulge out of their sockets.

It's a photo of Worth's still-hard cock wrapped in my thong, coated with his cum.

I stare at the picture for an embarrassingly long time.

"Mya?" Worth sounds amused.

"Uh—yeah. Wow. That's..."

"Hot," he supplies.

I giggle. "Yeah. I think so too. And unexpected."

"But very much needed."

As much as I want to stay in this little bubble, I have to pop it. "This doesn't change anything, though."

I hear the smile fade from his voice. "I know. Let's just enjoy it for now."

"Okay. Just for now."

We keep talking until it's stupid late in Paris and my eyes can barely stay open. It's as if we're both stretching out this tiny piece of heaven like we can make it last forever.

Eventually, I can't fight it anymore.

"Sleep, baby," he murmurs. "I'll stay right here while you drift off."

My heart actually hurts at how sweet he is. God, I love him.

I love you, Worth.

I think I hear Worth inhale sharply, but I'm too sleepy to wonder why.

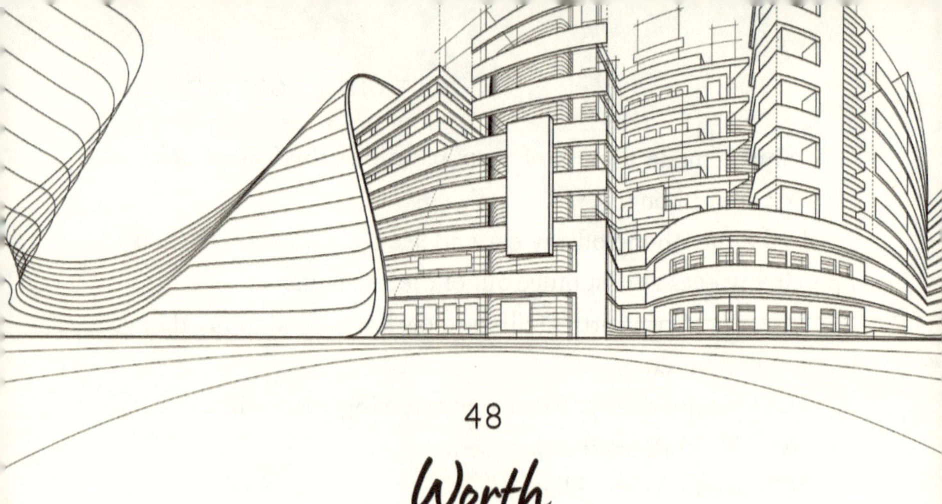

48

Worth

"*I love you, Worth.*"

I replay the words in my head for the hundredth time as I shut off the kitchen lights and head upstairs. Mya's voice was sleepy-soft, slurred at the edges, the way she gets when she's half under. But she said it. Not in a jokey or a "love ya, buddy" way. It was pulled from somewhere deep, a place she keeps locked up. And I got to hear it.

I'm grinning like an idiot. I can feel it on my face and I don't even care.

She might not remember it. I know that. She was on the verge of passing out, voice all warm and drowsy, barely aware she was still on the line. If I were to bring it up, it would probably spook her. So I won't.

But I heard it, and I'm going to sleep with it.

I crawl into my own bed and stare at the ceiling. It's become way too big and way too cold without Mya. I hadn't planned on calling her. I really hadn't. But then she answered my text.

And I was there, in my living room, with nothing but the

ache of missing her, and all I could think was: *I want to hear her voice.*

I was just going to check in. Instead, I heard Paris in the background, her laugh, and the way her breathing sped up when I flirted back. And then Mya went and set my whole world on fire with four sleepy words.

God, I miss her.

I roll onto my side and glance at my phone. I could've talked to her all night.

What I didn't tell her is that I'll be in Paris next week.

We were in that stupid perfect bubble where the annulment didn't matter and nothing else existed and we were just us.

I didn't want to shatter it or freak her out. She's finally happy. The last thing I want is for her to think I'm flying across the ocean to corner her.

I've got meetings with clients, a site walk, and lunch with the Paris partners.

Plus, Brianna will be with me this time. Spring break lines up, and she's been nagging me about the Eiffel Tower and croissants ever since Mya and I eloped, so I said yes.

There's another part of me that's picturing finding Mya on a Paris street and kissing her like no time has passed. Like that night in Nantucket didn't crack us all open.

I exhale, long and slow.

One step at a time, Miller.

Tonight, I got "I love you."

Next week, I go to Paris.

And if fate—God, universe, whatever—decides to put us in the same room again?

I'm not letting her leave without knowing exactly where I stand.

SUITCASES ARE LINED UP BY THE FRONT DOOR, PASSPORTS on the console, and Maggie is fussing in the kitchen like we're leaving for a year instead of a week. I'm in my room doing a last-minute check when there's a knock.

"Yeah?"

Brianna slips in, hands behind her back as if she's hiding something.

"What are you up to?" I narrow my eyes.

"Nothing." Which of course means *something*. She climbs onto my bed and finally brings her hands forward.

It's a small navy velvet box.

My chest tightens. "Where'd you get that?"

"In your closet," Bri says, unapologetic. "In the black box you thought was hidden."

I sigh. "You can't break into my stuff, Bri."

"You didn't lock it."

Touché.

I take the box from her and flip it open.

The ring catches the light. A simple gold band with a yellow pear diamond slightly off-center. It's elegant—and exactly Mya. I saw it one day and just knew it was made for her. Even though we were already separated, I still bought it, and stuck it in the back of the closet.

"Why are you giving me this?"

Bri shrugs, all innocent. "You should take it with you."

I huff out a laugh. "We are *not* at that level, Bri."

"But what if you *get* to ring level?" Her eyes go big. "What if you talk and you need it?"

"It doesn't happen like that."

Bri has been on me to talk to Mya ever since she left for

Paris, so I'm not even surprised my daughter is this optimistic about maybe seeing her while we're there.

"It could," Brianna says wisely, like she's been alive for forty years and seen things. "You always say to be prepared."

I point at her. "That's low. Using my own lines."

She grins. "Just bring it, Dad. You don't have to give it to her. But if you don't and then you *do* need it, you'll be mad."

My daughter is not wrong.

I look at the ring again. I bought it hoping that maybe one day Mya would look at me and not see the man who dragged her into a fake marriage—but the man she *chose*.

"Fine," I say finally, snapping the box shut. "But this is not for now. It's for when and if Mya's ready. Let's just bring it as a sort of lucky charm."

Brianna beams. "I like that."

I walk to my carry-on, unzip the inner pocket, and slip the box inside.

When I turn back, Bri is watching me, hopeful. "Do you think Mya'll be happy to see us?"

"I hope so."

"Me too," she says, hopping off the bed. "I miss her."

That one lands square in the center of my chest.

"Yeah," I say quietly. "I do too."

THE SECOND WE WALK OUT OF CHARLES DE GAULLE, Brianna is jumping about as if she just ate a boatload of sugar. By the time we're in the car and heading into the city, she's pressed to the window.

"Dad, look—look! That building has, like, gold on it."

"That's Les Invalides."

"It's shiny."

"It is."

We drive across the Seine and she practically climbs into my lap. "Dad, is that the tower? Is that it?"

"Yep," I say, grinning; her excitement is contagious. "That's the Eiffel Tower."

Bri straight-up *screams*. The driver laughs. I shake my head.

"It's so big. Can we go? Today? Now?"

"We'll see, we just got off a long flight."

My phone rings. It's Adrian.

I answer. "We're in the car."

"Great. I'm at the hotel. Your room is ready. Bring me my niece."

"Be there in ten minutes."

"See you soon," he says, and hangs up.

I glance at Bri. "Guess who's waiting?"

"Uncle A?" She lights up even more somehow.

"Yep."

We pull up to the hotel, one of those old Haussmann buildings with black iron balconies and too many mirrors in the lobby. Adrian is right there, in a tailored coat, leaning on the marble check-in desk with his cane.

"UNCLE A!" Brianna yells, bolting out before I can even thank the driver.

He opens his arms and she hugs him, carefully. He lifts her up just a tad off the floor. "Ah, mon petit loup. You've grown."

I clap his shoulder. "Nice to see you again, brother."

In the room, Bri runs straight to the balcony and gasps at the view.

Adrian watches her, before glancing at me. "I booked a private tour of the Louvre for me and my niece. Friend of a friend. We go now before the crowds."

I look at my kid, bouncing, jet-lag forgotten. "You want to go with Uncle A?"

"YES."

"Take her," I say. "Don't let her steal anything."

"I make no promises." He winks at Bri. "Come, we will look at naked statues."

"Ew." She squeals, delighted.

They leave in a rush and the suite goes quiet.

I sit on the edge of the bed in the master, looking out at Paris, and, of course, I think about Mya.

She's somewhere in this city. Maybe at the office, maybe on a site, maybe walking home with a baguette under her arm like every other person here. I'm in her city and she doesn't even know.

I pull out my phone. I could text her and ask her to come for dinner, but the other night was fragile, and I don't want to bulldoze it.

Still, I don't want to sit here and do nothing.

I scroll to my Paris concierge contact—someone the office uses—and type out a message.

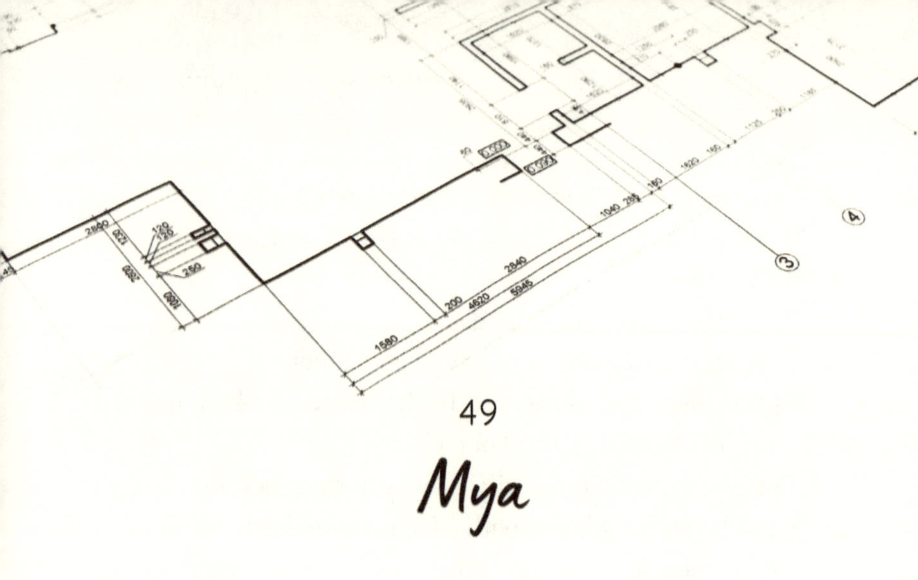

49

Mya

I'm halfway through redlining a plumbing layout when someone knocks.

I freeze.

No one ever comes over. The building is buzzer-only, and I'm not expecting a delivery. I glance at the time. 3:17 p.m. Then at the intercom, but whoever it is is already at my door.

I pad over and open it a crack.

"Bonjour, madame," the courier says, smiling. "Livraison."

He's holding a big, flat package wrapped in brown paper with a deep green ribbon tied around it like it's Christmas.

"Pour moi?" I ask, dumbly.

"Oui. Mlle Mya Dessen-Jones?"

"That's me."

He hands it over.

I close the door, and just stand there in my tiny entryway, staring at the package like it might explode.

I didn't order anything.

I carry it to the little bistro table I use as a desk and set it down. There's a card tied to the ribbon. I swallow, untie the bow, and open the card.

For your Paris walls, so you don't forget us.
Dinner tomorrow? 19 h. Loulou, Jardin des
Tuileries. Table is under Miller.
—W.

My heart lurches in my throat.

Worth is here.

In *Paris*.

And he wants dinner.

At Loulou. The same restaurant where we had our post-courthouse "wedding reception" dinner, where he fed me pasta and we pretended we were newlyweds.

My knees go a little soft.

He was just on the phone with me a few nights ago. He didn't say he was coming. He didn't even hint at it. And now he's here asking me to meet him.

Excitement fizzles, accompanied by a thin line of dread. I don't know what my heart is going to do when I see him again in person.

I drag the package closer and start tearing at the wrapper. As the brown paper falls away, my hand flies to my mouth.

It's the wolf sketch. Except this time it's not the crinkled pencil version I keep in my desk drawer and it features three wolves—a small pack. This one has been recreated with clean lines, soft watercolor wash behind it, and the moon fuller and brighter, like it's actually glowing. And it's been framed. At the bottom, in neat lettering:

A wolf always finds the moon again.

B. & M.

A tear slips out before I can stop it. I swipe at my cheek and laugh at myself.

Of course he'd send the one thing that would hit straight to the softest spot.

I stare at the note again. *Dinner tomorrow?*

I already know the answer.

I press the card to my chest and whisper, "You're a menace, Worth Miller."

WORTH

I wake up with an annoying little reminder in my brain: today would've been mine and Mya's first anniversary.

But I don't dwell on it.

We detonated that date so no point sitting in a hotel bed getting sentimental over a marriage that got ripped apart in public. Besides, I've got Bri today, and my daughter doesn't do brooding.

"Dad," she calls from the other room, "are we going to the office or are we just pretending to work and going around Paris instead?"

"Both," I call back. "Get ready."

We head to the Paris office late in the morning. Before we leave, I text Dre.

> Mya in the office today?

She replies in under a minute.

> DRE:
>
> No. She will be on site all day.

Good. Not because I don't want to see her. I don't want to crowd her or 'invade her territory' when she asked for space.

We take the company car over. Brianna is glued to her phone the whole ride, thumbs flying, making those half-smiles she makes when she's trying to be cool.

At the office, I set up in one of the glass conference rooms with a view over the courtyard. I pull up financials; Bri pulls out her sketchbook and a pack of markers. Every few minutes, her phone buzzes.

Finally I look over. "Who are you talking to?"

She goes pink immediately. "My friend."

I raise a brow. "Which friend?"

"Just... a friend."

"Mmm." I lean back, narrow my eyes at her in mock suspicion.

"Dad." She drags out the word. "It's *Kennedy*."

Ah, right. Kennedy.

"Uh huh. And what are you and *Kennedy* talking about at 11 a.m. on a school day?"

"He's on spring break too, remember? And we're talking about art."

"As long as you're being safe," I state, a slight frown pulling at my brows at the thought. "No sending weird stuff."

"Ew, gross, Dad."

I take a couple of calls. One with Seattle and one with the client I'm here to see, but part of my brain keeps drifting.

Did Mya remember today?

Brianna snaps her sketchbook shut after a while. "We should go to dinner tonight," she announces.

I glance up. "We can do dinner."

"A fancy dinner," she says, face bright.

I laugh. "In Paris, everything is fancy."

"You know what I mean. Somewhere special. Will you let me pick the spot?"

I think about it for half a second. "Sure."

She pulls out her phone again. "Okay. I'll make a reservation."

"You know how to do that?"

"It's 2025, Dad."

"Right."

We finish up around five and head back to the penthouse. I answer a couple more emails and Bri disappears into her room, resurfacing in a dress, tights and a beret she bought just for this trip.

"You look very French."

"Merci," Bri says with an exaggerated roll of her tongue.

On the way down, I ask, "Where are we going tonight?"

She smirks. "It's a surprise."

I chuckle. "Why the secrecy?"

"You'll see."

In the car, Brianna leans forward and whispers the address to the driver like we're in a spy movie. The man nods and pulls away.

I watch Paris roll by through the window, evening settling in. I wonder again if Mya has remembered this date or shoved it in the part of her brain marked *fake marriage, do not open.*

After a longer drive than I expected, we turn into the Tuileries side and slow near the entrance to the jardins.

My brows pull together.

The car stops. The driver gets out and opens my door.

No way.

MYA

I step out of the shower, my hair wrapped in a towel and my stomach in knots.

This is ridiculous. It's just dinner with my ex-husband, in Paris, on what would've been our first anniversary.

Totally casual.

I open my tiny wardrobe and immediately make a mess of it, pulling out dresses, blouses, and two pairs of heels I told myself I probably wouldn't wear here. I lay everything on the bed and stare at it.

Too sexy.

Too serious.

Too "look what you lost."

Too "I'm fine, actually."

Too *desperate.*

I don't want it to look like I dressed for him.

I'm also *very much* dressing for him.

After way too long, I land on a dress that's right in the middle.

I sit at my tiny table to put some light makeup on and cue up the Queen record Worth bought me months ago. I've been listening to it on repeat.

Freddie's voice fills the apartment, and for a minute, I close my eyes.

I wonder if my dad is looking down at me. If he'd be proud of me for how my life turned out.

I let myself think about him properly, not shoving the grief away because I'm scared. I miss him. And I finally accept that that's what this whole thing with Worth has been: me trying to outrun that first loss, thinking if I control the ending, it won't hurt as much.

Except it still does.

I grab my little black bag, shrug on a coat, and call a rideshare.

On the way to Loulou, I remember that day a year ago—Worth looking at me like I was really *his*. I remember thinking, *If this were real, I could fall so fast.*

How times have changed.

I don't know what to expect tonight.

The car pulls up to the restaurant, and my pulse skitters. I step out, inhale the cool air, and walk in.

"Bonsoir. Table for Miller, please."

The maître d' smiles knowingly. "Bien sûr, madame. This way."

My heels click against the floor as he leads me through the dining room. I smooth my dress, heart thudding in my throat.

We round the corner to the terrace, and I stop.

WORTH

I can't believe we got this table.

Out of all the places in Paris, and all the restaurants Bri could've picked, we're sitting at the exact table Mya and I sat at a year ago, when we were still figuring out how to pretend to be in love.

"Brianna..." I narrow my eyes at her.

She's stifling a smile so hard her cheeks puff. Then she lifts the menu to hide her face. "What?"

"What's going on?"

"Nothing. I just heard this place was, like, a staple."

"A staple," I repeat, deadpan. "Right. And this has nothing to do with a certain event that happened here last year?"

Brianna presses her lips into a thin line, stifling a smile. "I plead the fifth."

"And how exactly did you get a reservation on short notice?"

She shrugs without lowering the menu. "I guess they had a cancellation."

Uh huh.

The waiter comes over. "Bonsoir, Monsieur Miller. Would you like some champagne to begin?" He sets down two flutes.

I gesture to Bri. "She's underage."

"Dad, it's fine. He can leave it."

The waiter smiles, unbothered, and fills her another glass with water, leaving the extra flute on the side. "For mademoiselle."

"Merci," she says in her best French.

We give our appetizer order, and when the waiter leaves, I get a better look at my kid.

Bri is fidgety. Not bored-fidgety. Actually nervous, as if she's waiting for something to happen.

"Okay," I say slowly, leaning an elbow on the table. "What are you up to?"

"Nothing," she says again, too fast. "I'm just happy to be here with you."

Before I can press, I catch movement in my periphery.

A woman turns the corner onto the terrace.

I just see the outline of long, dark curls spilled over her shoulders, a deep red dress that hugs every single curve, and heels that make her legs look endless.

Jesus, she's gorgeous.

I immediately want to smack myself because what the hell am I doing checking out another woman when—

Shit.

It's not another woman. It's Mya.

My brain stutters. She's even more beautiful than the last

time I saw her, and she's walking toward our table like she doesn't quite believe what she's seeing either.

I flick my gaze to Bri.

She's watching me over the edge of her water glass, eyes bright, looking *very* proud of herself.

"Brianna," I mutter.

My daughter just grins.

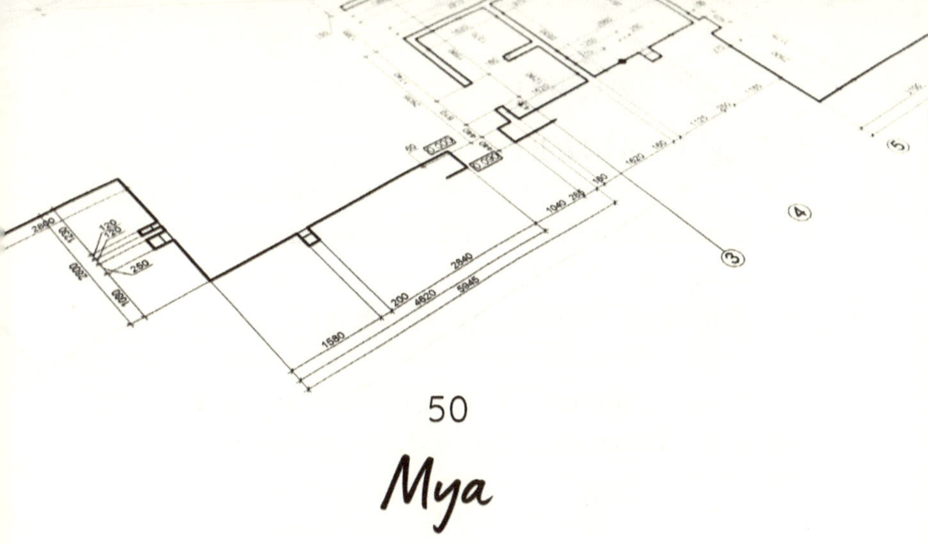

50

Mya

The maître d' pulls out the empty chair at the table.

"For you, madame."

I hesitate for half a beat, eyes traveling from Worth to Bri, but I sit. My brain is still trying to catch up.

No one says anything.

"So!" Brianna chirps. "We're all here!"

Worth drags a hand down his face. "Brianna."

"What?" she says, all fake-innocent.

He looks at me as I try to get my eyes to stop bugging out of my skull.

"Mya... what are you doing here?"

It comes out surprised, not accusing.

I blink. "You invited me."

"I—" Worth stops. "No, I didn't."

My brows knit. "You sent me a gift with a note." I narrow my eyes now. "You said, 'Dinner tomorrow, 19 h, Loulou, Jardin des Tuileries. Table is under Miller.'"

Worth stares at me.

Okay... Clearly he did not send me a gift.

We both look at Bri and she's already cracking. Her mouth starts to twitch, and then she just bursts out laughing.

"Oh my God," Worth says slowly. "What did you do?"

"Okay, okay," Brianna says, waving her hands because she can't breathe. "Don't be mad."

I'm smiling now too. "So, the gift wasn't actually from you," I say to her father, eyes dancing. "It was from *you?*" I point at Bri.

She nods, grinning. "Uncle Adrian helped me."

"Of course," Worth mutters. "I'm going to punch him for this. Is that who you kept texting earlier?"

"Yup!"

"Who's Adrian?" I ask, confused, but my question gets ignored.

"I told him I wanted to do something special because it was, you know..." Bri darts her eyes between us meaningfully. "And he said he knew people, so he helped me plan everything."

"Wait," Worth cuts in. "What gift?"

I'm still trying to process, but I manage to say, "The wolf and moon drawing. With the quote."

Worth blinks. "I definitely didn't send that."

"I know. Apparently your daughter did."

Bri bobs her head. "You guys needed to talk and you weren't talking and Dad kept not calling you and you kept not calling him, so I said, 'We're going to Paris anyway, let's just make them meet,' and here we are."

I stare at her.

Worth does too. Then I laugh, head tipping back—and I could kiss this kid, because I haven't genuinely laughed in months.

He shakes his head, fighting a smile. "You're not supposed to manipulate your father."

"You guys weren't doing it yourselves," Bri says, shrugging. "So I helped."

I look at Worth over the candle, eyes soft now. "For what it's worth... It was a really good gift."

He huffs out a laugh. "Yeah? I wish I could take credit." He holds my gaze, and for a second the noise of the restaurant fades.

Bri takes a sip of her water like she didn't just mastermind an international reunion. "Sooo, now that everybody's here... I have to pee," she announces, sliding off her chair, because subtlety is not in her vocabulary. She gives us both a pointed look. "Don't fight."

"We won't," Worth says.

She rolls her eyes, and disappears toward the bathrooms.

Suddenly it's just us.

I smooth my napkin over my lap. "Hi," I say, because what else do you say to your ex-husband-slash-still-somehow-love in the middle of a Paris restaurant on your fake anniversary?

Worth smiles, a little shy, which is so unlike him that my stomach flips.

"Hi." He glances in the direction Bri went. "Sorry about my conniving daughter."

"Don't be. She's persistent. Wonder where she got that from."

"Definitely not me," he deadpans.

I bite back another laugh. Then I figure I might as well tell him before Bri does. "I should probably admit something, though."

His brows lift. "Yeah?"

"Bri and I never really stopped talking." I watch his face carefully. "We've been texting this entire time. I hope you're not mad."

His expression softens immediately. "Mya. No. Of course

I'm not mad." He leans in, forearms on the table, candlelight catching in his eyes. "Brianna loves you. She was gutted when you left. We both were. I was just trying to give you space."

That stings, even though I knew. "I still feel guilty about that, and about leaving Bri without a goodbye... But she said she understood. I don't know how a fourteen-year-old can understand heartbreak better than some adults."

"She's had practice," Worth says quietly.

My throat tightens. I look around us. "It's kind of wild we're back here."

"Yeah."

"Whole different circumstances."

"Way different," he agrees.

A year ago, we were high on adrenaline. A year ago, I wasn't in love yet. Not like this. A year ago, there was just a man and a woman playing house and getting way too good at it.

"I don't regret it, though," he says.

My eyes flick back to him. "No?"

He shakes his head, gaze steady on mine. "Those six months we were married were some of the best months of my life."

I blink, thrown. "Have you gone soft, Mr. Miller?"

He chuckles, low. "Maybe."

The smile fades and he straightens, as if remembering something. "Actually, I promised myself that when I saw you in person again, I'd tell you. I'm not leaving it unsaid this time."

I swallow hard.

"Worth—"

"No, let me." He holds up a hand. "I'm not telling you this to make you stay, or to make you feel guilty, or to mess with the freedom you carved out for yourself. I'm telling you because I'd rather you walk away knowing it than not being aware of how I feel." He takes a deep breath.

"I love you, Mya."

My heart kicks in my chest.

"I fell in love with you somewhere in the midst of our pretending. You walked into my house and made it a home so fast I didn't even realize it had been missing something. You made me enjoy life again."

My eyes burn. I grip the edge of my napkin so I don't reach for him.

"You made me a better dad." Worth's eyes are shining now too. "You made me show up softer. You made me listen to Bri more. I didn't realize I'd been doing things on autopilot until you came in and started loving her like she was yours."

I blink, and tears slide down my cheeks.

"And you made me a better man," he adds, voice a little rough. "Not because you asked me to change. Because I wanted to be the kind of man you didn't want to run from."

God.

Worth takes a steadying breath. "Since you've been gone, the house hasn't felt like home. Bri and I are good, we always are. But it felt fuller with you. Complete. That's what you were. You were the missing piece to our puzzle."

I press my lips together to keep a sound in. My heart is hammering so hard I can hear it in my ears. This is everything I wanted him to say months ago. Everything I told myself I'd never get. Everything I was scared to hear, because once it's spoken, you can't pretend anymore that it was just sex and an arrangement.

"I'm not asking you for anything right now," he says softly, leaning in a little more. "I just didn't want to miss the chance to tell you. Because last time, I kept waiting for the perfect moment and we got blown up before I could."

I wipe under one eye, my laugh a little watery. "You're really not helping me keep my walls up here."

"Good," Worth says, eyes warm. "They were never that high with me, anyway."

Inside me, there's a war. I'm still scared—because once I say it, it's real. Once I say it, I'll have to let myself be happy, and happiness is what I'm terrified of losing.

But looking at Worth now, I realize what my mom said was right.

I didn't run because it wasn't real.

I ran because it *was*.

And I love Worth so much it hurts.

WORTH

I didn't realize how tight I'd been holding everything in until I said the words.

The second they were out, something in my chest loosened as if I'd been walking around with a fist around my ribcage.

And now I'm watching Mya like a hawk; I have no idea how she's going to take it.

She looks stunned. Wide-eyed, lashes wet, breathing a little too fast. Like a deer caught in headlights. Her fingers are trembling on the napkin, there are tears on her cheeks, and I can't tell if I just gave her the thing she was waiting for or if I've just scared her.

Shit.

Maybe I said too much. Maybe I should've eased her in.

Mya clears her throat, voice shaky. "Thank you for telling me this."

My heart drops.

Not the words you want to hear after a love declaration.

I manage a nod anyway, swallowing the sting. "Yeah. Of course."

Mya sees the hurt, because she's always seen right through me.

"No, Worth. I mean, thank you. Because I needed to hear everything you said. I love you too." Her eyes are fierce through the tears. "I've loved you since our first kiss. When I said I wasn't going to sleep in your bed and then I kept doing it. When I saw how you are with Bri. When you fought for her in court. When you bought me that stupid record." She laughs, wiping under her eye. "I fell for you and then I panicked. Because the only big love I've ever experienced got taken away. I thought if I ended it, at least it was *me* ending it."

I have to grip the table to keep from just hauling her across it to taste her mouth.

"I needed to know I could walk away," Mya whispers. "That I wasn't staying because I needed a savior. I needed to know that I could stand on my own and *then* choose you."

My throat burns.

"And I did. I proved I could do it, and I still missed you every night. I still texted your daughter. I still listened to the record. I still counted the days." She shakes her head, a small, desperate sound leaving her. "I can't stand being without you anymore, Worth. I don't want to."

I push my chair back and lean across the table. "Come here." I cup her face in both hands and kiss her.

It's not a careful kiss. It's months of missing her, weeks of restraint, a whole year of pretending we were temporary. She melts into it instantly, hands coming up to my wrists, mouth opening under mine like she was right there with me the whole time.

She tastes like wine and cinnamon and *Mya*. I groan against her, deepening it, and she makes that soft sound in her throat that always undoes me.

God, I missed this woman.

I could stay like that forever, bent over a restaurant table like a teenager, but then a small shape appears near us.

Brianna is back, quietly sliding into her chair. Without saying a damn word, she reaches into her little purse, pulls out the navy velvet box, and sets it on the table between us.

Then she winks at me.

I pull back from Mya with a breathless laugh, because of course my kid would do this.

Mya looks between us, eyes wide. "What is that?"

I pick up the box, thumb brushing the velvet.

"This might be crazy," I say, turning back to her, heart pounding like I just ran a marathon, "but I don't want to spend another moment apart from you."

Mya's eyes instantly fill again.

I stand. Chairs around us scrape as people notice what's happening. I don't care. I step around the table, take her hand and, like I should've done a year ago, I get down on one knee.

"Mya Dessen-Jones." I look up at her, every single thing I feel probably written all over my face. "Will you marry me? For real this time. No contracts. No timelines. No deals. Just us."

She gasps, hand flying to her mouth.

Behind me, I hear Bri whisper, "Say yes, say yes, say yes."

The restaurant quiets. Phones come out. Someone gasps in French.

Mya laughs through her tears, nodding so hard her curls bounce. "Yes," she chokes out. "Yes, Worth. Of course, yes."

The place erupts in applause, cheers, and someone actually whistles. Brianna is taking a thousand pictures on her phone, practically vibrating with happiness.

I slide the ring onto Mya's finger, then stand and pull her in, kissing her like the world paused just for us.

When we break, foreheads touching, breaths mingling, I whisper, "It's not just for now anymore."

Her eyes, full of happy tears, shine up at me as she shakes her head.

"It's just until forever."

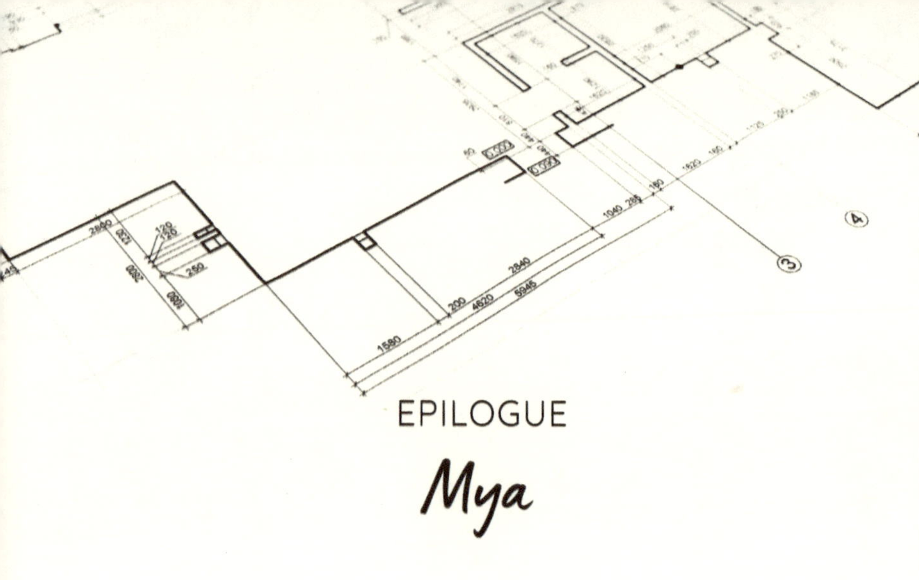

EPILOGUE

Mya

SOME MONTHS LATER

Project Rebuild stretches in front of me.

What was once a forgotten, broken stretch of aban-doned buildings now breathes with new life, colorful murals slowly being painted into existence.

This place is going to shelter people. Families. Girls who need somewhere safe. Kids who just need a chance. People who need proof that sometimes life *does* give you something back.

A worker jogs up to me, clipboard tucked under his arm. "We're finishing the south wing today. You want the final walk-through before the inspection tomorrow?"

"Yeah," I smile. "Let's do it."

He heads off and I take a second just to stand there and take it in.

When I first pitched this to the W.H.M. board, there were doubts. I had the ugly assumption that somehow Worth had handed me success on a silver platter. That the board would vote in favor of my project as some polite courtesy to the wife of a powerful man.

But I made them listen. I showed them research, layout plans, long-term projections, outreach integration, measurable impact. Programs tailored to real lives. I sold them the reality that this isn't charity—this is rebuilding a community with dignity.

And they didn't say yes because of my last name.

They said yes because I earned it.

It's empowering knowing that Worth stood on the sidelines and watched me fight without stepping in. He didn't clear the path for me.

He just believed I could walk it.

My phone buzzes in my pocket.

His name lights across the screen.

I brace a smile before I even answer. "Hey, playboy."

"Hey, pretty girl." Worth's voice is warm, silky, wrapped in a smile I can picture without seeing. "How's my brilliant fiancée?"

"Busy changing lives," I say, teasing.

"That's right. I'm proud of you, Mrs. Miller."

A laugh bubbles out of me, cheeks heating. "Not until tomorrow."

He hums. "Technicalities."

"Legalities," I correct.

"Still my girl."

Yeah. I always was. Even when I didn't know it.

"How's Bri?" I ask, glancing around as sun rays spills across the buildings.

"She's pretending not to be emotional about the rehearsal dinner," he chuckles. "Currently sitting on the floor eating cereal straight from the box."

I laugh softly.

"I'm proud of you," Worth adds.

My chest tightens. "You've said that already."

"I'll say it the rest of your life if I need to. Project Rebuild... it's you, Mya. Every inch of it. You did this. You fought for it. You didn't need me to make it happen, and that makes me love you even more."

Tears sting my eyes.

"That's funny," I breathe, "because building something real, choosing this life, choosing *you*... makes me love *you* more."

Worth exhales like I gave him something precious. "Tomorrow," he says softly.

"Tomorrow," I echo.

We hang up, and I slip the phone back into my pocket, pressing a hand against my chest for just a second before straightening my shoulders.

Across the courtyard, a group of local teens laughs while helping paint one of the murals. A woman watches with a stroller nearby.

This is community. Hope.

Today, I get to stand in the sunlight of what I built for myself.

Tomorrow I marry the love of my life.

And both things feel equally like destiny.

"Oh my God, Worth! Put me down."

"No chance." His voice is dark and amused as he carries me over the threshold of our honeymoon suite at the Thompson Hotel, his hand landing on my ass in a lingering sting that makes me squeak.

He finally sets me on my feet, only to crowd me back

against the wall, his body pressing into mine. His mouth is on my throat before I can even catch a breath, slow kisses trailing heat along my skin.

"Hi, husband," I whisper breathlessly.

"Hi, wife," he murmurs against my pulse, smiling. "God, I've been waiting for tonight."

Worth and I are finally married—again—and it was the best day of my life.

Technically, this was round two. But this time, it felt like our first. Today, we did it in front of our friends, family, and colleagues at Worth's—*our*—mansion. Even though it was a bigger celebration than the first time, I still wanted an intimate ceremony, and Worth didn't object.

We turned the backyard into something out of a dream. Soft white drapery hung from wooden beams, fairy lights threaded through the trees like fallen stars, and blush flowers lined the aisle and bloomed across the arch where we stood.

Brianna walked ahead of me, determined and proud, biting her lip to hold back tears. Tiana cried openly, fanning her face and whispering dramatic commentary that somehow made the moment even sweeter. My mom cried. My stepdad squeezed my hand as he walked me down the aisle, whispering that he had never seen me happier.

Worth waited under the arch, smiling at me. We kissed, and everything that had come before this moment finally found peace.

Now here we are.

Worth tilts my chin up, his forehead brushing mine. "Still with me, Mrs. Miller?"

"Yes," I breathe. "Always."

His fingers slide down my waist and he cups my hip, pulling me against him so I can feel exactly how much he wants me. He kisses me then—hungry and slow, tongue sliding into my mouth like he plans to devour me one taste at a time. I melt, gripping his shirt, feeling hard muscle underneath, feeling him everywhere.

Then he deepens the kiss. Harder. Rougher. It makes my knees weaken and my brain completely empty.

Worth backs me toward the bed, our mouths never breaking apart, as if he physically can't stand to not be touching me. His hands push into my hair, then down, then back up, mapping me greedily. I pull off his tux jacket and begin to unbutton his shirt, dragging my fingers down his torso, and he laughs against my lips before ripping it off himself and tossing it aside.

God, he's beautiful.

All power and warmth and *mine*.

He makes a low sound when my hands continue to explore his chest, sliding over firm muscle, nails lightly scraping his shoulders just to hear him groan. His grip tightens on my waist.

"Careful," he growls. "You start something, you'd better be ready to finish it."

"That's the plan, baby," I whisper.

His grin turns wicked.

Worth helps me take off my wedding dress. Then, our hands are everywhere. His mouth returns to my skin like he's starving, kissing, sucking, worshiping every inch he uncovers.

"Worth—" my voice breaks when his lips trail lower, slower, in a deliberate torture.

"Yeah. Say my name like that, pretty girl."

I tug him back up to me, crashing my mouth against his again, rolling him with me into the mattress, both of us laughing breathlessly before drowning in each other once more.

"My wife," he whispers against my lips. "My forever."

Worth disappears down my body, ripping my panties off, and his mouth is on my clit within seconds. His lips suck me in, my back arching off the mattress as a loud moan escapes my lips.

"Fuck. I'm already so close."

My husband laughs but doesn't stop, his tongue teasing and his mouth alternating between licking, nipping, and sucking at the sensitive nub. Every thought shatters, leaving nothing but the feel of him—overwhelming me in the best possible way.

And maybe that's why this feels even more intense. Because the first time we got married, we never made it here. We never consummated a damn thing. We barely had a wedding night at all. One phone call in Paris and we were on the first flight back to Seattle.

Worth slides two fingers inside me, and that's all it takes for the dam to finally break.

"Yes... yes... yes," I gasp, the orgasm cresting hard and fast, heat flooding through me, sparks racing all the way to my fingertips.

My breathing still hasn't settled when Worth lifts his head, his mouth slick with my cum and a wicked smile curving his lips.

"Come here," he murmurs, voice husky and commanding in a way that curls my toes. "On your knees for me, Mrs. Miller."

A shiver runs down my spine.

I slide off the bed slowly and kneel in front of him. His fingers thread through my hair, tender and possessive all at once, his thumb brushing my cheek.

"Open your mouth."

I obey, resting my hands on his thighs, feeling the coiled tension beneath his skin, knowing exactly how desperately he wants me and loving that I get to be the one to unravel him. His breathing stutters when I lean closer, his hand tightening just a little, like he's barely in control.

"That's it," he whispers. "So damn beautiful."

My lips part at his crown and I slide my mouth over every glorious inch of his cock, struggling to take him in.

"Slower, Kitten. I want to feel each second of you."

And I do exactly that, taking my time, savoring the way his body reacts, the low sounds he tries and fails to hold back, the way his composure fractures piece by piece until he's nothing but need and praise and shaking restraint beneath my hands.

"Fuck, Mya." His head falls back, a broken groan spilling from his lips. "I don't want to come like this but you make it so damn hard to stop."

His breathing turns ragged, and before I can push him any further, he slides his hand into my hair and pulls me away.

"Enough."

Worth helps me up, then turns me smoothly to face the bed, my palms pressed to the mattress, heart pounding in my throat. His body comes up behind mine, hands gliding slowly over my sides, my waist, my hips.

"Look at you," he breathes. "My beautiful wife."

His touch drags lower, unhurried, teasing, claiming, sending shivers through me. He leans in, his chest flush to my back, mouth finding my neck, marking a slow path of kisses up to my ear. I gasp when his cock slides against my entrance, using my slick arousal to push deep inside me.

"God, Worth... I'll never get used to your size." A moan escapes with the words.

He chuckles softly. "I've got you, baby. Take a deep breath for me."

I do, and he pulls out slowly, almost all the way, before pushing back in. I gasp—half squeal, half curse. "Oh, fuck!"

Worth's grip tightens on my hips as he sets the pace, guiding us until my body yields to him, stretching to accommodate the fullness of his cock. He presses in closer, murmuring praise and devotion against me.

His rhythm builds, slow at first, then deeper, harder. My fingers tighten against the mattress, my breath coming out in broken sounds I can't control.

"Look at me," Worth murmurs, voice wrecked.

I glance over my shoulder, and the way he stares at me—utterly undone—sends heat spiraling through my entire body.

"That's it. That's my girl."

His hand slides around to find my clit, fingers circling as pleasure coils tighter, impossible to hold back.

"I'm close," I moan.

"Good." His forehead drops to my shoulder. "Let go, Kitten."

The world fractures.

I come apart, his name on my lips, everything tightening, exploding into warmth and light that rushes through every nerve. Worth groans against my neck, his pace stuttering as he follows me over the edge.

For a moment, there's nothing but the sound of our breath and the wild thundering of our hearts. Then he softens, still wrapped around me, still holding me like he has no intention of ever letting go. He kisses my shoulder, my neck, the corner of my jaw, soothing where he's touched.

"Mine" he whispers, a smile in his voice. "My beautiful wife."

I laugh breathlessly, turning into his arms as he pulls me gently down with him, and we collapse onto the bed in a tangled, satisfied mess.

"I love you," I tell my husband.

"I love you back. So much," he replies.

We stay there, catching our breath, the world finally quiet.

Tonight, there's no rush. No fear or borrowed happiness.

Just us, finally getting the night we were always meant to have. Forever is ours.

WORTH

It's been one full year since Mya and I stood in our backyard under that arch, in front of everyone we love, and finally said *I do* for real.

I stand on our back terrace with a mug of coffee, watching the early morning sun roll across the yard. The world feels softer now. Or maybe I am. But I'd never tell anyone the latter.

The rumors feel like a lifetime ago. The arrangement whispers and the "she married him for money" headlines. Our PR team did what they do best, and slowly cracked the narrative apart and let the truth bleed through without ever once humiliating us. My legal counsel sealed every old wound and closed every door the world tried to pry open.

Gone are my blue collar playboy days.

Eventually, people stopped talking.

We let everyone believe our second wedding was just a "romantic renewal ceremony," nothing more. A symbolic recommitment. A sweet little celebration.

Let them have that version. We know the truth.

Behind me, I hear footsteps, then arms circle my waist.

"Morning, Mr. Miller," Mya murmurs, voice still warm from sleep.

I turn, pulling her into me and kissing her slowly. "Morning, Mrs. Miller."

She tucks into my side, head on my chest, like this is her favorite place to exist.

It definitely is mine.

Inside, I can hear Brianna rummaging in the kitchen, singing quietly under her breath. She's older and calmer these days, but every once in a while, I still catch glimpses of the little girl who used to cling to me like I was all she had left. Now, she has more.

She has us. She has her mother.

"Hey," Mya says gently, pulling back just enough to search my face. "Can we talk?"

"Of course. Is everything okay?"

We head to the outdoor couch, but she doesn't sit across from me, and instead curls into me, hand resting over my heart. That alone tells me this is safe news. Good news.

"So," she says softly, "I talked to Bri... And I asked how she'd feel if I... officially, legally... became her guardian."

The world stills. I smile wide.

Mya continues, nervous and glowing at the same time. "I told her it wouldn't change our dynamic. You'll always be her dad first. And she'll always have her mother. But I just want to be hers, too. Not just because I married you. Because I *choose* her as my daughter. Every day. Forever."

"And Bri said yes?" I choke out, the words barely making it past the lump in my throat.

Mya nods. "She said that it already feels like I'm her second mom, and this just makes it real."

My vision blurs.

I pull Mya in and bury my face in her shoulder, letting myself feel every ounce of relief, gratitude, and love I never thought I'd get to have again. Brianna will never question where she belongs again. She'll never worry the ground beneath her isn't permanent, now that she has three parents who would do anything for her.

When I finally find air again, I whisper, "Thank you."

Mya smiles. "You may want to stay seated for the next part."

I blink. "There's a next part?"

She nods, reaching into her pocket, and pulls out a tiny pacifier.

I stare at it. Then I choke on a breath because reality hits all at once.

"No."

"Yes." Her smile trembles. "We're going to have a baby."

I wrap Mya up in my arms instantly, lifting her, kissing her, probably holding her a bit too tight, but she just giggles and holds on.

My hand settles over her stomach instinctively, protectively.

"I already told Brianna," she whispers. "She cried. Then threatened any future sibling with violence if they ever steal her things."

I bark out a laugh.

That sounds exactly like my daughter.

I kiss Mya's forehead. We sit there in silence for a moment. Our wedding day feels like forever ago. Like we've lived a lifetime together already. But somehow, it also feels like just yesterday when we promised each other forever without fear or hesitation.

Time does something strange when you're where you belong.

I look at my wife.

I think of my daughter. Of the child on the way.

And I know with absolute certainty: It was worth everything.

This is just the beginning.

SNEAK PEAK OF BOOK 3

CHAPTER 1 - GRIFFIN

My alarm explodes and I groan, patting blindly across the sheet for my phone. I curse under my breath.

I sweep the blanket, finally catch the buzzing slab, kill it, and flop back onto the mattress. I rub the sleep from my eyes, then unlock the screen to check the time, only to land on the last page I was staring at before I crashed.

I sigh.

My thumb hovers over a sound-off reel I've already watched multiple times last night. Flour dusts her forearms, light slipping over satin shorts as she presses dough with the heel of her hand.

I'm not a man who lingers. I'm not a man who does... *this*.

The phone warms in my palm. The caption is nothing—three emojis and a caption: *cinnamon rolls tomorrow*—but my chest tightens like I've sprinted stairs.

Looking down at my sleep shorts, I notice a little tent forming. Goddamn it.

I readjust myself, scolding my cock to behave itself.

Five years taught me a lot about outrunning hunger and lust, but lately it's been catching me by the ankle.

I drag my thumb back to the beginning of the video.

Her laugh ghosts the room even when muted. She brushes hair off her mouth with the back of her wrist and a streak of flour kisses her cheek. It's harmless content. Still, it feels like a hand under my shirt.

I should put the phone down and take a cold shower.

"Dad?"

The spell detonates. I lock the screen so fast my hand almost cramps. "Yeah, bud?" I'm already on my feet, the phone face-down, the door open. Sylas stands there, his hair a storm, one fist rubbing an eye. "I think I had a bad dream last night," he says, small.

"C'mere."

He folds into me, and I squeeze him hard, giving his head a little kiss.

"Do you wanna talk about it?" I ask.

He shakes his head.

"Okay then. Let's get ready for the day shall we?"

Before heading out to the hallway, I pick up the phone and stare at my reflection in the blank screen: a man with work in the morning and a kid who needs structure more than I need a stupid distraction.

By seven, the house is loud. The TV is blaring, my dog's nails are ticking, and the coffee machine is whirring. I pour a mug, forget to drink it, then pour another.

One of Sylas's toys needs new batteries and he won't let it go until I change them, so I open the junk drawer, hunting for a screwdriver when a small white piece of paper snags against my knuckle. I stare at it for a few breaths.

If you find this, it means you woke up first for once. Kiss me before coffee. —L

Fuck.

I squeeze the note and rub my eyes with two fingers, letting out a rough exhale.

"What's for breakfast?" drifts down the hall, interrupting my thoughts.

"Cereal," I call back, tucking the note away like it belongs in the dark.

Sylas groans. "Again? We had cereal yesterday morning."

I rub my temple. "I know, buddy. I'm sorry. I'll do better tomorrow morning. Promise."

Our usual nanny had to step away last-minute to take care of a family member, and the precise little machine my life runs on threw a belt the same day. Joyce used to batch breakfast burritos, chop fruit into perfect stars, and leave sticky notes on the fridge with reminders. Since she left, I've been playing catch-up, badly.

"I miss Joyce," he says with a sigh.

"Same here, Sy." I state, scrawling my name on a permission slip I should've signed yesterday. "We'll try to find a new nanny in two weeks. Try to look harmless when we interview them."

He grins with all his teeth. "You first, Dad."

On the drive to school, Sylas tells me about the robot claw he's engineering. I nod, add a materials list to the notes app, and pretend I don't see the social media thumbnail trying to lure me back into the dark.

Knock it off, Griff.

The red light goes green, and I keep my eyes on the road.

As soon as we pull up, I kill the engine. Sylas is already unbuckled, door flying open, sprinting toward the schoolyard.

"Bye. Love you too!" I shout after him, and he gives me a backward thumbs-up without looking. Six going on sixteen.

My phone buzzes with the group thread that's been running since we were kids.

WORTH:

You alive, old man?

Look who's talking. You're the eldest of us three...

HENSON:

Haha. He got you there. You're late. Not for anything specific. Just late in general.

Just dropped Sy. Headed to the office now.

HENSON:

Good. We need your scary voice for the concrete sub at Tower South. He thinks 'timeline' is a suggestion.

WORTH:

Also, budget review at 10. Bring your red pen and that vein in your forehead.

I smirk despite myself. Nantucket feels like another life, but the salt lives in my bones. We were three idiots swinging hammers on summer decks, callused hands and a truck that only started if you swore at it. Years later, the Miller brothers came up to me with a pitch that sounded like a dare.

"Come build a firm with us."

I trusted them enough to pack a life into a storage unit and move across the country. First year, I was still blue collar, working as a union carpenter by day and draftsman by night, teaching myself CAD in a rented studio with bad heat. Then came night classes and licensure exams. Now I'm COO at

W.H.M. Construction, the guy who translates between the design team and the crews who actually make the drawings stand up.

It's been insane, but good.

I'll be there by ten.

HENSON:

Atta boy. I'll bring coffee.

WORTH:

I'll bring the actual agenda.

The lightness thins when the home screen flashes that same thumbnail again. I shouldn't. I really shouldn't. But I open the app anyway.

From my burner account, I type her name into the search bar and her profile blooms. She's always active, sunup to lights out, little squares of a life edited better than most movies.

I tap her story and watch. Then I watch the next. And the next.

The spell snaps. I toss the phone onto the passenger seat like it burned me and stare at my left hand, the gold band on my wedding finger catching a stripe of morning sun.

Guilt needles straight through the center of me.

I rub a palm over my mouth, jaw tight. Watching her is a habit I pretend I don't have. An itch I keep feeding.

Enough.

I turn the key, pull into traffic, and point the car toward the office, hating how much I'm already thinking about the next hit.

ACKNOWLEDGMENTS

Writing *Just Until Forever* happened in the middle of one the most intense, exhausting, beautiful seasons of my postpartum life.

This book was written between contact naps, late nights, early mornings, and moments where my brain was running on caffeine and pure adrenaline. If you're holding this book, just know it was powered by love, hormones, and a lot of determination.

To my beta readers: thank you for reading early, screaming in my messages, and making this story better with your honesty and enthusiasm. I'm endlessly grateful for you.

To my editor, Jennifer—thank you for your brilliance, and for helping me shape this book into what it was meant to be.

To my proofreader, Gill, thank you for catching what my tired eyes absolutely could not.

Thank you to my readers for choosing my stories, for trusting me, and for loving my characters as fiercely as I do.

To my PA and friend, Becca—there are not enough words. I would be lost without you. Thank you for holding everything together when my brain is elsewhere and for being such a constant support.

To my best friends, who never stop encouraging me, hyping me up, and reminding me why I started in the first place—thank you for believing in me even when I'm running on fumes.

And finally, to my husband—thank you for always supporting me, even while making fun of me for writing smut, and for laughing every single time you see the word *cock*.

Thank you for being here 🖤

STAY UP-TO-DATE WITH
NOUHA JULLIENNE

If you'd like to support me or keep up with my new projects,
scan the QR code below!